W9-CEH-708

H. G. WELLS

H. G. WELLS

Thirty Strange Stories

All rights reserved. No part of this work may be reproduced, transmitted in any form or by any means, electronic or mechanical, including photocopying, recording, or any information storage and retrieval system, without permission in writing from the publisher. All requests for permission to reproduce material from this work should be directed to Budget Book Service, Inc.

Published in 1993 by

Galahad Books
A division of Budget Book Service, Inc.
386 Park Avenue South
New York, NY 10016

Galahad Books is a registered trademark of Budget Book Service, Inc.

Library of Congress Catalog Card Number: 73-92546

ISBN: 0-88365-821-6

Designed by Hannah Lerner

Printed in the United States of America.

Contents

The Strange Orchid 1
Æpyornis Island 11
The Plattner Story 27
The Argonauts of the Air 51
The Story of the Late Mr. Elvesham 67
The Stolen Bacillus 89
The Red Room 99
A Moth (Genus Unknown) 111
In the Abyss 125
Under the Knife 145
The Reconciliation 163
A Slip under the Microscope 173
In the Avu Observatory 197
The Triumphs of a Taxidermist 207
A Deal in Ostriches 213
The Rajah's Treasure 219
The Story of Davidson's Eyes 233
The Cone 247
The Purple Pileus 261
A Catastrophe 277
Le Mari Terrible 289
The Apple 295
The Sad Story of a Dramatic Critic 307
The Jilting of Jane 317
The Lost Inheritance 327
Pollock and the Porroh Man 337
The Sea Raiders 357
In the Modern Vein 371
The Lord of the Dynamos 385
The Treasure in the Forest 397

The Strange Orchid

THE BUYING OF orchids always has in it a certain speculative flavour. You have before you the brown shrivelled lump of tissue, and for the rest you must trust your judgment, or the auctioneer, or your good-luck, as your taste may incline. The plant may be moribund or dead, or it may be just a respectable purchase, fair value for your money, or perhaps—for the thing has happened again and again—there slowly unfolds before the delighted eyes of the happy purchaser, day after day, some new variety, some novel richness, a strange twist of the labellum, or some subtler colouration or unexpected mimicry. Pride, beauty, and profit blossom together on one delicate green spike, and, it may be, even immortality. For the new miracle of Nature may stand in need of a new specific name, and what so convenient as that of its discoverer? "Johnsmithia"! There have been worse names.

It was perhaps the hope of some such happy discovery that made Winter-Wedderburn such a frequent attendant at these sales—that hope, and also, maybe, the fact that he had nothing else of the slightest interest to do in the world. He was a shy, lonely, rather ineffectual man, provided with just enough income to keep off the spur of necessity, and not enough nervous energy to make him seek any exacting employments. He might have collected stamps or coins, or translated Horace, or bound books, or invented new species of diatoms. But, as it happened, he grew orchids, and had one ambitious little hothouse.

"I have a fancy," he said over his coffee, "that something is going to happen to me to-day." He spoke—as he moved and thought—slowly.

"Oh, don't say *that!*" said his housekeeper—who was also his remote cousin. For "something happening" was a euphemism that meant only one thing to her.

"You misunderstand me. I mean nothing unpleasant—though what I do mean I scarcely know.

"To-day," he continued after a pause, "Peters are going to sell a batch of plants from the Andamans and the Indies. I shall go up and see what they have. It may be I shall buy something good, unawares. That may be it."

He passed his cup for his second cupful of coffee.

"Are these the things collected by that poor young fellow you told me of the other day?" asked his cousin as she filled his cup.

"Yes," he said, and became meditative over a piece of toast.

"Nothing ever does happen to me," he remarked presently, beginning to think aloud. "I wonder why? Things enough happen to other people. There is Harvey. Only the other week, on Monday he picked up sixpence, on Wednesday his chicks all had the staggers, on Friday his cousin came home from Australia, and on Saturday he broke his ankle. What a whirl of excitement!—compared to me."

"I think I would rather be without so much excitement," said his housekeeper. "It can't be good for you."

"I suppose it's troublesome. Still—you see, nothing ever happens to me. When I was a little boy I never had accidents. I never fell in love as I grew up. Never married—I wonder how it feels to have something happen to you, something really remarkable.

"That orchid-collector was only thirty-six—twenty years younger than myself—when he died. And he had been married twice and divorced once; he had had malarial fever four times, and once he broke his thigh. He killed a Malay once, and once he was wounded by a poisoned dart. And in the end he was killed by jungle-leeches. It must have all been very troublesome, but then it must have been very interesting, you know—except, perhaps, the leeches."

"I am sure it was not good for him," said the lady, with conviction.

"Perhaps not." And then Wedderburn looked at his watch. "Twenty-three minutes past eight. I am going up by the quarter to twelve train, so that there is plenty of time. I think I shall wear my alpaca jacket—it is quite warm enough—and my grey felt hat and brown shoes. I suppose—"

He glanced out of the window at the serene sky and sunlit garden, and then nervously at his cousin's face.

"I think you had better take an umbrella if you are going to London," she said in a voice that admitted of no denial. "There's all between here and the station coming back."

When he returned he was in a state of mild excitement. He had made a purchase. It was rare that he could make up his mind quickly enough to buy, but this time he had done so.

"There are Vandas," he said, "and a Dendrobe and some Palæonophis." He surveyed his purchases lovingly as he consumed his soup. They were laid out on the spotless tablecloth before him, and he was telling his cousin all about them as he slowly meandered through his dinner. It was his custom to live all his visits to London over again in the evening for her and his own entertainment.

"I knew something would happen to-day. And I have bought all these. Some of them—some of them—I feel sure, do you know, that some of them will be remarkable. I don't know how it is, but I feel just as sure as if some one had told me that some of these will turn out remarkable.

"That one"—he pointed to a shrivelled rhizome—"was not identified. It may be a Palæonophis—or it may not. It may be a new species, or even a new genus. And it was the last that poor Batten ever collected."

"I don't like the look of it," said his housekeeper. "It's such an ugly shape."

"To me it scarcely seems to have a shape."

"I don't like those things that stick out," said his housekeeper.

"It shall be put away in a pot to-morrow."

"It looks," said the housekeeper, "like a spider shamming dead."

Wedderburn smiled and surveyed the root with his head on one side. "It is certainly not a pretty lump of stuff. But you can never judge of these things from their dry appearance. It may turn out to be a very beautiful orchid indeed. How busy I shall be to-morrow! I must see to-night just exactly what to do with these things, and to-morrow I shall set to work.

"They found poor Batten lying dead, or dying, in a mangrove swamp—I forget which," he began again presently, "with one of these very orchids crushed up under his body. He had been unwell for some days with some kind of native fever, and I suppose he fainted. These mangrove swamps are very unwholesome. Every drop of blood, they say, was taken out of him by the jungle-leeches. It may be that very plant that cost him his life to obtain."

"I think none the better of it for that."

"Men must work though women may weep," said Wedderburn, with profound gravity.

"Fancy dying away from every comfort in a nasty swamp! Fancy being ill of fever with nothing to take but chlorodyne and quinine—if men were left to themselves they would live on chlorodyne and quinine—and no one round you but horrible natives! They say the Andaman islanders are most disgusting wretches—and, anyhow, they can scarcely make good nurses, not having the necessary training. And just for people in England to have orchids!"

"I don't suppose it was comfortable, but some men seem to enjoy that kind of thing," said Wedderburn. "Anyhow, the natives of his party were sufficiently civilised to take care of all his collection until his colleague, who was an ornithologist, came back again from the interior; though they could not tell the species of the orchid, and had let it wither. And it makes these things more interesting."

"It makes them disgusting. I should be afraid of some of the malaria clinging to them. And just think, there has been a dead body lying across that ugly thing! I never thought of that before. There! I declare I cannot eat another mouthful of dinner."

"I will take them off the table if you like, and put them in the window-seat. I can see them just as well there."

The next few days he was indeed singularly busy in his steamy little hothouse, fussing about with charcoal, lumps of teak, moss, and all the other mysteries of the orchid cultivator. He considered he was having a wonderfully eventful time. In the evening he would talk about these new orchids to his friends, and over and over again he reverted to his expectation of something strange.

Several of the Vandas and the Dendrobium died under his care, but presently the strange orchid began to show signs of life. He was delighted, and took his housekeeper right away from jam-making to see it at once, directly he made the discovery.

"That is a bud," he said, "and presently there will be a lot of leaves there, and those little things coming out here are aërial rootlets."

"They look to me like little white fingers poking out of the brown. I don't like them," said his housekeeper.

"Why not?"

"I don't know. They look like fingers trying to get at you. I can't help my likes and dislikes."

"I don't know for certain, but I don't *think* there are any orchids I know that have aërial rootlets quite like that. It may be my fancy, of course. You see they are a little flattened at the ends."

"I don't like 'em," said his housekeeper, suddenly shivering and turning away. "I know it's very silly of me—and I'm very sorry, particularly as you like the thing so much. But I can't help thinking of that corpse."

"But it may not be that particular plant. That was merely a guess of mine."

His housekeeper shrugged her shoulders.

"Anyhow I don't like it," she said.

Wedderburn felt a little hurt at her dislike to the plant. But that did not prevent his talking to her about orchids generally, and this orchid in particular, whenever he felt inclined.

"There are such queer things about orchids," he said one day; "such possibilities of surprises. You know, Darwin studied their fertilisation, and showed that the whole structure of an ordinary orchid-flower was contrived in order that moths might carry the pollen from plant to plant. Well, it seems that there are lots of orchids known the flower of which cannot possibly be used for fertilisation in that way. Some of the Cypripediums, for instance; there are no insects known that can possibly fertilise them, and some of them have never been found with seed."

"But how do they form new plants?"

"By runners and tubers, and that kind of outgrowth. That is easily explained. The puzzle is, what are the flowers for?

"Very likely," he added, "*my* orchid may be something extraordinary in that way. If so, I shall study it. I have often thought of making researches as Darwin did. But hitherto I have not found the time, or something else has happened to prevent it. The leaves are beginning to unfold now. I do wish you would come and see them!"

But she said that the orchid-house was so hot it gave her the headache. She had seen the plant once again, and the aërial rootlets, which were now some of them more than a foot long, had unfortunately reminded her of tentacles reaching out after something; and they got into her dreams, growing after her with incredible rapidity. So that she had settled to her entire satisfaction that she would not see that plant again, and Wedderburn had to admire its leaves alone. They were of the ordinary broad form, and a deep glossy green, with splashes and dots of deep red towards the base. He knew of no other leaves quite like them. The plant was placed on a low bench near the thermometer, and close by was a simple arrangement by which a tap dripped on the hot-water pipes and kept the air steamy. And he spent his afternoons now with some regularity meditating on the approaching flowering of this strange plant.

And at last the great thing happened. Directly he entered

the little glass house he knew that the spike had burst out, although his great *Palæonophis Lowii* hid the corner where his new darling stood. There was a new odour in the air, a rich, intensely sweet scent, that overpowered every other in that crowded, steaming little greenhouse.

Directly he noticed this he hurried down to the strange orchid. And, behold! the trailing green spikes bore now three great splashes of blossom, from which this overpowering sweetness proceeded. He stopped before them in an ecstasy of admiration.

The flowers were white, with streaks of golden orange upon the petals; the heavy labellum was coiled into an intricate projection, and a wonderful bluish purple mingled there with the gold. He could see at once that the genus was altogether a new one. And the insufferable scent! How hot the place was! The blossoms swam before his eyes.

He would see if the temperature was right. He made a step towards the thermometer. Suddenly everything appeared unsteady. The bricks on the floor were dancing up and down. Then the white blossoms, the green leaves behind them, the whole greenhouse, seemed to sweep sideways, and then in a curve upward.

At half-past four his cousin made the tea, according to their invariable custom. But Wedderburn did not come in for his tea.

"He is worshipping that horrid orchid," she told herself, and waited ten minutes. "His watch must have stopped. I will go and call him."

She went straight to the hothouse, and, opening the door, called his name. There was no reply. She noticed that the air was very close, and loaded with an intense perfume. Then she saw something lying on the bricks between the hotwater pipes.

For a minute, perhaps, she stood motionless.

He was lying, face upward, at the foot of the strange orchid. The tentacle-like aërial rootlets no longer swayed freely in the air, but were crowded together, a tangle of grey ropes, and stretched tight with their ends closely applied to his chin and neck and hands.

She did not understand. Then she saw from under one of the exultant tentacles upon his cheek there trickled a little thread of blood.

With an inarticulate cry she ran towards him, and tried to pull him away from the leech-like suckers. She snapped two of these tentacles, and their sap dripped red.

Then the overpowering scent of the blossom began to make her head reel. How they clung to him! She tore at the tough ropes, and he and the white inflorescence swam about her. She felt she was fainting, knew she must not. She left him and hastily opened the nearest door, and, after she had panted for a moment in the fresh air, she had a brilliant inspiration. She caught up a flower-pot and smashed in the windows at the end of the greenhouse. Then she re-entered. She tugged now with renewed strength at Wedderburn's motionless body, and brought the strange orchid crashing to the floor. It still clung with the grimmest tenacity to its victim. In a frenzy, she lugged it and him into the open air.

Then she thought of tearing through the sucker rootlets one by one, and in another minute she had released him and was dragging him away from the horror.

He was white and bleeding from a dozen circular patches.

The odd-job man was coming up the garden, amazed at the smashing of glass, and saw her emerge, hauling the inanimate body with red-stained hands. For a moment he thought impossible things.

"Bring some water!" she cried, and her voice dispelled his fancies. When, with unnatural alacrity, he returned with the water, he found her weeping with excitement, and with Wedderburn's head upon her knee, wiping the blood from his face.

"What's the matter?" said Wedderburn, opening his eyes feebly, and closing them again at once.

"Go and tell Annie to come out here to me, and then go for Dr. Haddon at once," she said to the odd-job man so soon as he brought the water; and added, seeing he hesitated, "I will tell you all about it when you come back."

Presently Wedderburn opened his eyes again, and, seeing that he was troubled by the puzzle of his position, she explained to him, "You fainted in the hothouse."

"And the orchid?"

"I will see to that," she said.

Wedderburn had lost a good deal of blood, but beyond that he had suffered no very great injury. They gave him brandy mixed with some pink extract of meat, and carried him upstairs to bed. His housekeeper told her incredible story in fragments to Dr. Haddon. "Come to the orchid-house and see," she said.

The cold outer air was blowing in through the open door, and the sickly perfume was almost dispelled. Most of the torn aërial rootlets lay already withered amidst a number of dark stains upon the bricks. The stem of the inflorescence was broken by the fall of the plant, and the flowers were growing limp and brown at the edges of the petals. The doctor stooped towards it, then saw that one of the aërial rootlets still stirred feebly, and hesitated.

The next morning the strange orchid still lay there, black now and putrescent. The door banged intermittingly in the morning breeze, and all the array of Wedderburn's orchids was shrivelled and prostrate. But Wedderburn himself was bright and garrulous upstairs in the story of his strange adventure.

Æpyornis Island

THE MAN WITH the scarred face leant over the table and looked at my bundle.

"Orchids?" he asked.

"A few," I said.

"Cypripediums?" he said.

"Chiefly," said I.

"Anything new?—I thought not. *I* did these islands twenty-five—twenty-seven years ago. If you find anything new here—well, it's brand new. I didn't leave much."

"I'm not a collector," said I.

"I was young then," he went on. "Lord! how I used to fly round." He seemed to take my measure. "I was in the East Indies two years, and in Brazil seven. Then I went to Madagascar."

"I know a few explorers by name," I said anticipating a yarn. "Who did you collect for?"

"Dawsons. I wonder if you've heard the name of Butcher ever?"

"Butcher—Butcher?" The name seemed vaguely present in my memory; then I recalled *Butcher v. Dawson.* "Why!" said I, "you are the man who sued them for four years' salary—got cast away on a desert island—"

"Your servant," said the man with the scar, bowing. "Funny case, wasn't it? Here was me, making a little fortune on that island, doing nothing for it neither, and them quite unable to give me notice. It often used to amuse me thinking over it while I was there. I did calculations of it—big—all over the blessed atoll in ornamental figuring."

"How did it happen? "said I. "I don't rightly remember the case."

"Well—you've heard of the Æpyornis?"

"Rather. Andrews was telling me of a new species he was working on only a month or so ago. Just before I sailed. They've got a thigh bone, it seems, nearly a yard long. Monster the thing must have been!"

"I believe you," said the man with the scar. "It *was* a monster. Sinbad's roc was just a legend of 'em. But when did they find these bones?"

"Three or four years ago—'91 I fancy. Why?"

"Why?—Because *I* found 'em—Lord!—it's nearly twenty years ago. If Dawsons hadn't been silly about that salary they might have made a perfect ring in 'em.—*I* couldn't help the infernal boat going adrift."

He paused. "I suppose it's the same place. A kind of swamp about ninety miles north of Antananarivo. Do you happen to know? You have to go to it along the coast by boats. You don't happen to remember, perhaps?"

"I don't. I fancy Andrews said something about a swamp."

"It must be the same. It's on the east coast. And somehow there's something in the water that keeps things from decaying. Like creosote it smells. It reminded me of Trinidad. Did they get any more eggs? Some of the eggs I found were a foot and a half long. The swamp goes circling round, you know, and cuts off this bit. It's mostly salt, too. Well—What a time I had of it! I found the things quite by accident. We went for eggs, me and two native chaps, in one of those rum canoes all tied together, and found the bones at the same time. We had a tent and provisions for four days, and we pitched on one of the firmer places. To think of it brings that odd tarry smell back even now. It's funny work. You go probing into the mud with iron rods, you know. Usually the egg gets smashed. I wonder how long it is since these Æpyornises really lived. The missionaries say the natives have legends about when they were alive, but I never heard any such stories myself.[1] But certainly those eggs we got were as fresh as if they had been new-laid. Fresh! Carrying them down to the boat one of my nigger chaps dropped one on a rock and it smashed. How I lammed into the beggar! But sweet it was as if it was new-laid, not even smelly, and its mother dead these four hundred years perhaps. Said a centipede had bit him. However, I'm getting off the straight with the story. It had taken us all day to dig into the slush and get these eggs out unbroken, and we were all covered with beastly black mud, and naturally I was cross. So far as I knew they were the only eggs that had ever been got out not even cracked. I went afterwards to see the ones they have at the Natural History Museum in London: all of them were cracked and just stuck together like a mosaic, and bits missing. Mine were perfect, and I meant to blow them when I got back. Naturally I was annoyed at the silly devil dropping three hours' work just on account of a centipede. I hit him about rather."

The man with the scar took out a clay pipe. I placed my pouch before him. He filled up absent-mindedly.

[1]No European is known to have seen a live Æpyornis, with the doubtful exception of MacAndrew, who visited Madagascar in 1745. H. G. W.

"How about the others? Did you get those home? I don't remember—"

"That's the queer part of the story. I had three others. Perfectly fresh eggs. Well, we put 'em in the boat, and then I went up to the tent to make some coffee, leaving my two heathens down by the beach—the one fooling about with his sting and the other helping him. It never occurred to me that the beggars would take advantage of the peculiar position I was in to pick a quarrel. But I suppose the centipede poison and the kicking I'd given him had upset the one—he was always a cantankerous sort—and he persuaded the other.

"I remember I was sitting and smoking and boiling up the water over a spirit-lamp business I used to take on these expeditions. Incidentally I was admiring the swamp under the sunset. All black and blood red it was, in streaks—a beautiful sight. And up beyond, the land rose grey and hazy to the hills, and the sky behind them red, like a furnace mouth. And fifty yards behind the back of me was these blessed heathen—quite regardless of the tranquil air of things—plotting to cut off with the boat and leave me all alone with three days' provisions and a canvas tent, and nothing to drink whatsoever, beyond a little keg of water. I heard a kind of yelp behind me, and there they were in this canoe affair—it wasn't properly a boat—and perhaps twenty yards from land. I realised what was up in a moment. My gun was in the tent, and besides I had no bullets—only duck shot. They knew that. But I had a little revolver in my pocket and I pulled that out as I ran down to the beach.

"'Come back!' says I, flourishing it.

"They jabbered something at me, and the man that broke the egg jeered. I aimed at the other—because he was unwounded and had the paddle, and I missed. They laughed. However, I was n't beat. I knew I had to keep cool, and I tried him again and made him jump with the whang of it. The third time I got his head, and over he went, and the paddle with him. It was a precious lucky shot for a revolver. I reckon it was fifty yards. He went right under. I don't know if he was shot, or simply stunned and drowned. Then I began to shout to the other chap to come back, but he huddled up in the canoe and refused to answer. So I fired out my revolver at him and never got near him.

"I felt a precious fool, I can tell you. There I was on this rotten, black beach, flat swamp all behind me, and the flat sea, cold after the sunset, and just this black canoe drifting steadily out to sea. I tell you I damned Dawsons and Jamrachs and Museums and all the rest of it just to rights. I bawled to this nigger to come back, until my voice went up into a scream.

"There was nothing for it but to swim after him and take my luck with the sharks. So I opened my clasp-knife and put it in my mouth and took off my clothes and waded in. As soon as I was in the water I lost sight of the canoe, but I aimed, as I judged, to head it off. I hoped the man in it was too bad to navigate it, and that it would keep on drifting in the same direction. Presently it came up over the horizon again to the south-westward about. The afterglow of sunset was well over now and the dim of night creeping up. The stars were coming through the blue. I swam like a champion, though my legs and arms were soon aching.

"However, I came up to him by the time the stars were fairly out. As it got darker I began to see all manner of glowing things in the water—phosphorescence, you know. At times it made me giddy. I hardly knew which was stars and which was phosphorescence, and whether I was swimming on my head or my heels. The canoe was as black as sin, and the ripple under the bows like liquid fire. I was naturally chary of clambering up into it. I was anxious to see what he was up to first. He seemed to be lying cuddled up in a lump in the bows, and the stern was all out of water. The thing kept turning round slowly as it drifted—kind of waltzing, don't you know. I went to the stern and pulled it down, expecting him to wake up. Then I began to clamber in with my knife in my hand, and ready for a rush. But he never stirred. So there I sat in the stern of the little canoe, drifting away over the calm phosphorescent sea, and with all the host of the stars above me, waiting for something to happen.

"After a long time I called him by name, but he never answered. I was too tired to take any risks by going along to him. So we sat there. I fancy I dozed once or twice. When the dawn came I saw he was as dead as a doornail and all puffed up and purple. My three eggs and the bones were lying in the middle of the canoe, and the keg of water and some coffee and biscuits wrapped in a Cape 'Argus' by his feet, and a tin of methylated spirit underneath him. There was no paddle, nor in fact anything except the spirit tin that one could use as one, so I settled to drift until I was picked up. I held an inquest on him, brought in a verdict against some snake, scorpion, or centipede unknown, and sent him overboard.

"After that I had a drink of water and a few biscuits, and took a look round. I suppose a man low down as I was don't see very far; leastways, Madagascar was clean out of sight, and any trace of land at all. I saw a sail going south-westward—looked like a schooner, but her hull never came up. Presently the sun got high in the sky and began to beat down upon me. Lord!—it pretty near made my brains boil.

I tried dipping my head in the sea, but after a while my eye fell on the Cape 'Argus,' and I lay down flat in the canoe and spread this over me. Wonderful things these newspapers. I never read one through thoroughly before, but it's odd what you get up to when you're alone, as I was. I suppose I read that blessed old Cape 'Argus' twenty times. The pitch in the canoe simply reeked with the heat and rose up into big blisters.

"I drifted ten days," said the man with the scar. "It's a little thing in the telling, is n't it? Every day was like the last. Except in the morning and the evening I never kept a look-out even—the blaze was so infernal. I didn't see a sail after the first three days, and those I saw took no notice of me. About the sixth night a ship went by scarcely half a mile away from me, with all its lights ablaze and its ports open, looking like a big firefly. There was music aboard. I stood up and shouted and screamed at it. The second day I broached one of the Æpyornis eggs, scraped the shell away at the end bit by bit, and tried it, and I was glad to find it was good enough to eat. A bit flavoury—not bad, I mean, but with something of the taste of a duck's egg. There was a kind of circular patch about six inches across on one side of the yolk, and with streaks of blood and a white mark like a ladder in it that I thought queer, but I did n't understand what this meant at the time, and I was n't inclined to be particular. The egg lasted me three days, with biscuits and a drink of water. I chewed coffee berries too—invigorating stuff. The second egg I opened about the eighth day. And it scared me."

The man with the scar paused. "Yes," he said —"developing.

"I daresay you find it hard to believe. *I* did, with the thing before me. There the egg had been, sunk in that cold black mud, perhaps three hundred years. But there was no mistaking it. There was the—what is it?—embryo, with its big head and curved back and its heart beating under its throat, and the yolk shrivelled up and great membranes spreading inside of the shell and all over the yolk. Here was I hatching out the eggs of the biggest of all extinct birds, in a little canoe in the midst of the Indian Ocean. If old Dawson had known that! It was worth four years' salary. What do *you* think?

"However, I had to eat that precious thing up, every bit of it, before I sighted the reef, and some of the mouthfuls were beastly unpleasant. I left the third one alone. I held it up to the light, but the shell was too thick for me to get any notion of what might be happening inside; and though I fancied I heard blood pulsing, it might have been the rustle in my own ears, like what you listen to in a seashell.

"Then came the atoll. Came out of the sunrise, as it were, suddenly, close up to me. I drifted straight towards it until I was about half a mile from shore—not more, and then the current took a turn, and I had to paddle as hard as I could with my hands and bits of the Æpyornis shell to make the place. However, I got there. It was just a common atoll about four miles round, with a few trees growing and a spring in one place and the lagoon full of parrot fish. I took the egg ashore and put it in a good place well above the tide lines and in the sun, to give it all the chance I could, and pulled the canoe up safe, and loafed about prospecting. It's rum how dull an atoll is. When I was a kid I thought nothing could be finer or more adventurous than the Robinson Crusoe business, but that place was as monotonous as a book of sermons. I went round finding eatable things and generally thinking; but I tell you I was bored to death before the first day was out. It shows my luck—the very day I landed the weather changed. A thunderstorm went by to the north and flicked its wing over the island, and in the night there came a drencher and a howling wind slap over us. It wouldn't have taken much, you know, to upset that canoe.

"I was sleeping under the canoe, and the egg was luckily among the sand higher up the beach, and the first thing I remember was a sound like a hundred pebbles hitting the boat at once and a rush of water over my body. I'd been dreaming of Antananarivo, and I sat up and holloaed to Intoshi to ask her what the devil was up, and clawed out at the chair where the matches used to be. Then I remembered where I was. There were phosphorescent waves rolling up as if they meant to eat me, and all the rest of the night as black as pitch. The air was simply yelling. The clouds seemed down on your head almost, and the rain fell as if heaven was sinking and they were baling out the waters above the firmament. One great roller came writhing at me, like a fiery serpent, and I bolted. Then I thought of the canoe, and ran down to it as the water went hissing back again, but the thing had gone. I wondered about the egg then, and felt my way to it. It was all right and well out of reach of the maddest waves, so I sat down beside it and cuddled it for company. Lord! What a night that was!

"The storm was over before the morning. There wasn't a rag of cloud left in the sky when the dawn came, and all along the beach there were bits of plank scattered—which was the disarticulated skeleton, so to speak, of my canoe. However, that gave me something to do, for, taking advantage of two of the trees being together, I rigged up a kind of storm shelter with these vestiges. And that day the egg hatched.

"Hatched, sir, when my head was pillowed on it and I was asleep. I heard a whack and felt a jar and sat up, and there was the end of the egg pecked out and a rum little brown head looking out at me. 'Lord!' I said, 'you're welcome,' and with a little difficulty he came out.

"He was a nice friendly little chap, at first, about the size of a small hen—very much like most other young birds, only bigger. His plumage was a dirty brown to begin with, with a sort of grey scab that fell off it very soon, and scarcely feathers—a kind of downy hair. I can hardly express how pleased I was to see him. I tell you, Robinson Crusoe don't make near enough of his loneliness. But here was interesting company. He looked at me and winked his eye from the front backwards like a hen, and gave a chirp and began to peck about at once, as though being hatched three hundred years too late was just nothing. 'Glad to see you, Man Friday!' says I, for I had naturally settled he was to be called Man Friday if ever he was hatched, as soon as ever I found the egg in the canoe had developed. I was a bit anxious about his feed, so I gave him a lump of raw parrot fish at once. He took it and opened his beak for more. I was glad of that, for, under the circumstances, if he'd been fanciful, I should have had to eat him after all.

"You'd be surprised what an interesting bird that Æpyornis chick was. He followed me about from the very beginning. He used to stand by me and watch while I fished in the lagoon and go shares in anything I caught. And he was sensible, too. There were nasty green warty things, like pickled gherkins, used to lie about on the beach, and he tried one of these and it upset him. He never even looked at any of them again.

"And he grew. You could almost see him grow. And as I was never much of a society man, his quiet, friendly ways suited me to a T. For nearly two years we were as happy as we could be on that island. I had no business worries, for I knew my salary was mounting up at Dawsons'. We would see a sail now and then, but nothing ever came near us. I amused myself too by decorating the island with designs worked in sea-urchins and fancy shells of various kinds. I put ÆPYORNIS ISLAND all round the place very nearly, in big letters, like what you see done with coloured stones at railway stations in the old country. And I used to lie watching the blessed bird stalking round and growing, growing, and think how I could make a living out of him by showing him about if ever I got taken off. After his first moult he began to get handsome, with a crest and a blue wattle, and a lot of green feathers at the behind of him. And then I used to puzzle whether Dawsons had any right to claim him or not. Stormy weather and in the rainy season we lay snug under the shelter I had made out of the old canoe, and I used to tell him lies about my friends at home. It was a kind of idyll, you might say. If only I had had some tobacco it would have been simply just like Heaven.

"It was about the end of the second year our little Paradise went wrong. Friday was then about fourteen feet high to the bill of him, with a big broad head like the end of a pickaxe, and two huge brown eyes with yellow rims set together like a man's—not out of sight of each other like a hen's. His plumage was fine—none of the half mourning style of your ostrich—more like a cassowary as far as colour and texture go. And then it was he began to cock his comb at me and give himself airs and show signs of a nasty temper.

"At last came a time when my fishing had been rather unlucky and he began to hang about me in a queer, meditative way. I thought he might have been eating sea-cucumbers or something, but it was really just discontent on his part. I was hungry too, and when at last I landed a fish I wanted it for myself. Tempers were short that morning on both sides. He pecked at it and grabbed it, and I gave him a whack on the head to make him leave go. And at that he went for me. Lord!

"He gave me this in the face." The man indicated his scar. "Then he kicked me. It was like a cart horse. I got up, and seeing he hadn't finished I started off full tilt with my arms doubled up over my face. But he ran on those gawky legs of his faster than a race horse, and kept landing out at me with sledge-hammer kicks, and bringing his pickaxe down on the back of my head. I made for the lagoon, and went in up to my neck. He stopped at the water, for he hated getting his feet wet, and began to make a shindy, something like a peacock's, only hoarser. He started strutting up and down the beach. I'll admit I felt small to see this blessed fossil lording it there. And my head and face were all bleeding, and—well, my body just one jelly of bruises.

"I decided to swim across the lagoon and leave him alone for a bit, until the affair blew over. I shinned up the tallest palm-tree and sat there thinking of it all. I don't suppose I ever felt so hurt by anything before or since. It was the brutal ingratitude of the creature. I'd been more than a brother to him. I'd hatched him. Educated him. A great, gawky, out-of-date bird! And me a human being—heir of the ages and all that.

"I thought after a time he'd begin to see things in that light himself, and feel a little sorry for his behaviour. I thought if I was to catch some nice little bits of fish, perhaps, and go to him presently in a casual kind of way, and offer them to him, he might do the sensible thing. It took me some time to learn how unforgiving and cantankerous an extinct bird can be. Malice!

"I won't tell you all the little devices I tried to get that bird round again. I simply can't. It makes my cheek burn with shame even now to think of the snubs and buffets I had from this infernal curiosity. I tried violence. I chucked lumps of coral at him from a safe distance, but he only swallowed them. I shied my open knife at him and almost lost it, though it was too big for him to swallow. I tried starving him out and struck fishing, but he took to picking along the beach at low water after worms, and rubbed along on that. Half my time I spent up to my neck in the lagoon, and the rest up the palm-trees. One of them was scarcely high enough, and when he caught me up it he had a regular Bank Holiday with the calves of my legs. It got unbearable. I don't know if you have ever tried sleeping up a palm-tree. It gave me the most horrible nightmares. Think of the shame of it too! Here was this extinct animal mooning about my island like a sulky duke, and me not allowed to rest the sole of my foot on the place. I used to cry with weariness and vexation. I told him straight that I didn't mean to be chased about a desert island by any damned anachronisms. I told him to go and peck a navigator of his own age. But he only snapped his beak at me. Great ugly bird—all legs and neck!

"I shouldn't like to say how long that went on altogether. I'd have killed him sooner if I'd known how. However, I hit on a way of settling him at last. It's a South American dodge. I joined all my fishing lines together with stems of seaweed and things, and made a stoutish string, perhaps twelve yards in length or more, and I fastened two lumps of coral rock to the ends of this. It took me some time to do, because every now and then I had to go into the lagoon or up a tree as the fancy took me. This I whirled rapidly round my head and then let it go at him. The first time I missed, but the next time the string caught his legs beautifully and wrapped round them again and again. Over he went. I threw it standing waist-deep in the lagoon, and as soon as he went down I was out of the water and sawing at his neck with my knife—

"I don't like to think of that even now. I felt like a murderer while I did it, though my anger was hot against him. When I stood over him and saw him bleeding on the white sand and his beautiful great legs and neck writhing in his last agony—Pah!

"With that tragedy, Loneliness came upon me like a curse. Good Lord! you can't imagine how I missed that bird. I sat by his corpse and sorrowed over him, and shivered as I looked round the desolate, silent reef. I thought of what a jolly little bird he had been when he was hatched, and of a thousand pleasant tricks he had played before he went wrong. I thought if I'd only wounded him I might have nursed him round into a better understanding. If I'd had any means of digging into the coral rock I'd have buried him. I felt exactly as if he was human. As it was I couldn't think of eating him, so I put him in the lagoon and the little fishes picked him clean. Then one day a chap cruising about in a yacht had a fancy to see if my atoll still existed.

"He didn't come a moment too soon, for I was about sick enough of the desolation of it, and only hesitating whether I should walk out into the sea and finish up the business that way, or fall back on the green things.

"I sold the bones to a man named Winslow—a dealer near the British Museum, and he says he sold them to old Havers. It seems Havers didn't understand they were extra large, and it was only after his death they attracted attention. They called 'em Æpyornis—what was it?"

"*Æpyornis vastus,*" said I. "It's funny, the very thing was mentioned to me by a friend of mine. When they found an Æpyornis with a thigh a yard long they thought they had reached the top of the scale and called him *Æpyornis maximus*. Then some one turned up another thigh bone four feet six or more, and that they called *Æpyornis Titan*. Then your *vastus* was found after old Havers died, in his collection, and then a *vastissimus* turned up."

"Winslow was telling me as much," said the man with the scar. "If they get any more Æpyornises, he reckons some scientific swell will go and burst a blood-vessel. But it was a queer thing to happen to a man; wasn't it—altogether?"

The Plattner Story

WHETHER THE STORY of Gottfried Plattner is to be credited or not, is a pretty question in the value of evidence. On the one hand, we have seven witnesses—to be perfectly exact, we have six and a half pairs of eyes, and one undeniable fact; and on the other we have—what is it?—prejudice, common sense, the inertia of opinion. Never were there seven more honest-seeming witnesses; never was there a more undeniable fact than the inversion of Gottfried Plattner's anatomical structure, and—never was there a more preposterous story than the one they have to tell! The most preposterous part of the story is the worthy Gottfried's contribution (for I count him as one of the seven). Heaven forbid that I should be led into giving countenance to superstition by a passion for impartiality, and so come to share the fate of Eusapia's patrons! Frankly, I believe there is something crooked about this business of Gottfried Plattner; but what that crooked factor is, I will admit as frankly, I do not know. I have been surprised at the credit accorded to the story in the most unexpected and authoritative quarters.

The fairest way to the reader, however, will be for me to tell it without further comment.

Gottfried Plattner is, in spite of his name, a freeborn Englishman. His father was an Alsatian who came to England in the Sixties, married a respectable English girl of unexceptionable antecedents, and died, after a wholesome and uneventful life (devoted, I understand, chiefly to the laying of parquet flooring), in 1887. Gottfried's age is seven-and-twenty. He is, by virtue of his heritage of three languages, Modern Languages Master in a small private school in the South of England. To the casual observer he is singularly like any other Modern Languages Master in any other small private school. His costume is neither very costly nor very fashionable, but, on the other hand, it is not markedly cheap or shabby; his complexion, like his height and his bearing, is inconspicuous. You would notice, perhaps, that, like the majority of people, his face was not absolutely symmetrical, his right eye a little larger than the left, and his jaw a trifle heavier on the right side. If you, as an ordinary careless person, were to bare his chest and feel his heart beating, you would probably find it quite like the heart of any one else. But here you and the trained observer would part company. If you found his heart quite ordinary, the trained observer would find it quite otherwise. And once the thing was pointed out to you, you too would perceive the peculiarity easily enough. It is that Gottfried's heart beats on the right side of his body.

Now, that is not the only singularity of Gottfried's structure, although it is the only one that would appeal to the untrained mind. Careful sounding of Gottfried's internal arrangements, by a well-known surgeon, seems to point to the fact that all the other unsymmetrical parts of his body are similarly misplaced. The right lobe of his liver is on the left side, the left on his right; while his lungs, too, are similarly contraposed. What is still more singular, unless Gottfried is a consummate actor, we must believe that his right hand has recently become his left. Since the occurrences we are about to consider (as impartially as possible), he has found the utmost difficulty in writing, except from right to left across the paper with his left hand. He cannot throw with his right hand, he is perplexed at meal times between knife and fork, and his ideas of the rule of the road—he is a cyclist—are still a dangerous confusion. And there is not a scrap of evidence to show that before these occurrences Gottfried was at all left-handed.

There is yet another wonderful fact in this preposterous business. Gottfried produces three photographs of himself. You have him at the age of five or six, thrusting fat legs at you from under a plaid frock, and scowling. In that photograph his left eye is a little larger than his right, and his jaw is a trifle heavier on the left side. This is the reverse of his present living conditions. The photograph of Gottfried at fourteen seems to contradict these facts, but that is because it is one of those cheap "Gem" photographs that were then in vogue, taken direct upon metal, and therefore reversing things just as a looking-glass would. The third photograph represents him at one-and-twenty, and confirms the record of the others. There seems here evidence of the strongest confirmatory character that Gottfried has exchanged his left side for his right. Yet how a human being can be so changed, short of a fantastic and pointless miracle, it is exceedingly hard to suggest.

In one way, of course, these facts might be explicable on the supposition that Plattner has undertaken an elaborate mystification, on the strength of his heart's displacement. Photographs may be fudged, and left-handedness imitated. But the character of the man does not lend itself to any such theory. He is quiet, practical, unobtrusive, and thoroughly sane, from the Nordau standpoint. He likes beer, and smokes moderately, takes walking exercise daily, and has a healthily high estimate of the value of his teaching. He has a good but untrained tenor voice, and takes a pleasure in singing airs of a popular and cheerful character. He is fond, but not morbidly fond, of reading,—chiefly fiction pervaded with a vaguely pious optimism,—sleeps well, and rarely dreams. He is, in fact, the very last person to evolve a fantastic fable. Indeed, so far from forcing this story upon the world, he has been singularly reticent on the matter. He meets enquirers with a certain engaging—bashfulness is almost the word, that disarms the most suspicious. He seems genuinely ashamed that anything so unusual has occurred to him.

It is to be regretted that Plattner's aversion to the idea of post-mortem dissection may postpone, perhaps for ever, the positive proof that his entire body has had its left and right sides transposed. Upon that fact mainly the credibility of his story hangs. There is no way of taking a man and moving him about *in space*, as ordinary people understand space, that will result in our changing his sides. Whatever you do, his right is still his right, his left his left. You can do that with a perfectly thin and flat thing, of course. If you were to cut a figure out of paper, any figure with a right and left side, you could change its sides simply by lifting it up and turning it over. But with a solid it is different. Mathematical theorists tell us that the only way in which the right and left sides of a solid body can be changed is by taking that body clean out of space as we know it,—taking it out of ordinary existence, that is, and turning it somewhere outside space. This is a little abstruse, no doubt, but any one with any knowledge of mathematical theory will assure the reader of its truth. To put the thing in technical language, the curious inversion of Plattner's right and left sides is proof that he has moved out of our space into what is called the Fourth Dimension, and that he has returned again to our world. Unless we choose to consider ourselves the victims of an elaborate and motiveless fabrication, we are almost bound to believe that this has occurred.

So much for the tangible facts. We come now to the account of the phenomena that attended his temporary disappearance from the world. It appears that in the Sussexville Proprietary School Plattner not only discharged the duties of Modern Languages Master, but also taught chemistry, commercial geography, book-keeping, shorthand, drawing, and any other additional subject to which the changing fancies of the boys' parents might direct attention. He knew little or nothing of these various subjects, but in secondary as distinguished from Board or elementary schools, knowledge in the teacher is, very properly, by no means so necessary as high moral character and gentlemanly tone. In chemistry he was particularly deficient, knowing, he says, nothing beyond the Three Gases (whatever the three gases may be). As, however, his pupils began by knowing nothing, and derived all their information from him, this caused him (or any one) but little inconvenience for several terms. Then a little boy named Whibble joined the school, who had been educated (it seems) by some mischievous relative into an enquiring habit of mind. This little boy followed Plattner's lessons with marked and sustained interest, and in order to exhibit his zeal on the subject, brought, at various times, substances for Plattner to analyse. Plattner, flattered by this evidence of his power of awakening interest, and trusting to the boy's ignorance, analysed these, and even made general statements as to their composition. Indeed, he was so far stimulated by his pupil as to obtain a work upon analytical chemistry and study it during his supervision of the evening's preparation. He was surprised to find chemistry quite an interesting subject.

So far the story is absolutely commonplace. But now the greenish powder comes upon the scene. The source of that greenish powder seems, unfortunately, lost. Master Whibble tells a tortuous story of finding it done up in a packet in a disused limekiln near the Downs. It would have been an excellent thing for Plattner, and possibly for Master Whibble's family, if a match could have been applied to that powder there and then. The young gentleman certainly did not bring it to school in a packet, but in a common eight-ounce graduated medicine bottle, plugged with masticated newspaper. He gave it to Plattner at the end of the afternoon school. Four boys had been detained after school prayers in order to complete some neglected tasks, and Plattner was supervising these in the small classroom in which the chemical teaching was conducted. The appliances for the practical teaching of chemistry in the Sussexville Proprietary School, as in most small schools in this country, are characterised by a severe simplicity. They are kept in a small cupboard standing in a recess, and having about the same capacity as a common traveling trunk. Plattner, being bored with his passive superintendence, seems to have welcomed the intervention of Whibble with his green powder as an agreeable diversion, and, unlocking this cupboard, proceeded at once with his analytical experiments. Whibble sat, luckily for himself, at a safe distance, regarding him. The four malefactors, feigning a profound absorption in their work, watched him furtively with the keenest interest. For even within the limits of the Three Gases, Plattner's practical chemistry was, I understand, temerarious.

They are practically unanimous in their account of Plattner's proceedings. He poured a little of the green powder into a test-tube, and tried the substance with water, hydrochloric acid, nitric acid, and sulphuric acid in succession. Getting no result, he emptied out a little heap—nearly half the bottleful, ill fact—upon a slate and tried a match. He held the medicine bottle in his left hand. The stuff began to smoke and melt, and then—exploded with deafening violence and a blinding flash.

The five boys, seeing the flash and being prepared for catastrophes, ducked below their desks, and were none of them seriously hurt. The window was blown out into the playground, and the blackboard on its easel was upset. The slate was smashed to atoms. Some plaster fell from the ceiling. No other damage was done to the school edifice or appliances, and the boys at first, seeing nothing of Plattner, fancied he was knocked down and lying out of their sight below the desks. They jumped out of their places to go to his assistance, and were amazed to find the space empty. Being still confused by the sudden violence of the report, they hurried to the open door, under the impression that he must have been hurt, and have rushed out of the room. But Carson, the foremost, nearly collided in the doorway with the principal, Mr. Lidgett.

Mr. Lidgett is a corpulent, excitable man with one eye. The boys describe him as stumbling into the room mouthing some of those tempered expletives irritable schoolmasters accustom themselves to use—lest worse befall. "Wretched mumchancer!" he said. "Where's Mr. Plattner?" The boys are agreed on the very words. ("Wobbler," "snivelling puppy," and "mumchancer" are, it seems, among the ordinary small change of Mr. Lidgett's scholastic commerce.)

Where's Mr. Plattner? That was a question that was to be repeated many times in the next few days. It really seemed as though that frantic hyperbole, "blown to atoms," had for once realised itself. There was not a visible particle of Plattner to be seen; not a drop of blood nor a stitch of clothing to be found. Apparently he had been blown clean out of existence and left not a wrack behind. Not so much as would cover a sixpenny piece, to quote a proverbial expression! The evidence of his absolute disappearance, as a consequence of that explosion, is indubitable.

It is not necessary to enlarge here upon the commotion excited in the Sussexville Proprietary School, and in Sussexville and elsewhere, by this event. It is quite possible, indeed, that some of the readers of these pages may recall the hearing of some remote and dying version of that excitement during the last summer holidays. Lidgett, it would seem, did everything in his power to suppress and minimise the story. He instituted a penalty of twenty-five lines for any mention of Plattner's name among the boys, and stated in the schoolroom that he was clearly aware of his assistant's whereabouts. He was afraid, he explains, that the possibility of an explosion happening, in spite of the elaborate precautions taken to minimise the practical teaching of chemistry, might injure the reputation of the school; and so might any mysterious quality in Plattner's departure. Indeed, he did everything in his power to make the occurrence seem as ordinary as possible. In particular, he cross-examined the five eye-witnesses of the occurrence so searchingly that they began to doubt the plain evidence of their senses. But, in spite of these efforts, the tale, in a magnified and distorted state, made a nine days' wonder in the district, and several parents withdrew their sons on colourable pretexts. Not the least remarkable point in the matter is the fact that a large number of people in the neighbourhood dreamed singularly vivid dreams of Plattner during the period of excitement before his return, and that these dreams had a curious uniformity. In almost all of them Plattner was seen, sometimes singly, sometimes in company, wandering about through a coruscating iridescence. In all cases his face was pale and distressed, and in some he gesticulated towards the dreamer. One or two of the boys, evidently under the influence of nightmare, fancied that Plattner approached them with remarkable swiftness, and seemed to look closely into their very eyes. Others fled with Plattner from the pursuit of vague and extraordinary creatures of a globular shape. But all these fancies were forgotten in enquiries and speculations when, on the Wednesday next but one after the Monday of the explosion, Plattner returned.

The circumstances of his return were as singular as those of his departure. So far as Mr. Lidgett's somewhat choleric outline can be filled in from Plattner's hesitating statements, it would appear that on Wednesday evening, towards the hour of sunset, the former gentleman, having dismissed evening preparation, was engaged in his garden, picking and eating strawberries, a fruit of which he is inordinately fond. It is a large old-fashioned garden, secured from observation, fortunately, by a high and ivy-covered red-brick wall. Just as he was stooping over a particularly prolific plant, there was a flash in the air and a heavy thud, and before he could look round, some heavy body struck him violently from behind. He was pitched forward, crushing the strawberries he held in his hand, and that so roughly, that his silk hat—Mr. Lidgett adheres to the older ideas of scholastic costume—was driven violently down upon his forehead, and almost over one eye. This heavy missile, which slid over him sideways and collapsed into a sitting posture among the strawberry plants, proved to be our long-lost Mr. Gottfried Plattner, in an extremely dishevelled condition. He was collarless and hatless, his linen was dirty, and there was blood upon his hands. Mr. Lidgett was so indignant and surprised that he remained on all-fours, and with his hat jammed down on his eye, while he expostulated vehemently with Plattner for his disrespectful and unaccountable conduct.

This scarcely idyllic scene completes what I may call the exterior version of the Plattner story—its exoteric aspect. It is quite unnecessary to enter here into all the details of his dismissal by Mr. Lidgett. Such details, with the full names and dates and references, will be found in the larger report of these occurrences that was laid before the Society for the Investigation of Abnormal Phenomena. The singular transposition of Plattner's right and left sides was scarcely observed for the first day or so, and then first in connection with his disposition to write from right to left across the blackboard. He concealed rather than ostended this curious confirmatory circumstance, as he considered it would unfavourably affect his prospects in a new situation. The displacement of his heart was discovered some months after, when he was having a tooth extracted under anæsthetics. He then, very unwillingly, allowed a cursory surgical examination to be made of himself, with a view to a brief account in the "Journal of Anatomy." That exhausts the statement of the material facts; and we may now go on to consider Plattner's account of the matter.

But first let us clearly differentiate between the preceding portion of this story and what is to follow. All I have told thus far is established by such evidence as even a criminal lawyer would approve. Every one of the witnesses is still alive; the reader, if he have the leisure, may hunt the lads out to-morrow, or even brave the terrors of the redoubtable Lidgett, and cross-examine and trap and test to his heart's content; Gottfried Plattner, himself, and his twisted heart and his three photographs are producible. It may be taken as proved that he did disappear for nine days as the consequence of an explosion; that he returned almost as violently, under circumstances in their nature annoying to Mr. Lidgett, whatever the details of those circumstances may be; and that he returned inverted, just as a reflection returns from a mirror. From the last fact, as I have already stated, it follows almost inevitably that Plattner, during those nine days, must have been in some state of existence altogether out of space. The evidence to these statements is, indeed, far stronger than that upon which most murderers are hanged. But for his own particular account of where he had been, with its confused explanations and well-nigh self-contradictory details, we have only Mr. Gottfried Plattner's word. I do not wish to discredit that, but I must point out—what so many writers upon obscure psychic phenomena fail to do—that we are passing here from the practically undeniable to that kind of matter which any reasonable man is entitled to believe or reject as he thinks proper. The previous statements render it plausible; its discordance with common experience tilts it towards the incredible. I would prefer not to sway the beam of the reader's judgment either way, but simply to tell the story as Plattner told it me.

He gave me his narrative, I may state, at my house at Chislehurst, and so soon as he had left me that evening, I went into my study and wrote down everything as I remembered it. Subsequently he was good enough to read over a typewritten copy, so that its substantial correctness is undeniable.

He states that at the moment of the explosion he distinctly thought he was killed. He felt lifted off his feet and driven forcibly backward. It is a curious fact for psychologists that he thought clearly during his backward flight, and wondered whether he should hit the chemistry cupboard or the blackboard easel. His heels struck ground, and he staggered and fell heavily into a sitting position on something soft and firm. For a moment the concussion stunned him. He became aware at once of a vivid scent of singed hair, and he seemed to hear the voice of Lidgett asking for him. You will understand that for a time his mind was greatly confused.

At first he was distinctly under the impression that he was still in the classroom. He perceived quite distinctly the surprise of the boys and the entry of Mr. Lidgett. He is quite positive upon that score. He did not hear their remarks; but that he ascribed to the deafening effect of the experiment. Things about him seemed curiously dark and faint, but his mind explained that on the obvious but mistaken idea that the explosion had engendered a huge volume of dark smoke. Through the dimness the figures of Lidgett and the boys moved, as faint and silent as ghosts. Plattner's face still tingled with the stinging heat of the flash. He was, he says, "all muddled." His first definite thoughts seem to have been of his personal safety. He thought he was perhaps blinded and deafened. He felt his limbs and face in a gingerly manner. Then his perceptions grew clearer, and he was astonished to miss the old familiar desks and other schoolroom furniture about him. Only dim, uncertain, grey shapes stood in the place of these. Then came a thing that made him shout aloud, and awoke his stunned faculties to instant activity. *Two of the boys, gesticulating, walked one after the other clean through him!* Neither manifested the slightest consciousness of his presence. It is difficult to imagine the sensation he felt. They came against him, he says, with no more force than a wisp of mist.

Plattner's first thought after that was that he was dead. Having been brought up with thoroughly sound views in these matters, however, he was a little surprised to find his body still about him. His second conclusion was that he was not dead, but that the others were: that the explosion had destroyed the Sussexville Proprietary School and every soul in it except himself. But that, too, was scarcely satisfactory. He was thrown back upon astonished observation.

Everything about him was extraordinarily dark: at first it seemed to have an altogether ebony blackness. Overhead was a black firmament. The only touch of light in the scene was a faint greenish glow at the edge of the sky in one direction, which threw into prominence a horizon of undulating black hills. This, I say, was his impression at first. As his eye grew accustomed to the darkness, he began to distinguish a faint quality of differentiating greenish colour in the circumambient night. Against this background the furniture and occupants of the classroom, it seems, stood out like phosphorescent spectres, faint and impalpable. He extended his hand, and thrust it without an effort through the wall of the room by the fireplace.

He describes himself as making a strenuous effort to attract attention. He shouted to Lidgett, and tried to seize the boys as they went to and fro. He only desisted from these attempts when Mrs. Lidgett, whom he (as an Assistant Master) naturally disliked, entered the room. He says the sensation of being in the world, and yet not a part of it, was an extraordinarily disagreeable one. He compared his feelings, not inaptly, to those of a cat watching a mouse through a window. Whenever he made a motion to communicate with the dim, familiar world about him, he found an invisible, incomprehensible barrier preventing intercourse.

He then turned his attention to his solid environment. He found the medicine bottle still unbroken in his hand, with the remainder of the green powder therein. He put this in his pocket, and began to feel about him. Apparently, he was sitting on a boulder of rock covered with a velvety moss. The dark country about him he was unable to see, the faint, misty picture of the schoolroom blotting it out, but he had a feeling (due perhaps to a cold wind) that he was near the crest of a hill, and that a steep valley fell away beneath his feet. The green glow along the edge of the sky seemed to be growing in extent and intensity. He stood up, rubbing his eyes.

It would seem that he made a few steps, going steeply downhill, and then stumbled, nearly fell, and sat down again upon a jagged mass of rock to watch the dawn. He became aware that the world about him was absolutely silent. It was as still as it was dark, and though there was a cold wind blowing up the hill-face, the rustle of grass, the soughing of the boughs that should have accompanied it, were absent. He could hear, therefore, if he could not see, that the hillside upon which he stood was rocky and desolate. The green grew brighter every moment, and as it did so, a faint, transparent blood-red mingled with, but did not mitigate, the blackness of the sky overhead and the rocky desolations about him. Having regard to what follows, I am inclined to think that that redness may have been an optical effect due to contrast. Something black fluttered momentarily against the livid yellow-green of the lower sky, and then the thin and penetrating voice of a bell rose out of the black gulf below him. An oppressive expectation grew with the growing light.

It is probable that an hour or more elapsed while he sat there, the strange green light growing brighter every moment, and spreading slowly, in flamboyant fingers, upward towards the zenith. As it grew, the spectral vision of *our* world became relatively or absolutely fainter. Probably both, for the time must have been about that of our earthly sunset. So far as his vision of our world went, Plattner, by his few steps downhill, had passed through the floor of the classroom, and was now, it seemed, sitting in mid-air in the larger schoolroom downstairs. He saw the boarders distinctly, but much more faintly than he had seen

Lidgett. They were preparing their evening tasks, and he noticed with interest that several were cheating with their Euclid riders by means of a crib, a compilation whose existence he had hitherto never suspected. As the time passed, they faded steadily, as steadily as the light of the green dawn increased.

Looking down into the valley, he saw that the light had crept far down its rocky sides, and that the profound blackness of the abyss was now broken by a minute green glow, like the light of a glowworm. And almost immediately the limb of a huge heavenly body of blazing green rose over the basaltic undulations of the distant hills, and the monstrous hill-masses about him came out gaunt and desolate, in green light and deep, ruddy black shadows. He became aware of a vast number of ball-shaped objects drifting as thistledown drifts over the high ground. There were none of these nearer to him than the opposite side of the gorge. The bell below twanged quicker and quicker, with something like impatient insistence, and several lights moved hither and thither. The boys at work at their desks were now almost imperceptibly faint.

This extinction of our world, when the green sun of this other universe rose, is a curious point upon which Plattner insists. During the Other-World night, it is difficult to move about, on account of the vividness with which the things of this world are visible. It becomes a riddle to explain why, if this is the case, we in this world catch no glimpse of the Other-World. It is due, perhaps, to the comparatively vivid illumination of this world of ours. Plattner describes the midday of the Other-World, at its brightest, as not being nearly so bright as this world at full moon, while its night is profoundly black. Consequently, the amount of light, even in an ordinary dark room, is sufficient to render the things of the Other-World invisible, on the same principle that faint phosphorescence is only visible in the profoundest darkness. I have tried, since he told me his story, to see something of the Other-World by sitting for a long space in a photographer's dark room at night. I have certainly seen indistinctly the form of greenish slopes and rocks, but only, I must admit, very indistinctly indeed. The reader may possibly be more successful. Plattner tells me that since his return he has dreamt and seen and recognised places in the Other-World, but this is probably due to his memory of these scenes. It seems quite possible that people with unusually keen eyesight may occasionally catch a glimpse of this strange Other-World about us.

However, this is a digression. As the green sun rose, a long street of black buildings became perceptible, though only darkly and indistinctly, in the gorge, and, after some hesitation, Plattner began to clamber down the precipitous descent towards them. The descent was long and exceedingly tedious, being so not only by the extraordinary steepness, but also by reason of the looseness of the boulders with which the whole face of the hill was strewn. The noise of his descent—now and then his heels struck fire from the rocks—seemed now the only sound in the universe, for the beating of the bell had ceased. As he drew nearer, he perceived that the various edifices had a singular resemblance to tombs and mausoleums and monuments, saving only that they were all uniformly black instead of being white, as most sepulchres are. And then he saw, crowding out of the largest building, very much as people disperse from church, a number of pallid, rounded, pale-green figures. These dispersed in several directions about the broad street of the place, some going through side alleys and reappearing upon the steepness of the hill, others entering some of the small black buildings which lined the way.

At the sight of these things drifting up towards him, Plattner stopped, staring. They were not walking, they were indeed limbless, and they had the appearance of human heads, beneath which a tadpole-like body swung. He was too astonished at their strangeness, too full, indeed, of strangeness, to be seriously alarmed by them. They drove towards him, in front of the chill wind that was blowing uphill, much as soap-bubbles drive before a draught. And as he looked at the nearest of those approaching, he saw it was indeed a human head, albeit with singularly large eyes, and wearing such an expression of distress and anguish as he had never seen before upon mortal countenance. He was surprised to find that it did not turn to regard him, but seemed to be watching and following some unseen moving thing. For a moment he was puzzled, and then it occurred to him that this creature was watching with its enormous eyes something that was happening in the world he had just left. Nearer it came, and nearer, and he was too astonished to cry out. It made a very faint fretting sound as it came close to him. Then it struck his face with a gentle pat,—its touch was very cold,—and drove past him, and upward towards the crest of the hill.

An extraordinary conviction flashed across Plattner's mind that this head had a strong likeness to Lidgett. Then he turned his attention to the other heads that were now swarming thickly up the hillside. None made the slightest sign of recognition. One or two, indeed, came close to his head and almost followed the example of the first, but he dodged convulsively out of the way. Upon most of them he saw the same expression of unavailing regret he had seen upon the first, and heard the same faint sounds of wretchedness from them. One or two wept, and one rolling swiftly uphill wore an expression of diabolical rage. But others were cold, and several had a look of gratified interest in their eyes.

One, at least, was almost in an ecstasy of happiness. Plattner does not remember that he recognised any more likenesses in those he saw at this time.

For several hours, perhaps, Plattner watched these strange things dispersing themselves over the hills, and not till long after they had ceased to issue from the clustering black buildings in the gorge, did he resume his downward climb. The darkness about him increased so much that he had a difficulty in stepping true. Overhead the sky was now a bright, pale green. He felt neither hunger nor thirst. Later, when he did, he found a chilly stream running down the centre of the gorge, and the rare moss upon the boulders, when he tried it at last in desperation, was good to eat.

He groped about among the tombs that ran down the gorge, seeking vaguely for some clue to these inexplicable things. After a long time he came to the entrance of the big mausoleum-like building from which the heads had issued. In this he found a group of green lights burning upon a kind of basaltic altar, and a bell-rope from a belfry overhead hanging down into the centre of the place. Round the wall ran a lettering of fire in a character unknown to him. While he was still wondering at the purport of these things, he heard the receding tramp of heavy feet echoing far down the street. He ran out into the darkness again, but he could see nothing. He had a mind to pull the bell-rope, and finally decided to follow the footsteps. But, although he ran far, he never overtook them; and his shouting was of no avail. The gorge seemed to extend an interminable distance. It was as dark as earthly starlight throughout its length, while the ghastly green day lay along the upper edge of its precipices. There were none of the heads, now, below. They were all, it seemed, busily occupied along the upper slopes. Looking up, he saw them drifting hither and thither, some hovering stationary, some flying swiftly through the air. It reminded him, he said, of "big snowflakes;" only these were black and pale green.

In pursuing the firm, undeviating footsteps that he never overtook, in groping into new regions of this endless devil's dyke, in clambering up and down the pitiless heights, in wandering about the summits, and in watching the drifting faces, Plattner states that he spent the better part of seven or eight days. He did not keep count, he says. Though once or twice he found eyes watching him, he had word with no living soul. He slept among the rocks on the hillside. In the gorge things earthly were invisible, because, from the earthly standpoint, it was far underground. On the altitudes, so soon as the earthly day began, the world became visible to him. He found himself sometimes stumbling over the dark-green rocks, or arresting himself on a precipitous brink, while all about him the green branches of the Sussexville lanes were swaying; or, again, he seemed to be walking through the Sussexville streets, or watching unseen the private business of some household. And then it was he discovered, that to almost every human being in our world there pertained some of these drifting heads: that every one in the world is watched intermittently by these helpless disembodiments.

What are they—these Watchers of the Living? Plattner never learned. But two, that presently found and followed him, were like his childhood's memory of his father and mother. Now and then other faces turned their eyes upon him: eyes like those of dead people who had swayed him, or injured him, or helped him in his youth and manhood. Whenever they looked at him, Plattner was overcome with a strange sense of responsibility. To his mother he ventured to speak; but she made no answer. She looked sadly, steadfastly, and tenderly—a little reproachfully, too, it seemed—into his eyes.

He simply tells this story: he does not endeavour to explain. We are left to surmise who these Watchers of the Living may be, or if they are indeed the Dead, why they should so closely and passionately watch a world they have left for ever. It may be—indeed to my mind it seems just—that, when our life has closed, when evil or good is no longer a choice for us, we may still have to witness the working out of the train of consequences we have laid. If human souls continue after death, then surely human interests continue after death. But that is merely my own guess at the meaning of the things seen. Plattner offers no interpretation, for none was given him. It is well the reader should understand this clearly. Day after day, with his head reeling, he wandered about this strange-lit world outside the world, weary and, towards the end, weak and hungry. By day—by our earthly day, that is—the ghostly vision of the old familiar scenery of Sussexville, all about him, irked and worried him. He could not see where to put his feet, and ever and again with a chilly touch one of these Watching Souls would come against his face. And after dark the multitude of these Watchers about him, and their intent distress, confused his mind beyond describing. A great longing to return to the earthly life that was so near and yet so remote consumed him. The unearthliness of things about him produced a positively painful mental distress. He was worried beyond describing by his own particular followers. He would shout at them to desist from staring at him, scold at them, hurry away from them. They were always mute and intent. Run as he might over the uneven ground, they followed his destinies.

On the ninth day, towards evening, Plattner heard the invisible footsteps approaching, far away down the gorge. He was then wandering over the broad crest of the same hill upon which he had fallen in his entry into this strange

Other-World of his. He turned to hurry down into the gorge, feeling his way hastily, and was arrested by the sight of the thing that was happening in a room in a back street near the school. Both of the people in the room he knew by sight. The windows were open, the blinds up, and the setting sun shone clearly into it, so that it came out quite brightly at first, a vivid oblong of room, lying like a magic-lantern picture upon the black landscape and the livid green dawn. In addition to the sunlight, a candle had just been lit in the room.

On the bed lay a lank man, his ghastly white face terrible upon the tumbled pillow. His clenched hands were raised above his head. A little table beside the bed carried a few medicine bottles, some toast and water, and an empty glass. Every now and then the lank man's lips fell apart, to indicate a word he could not articulate. But the woman did not notice that he wanted anything, because she was busy turning out papers from an old-fashioned bureau in the opposite corner of the room. At first the picture was very vivid indeed, but as the green dawn behind it grew brighter and brighter, so it became fainter and more and more transparent.

As the echoing footsteps paced nearer and nearer, those footsteps that sound so loud in that Other-World and come so silently in this, Plattner perceived about him a great multitude of dim faces gathering together out of the darkness and watching the two people in the room. Never before had he seen so many of the Watchers of the Living. A multitude had eyes only for the sufferer in the room, another multitude, in infinite anguish, watched the woman as she hunted with greedy eyes for something she could not find. They crowded about Plattner, they came across his sight and buffeted his face, the noise of their unavailing regrets was all about him. He saw clearly only now and then. At other times the picture quivered dimly, through the veil of green reflections upon their movements. In the room it must have been very still, and Plattner says the candle flame streamed up into a perfectly vertical line of smoke, but in his ears each footfall and its echoes beat like a clap of thunder. And the faces! Two, more particularly near the woman's: one a woman's also, white and clear-featured, a face which might have once been cold and hard, but which was now softened by the touch of a wisdom strange to earth. The other might have been the woman's father. Both were evidently absorbed in the contemplation of some act of hateful meanness, so it seemed, which they could no longer guard against and prevent. Behind were others, teachers, it may be, who had taught ill, friends whose influence had failed. And over the man, too—a multitude, but none that seemed to be parents or teachers! Faces that might once have been coarse, now purged to strength by sorrow! And in the forefront one face, a girlish one, neither angry nor remorseful, but merely patient and weary, and, as it seemed to Plattner, waiting for relief. His powers of description fail him at the memory of this multitude of ghastly countenances. They gathered on the stroke of the bell. He saw them all in the space of a second. It would seem that he was so worked on by his excitement that, quite involuntarily, his restless fingers took the bottle of green powder out of his pocket and held it before him. But he does not remember that.

Abruptly the footsteps ceased. He waited for the next, and there was silence, and then suddenly, cutting through the unexpected stillness like a keen, thin blade, came the first stroke of the bell. At that the multitudinous faces swayed to and fro and a louder crying began all about him. The woman did not hear; she was burning something now in the candle flame. At the second stroke everything grew dim, and a breath of wind, icy cold, blew through the host of watchers. They swirled about him like an eddy of dead leaves in the spring, and at the third stroke something was extended through them to the bed. You have heard of a beam of light. This was like a beam of darkness, and looking again at it, Plattner saw that it was a shadowy arm and hand.

The green sun was now topping the black desolations of the horizon, and the vision of the room was very faint. Plattner could see that the white of the bed struggled, and was convulsed; and that the woman looked round over her shoulder at it, startled.

The cloud of watchers lifted high like a puff of green dust before the wind, and swept swiftly downward towards the temple in the gorge. Then suddenly Plattner understood the meaning of the shadowy black arm that stretched across his shoulder and clutched its prey. He did not dare turn his head to see the Shadow behind the arm. With a violent effort, and covering his eyes, he set himself to run, made, perhaps, twenty strides, then slipped on a boulder, and fell. He fell forward on his hands; and the bottle smashed and exploded as he touched the ground.

In another moment he found himself, stunned and bleeding, sitting face to face with Lidgett in the old walled garden behind the school.

There the story of Plattner's experiences ends. I have resisted, I believe successfully, the natural disposition of a writer of fiction to dress up incidents of this sort. I have told the thing as far as possible in the order in which Plattner told it to me. I have carefully avoided any attempt at style, effect, or construction. It would have been easy, for instance, to have worked the scene of the death-bed into a kind of plot in which Plattner might have been involved. But, quite apart from the objectionableness of falsifying a most extraordinary true story, any such trite devices would spoil, to my mind, the peculiar effect of this dark world, with its livid green illumination and its drifting Watchers of the Living, which, unseen and unapproachable to us, is yet lying all about us.

It remains to add, that a death did actually occur in Vincent Terrace, just beyond the school garden, and, so far as can be proved, at the moment of Plattner's return. Deceased was a rate-collector and insurance agent. His widow, who was much younger than himself, married last month a Mr. Whymper, a veterinary surgeon of Allbeeding. As the portion of this story given here has in various forms circulated orally in Sussexville, she has consented to my use of her name, on condition that I make it distinctly known that she emphatically contradicts every detail of Plattner's account of her husband's last moments. She burnt no will, she says, although Plattner never accused her of doing so; her husband made but one will, and that just after their marriage. Certainly, from a man who had never seen it, Plattner's account of the furniture of the room was curiously accurate.

One other thing, even at the risk of an irksome repetition, I must insist upon, lest I seem to favour the credulous, superstitious view. Plattner's absence from the world for nine days is, I think, proved. But that does not prove his story. It is quite conceivable that even outside space hallucinations may be possible. That, at least, the reader must bear distinctly in mind.

The Argonauts of the Air

ONE SAW MONSON'S flying-machine from the windows of the trains passing either along the South-Western main line or along the line between Wimbledon and Worcester Park,—to be more exact, one saw the huge scaffoldings which limited the flight of the apparatus. They rose over the tree-tops, a massive alley of interlacing iron and timber, and an enormous web of ropes and tackle, extending the best part of two miles. From the Leatherhead branch this alley was foreshortened and in part hidden by a hill with villas; but from the main line one had it in profile, a complex tangle of girders and curving bars, very impressive to the excursionists from Portsmouth and Southampton and the West. Monson had taken up the work where Maxim had left it, had gone on at first with an utter contempt for the journalistic wit and ignorance that had irritated and hampered his predecessor, and had spent (it was said) rather more than half his immense fortune upon his experiments. The results, to an impatient generation, seemed inconsiderable. When some five years had passed after the growth of the colossal iron groves at Worcester Park, and Monson still failed to put in a fluttering appearance over Trafalgar Square, even the Isle of Wight trippers felt their liberty to smile. And such intelligent people as did not consider Monson a fool stricken with the mania for invention, denounced him as being (for no particular reason) a self-advertising quack.

Yet now and again a morning trainload of season-ticket holders would see a white monster rush headlong through the airy tracery of guides and bars, and hear the further stays, nettings, and buffers snap, creak, and groan with the impact of the blow. Then there would be an efflorescence of black-set white-rimmed faces along the sides of the train, and the morning papers would be neglected for a vigorous discussion of the possibility of flying (in which nothing new was ever said by any chance), until the train reached Waterloo, and its cargo of season-ticket holders dispersed themselves over London. Or the fathers and mothers in some multitudinous train of weary excursionists returning exhausted from a day of rest by the sea, would find the dark fabric, standing out against the evening sky, useful in diverting some bilious child from its introspection, and be suddenly startled by the swift transit of a huge black flapping shape that strained upward against the guides. It was a great and forcible thing beyond dispute, and excellent for conversation; yet, all the same, it was but flying in leading-strings, and most of those who witnessed it scarcely counted its flight as flying. More of a switchback it seemed to the run of the folk.

Monson, I say, did not trouble himself very keenly about the opinions of the press at first. But possibly he, even, had formed but a poor idea of the time it would take before the tactics of flying were mastered, the swift assured adjustment of the big soaring shape to every gust and chance movement of the air; nor had he clearly reckoned the money this prolonged struggle against gravitation would cost him. And he was not so pachydermatous as he seemed. Secretly he had his periodical bundles of cuttings sent him by Romeike, he had his periodical reminders from his banker; and if he did not mind the initial ridicule and scepticism, he felt the growing neglect as the months went by and the money dribbled away. Time was when Monson had sent the enterprising journalist, keen after readable matter, empty from his gates. But when the enterprising journalist ceased from troubling, Monson was anything but satisfied in his heart of hearts. Still day by day the work went on, and the multitudinous subtle difficulties of the steering diminished in number. Day by day, too, the money trickled away, until his balance was no longer a matter of hundreds of thousands, but of tens. And at last came an anniversary.

Monson, sitting in the little drawing-shed, suddenly noticed the date on Woodhouse's calendar.

"It was five years ago to-day that we began," he said to Woodhouse suddenly.

"Is it?" said Woodhouse.

"It's the alterations play the devil with us," said Monson, biting a paper-fastener.

The drawings for the new vans to the hinder screw lay on the table before him as he spoke. He pitched the mutilated brass paper-fastener into the waste-paper basket and drummed with his fingers. "These alterations! Will the mathematicians ever be clever enough to save us all this patching and experimenting. Five years—learning by rule of thumb, when one might think that it was possible to calculate the whole thing out beforehand. The cost of it! I might have hired three senior wranglers for life. But they'd only have developed some beautifully useless theorems in pneumatics. What a time it has been, Woodhouse!"

"These mouldings will take three weeks," said Woodhouse. "At special prices."

"Three weeks!" said Monson, and sat drumming.

"Three weeks certain," said Woodhouse, an excellent engineer, but no good as a comforter. He drew the sheets towards him and began shading a bar.

Monson stopped drumming and began to bite his finger-nails, staring the while at Woodhouse's head.

"How long have they been calling this Monson's Folly?" he said suddenly.

"*Oh!* Year or so," said Woodhouse, carelessly, without looking up.

Monson sucked the air in between his teeth, and went to the window. The stout iron columns carrying the elevated rails upon which the start of the machine was made rose up close by, and the machine was hidden by the upper edge of the window. Through the grove of iron pillars, red painted and ornate with rows of bolts, one had a glimpse of the pretty scenery towards Esher. A train went gliding noiselessly across the middle distance, its rattle drowned by the hammering of the workmen overhead. Monson could imagine the grinning faces at the windows of the carriages. He swore savagely under his breath, and dabbed viciously at a blowfly that suddenly became noisy on the window-pane.

"What's up?" said Woodhouse, staring in surprise at his employer.

"I'm about sick of this."

Woodhouse scratched his cheek. "Oh!" he said, after an assimilating pause. He pushed the drawing away from him.

"Here these fools—I'm trying to conquer a new element—trying to do a thing that will revolutionise life. And instead of taking an intelligent interest, they grin and make their stupid jokes, and call me and my appliances names."

"Asses!" said Woodhouse, letting his eye fall again on the drawing.

The epithet, curiously enough, made Monson wince. "I'm about sick of it, Woodhouse, anyhow," he said, after a pause.

Woodhouse shrugged his shoulders.

"There's nothing for it but patience, I suppose," said Monson, sticking his hands in his pockets. "I've started. I've made my bed, and I've got to lie on it. I can't go back. I'll see it through, and spend every penny I have and every penny I can borrow. But I tell you, Woodhouse, I'm infernally sick of it, all the same. If I'd paid a tenth part of the money towards some political greaser's expenses—I'd have been a baronet before this."

Monson paused. Woodhouse stared in front of him with a blank expression he always employed to indicate sympathy, and tapped his pencil-case on the table. Monson stared at him for a minute.

"Oh, *damn!*" said Monson, suddenly, and abruptly rushed out of the room.

Woodhouse continued his sympathetic rigour for perhaps half a minute. Then he sighed and resumed the shading of the drawings. Something had evidently upset Monson. Nice chap, and generous, but difficult to get on with. It was the way with every amateur who had anything to do with engineering—wanted everything finished at once. But Monson had usually the patience of the expert. Odd he was so irritable. Nice and round that aluminum rod did look now! Woodhouse threw back his head, and put it, first this side and then that, to appreciate his bit of shading better.

"Mr. Woodhouse," said Hooper, the foreman of the labourers, putting his head in at the door.

"Hullo!" said Woodhouse, without turning round.

"Nothing happened, sir?" said Hooper.

"Happened?" said Woodhouse.

"The governor just been up the rails swearing like a tornader."

"*Oh!*" said Woodhouse.

"It ain't like him, sir."

"No?"

"And I was thinking perhaps—"

"Don't think," said Woodhouse, still admiring the drawings.

Hooper knew Woodhouse, and he shut the door suddenly with a vicious slam. Woodhouse stared stonily before him for some further minutes, and then made an ineffectual effort to pick his teeth with his pencil. Abruptly he desisted, pitched that old, tried, and stumpy servitor across the room, got up, stretched himself, and followed Hooper.

He looked ruffled—it was visible to every workman he met. When a millionaire who has been spending thousands on experiments that employ quite a little army of people suddenly indicates that he is sick of the undertaking, there is almost invariably a certain amount of mental friction in the ranks of the little army he employs. And even before he indicates his intentions there are speculations and murmurs, a watching of faces and a study of straws. Hundreds of people knew before the day was out that Monson was ruffled, Woodhouse ruffled, Hooper ruffled. A workman's wife, for instance (whom Monson had never seen), decided to keep her money in the savings-bank instead of buying a velveteen dress. So far-reaching are even the casual curses of a millionaire.

Monson found a certain satisfaction in going on the works and behaving disagreeably to as many people as possible. After a time even that palled upon him, and he rode off the grounds, to every one's relief there, and through the lanes south-eastward, to the infinite tribulation of his house steward at Cheam.

And the immediate cause of it all, the little grain of annoyance that had suddenly precipitated all this discontent with his life-work was—these trivial things that direct all our great decisions!—half a dozen ill-considered remarks made by a pretty girl, prettily dressed, with a beautiful voice and something more than prettiness in her soft grey eyes. And of these half-dozen remarks, two words especially—"Monson's Folly." She had felt she was behaving charmingly to Monson; she reflected the next day how exceptionally effective she had been, and no one would have been more amazed than she, had she learned the effect she had left on Monson's mind. I hope, considering everything, that she never knew.

"How are you getting on with your flying-machine?" she asked. ("I wonder if I shall ever meet any one with the sense not to ask that," thought Monson.) "It will be very dangerous at first, will it not?" ("Thinks I'm afraid.") "Jorgon is going to play presently; have you heard him before?" ("My mania being attended to, we turn to rational conversation.") Gush about Jorgon; gradual decline of conversation, ending with—"You must let me know when your flying-machine is finished, Mr. Monson, and then I will consider the advisability of taking a ticket." ("One would think I was still playing inventions in the nursery.") But the bitterest thing she said was not meant for Monson's ears. To Phlox, the novelist, she was always conscientiously brilliant. "I have been talking to Mr. Monson, and he can think of nothing, positively nothing, but that flying-machine of his. Do you know, all his workmen call that place of his 'Monson's Folly'? He is quite impossible. It is really very, very sad. I always regard him myself in the light of sunken treasure —the Lost Millionaire, you know."

She was pretty and well educated,—indeed, she had written an epigrammatic novelette; but the bitterness was that she was typical. She summarised what the world thought of the man who was working sanely, steadily, and surely towards a more tremendous revolution in the appliances of civilisation, a more far-reaching alteration in the ways of humanity than has ever been effected since history began. They did not even take him seriously. In a little while he would be proverbial. "I *must* fly now," he said on his way home, smarting with a sense of absolute social failure. "I must fly soon. If it doesn't come off soon, by God! I shall run amuck."

He said that before he had gone through his pass-book and his litter of papers. Inadequate as the cause seems, it was that girl's voice and the expression of her eyes that precipitated his discontent. But certainly the discovery that he had no longer even one hundred thousand pounds' worth of realisable property behind him was the poison that made the wound deadly.

It was the next day after this that he exploded upon Woodhouse and his workmen, and thereafter his bearing was consistently grim for three weeks, and anxiety dwelt in Cheam and Ewell, Malden, Morden, and Worcester Park, places that had thriven mightily on his experiments.

Four weeks after that first swearing of his, he stood with Woodhouse by the reconstructed machine as it lay across the elevated railway, by means of which it gained its initial impetus. The new propeller glittered a brighter white than the rest of the machine, and a gilder, obedient to a whim of Monson's, was picking out the aluminium bars with gold. And looking down the long avenue between the ropes (gilded now with the sunset), one saw red signals, and two miles away an anthill of workmen busy altering the last falls of the run into a rising slope.

"I'll *come*," said Woodhouse. "I'll come right enough. But I tell you it's infernally foolhardy. If only you would give another year—"

"I tell you I won't. I tell you the thing works. I've given years enough—"

"It's not that," said Woodhouse. "We're all right with the machine. But it's the steering—"

"Haven't I been rushing, night and morning, backwards and forwards, through this squirrel's cage? If the thing steers true here, it will steer true all across England. It's just funk, I tell you, Woodhouse. We could have gone a year ago. And besides—"

"Well?" said Woodhouse.

"The money!" snapped Monson, over his shoulder.

"Hang it! I never thought of the money," said Woodhouse, and then, speaking now in a very different tone to that with which he had said the words before, he repeated, "I'll come. Trust me."

Monson turned suddenly, and saw all that Woodhouse had not the dexterity to say, shining on his sunset-lit face. He looked for a moment, then impulsively extended his hand. "Thanks," he said.

"All right," said Woodhouse, gripping the hand, and with a queer softening of his features. "Trust me."

Then both men turned to the big apparatus that lay with its flat wings extended upon the carrier, and stared at it meditatively. Monson, guided perhaps by a photographic study of the flight of birds, and by Lilienthal's methods, had gradually drifted from Maxim's shapes towards the bird form again. The thing, however, was driven by a huge screw behind in the place of the tail; and so hovering, which needs an almost vertical adjustment of a flat tail, was rendered impossible. The body of the machine was small, almost cylindrical, and pointed. Forward and aft on the pointed ends were two small petroleum engines for the screw, and the navigators sat deep in a canoe-like recess, the foremost one steering, and being protected by a low screen, with two plate-glass windows, from the blinding rush of air. On either side a monstrous flat framework with a curved front border could be adjusted so as either to lie horizontally, or to be tilted upward or down. These wings worked rigidly together, or, by releasing a pin, one could be tilted through a small angle independently of its fellow. The front edge of either wing could also be shifted back so as to diminish the wing-area about one-sixth. The machine was not only not designed to hover, but it was also incapable of fluttering. Monson's idea was to get into the air with the initial rush of the apparatus, and then to skim, much as a playing-card may be skimmed, keeping up the rush by means of the screw at the stern. Rooks and gulls fly enormous distances in that way with scarcely a perceptible movement of the wings. The bird really drives along on an aërial switch-back. It glides slanting downward for a space, until it has gained considerable momentum, and then altering the inclination of its wings, glides up again almost to its original altitude. Even a Londoner who has watched the birds in the aviary in Regent's Park knows that.

But the bird is practicing this art from the moment it leaves its nest. It has not only the perfect apparatus, but the perfect instinct to use it. A man off his feet has the poorest skill in balancing. Even the simple trick of the bicycle costs him some hours of labour. The instantaneous adjustments of the wings, the quick response to a passing breeze, the swift recovery of equilibrium, the giddy, eddying movements that require such absolute precision—all that he must learn, learn with infinite labour and infinite danger, if ever he is to conquer flying. The flying-machine that will start off some fine day, driven by neat "little levers," with a nice open deck like a liner, and all loaded up with bomb-shells and guns, is the easy dreaming of a literary man. In lives and in treasure the cost of the conquest of the empire of the air may even exceed all that has been spent in man's great conquest of the sea. Certainly it will be costlier than the greatest war that has ever devastated the world.

No one knew these things better than these two practical men. And they knew they were in the front rank of the coming army. Yet there is hope even in a forlorn hope. Men are killed outright in the reserves sometimes, while others who have been left for dead in the thickest corner crawl out and survive.

"If we miss these meadows—" said Woodhouse, presently in his slow way.

"My dear chap," said Monson, whose spirits had been rising fitfully during the last few days, "we mustn't miss these meadows. There's a quarter of a square mile for us to hit, fences removed, ditches levelled. We shall come down all right—rest assured. And if we don't—"

"Ah!" said Woodhouse. "If we don't!"

Before the day of the start, the newspaper people got wind of the alterations at the northward end of the framework, and Monson was cheered by a decided change in the comments Romeike forwarded him. "He will be off some day," said the papers. "He will be off some day," said the South-Western season-ticket holders one to another; the seaside excursionists, the Saturday-to-Monday trippers from Sussex and Hampshire and Dorset and Devon, the eminent literary people from Hazlemere, all remarked eagerly one to another, "He will be off some day," as the familiar scaffolding came in sight. And actually, one bright morning, in full view of the ten-past-ten train from Basingstoke, Monson's flying-machine started on its journey.

They saw the carrier running swiftly along its rail, and the white-and-gold screw spinning in the air. They heard the rapid rumble of wheels, and a thud as the carrier reached the buffers at the end of its run. Then a whirr as the flying-machine was shot forward into the networks. All that the majority of them had seen and heard before. The thing went with a drooping flight through the framework and rose again, and then every beholder shouted, or screamed, or yelled, or shrieked after his kind. For instead of the customary concussion and stoppage, the flying-machine flew out of its five years' cage like a bolt from a crossbow, and drove slantingly upward into the air, curved round a little, so as to cross the line, and soared in the direction of Wimbledon Common.

It seemed to hang momentarily in the air and grow smaller, then it ducked and vanished over the clustering blue tree-tops to the east of Coombe Hill, and no one stopped staring and gasping until long after it had disappeared.

That was what the people in the train from Basingstoke saw. If you had drawn a line down the middle of that train, from engine to guard's van, you would not have found a living soul on the opposite side to the flying-machine. It was a mad rush from window to window as the thing crossed the line. And the engine-driver and stoker never took their eyes off the low hills about Wimbledon, and never noticed that they had run clean through Coombe and Malden and Raynes Park, until, with returning animation, they found themselves pelting, at the most indecent pace, into Wimbledon station.

From the moment when Monson had started the carrier with a "*Now!*" neither he nor Woodhouse said a word. Both men sat with clenched teeth. Monson had crossed the line with a curve that was too sharp, and Woodhouse had opened and shut his white lips; but neither spoke. Woodhouse simply gripped his seat, and breathed sharply through his teeth, watching the blue country to the west rushing past, and down, and away from him. Monson knelt at his post forward, and his hands trembled on the spoked wheel that moved the wings. He could see nothing before him but a mass of white clouds in the sky.

The machine went slanting upward, travelling with an enormous speed still, but losing momentum every moment. The land ran away underneath with diminishing speed.

"Now!" said Woodhouse at last, and with a violent effort Monson wrenched over the wheel and altered the angle of the wings. The machine seemed to hang for half a minute motionless in mid-air, and then he saw the hazy blue house-covered hills of Kilburn and Hampstead jump up before his eyes and rise steadily, until the little sunlit dome of the Albert Hall appeared through his windows. For a moment he scarcely understood the meaning of this upward rush of the horizon, but as the nearer and nearer houses came into view, he realised what he had done. He had turned the wings over too far, and they were swooping steeply downward towards the Thames.

The thought, the question, the realisation were all the business of a second of time. "Too much!" gasped Woodhouse. Monson brought the wheel half-way back with a jerk, and forthwith the Kilburn and Hampstead ridge dropped again to the lower edge of his windows. They had been a thousand feet above Coombe and Malden station; fifty seconds after they whizzed, at a frightful pace, not eighty feet above the East Putney station, on the Metropolitan District line, to the screaming astonishment of a platformful of people. Monson flung up the vans against the air, and over Fulham they rushed up their atmospheric switchback again, steeply—too steeply. The 'busses went floundering across the Fulham Road, the people yelled.

Then down again, too steeply still, and the distant trees and houses about Primrose Hill leapt up across Monson's window, and then suddenly he saw straight before him the greenery of Kensington Gardens and the towers of the Imperial Institute. They were driving straight down upon South Kensington. The pinnacles of the Natural History Museum rushed up into view. There came one fatal second of swift thought, a moment of hesitation. Should he try and clear the towers, or swerve eastward?

He made a hesitating attempt to release the right wing, left the catch half released, and gave a frantic clutch at the wheel.

The nose of the machine seemed to leap up before him. The wheel pressed his hand with irresistible force, and jerked itself out of his control.

Woodhouse, sitting crouched together, gave a hoarse cry, and sprang up towards Monson. "Too far!" he cried, and then he was clinging to the gunwale for dear life, and Monson had been jerked clean overhead, and was falling backwards upon him.

So swiftly had the thing happened that barely a quarter of the people going to and fro in Hyde Park, and Brompton Road, and the Exhibition Road saw anything of the aërial catastrophe. A distant winged shape had appeared above the clustering houses to the south, had fallen and risen, growing larger as it did so; had swooped swiftly down towards the Imperial Institute, a broad spread of flying wings, had swept round in a quarter circle, dashed eastward, and then suddenly sprang vertically into the air. A black object shot out of it, and came spinning downward. A man! Two men clutching each other! They came whirling down, separated as they struck the roof of the Students' Club, and bounded off into the green bushes on its southward side.

For perhaps half a minute, the pointed stem of the big machine still pierced vertically upward, the screw spinning desperately. For one brief instant, that yet seemed an age to all who watched, it had hung motionless in mid-air. Then a spout of yellow flame licked up its length from the stern engine, and swift, swifter, swifter, and flaring like a rocket, it rushed down upon the solid mass of masonry which was formerly the Royal College of Science. The big screw of white and gold touched the parapet, and crumpled up like wet linen. Then the blazing spindle-shaped body smashed and splintered, smashing and splintering in its fall, upon the north-westward angle of the building.

But the crash, the flame of blazing paraffin that shot heavenward from the shattered engines of the machine, the crushed horrors that were found in the garden beyond the Students' Club, the masses of yellow parapet and red brick that fell headlong into the roadway, the running to and fro of people like ants in a broken anthill, the galloping of fire-engines, the gathering of crowds—all these things do not belong to this story, which was written only to tell how the first of all successful flying-machines was launched and flew. Though he failed, and failed disastrously, the record of Monson's work remains—a sufficient monument—to guide the next of that band of gallant experimentalists who will sooner or later master this great problem of flying. And between Worcester Park and Malden there still stands that portentous avenue of iron-work, rusting now, and dangerous here and there, to witness to the first desperate struggle for man's right of way through the air.

The Story of The Late Mr. Elvesham

I SET THIS story down, not expecting it will be believed, but, if possible, to prepare a way of escape for the next victim. He, perhaps, may profit by my misfortune. My own case, I know, is hopeless, and I am now in some measure prepared to meet my fate.

My name is Edward George Eden. I was born at Trentham, in Staffordshire, my father being employed in the gardens there. I lost my mother when I was three years old, and my father when I was five, my uncle, George Eden, then adopting me as his own son. He was a single man, self-educated, and well known in Birmingham as an enterprising journalist; he educated me generously, fired my ambition to succeed in the world, and at his death, which happened four years ago, left me his entire fortune, a matter of about five hundred pounds after all outgoing charges were paid. I was then eighteen. He advised me in his will to expend the money in completing my education. I had already chosen the profession of medicine, and through his posthumous generosity, and my good fortune in a scholarship competition, I became a medical student at University College, London. At the time of the beginning of my story I lodged at 11A University Street, in a little upper room, very shabbily furnished, and draughty, overlooking the back of Shoolbred's premises. I used this little room both to live in and sleep in, because I was anxious to eke out my means to the very last shillingsworth.

I was taking a pair of shoes to be mended at a shop in the Tottenham Court Road when I first encountered the little old man with the yellow face, with whom my life has now become so inextricably entangled. He was standing on the kerb, and staring at the number on the door in a doubtful way, as I opened it. His eyes—they were dull grey eyes, and reddish under the rims—fell to my face, and his countenance immediately assumed an expression of corrugated amiability.

"You come," he said, "apt to the moment. I had forgotten the number of your house. How do you do, Mr. Eden?"

I was a little astonished at his familiar address, for I had never set eyes on the man before. I was a little annoyed, too, at his catching me with my boots under my arm. He noticed my lack of cordiality.

"Wonder who the deuce I am, eh? A friend, let me assure you. I have seen you before, though you haven't seen me. Is there anywhere where I can talk to you?"

I hesitated. The shabbiness of my room upstairs was not a matter for every stranger. "Perhaps," said I, "we might walk down the street. I'm unfortunately prevented—" My gesture explained the sentence before I had spoken it.

"The very thing," he said, and faced this way and then that. "The street? Which way shall we go?" I slipped my boots down in the passage. "Look here!" he said abruptly; "this business of mine is a rigmarole. Come and lunch with me, Mr. Eden. I'm an old man, a very old man, and not good at explanations, and what with my piping voice and the clatter of the traffic—"

He laid a persuasive, skinny hand that trembled a little upon my arm.

I was not so old that an old man might not treat me to a lunch. Yet at the same time I was not altogether pleased by this abrupt invitation. "I had rather—" I began. "But *I* had rather," he said, catching me up, "and a certain civility is surely due to my grey hairs." And so I consented, and went with him.

He took me to Blavitski's; I had to walk slowly to accommodate myself to his paces; and over such a lunch as I had never tasted before, he fended off my leading questions, and I took a better note of his appearance. His clean-shaven face was lean and wrinkled, his shrivelled lips fell over a set of false teeth, and his white hair was thin and rather long; he seemed small to me,—though, indeed, most people seemed small to me,—and his shoulders were rounded and bent. And watching him, I could not help but observe that he too was taking note of me, running his eyes, with a curious touch of greed in them, over me, from my broad shoulders to my sun-tanned hands, and up to my freckled face again. "And now," said he, as we lit our cigarettes, "I must tell you of the business in hand.

"I must tell you, then, that I am an old man, a very old man." He paused momentarily. "And it happens that I have money that I must presently be leaving, and never a child have I to leave it to." I thought of the confidence trick, and resolved I would be on the alert for the vestiges of my five hundred pounds. He proceeded to enlarge on his loneliness, and the trouble he had to find a proper disposition of his money. "I have weighed this plan and that plan, charities, institutions, and scholarships, and libraries, and I have come to this conclusion at last,"—he fixed his eyes on my face,—

"that I will find some young fellow, ambitious, pure-minded, and poor, healthy in body and healthy in mind, and, in short, make him my heir, give him all that I have." He repeated, "Give him all that I have. So that he will suddenly be lifted out of all the trouble and struggle in which his sympathies have been educated, to freedom and influence."

I tried to seem disinterested. With a transparent hypocrisy, I said, "And you want my help, my professional services, maybe, to find that person."

He smiled, and looked at me over his cigarette, and I laughed at his quiet exposure of my modest pretence.

"What a career such a man might have!" he said. "It fills me with envy to think how I have accumulated that another man may spend—

"But there are conditions, of course, burdens to be imposed. He must, for instance, take my name. You cannot expect everything without some return. And I must go into all the circumstances of his life before I can accept him. He *must* be sound. I must know his heredity, how his parents and grandparents died, have the strictest inquiries made into his private morals—"

This modified my secret congratulations a little. "And do I understand," said I, "that I—?"

"Yes," he said, almost fiercely. "You. *You.*"

I answered never a word. My imagination was dancing wildly, my innate scepticism was useless to modify its transports. There was not a particle of gratitude in my mind—I did not know what to say nor how to say it. "But why me in particular?" I said at last.

He had chanced to hear of me from Professor Haslar, he said, as a typically sound and sane young man, and he wished, as far as possible, to leave his money where health and integrity were assured.

That was my first meeting with the little old man. He was mysterious about himself; he would not give his name yet, he said, and after I had answered some questions of his, he left me at the Blavitski portal. I noticed that he drew a handful of gold coins from his pocket when it came to paying for the lunch. His insistence upon bodily health was curious. In accordance with an arrangement we had made I applied that day for a life policy in the Loyal Insurance Company for a large sum, and I was exhaustively overhauled by the medical advisers of that company in the subsequent week. Even that did not satisfy him, and he insisted I must be re-examined by the great Dr. Henderson. It was Friday in Whitsun week before he came to a decision. He called me down, quite late in the evening,—nearly nine it was,—from cramming chemical equations for my Preliminary Scientific examination. He was standing in the passage under the feeble gas-lamp, and his face was a grotesque interplay of shadows. He seemed more bowed than when I had first seen him, and his cheeks had sunk in a little.

His voice shook with emotion. "Everything is satisfactory, Mr. Eden," he said. "Everything is quite, quite satisfactory. And this night of all nights, you must dine with me and celebrate your—accession." He was interrupted by a cough. "You won't have long to wait, either," he said, wiping his handkerchief across his lips, and gripping my hand with his long bony claw that was disengaged. "Certainly not very long to wait."

We went into the street and called a cab. I remember every incident of that drive vividly, the swift, easy motion, the vivid contrast of gas, and oil, and electric light, the crowds of people in the streets, the place in Regent Street to which we went, and the sumptuous dinner we were served there. I was disconcerted at first by the well-dressed waiters' glances at my rough clothes, bothered by the stones of the olives, but as the champagne warmed my blood, my confidence revived. At first the old man talked of himself. He had already told me his name in the cab; he was Egbert Elvesham, the great philosopher, whose name I had known since I was a lad at school. It seemed incredible to me that this man, whose intelligence had so early dominated mine, this great abstraction, should suddenly realise itself as this decrepit, familiar figure. I daresay every young fellow who has suddenly fallen among celebrities has felt something of my disappointment. He told me now of the future that the feeble streams of his life would presently leave dry for me, houses, copyrights, investments; I had never suspected that philosophers were so rich. He watched me drink and eat with a touch of envy. "What a capacity for living you have!" he said; and then, with a sigh, a sigh of relief I could have thought it, "It will not be long."

"Ay," said I, my head swimming now with champagne; "I have a future perhaps—of a passing agreeable sort, thanks to you. I shall now have the honour of your name. But you have a past. Such a past as is worth all my future."

He shook his head and smiled, as I thought, with half-sad appreciation of my flattering admiration. "That future," he said, "would you in truth change it?" The waiter came with liqueurs. "You will not perhaps mind taking my name, taking my position, but would you indeed—willingly—take my years?"

"With your achievements," said I, gallantly.

He smiled again. "Kummel—both," he said to the waiter, and turned his attention to a little paper packet he had taken from his pocket. "This hour," said he, "this after-dinner hour is the hour of small things. Here is a scrap of my unpublished wisdom." He opened the packet with his shaking yellow fingers, and showed a little pinkish powder on the paper. "This," said he —"well, you must guess what it is.

But Kummel—put but a dash of this powder in it—is Himmel." His large greyish eyes watched mine with an inscrutable expression.

It was a bit of a shock to me to find this great teacher gave his mind to the flavour of liqueurs. However, I feigned a great interest in his weakness, for I was drunk enough for such small sycophancy.

He parted the powder between the little glasses, and, rising suddenly, with a strange, unexpected dignity, held out his hand towards me. I imitated his action, and the glasses rang. "To a quick succession," said he, and raised his glass towards his lips.

"Not that," I said hastily. "Not that."

He paused, with the liqueur at the level of his chin, and his eyes blazing into mine.

"To a long life," said I.

He hesitated. "To a long life," said he, with a sudden bark of laughter, and with eyes fixed on one another we tilted the little glasses. His eyes looked straight into mine, and as I drained the stuff off, I felt a curiously intense sensation. The first touch of it set my brain in a furious tumult; I seemed to feel an actual physical stirring in my skull, and a seething humming filled my ears. I did not notice the flavour in my mouth, the aroma that filled my throat; I saw only the grey intensity of his gaze that burnt into mine. The draught, the mental confusion, the noise and stirring in my head, seemed to last an interminable time. Curious vague impressions of half-forgotten things danced and vanished on the edge of my consciousness. At last he broke the spell. With a sudden explosive sigh he put down his glass.

"Well?" he said.

"It's glorious," said I, though I had not tasted the stuff.

My head was spinning. I sat down. My brain was chaos. Then my perception grew clear and minute as though I saw things in a concave mirror. His manner seemed to have changed into something nervous and hasty. He pulled out his watch and grimaced at it. "Eleven-seven! And to-night I must—Seven—twenty-five. Waterloo! I must go at once." He called for the bill, and struggled with his coat. Officious waiters came to our assistance. In another moment I was wishing him good-bye, over the apron of a cab, and still with an absurd feeling of minute distinctness, as though—how can I express it?—I not only saw but *felt* through an inverted opera-glass.

"That stuff," he said. He put his hand to his forehead. "I ought not to have given it to you. It will make your head split to-morrow. Wait a minute. Here." He handed me out a little flat thing like a seidlitz-powder. "Take that in water as you are going to bed. The other thing was a drug. Not till you're ready to go to bed, mind. It will clear your head. That's all. One more shake—Futurus!"

I gripped his shrivelled claw. "Good-bye," he said, and by the droop of his eyelids I judged he too was a little under the influence of that brain-twisting cordial.

He recollected something else with a start, felt in his breast-pocket, and produced another packet, this time a cylinder the size and shape of a shaving-stick. "Here," said he. "I'd almost forgotten. Don't open this until I come to-morrow—but take it now."

It was so heavy that I well-nigh dropped it. "All ri'!" said I, and he grinned at me through the cab-window as the cabman flicked his horse into wakefulness. It was a white packet he had given me, with red seals at either end and along its edge. "If this isn't money," said I, "it's platinum or lead."

I stuck it with elaborate care into my pocket, and with a whirling brain walked home through the Regent Street loiterers and the dark back streets beyond Portland Road. I remember the sensations of that walk very vividly, strange as they were. I was still so far myself that I could notice my strange mental state, and wonder whether this stuff I had had was opium—a drug beyond my experience. It is hard now to describe the peculiarity of my mental strangeness—mental doubling vaguely expresses it. As I was walking up Regent Street I found in my mind a queer persuasion that it was Waterloo station, and had an odd impulse to get into the Polytechnic as a man might get into a train. I put a knuckle in my eye, and it was Regent Street. How can I express it? You see a skilful actor looking quietly at you, he pulls a grimace, and lo!—another person. Is it too extravagant if I tell you that it seemed to me as if Regent Street had, for the moment, done that? Then, being persuaded it was Regent Street again, I was oddly muddled about some fantastic reminiscences that cropped up. "Thirty years ago," thought I, "it was here that I quarrelled with my brother." Then I burst out laughing, to the astonishment and encouragement of a group of night prowlers. Thirty years ago I did not exist, and never in my life had I boasted a brother. The stuff was surely liquid folly, for the poignant regret for that lost brother still clung to me. Along Portland Road the madness took another turn. I began to recall vanished shops, and to compare the street with what it used to be. Confused, troubled thinking is comprehensible enough after the drink I had taken, but what puzzled me were these curiously vivid phantasm memories that had crept into my mind, and not only the memories that had crept in, but also the memories that had slipped out. I stopped opposite Stevens', the natural history dealer's, and cudgelled my brains to think what he had to do with me. A 'bus went by, and sounded exactly like the rumbling of a train. I seemed to be dipped into some dark, remote pit for the recollection. "Of course," said I, at last, "he has promised me three frogs to-morrow. Odd I should have forgotten.

Do they still show children dissolving views? In those I remember one view would begin like a faint ghost, and grow and oust another. In just that way it seemed to me that a ghostly set of new sensations was struggling with those of my ordinary self.

I went on through Euston Road to Tottenham Court Road, puzzled, and a little frightened, and scarcely noticed the unusual way I was taking, for commonly I used to cut through the intervening network of back streets. I turned into University Street, to discover that I had forgotten my number. Only by a strong effort did I recall 11A, and even then it seemed to me that it was a thing some forgotten person had told me. I tried to steady my mind by recalling the incidents of the dinner, and for the life of me I could conjure up no picture of my host's face; I saw him only as a shadowy outline, as one might see oneself reflected in a window through which one was looking. In his place, however, I had a curious exterior vision of myself sitting at a table, flushed, bright-eyed, and talkative.

"I must take this other powder," said I. "This is getting impossible."

I tried the wrong side of the hall for my candle and the matches, and had a doubt of which landing my room might be on. "I'm drunk," I said, "that's certain," and blundered needlessly on the staircase to sustain the proposition.

At the first glance my room seemed unfamiliar. "What rot!" I said, and stared about me. I seemed to bring myself back by the effort, and the odd phantasmal quality passed into the concrete familiar. There was the old glass still, with my notes on the albumens stuck in the corner of the frame, my old everyday suit of clothes pitched about the floor. And yet it was not so real after all. I felt an idiotic persuasion trying to creep into my mind, as it were, that I was in a railway carriage in a train just stopping, that I was peering out of the window at some unknown station. I gripped the bed-rail firmly to reassure myself. "It's clairvoyance, perhaps," I said. "I must write to the Psychical Research Society."

I put the rouleau on my dressing-table, sat on my bed and began to take off my boots. It was as if the picture of my present sensations was painted over some other picture that was trying to show through. "Curse it!" said I; "my wits are going, or am I in two places at once?" Half-undressed, I tossed the powder into a glass and drank it off. It effervesced, and became a fluorescent amber colour. Before I was in bed my mind was already tranquillised. I felt the pillow at my cheek, and thereupon I must have fallen asleep.

I awoke abruptly out of a dream of strange beasts, and found myself lying on my back. Probably every one knows that dismal, emotional dream from which one escapes, awake indeed, but strangely cowed. There was a curious taste in my mouth, a tired feeling in my limbs, a sense of cutaneous discomfort. I lay with my head motionless on my pillow, expecting that my feeling of strangeness and terror would probably pass away, and that I should then doze off again to sleep. But instead of that, my uncanny sensations increased. At first I could perceive nothing wrong about me. There was a faint light in the room, so faint that it was the very next thing to darkness, and the furniture stood out in it as vague blots of absolute darkness. I stared with my eyes just over the bedclothes.

It came into my mind that some one had entered the room to rob me of my rouleau of money, but after lying for some moments, breathing regularly to simulate sleep, I realised this was mere fancy. Nevertheless, the uneasy assurance of something wrong kept fast hold of me. With an effort I raised my head from the pillow, and peered about me at the dark. What it was I could not conceive. I looked at the dim shapes around me, the greater and lesser darknesses that indicated curtains, table, fireplace, bookshelves, and so forth. Then I began to perceive something unfamiliar in the forms of the darkness. Had the bed turned round? Yonder should be the bookshelves, and something shrouded and pallid rose there, something that would not answer to the bookshelves, however I looked at it. It was far too big to be my shirt thrown on a chair.

Overcoming a childish terror, I threw back the bedclothes and thrust my leg out of bed. Instead of coming out of my truckle-bed upon the floor, I found my foot scarcely reached the edge of the mattress. I made another step, as it were, and sat up on the edge of the bed. By the side of my bed should be the candle, and the matches upon the broken chair. I put out my hand and touched—nothing. I waved my hand in the darkness, and it came against some heavy hanging, soft and thick in texture, which gave a rustling noise at my touch. I grasped this and pulled it; it appeared to be a curtain suspended over the head of my bed.

I was now thoroughly awake, and beginning to realise that I was in a strange room. I was puzzled. I tried to recall the overnight circumstances, and I found them now, curiously enough, vivid in my memory: the supper, my reception of the little packages, my wonder whether I was intoxicated, my slow undressing, the coolness to my flushed face of my pillow. I felt a sudden distrust. Was that last night, or the night before? At any rate, this room was strange to me, and I could not imagine how I had got into it. The dim, pallid outline was growing paler, and I perceived it was a window, with the dark shape of an oval toilet-glass against the weak intimation of the dawn that filtered through the blind. I stood up, and was surprised by a curious feeling of weakness and unsteadiness. With trembling hands outstretched, I walked slowly towards the window, getting, nevertheless, a bruise on the knee from a chair by the way. I fumbled round the glass, which was large, with handsome brass sconces, to find the blind-cord. I could not find any. By chance I took hold of the tassel, and with the click of a spring the blind ran up.

I found myself looking out upon a scene that was altogether strange to me. The night was overcast, and through the flocculent grey of the heaped clouds there filtered a faint half-light of dawn. Just at the edge of the sky, the cloud-canopy had a blood-red rim. Below, everything was dark and indistinct, dim hills in the distance, a vague mass of buildings running up into pinnacles, trees like spilt ink, and below the window a tracery of black bushes and pale grey paths. It was so unfamiliar that for the moment I thought myself still dreaming. I felt the toilet-table; it appeared to be made of some polished wood, and was rather elaborately furnished—there were little cut-glass bottles and a brush upon it. There was also a queer little object, horse-shoe-shaped it felt, with smooth, hard projections, lying in a saucer. I could find no matches nor candlestick.

I turned my eyes to the room again. Now the blind was up, faint spectres of its furnishing came out of the darkness. There was a huge curtained bed, and the fireplace at its foot had a large white mantel with something of the shimmer of marble.

I leant against the toilet-table, shut my eyes and opened them again, and tried to think. The whole thing was far too real for dreaming. I was inclined to imagine there was still some hiatus in my memory, as a consequence of my draught of that strange liqueur; that I had come into my inheritance perhaps, and suddenly lost my recollection of everything since my good fortune had been announced. Perhaps if I waited a little, things would be clearer to me again. Yet my dinner with old Elvesham was now singularly vivid and recent. The champagne, the observant waiters, the powder, and the liqueurs—I could have staked my soul it all happened a few hours ago.

And then occurred a thing so trivial and yet so terrible to me that I shiver now to think of that moment. I spoke aloud. I said, "How the devil did I get here?"—*And the voice was not my own.*

It was not my own, it was thin, the articulation was slurred, the resonance of my facial bones was different. Then, to reassure myself, I ran one hand over the other, and felt loose folds of skin, the bony laxity of age. "Surely," I said, in that horrible voice that had somehow established itself in my throat, "surely this thing is a dream!" Almost as quickly as if I did it involuntarily, I thrust my fingers into my mouth. My teeth had gone. My finger-tips ran on the flaccid surface of an even row of shrivelled gums. I was sick with dismay and disgust.

I felt then a passionate desire to see myself, to realise at once in its full horror the ghastly change that had come upon me. I tottered to the mantel, and felt along it for matches. As I did so, a barking cough sprang up in my throat, and I clutched the thick flannel nightdress I found about me. There were no matches there, and I suddenly realised that my extremities were cold. Sniffing and coughing, whimpering, a little, perhaps, I fumbled back to bed. "It is surely a dream," I whimpered to myself as I clambered back, "surely a dream." It was a senile repetition. I pulled the bedclothes over my shoulders, over my ears, I thrust my withered hand under the pillow, and determined to compose myself to sleep. Of course it was a dream. In the morning the dream would be over, and I should wake up strong and vigorous again to my youth and studies. I shut my eyes, breathed regularly, and, finding myself wakeful, began to count slowly through the powers of three.

But the thing I desired would not come. I could not get to sleep. And the persuasion of the inexorable reality of the change that had happened to me grew steadily. Presently I found myself with my eyes wide open, the powers of three forgotten, and my skinny fingers upon my shrivelled gums. I was, indeed, suddenly and abruptly, an old man. I had in some unaccountable manner fallen through my life and come to old age, in some way I had been cheated of all the best of my life; of love, of struggle, of strength, and hope. I grovelled into the pillow and tried to persuade myself that such hallucination was possible. Imperceptibly, steadily, the dawn grew clearer.

At last, despairing of further sleep, I sat up in bed and looked about me. A chill twilight rendered the whole chamber visible. It was spacious and well-furnished, better furnished than any room I had ever slept in before. A candle and matches became dimly visible upon a little pedestal in a recess. I threw back the bedclothes, and, shivering with the rawness of the early morning, albeit it was summer-time, I got out and lit the candle. Then, trembling horribly, so that the extinguisher rattled on its spike, I tottered to the glass and saw—*Elvesham's face*! It was none the less horrible because I had already dimly feared as much. He had already seemed physically weak and pitiful to me, but seen now, dressed only in a coarse flannel nightdress that fell apart and showed the stringy neck, seen now as my own body, I cannot describe its desolate decrepitude. The hollow cheeks, the straggling tail of dirty grey hair, the rheumy bleared eyes, the quivering, shrivelled lips, the lower displaying a gleam of the pink interior lining, and those horrible dark gums showing. You who are mind and body together, at your natural years, cannot imagine what this fiendish imprisonment meant to me. To be young and full of the desire and energy of youth, and to be caught, and presently to be crushed in this tottering ruin of a body. . . .

But I wander from the course of my story. For some time I must have been stunned at this change that had come upon me. It was daylight when I did so far gather myself together as to think. In some inexplicable way I had been changed, though how, short of magic, the thing had been done, I could not say. And as I thought, the diabolical ingenuity of Elvesham came home to me. It seemed plain to me that as I found myself in his, so he must be in possession of *my* body, of my strength, that is, and my future. But how to prove it? Then, as I thought, the thing became so incredible, even to me, that my mind reeled, and I had to pinch myself, to feel my toothless gums, to see myself in the glass, and touch the things about me, before I could steady myself to face the facts again. Was all life hallucination? Was I indeed Elvesham, and he me? Had I been dreaming of Eden overnight? Was there any Eden? But if I was Elvesham, I should remember where I was on the previous morning, the name of the town in which I lived, what happened before the dream began. I struggled with my thoughts. I recalled the queer doubleness of my memories overnight. But now my mind was clear. Not the ghost of any memories but those proper to Eden could I raise.

"This way lies insanity!" I cried in my piping voice. I staggered to my feet, dragged my feeble, heavy limbs to the washhand-stand, and plunged my grey head into a basin of cold water. Then, towelling myself, I tried again. It was no good. I felt beyond all question that I was indeed Eden, not Elvesham. But Eden in Elvesham's body.

Had I been a man of any other age, I might have given myself up to my fate as one enchanted. But in these sceptical days miracles do not pass current. Here was some trick of psychology. What a drug and a steady stare could do, a drug and a steady stare, or some similar treatment, could surely undo. Men have lost their memories before. But to exchange memories as one does umbrellas! I laughed. Alas! not a healthy laugh, but a wheezing, senile titter. I could have fancied old Elvesham laughing at my plight, and a gust of petulant anger, unusual to me, swept across my feelings. I began dressing eagerly in the clothes I found lying about on the floor, and only realised when I was dressed that it was an evening suit I had assumed. I opened the wardrobe and found some more ordinary clothes, a pair of plaid trousers, and an old-fashioned dressing-gown. I put a venerable smoking-cap on my venerable head, and, coughing a little from my exertions, tottered out upon the landing.

It was then, perhaps, a quarter to six, and the blinds were closely drawn and the house quite silent. The landing was a spacious one, a broad, richly-carpeted staircase went down into the darkness of the hall below, and before me a door ajar showed me a writing-desk, a revolving bookcase, the back of a study chair, and a fine array of bound books, shelf upon shelf.

"My study," I mumbled, and walked across the landing. Then at the sound of my voice a thought struck me, and I went back to the bedroom and put in the set of false teeth. They slipped in with the ease of old habit. "That's better," said I, gnashing them, and so returned to the study.

The drawers of the writing-desk were locked. Its revolving top was also locked. I could see no indications of the keys, and there were none in the pockets of my trousers. I shuffled back at once to the bedroom, and went through the dress suit, and afterwards the pockets of all the garments I could find. I was very eager, and one might have imagined that burglars had been at work, to see my room when I had done. Not only were there no keys to be found, but not a coin, nor a scrap of paper—save only the receipted bill of the overnight dinner.

A curious weariness asserted itself. I sat down and stared at the garments flung here and there, their pockets turned inside out. My first frenzy had already flickered out. Every moment I was beginning to realise the immense intelligence of the plans of my enemy, to see more and more clearly the hopelessness of my position. With an effort I rose and hurried hobbling into the study again. On the staircase was a housemaid pulling up the blinds. She stared, I think, at the expression of my face. I shut the door of the study behind me, and, seizing a poker, began an attack upon the desk. That is how they found me. The cover of the desk was split, the lock smashed, the letters torn out of the pigeon-holes and tossed about the room. In my senile rage I had flung about the pens and other such light stationery, and overturned the ink. Moreover, a large vase upon the mantel had got broken—I do not know how. I could find no cheque-book, no money, no indications of the slightest use for the recovery of my body. I was battering madly at the drawers, when the butler, backed by two women-servants, intruded upon me.

That simply is the story of my change. No one will believe my frantic assertions. I am treated as one demented, and even at this moment I am under restraint. But I am sane, absolutely sane, and to prove it I have sat down to write this story minutely as the things happened to me. I appeal to the reader, whether there is any trace of insanity in the style or method of the story he has been reading. I am a young man locked away in an old man's body. But the clear fact is incredible to every one. Naturally I appear demented to those who will not believe this, naturally I do not know the names of my secretaries, of the doctors who come to see me, of my servants and neighbours, of this town (wherever it is) where I find myself. Naturally I lose myself in my own house, and suffer inconveniences of every sort. Naturally I ask the oddest questions. Naturally I weep and cry out, and have paroxysms of despair. I have no money and no cheque-book. The bank will not recognise my signature, for I suppose that, allowing for the feeble muscles I now have, my handwriting is still Eden's. These people about me will not let me go to the bank personally. It seems, indeed, that there is no bank in this town, and that I have an account in some part of London. It seems that Elvesham kept the name of his solicitor secret from all his household—I can ascertain nothing. Elvesham was, of course, a profound student of mental science, and all my declarations of the facts of the case merely confirm the theory that my insanity is the outcome of overmuch brooding upon psychology. Dreams of the personal identity indeed! Two days ago I was a healthy youngster, with all life before me; now I am a furious old man, unkempt, and desperate, and miserable, prowling about a great luxurious strange house, watched, feared, and avoided as a lunatic by every one about me. And in London is Elvesham beginning life again in a vigorous body, and with all the accumulated knowledge and wisdom of threescore and ten. He has stolen my life.

What has happened I do not clearly know. In the study are volumes of manuscript notes referring chiefly to the psychology of memory, and parts of what may be either calculations or ciphers in symbols absolutely strange to me. In some passages there are indications that he was also occupied with the philosophy of mathematics. I take it he has transferred the whole of his memories, the accumulation that makes up his personality, from this old withered brain of his to mine, and, similarly, that he has transferred mine to his discarded tenement. Practically, that is, he has changed bodies. But how such a change may be possible is without the range of my philosophy. I have been a materialist for all my thinking life, but here, suddenly, is a clear case of man's detachability from matter.

One desperate experiment I am about to try. I sit writing here before putting the matter to issue. This morning, with the help of a table-knife that I had secreted at breakfast, I succeeded in breaking open a fairly obvious secret drawer in this wrecked writing-desk. I discovered nothing save a little green glass phial containing a white powder. Round the neck of the phial was a label, and thereon was written this one word, "*Release*." This may be—is most probably, poison. I can understand Elvesham placing poison in my way, and I should be sure that it was his intention so to get rid of the only living witness against him, were it not for this careful concealment. The man has practically solved the problem of immortality. Save for the spite of chance, he will live in my body until it has aged, and then, again, throwing that aside, he will assume some other victim's youth and strength. When one remembers his heartlessness, it is terrible to think of the ever-growing experience, that—How long has he been leaping from body to body? But I tire of writing. The powder appears to be soluble in water. The taste is not unpleasant.

There the narrative found upon Mr. Elvesham's desk ends. His dead body lay between the desk and the chair. The latter had been pushed back, probably by his last convulsions. The story was written in pencil, and in a crazy hand, quite unlike his usual minute characters. There remain only two curious facts to record. Indisputably there was some connection between Eden and Elvesham, since the whole of Elvesham's property was bequeathed to the young man. But he never inherited. When Elvesham committed suicide, Eden was, strangely enough, already dead. Twenty-four hours before, he had been knocked down by a cab and killed instantly, at the crowded crossing at the intersection of Gower Street and Euston Road. So that the only human being who could have thrown light upon this fantastic narrative is beyond the reach of questions. Without further comment I leave this extraordinary matter to the reader's individual judgment.

The

Stolen Bacillus

"THIS AGAIN," SAID the Bacteriologist, slipping a glass slide under the microscope, "is a preparation of the celebrated Bacillus of cholera—the cholera germ."

The pale-faced man peered down the microscope. He was evidently not accustomed to that kind of thing, and held a limp white hand over his disengaged eye. "I see very little," he said.

"Touch this screw," said the Bacteriologist; "perhaps the microscope is out of focus for you. Eyes vary so much. Just the fraction of a turn this way or that."

"Ah! now I see," said the visitor. "Not so very much to see, after all. Little streaks and shreds of pink. And yet those little particles, those mere atomies, might multiply and devastate a city! Wonderful!"

He stood up, and releasing the glass slip from the microscope, held it in his hand towards the window. "Scarcely visible," he said, scrutinising the preparation. He hesitated. "Are these—alive? Are they dangerous now?"

"Those have been stained and killed," said the Bacteriologist. "I wish, for my own part, we could kill and stain every one of them in the universe."

"I suppose," the pale man said with a slight smile, "that you scarcely care to have such things about you in the living—in the active state?"

"On the contrary, we are obliged to," said the Bacteriologist. "Here, for instance—" He walked across the room and took up one of several sealed tubes. "Here is the living thing. This is a cultivation of the actual living disease bacteria." He hesitated. "Bottled cholera, so to speak."

A slight gleam of satisfaction appeared momentarily in the face of the pale man. "It's a deadly thing to have in your possession," he said, devouring the little tube with his eyes. The Bacteriologist watched the morbid pleasure in his visitor's expression. This man, who had visited him that afternoon with a note of introduction from an old friend, interested him from the very contrast of their dispositions. The lank black hair and deep grey eyes, the haggard expression and nervous manner, the fitful yet keen interest of his visitor were a novel change from the phlegmatic deliberations of the ordinary scientific worker with whom the Bacteriologist chiefly associated. It was perhaps natural, with a hearer evidently so impressionable to the lethal nature of his topic, to take the most effective aspect of the matter.

He held the tube in his hand thoughtfully. "Yes, here is the pestilence imprisoned. Only break such a little tube as this into a supply of drinking-water, say to these minute particles of life that one must needs stain and examine with the highest powers of the microscope even to see, and that one can neither smell nor taste—say to them, 'Go forth, increase and multiply, and replenish the cisterns,' and Death—mysterious, untraceable Death, Death swift and terrible, Death full of pain and indignity—would be released upon this city, and go hither and thither seeking his victims. Here he would take the husband from the wife, here the child from its mother, here the statesman from his duty, and here the toiler from his trouble. He would follow the water-mains, creeping along streets, picking out and punishing a house here and a house there where they did not boil their drinking-water, creeping into the wells of the mineral-water makers, getting washed into salad, and lying dormant in ices. He would wait ready to be drunk in the horse-troughs, and by unwary children in the public fountains. He would soak into the soil, to reappear in springs and wells at a thousand unexpected places. Once start him at the water-supply, and before we could ring him in and catch him again he would have decimated the metropolis."

He stopped abruptly. He had been told rhetoric was his weakness.

"But he is quite safe here, you know—quite safe."

The pale-faced man nodded. His eyes shone. He cleared his throat. "These Anarchist—rascals," said he, "are fools, blind fools—to use bombs when this kind of thing is attainable. I think—"

A gentle rap, a mere light touch of the fingernails was heard at the door. The Bacteriologist opened it. "Just a minute, dear," whispered his wife.

When he re-entered the laboratory his visitor was looking at his watch. "I had no idea I had wasted an hour of your time," he said. "Twelve minutes to four. I ought to have left here by half-past three. But your things were really too interesting. No, positively, I cannot stop a moment longer. I have an engagement at four."

He passed out of the room reiterating his thanks, and the Bacteriologist accompanied him to the door, and then returned thoughtfully along the passage to his laboratory. He was musing on the ethnology of his visitor. Certainly the man was not a Teutonic type nor a common Latin one. "A morbid product, anyhow, I am afraid," said the Bacteriologist to himself. "How he gloated on those cultivations of disease-germs!" A disturbing thought struck him. He turned to the bench by the vapour-bath, and then very quickly to his writing-table. Then he felt hastily in his pockets, and then rushed to the door. "I may have put it down on the hall table," he said.

"Minnie!" he shouted hoarsely in the hall.

"Yes, dear," came a remote voice.

"Had I anything in my hand when I spoke to you, dear, just now?"

Pause.

"Nothing, dear, because I remember—"

"Blue ruin!" cried the Bacteriologist, and incontinently ran to the front door and down the steps of his house to the street.

Minnie, hearing the door slam violently, ran in alarm to the window. Down the street a slender man was getting into a cab. The Bacteriologist, hatless, and in his carpet slippers, was running and gesticulating wildly towards this group. One slipper came off, but he did not wait for it. "He has gone *mad*!"said Minnie; "it's that horrid science of his;" and, opening the window, would have called after him. The slender man, suddenly glancing round, seemed struck with the same idea of mental disorder. He pointed hastily to the Bacteriologist, said something to the cabman, the apron of the cab slammed, the whip swished, the horse's feet clattered, and in a moment cab, and Bacteriologist hotly in pursuit, had receded up the vista of the roadway and disappeared round the corner.

Minnie remained straining out of the window for a minute. Then she drew her head back into the room again. She was dumbfounded. "Of course he is eccentric," she meditated. "But running about London—in the height of the season, too—in his socks!" A happy thought struck her. She hastily put her bonnet on, seized his shoes, went into the hall, took down his hat and light overcoat from the pegs, emerged upon the doorstep, and hailed a cab that opportunely crawled by. "Drive me up the road and round Havelock Crescent, and see if we can find a gentleman running about in a velveteen coat and no hat."

"Velveteen coat, ma'am, and no 'at. Very good, ma'am." And the cabman whipped up at once in the most matter-of-fact way, as if he drove to this address every day in his life.

Some few minutes later the little group of cabmen and loafers that collects round the cabmen's shelter at Haverstock Hill were startled by the passing of a cab with a ginger-coloured screw of a horse, driven furiously.

They were silent as it went by, and then as it receded—"That's 'Arry 'Icks. Wot's *he* got?" said the stout gentleman known as Old Tootles.

"He's a-using his whip, he is, *to* rights," said the ostler boy.

"Hullo!" said poor old Tommy Byles; "here's another bloomin' loonattic. Blowed if there ain't."

"It's old George," said Old Tootles, "and he's drivin' a loonattic, *as* you say. Ain't he a-clawin' out of the keb? Wonder if he's after 'Arry 'Icks?"

The group round the cabmen's shelter became animated. Chorus: "Go it, George!" "It's a race." "You'll ketch 'em!" "Whip up!"

"She's a goer, she is!" said the ostler boy.

"Strike me giddy!" cried Old Tootles. "Here! *I'm* a-goin' to begin in a minute. Here's another comin'. If all the kebs in Hampstead ain't gone mad this morning!"

"It's a fieldmale this time," said the ostler boy.

"She's a followin' *him,*" said Old Tootles. "Usually the other way about."

"What's she got in her 'and?"

"Looks like a 'igh 'at."

"What a bloomin' lark it is! Three to one on old George," said the ostler boy. "Nexst!"

Minnie went by in a perfect roar of applause. She did not like it, but she felt that she was doing her duty, and whirled on down Haverstock Hill and Camden Town High Street, with her eyes ever intent on the animated back view of old George, who was driving her vagrant husband so incomprehensibly away from her.

The man in the foremost cab sat crouched in the corner, his arms tightly folded, and the little tube that contained such vast possibilities of destruction gripped in his hand. His mood was a singular mixture of fear and exultation. Chiefly he was afraid of being caught before he could accomplish his purpose, but behind this was a vaguer but larger fear of the awfulness of his crime. But his exultation far exceeded his fear. No Anarchist before him had ever approached this conception of his. Ravachol, Vaillant, all those distinguished persons whose fame he had envied dwindled into insignificance beside him. He had only to make sure of the water-supply, and break the little tube into a reservoir. How brilliantly he had planned it, forged the letter of introduction and got into the laboratory, and how brilliantly he had seized his opportunity! The world should hear of him at last. All those people who had sneered at him, neglected him, preferred other people to him, found his company undesirable, should consider him at last. Death, death, death! They had always treated him as a man of no importance. All the world had been in a conspiracy to keep him under. He would teach them yet what it is to isolate a man. What was this familiar street? Great Saint Andrew's

Street, of course! How fared the chase? He craned out of the cab. The Bacteriologist was scarcely fifty yards behind. That was bad. He would be caught and stopped yet. He felt in his pocket for money, and found half-a-sovereign. This he thrust up through the trap in the top of the cab into the man's face. "More," he shouted, "if only we get away."

The money was snatched out of his hand. "Right you are," said the cabman, and the trap slammed, and the lash lay along the glistening side of the horse. The cab swayed, and the Anarchist, half-standing under the trap, put the hand containing the little glass tube upon the apron to preserve his balance. He felt the brittle thing crack, and the broken half of it rang upon the floor of the cab. He fell back into the seat with a curse, and stared dismally at the two or three drops of moisture on the apron.

He shuddered.

"Well! I suppose I shall be the first. *Phew*! Anyhow, I shall be a Martyr. That's something. But it is a filthy death, nevertheless. I wonder if it hurts as much as they say."

Presently a thought occurred to him—he groped between his feet. A little drop was still in the broken end of the tube, and he drank that to make sure. It was better to make sure. At any rate, he would not fail.

Then it dawned upon him that there was no further need to escape the Bacteriologist. In Wellington Street he told the cabman to stop, and got out. He slipped on the step, and his head felt queer. It was rapid stuff, this cholera poison. He waved his cabman out of existence, so to speak, and stood on the pavement with his arms folded upon his breast awaiting the arrival of the Bacteriologist. There was something tragic in his pose. The sense of imminent death gave him a certain dignity. He greeted his pursuer with a defiant laugh.

"Vive l'Anarchie! You are too late, my friend. I have drunk it. The cholera is abroad!"

The Bacteriologist from his cab beamed curiously at him through his spectacles. "You have drunk it! An Anarchist! I see now." He was about to say something more, and then checked himself. A smile hung in the corner of his mouth. He opened the apron of his cab as if to descend, at which the Anarchist waved him a dramatic farewell and strode off towards Waterloo Bridge, carefully jostling his infected body against as many people as possible. The Bacteriologist was so preoccupied with the vision of him that he scarcely manifested the slightest surprise at the appearance of Minnie upon the pavement with his hat and shoes and overcoat. "Very good of you to bring my things," he said, and remained lost in contemplation of the receding figure of the Anarchist.

"You had better get in," he said, still staring. Minnie felt absolutely convinced now that he was mad, and directed the cabman home on her own responsibility. "Put on my shoes? Certainly, dear," said he, as the cab began to turn, and hid the strutting black figure, now small in the distance, from his eyes. Then suddenly something grotesque struck him, and he laughed. Then he remarked, "It is really very serious, though.

"You see, that man came to my house to see me, and he is an Anarchist. No—don't faint, or I cannot possibly tell you the rest. And I wanted to astonish him, not knowing he was an Anarchist, and took up a cultivation of that new species of Bacterium I was telling you of, that infest, and I think cause, the blue patches upon various monkeys; and, like a fool, I said it was Asiatic cholera. And he ran away with it to poison the water of London, and he certainly might have made things look blue for this civilised city. And now he has swallowed it. Of course I cannot say what will happen, but you know it turned that kitten blue, and the three puppies—in patches, and the sparrow—bright blue. But the bother is I shall have all the trouble and expense of preparing some more.

"Put on my coat on this hot day! Why? Because we might meet Mrs. Jabber. My dear, Mrs. Jabber is not a draught. But why should I wear a coat on a hot day because of Mrs.———. Oh! *very* well."

The Red Room

"I CAN ASSURE you," said I, "that it will take a very tangible ghost to frighten me." And I stood up before the fire with my glass in my hand.

"It is your own choosing," said the man with the withered arm, and glanced at me askance.

"Eight-and-twenty years," said I, "I have lived, and never a ghost have I seen as yet."

The old woman sat staring hard into the fire, her pale eyes wide open. "Ay," she broke in; "and eight-and-twenty years you have lived and never seen the likes of this house, I reckon. There's a many things to see, when one's still but eight-and-twenty." She swayed her head slowly from side to side. "A many things to see and sorrow for."

I half-suspected the old people were trying to enhance the spiritual terrors of their house by their droning insistence. I put down my empty glass on the table and looked about the room, and caught a glimpse of myself, abbreviated and broadened to an impossible sturdiness, in the queer old mirror at the end of the room. "Well," I said, "if I see anything to-night, I shall be so much the wiser. For I come to the business with an open mind."

"It's your own choosing," said the man with the withered arm once more.

I heard the sound of a stick and a shambling step on the flags in the passage outside, and the door creaked on its hinges as a second old man entered, more bent, more wrinkled, more aged even than the first. He supported himself by a single crutch, his eyes were covered by a shade, and his lower lip, half-averted, hung pale and pink from his decaying yellow teeth. He made straight for an arm-chair on the opposite side of the table, sat down clumsily, and began to cough. The man with the withered arm gave this new-comer a short glance of positive dislike; the old woman took no notice of his arrival, but remained with her eyes fixed steadily on the fire.

"I said—it's your own choosing," said the man with the withered arm, when the coughing had ceased for awhile.

"It's my own choosing," I answered.

The man with the shade became aware of my presence for the first time, and threw his head back for a moment and sideways, to see me. I caught a momentary glimpse of his eyes, small and bright and inflamed. Then he began to cough and splutter again.

"Why don't you drink?" said the man with the withered arm, pushing the beer towards him. The man with the shade poured out a glassful with a shaky arm that splashed half as much again on the deal table. A monstrous shadow of him crouched upon the wall and mocked his action as he poured and drank. I must confess I had scarce expected these grotesque custodians. There is to my mind something inhuman in senility, something crouching and atavistic; the human qualities seem to drop from old people insensibly day by day. The three of them made me feel uncomfortable, with their gaunt silences, their bent carriage, their evident unfriendliness to me and to one another.

"If," said I, "you will show me to this haunted room of yours, I will make myself comfortable there."

The old man with the cough jerked his head back so suddenly that it startled me, and shot another glance of his red eyes at me from under the shade; but no one answered me. I waited a minute, glancing from one to the other.

"If," I said a little louder, "if you will show me to this haunted room of yours, I will relieve you from the task of entertaining me."

"There's a candle on the slab outside the door," said the man with the withered arm, looking at my feet as he addressed me. "But if you go to the red room to-night—"

("This night of all nights!" said the old woman.)

"You go alone."

"Very well," I answered. "And which way do I go?"

You go along the passage for a bit," said he, "until you come to a door, and through that is a spiral staircase, and half-way up that is a landing and another door covered with baize. Go through that and down the long corridor to the end, and the red room is on your left up the steps."

"Have I got that right?" I said, and repeated his directions. He corrected me in one particular.

"And are you really going?" said the man with the shade, looking at me again for the third time, with that queer, unnatural tilting of the face.

("This night of all nights!" said the old woman.)

"It is what I came for," I said, and moved towards the door. As I did so, the old man with the shade rose and staggered round the table, so as to be closer to the others and to the fire. At the door I turned and looked at them, and saw they were all close together, dark against the firelight, staring at me over their shoulders, with an intent expression on their ancient faces.

"Good-night," I said, setting the door open.

"It's your own choosing," said the man with the withered arm.

I left the door wide open until the candle was well alight, and then I shut them in and walked down the chilly, echoing passage.

I must confess that the oddness of these three old pensioners in whose charge her ladyship had left the castle, and the deep-toned, old-fashioned furniture of the housekeeper's room in which they foregathered, affected me in spite of my efforts to keep myself at a matter-of-fact phase. They seemed to belong to another age, an older age, an age when things spiritual were different from this of ours, less certain; an age when omens and witches were credible, and ghosts beyond denying. Their very existence was spectral; the cut of their clothing, fashions born in dead brains. The ornaments and conveniences of the room about them were ghostly—the thoughts of vanished men, which still haunted rather than participated in the world of to-day. But with an effort I sent such thoughts to the right-about. The long, draughty subterranean passage was chilly and dusty, and my candle flared and made the shadows cower and quiver. The echoes rang up and down the spiral staircase, and a shadow came sweeping up after me, and one fled before me into the darkness overhead. I came to the landing and stopped there for a moment, listening to a rustling that I fancied I heard; then, satisfied of the absolute silence, I pushed open the baize-covered door and stood in the corridor.

The effect was scarcely what I expected, for the moonlight, coming in by the great window on the grand staircase, picked out everything in vivid black shadow or silvery illumination. Everything was in its place: the house might have been deserted on the yesterday instead of eighteen months ago. There were candles in the sockets of the sconces, and whatever dust had gathered on the carpets or upon the polished flooring was distributed so evenly as to be invisible in the moonlight. I was about to advance, and stopped abruptly. A bronze group stood upon the landing, hidden from me by the corner of the wall, but its shadow fell with marvelous distinctness upon the white panelling, and gave me the impression of some one crouching to waylay me. I stood rigid for half a minute perhaps. Then, with my hand in the pocket that held my revolver, I advanced, only to discover a Ganymede and Eagle glistening in the moonlight. That incident for a time restored my nerve, and a porcelain Chinaman on a buhl table, whose head rocked silently as I passed him, scarcely startled me.

The door to the red room and the steps up to it were in a shadowy corner. I moved my candle from side to side, in order to see clearly the nature of the recess in which I stood before opening the door. Here it was, thought I, that my predecessor was found, and the memory of that story gave me a sudden twinge of apprehension. I glanced over my shoulder at the Ganymede in the moonlight, and opened the door of the red room rather hastily, with my face half turned to the pallid silence of the landing.

I entered, closed the door behind me at once, turned the key I found in the lock within, and stood with the candle held aloft, surveying the scene of my vigil, the great red room of Lorraine Castle, in which the young duke had died. Or, rather, in which he had begun his dying, for he had opened the door and fallen headlong down the steps I had just ascended. That had been the end of his vigil, of his gallant attempt to conquer the ghostly tradition of the place, and never, I thought, had apoplexy better served the ends of superstition. And there were other and older stories that clung to the room, back to the half-credible beginning of it all, the tale of a timid wife and the tragic end that came to her husband's jest of frightening her. And looking around that large shadowy room, with its shadowy window bays, its recesses and alcoves, one could well understand the legends that had sprouted in its black corners, its germinating darkness. My candle was a little tongue of light in its vastness, that failed to pierce the opposite end of the room, and left an ocean of mystery and suggestion beyond its island of light.

I resolved to make a systematic examination of the place at once, and dispel the fanciful suggestions of its obscurity before they obtained a hold upon me. After satisfying myself of the fastening of the door, I began to walk about the room, peering round each article of furniture, tucking up the valances of the bed, and opening its curtains wide. I pulled up the blinds and examined the fastenings of the several windows before closing the shutters, leant forward and looked up the blackness of the wide chimney, and tapped the dark oak panelling for any secret opening. There were two big mirrors in the room, each with a pair of sconces bearing candles, and on the mantel-shelf, too, were more candles in china candlesticks. All these I lit one after the other. The fire was laid,—an unexpected consideration from the old housekeeper,—and I lit it, to keep down any disposition to shiver, and when it was burning well, I stood round with my back to it and regarded the room again. I had pulled up a chintz-covered armchair and a table, to form a kind of barricade before me, and on this lay my revolver ready to hand. My precise examination had done me good, but I still found the remoter darkness of the place, and its perfect stillness, too stimulating for the imagination. The echoing of the stir and crackling of the fire was no sort of comfort to me. The shadow in the alcove, at the end in particular, had that undefinable quality of a presence, that odd suggestion of a lurking living thing, that comes so easily in silence and solitude. At last, to reassure myself, I walked with a candle into it, and satisfied myself that there was nothing tangible there. I stood that candle upon the floor of the alcove, and left it in that position.

By this time I was in a state of considerable nervous tension, although to my reason there was no adequate cause for the condition. My mind, however, was perfectly clear. I postulated quite unreservedly that nothing supernatural could happen, and to pass the time I began to string some rhymes together, Ingoldsby fashion, of the original legend of the place. A few I spoke aloud, but the echoes were not pleasant. For the same reason I also abandoned, after a time, a conversation with myself upon the impossibility of ghosts and haunting. My mind reverted to the three old and distorted people downstairs, and I tried to keep it upon that topic. The sombre reds and blacks of the room troubled me; even with seven candles the place was merely dim. The one in the alcove flared in a draught, and the fire-flickering kept the shadows and penumbra perpetually shifting and stirring. Casting about for a remedy, I recalled the candles I had seen in the passage, and, with a slight effort, walked out into the moonlight, carrying a candle and leaving the door open, and presently returned with as many as ten. These I put in various knick-knacks of china with which the room was sparsely adorned, lit and placed where the shadows had lain deepest, some on the floor, some in the window recesses, until at last my seventeen candles were so arranged that not an inch of the room but had the direct light of at least one of them. It occurred to me that when the ghost came, I could warn him not to trip over them. The room was now quite brightly illuminated. There was something very cheery and reassuring in these little streaming flames, and snuffing them gave me an occupation, and afforded a reassuring sense of the passage of time.

Even with that, however, the brooding expectation of the vigil weighed heavily upon me. It was after midnight that the candle in the alcove suddenly went out, and the black shadow sprang back to its place there. I did not see the candle go out; I simply turned and saw that the darkness was there, as one might start and see the unexpected presence of a stranger. "By Jove!" said I aloud; "that draught's a strong one!" and, taking the matches from the table, I walked across the room in a leisurely manner to relight the corner again. My first match would not strike, and as I succeeded with the second, something seemed to blink on the wall before me. I turned my head involuntarily, and saw that the two candles on the little table by the fireplace were extinguished. I rose at once to my feet.

"Odd!" I said. "Did I do that myself in a flash of absent-mindedness?"

I walked back, relit one, and as I did so, I saw the candle in the right sconce of one of the mirrors wink and go right out, and almost immediately its companion followed it. There was no mistake about it. The flame vanished, as if the wicks had been suddenly nipped between a finger and a thumb, leaving the wick neither glowing nor smoking, but black. While I stood gaping, the candle at the foot of the bed went out, and the shadows seemed to take another step towards me.

"This won't do!" said I, and first one and then another candle on the mantel-shelf followed.

"What's up?" I cried, with a queer high note getting into my voice somehow. At that the candle on the wardrobe went out, and the one I had relit in the alcove followed.

"Steady on!" I said. "These candles are wanted," speaking with a half-hysterical facetiousness, and scratching away at a match the while for the mantel candlesticks. My hands trembled so much that twice I missed the rough paper of the matchbox. As the mantel emerged from darkness again, two candles in the remoter end of the window were eclipsed. But with the same match I also relit the larger mirror candles, and those on the floor near the doorway, so that for the moment I seemed to gain on the extinctions. But then in a volley there vanished four lights at once in different corners of the room, and I struck another match in quivering haste, and stood hesitating whither to take it.

As I stood undecided, an invisible hand seemed to sweep out the two candles on the table. With a cry of terror, I dashed at the alcove, then into the corner, and then into the window, relighting three, as two more vanished by the fireplace; then, perceiving a better way, I dropped the matches on the iron-bound deed-box in the corner, and caught up the bedroom candlestick. With this I avoided the delay of striking matches; but for all that the steady process of extinction went on, and the shadows I feared and fought against returned, and crept in upon me, first a step gained on this side of me and then on that. It was like a ragged stormcloud sweeping out the stars. Now and then one returned for a minute, and was lost again. I was now almost frantic with the horror of the coming darkness, and my self-possession deserted me. I leaped, panting and dishevelled, from candle to candle, in a vain struggle against that remorseless advance.

I bruised myself on the thigh against the table, I sent a chair headlong, I stumbled and fell and whisked the cloth from the table in my fall. My candle rolled away from me, and I snatched another as I rose. Abruptly this was blown out, as I swung it off the table, by the wind of my sudden movement, and immediately the two remaining candles followed. But there was light still in the room, a red light that staved off the shadows from me. The fire! Of course, I could still thrust my candle between the bars and relight it!

I turned to where the flames were still dancing between the glowing coals, and splashing red reflections upon the furniture, made two steps towards the grate, and incontinently the flames dwindled and vanished, the glow vanished, the reflections rushed together and vanished, and as I thrust the candle between the bars, darkness closed upon me like the shutting of an eye, wrapped about me in a stifling embrace, sealed my vision, and crushed the last vestiges of reason from my brain. The candle fell from my hand. I flung out my arms in a vain effort to thrust that ponderous blackness away from me, and, lifting up my voice, screamed with all my might—once, twice, thrice. Then I think I must have staggered to my feet. I know I thought suddenly of the moonlit corridor, and, with my head bowed and my arms over my face, made a run for the door.

But I had forgotten the exact position of the door, and struck myself heavily against the corner of the bed. I staggered back, turned, and was either struck or struck myself against some other bulky furniture. I have a vague memory of battering myself thus, to and fro in the darkness, of a cramped struggle, and of my own wild crying as I darted to and fro, of a heavy blow at last upon my forehead, a horrible sensation of falling that lasted an age, of my last frantic effort to keep my footing, and then I remember no more.

I opened my eyes in daylight. My head was roughly bandaged, and the man with the withered arm was watching my face. I looked about me, trying to remember what had happened, and for a space I could not recollect. I rolled my eyes into the corner, and saw the old woman, no longer abstracted, pouring out some drops of medicine from a little blue phial into a glass. "Where am I?" I asked. "I seem to remember you, and yet I cannot remember who you are."

They told me then, and I heard of the haunted red room as one who hears a tale. "We found you at dawn," said he, "and there was blood on your forehead and lips."

It was very slowly I recovered my memory of my experience. "You believe now," said the old man, "that the room is haunted?" He spoke no longer as one who greets an intruder, but as one who grieves for a broken friend.

"Yes," said I; "the room is haunted."

"And you have seen it. And we, who have lived here all our lives, have never set eyes upon it. Because we have never dared.—Tell us, is it truly the old earl who—"

"No," said I; "it is not."

"I told you so," said the old lady, with the glass in her hand. "It is his poor young countess who was frightened—"

"It is not," I said. "There is neither ghost of earl nor ghost of countess in that room, there is no ghost there at all; but worse, far worse—"

"Well?" they said.

"The worst of all the things that haunt poor mortal man," said I; "and that is, in all its nakedness—*Fear!* Fear that will not have light nor sound, that will not bear with reason, that deafens and darkens and overwhelms. It followed me through the corridor, it fought against me in the room—"

I stopped abruptly. There was an interval of silence. My hand went up to my bandages.

Then the man with the shade sighed and spoke. "That is it," said he. "I knew that was it. A Power of Darkness. To put such a curse upon a woman! It lurks there always. You can feel it even in the daytime, even of a bright summer's day, in the hangings, in the curtains, keeping behind you however you face about. In the dusk it creeps along the corridor and follows you, so that you dare not turn. There is Fear in that room of hers—black Fear, and there will be—so long as this house of sin endures."

A Moth
(Genus Unknown)

PROBABLY YOU HAVE heard of Hapley—not W. T. Hapley, the son, but the celebrated Hapley, the Hapley of *Periplaneta Hapliia,* Hapley the entomologist. If so, you know at least of the great feud between Hapley and Professor Pawkins, though certain of its consequences may be new to you. For those who have not, a word or two of explanation is necessary, which the idle reader may go over with a glancing eye, if his indolence so incline him.

It is amazing how very widely diffused is the ignorance of such really important matters as this Hapley-Pawkins feud. Those epoch-making controversies, again, that have convulsed the Geological Society, are, I verily believe, almost entirely unknown outside the fellowship of that body. I have heard men of fair general education even refer to the great scenes at these meetings as vestry-meeting squabbles. Yet the great Hate of the English and Scotch geologists has lasted now half a century, and has "left deep and abundant marks upon the body of the science." And this Hapley-Pawkins business, though perhaps a more personal affair, stirred passions as profound, if not profounder. Your common man has no conception of the zeal that animates a scientific investigator, the fury of contradiction you can arouse in him. It is the *odium theologicum* in a new form. There are men, for instance, who would gladly burn Professor Ray Lankester at Smithfield for his treatment of the Mollusca in the Encyclopædia. That fantastic extension of the Cephalopods to cover the Pterpodos—But I wander from Hapley and Pawkins.

It began years and years ago, with a revision of the Microlepidoptera (whatever these may be) by Pawkins, in which he extinguished a new species created by Hapley. Hapley, who was always quarrelsome, replied by a stinging impeachment of the entire classification of Pawkins.[1] Pawkins, in his "Rejoinder,"[2] suggested that Hapley's microscope was as defective as his powers of observation, and called him an "irresponsible meddler"—Hapley was not a professor at that time. Hapley, in his retort,[3] spoke of "blundering collectors," and described, as if inadvertently, Pawkins's revision as a "miracle of ineptitude." It was war to the knife. However, it would scarcely interest the reader to detail how these two great men quarrelled, and how the split between them widened until from the Microlepidoptera, they were at war upon every open question in entomology. There were memorable occasions. At times the Royal Entomological Society meetings resembled nothing so much as the Chamber of Deputies. On the whole, I fancy Pawkins was nearer the truth than Hapley. But Hapley was skilful with his rhetoric, had a turn for ridicule rare in a scientific man, was endowed with vast energy, and had a fine sense

[1]"Remarks on a Recent Revision of Microlepidoptera." *Quart. Journ. Entomological Soc.* 1863.
[2]"Rejoinder to certain Remarks," &c. *Ibid.* 1864.
[3]"Further Remarks," &c. *Ibid.*

of injury in the matter of the extinguished species; while Pawkins was a man of dull presence, prosy of speech, in shape not unlike a water-barrel, overconscientious with testimonials, and suspected of jobbing museum appointments. So the young men gathered round Hapley and applauded him. It was a long struggle, vicious from the beginning, and growing at last to pitiless antagonism. The successive turns of fortune, now an advantage to one side and now to another—now Hapley tormented by some success of Pawkins, and now Pawkins outshone by Hapley—belong rather to the history of entomology than to this story.

But in 1891 Pawkins, whose health had been bad for some time, published some work upon the "mesoblast" of the Death's Head Moth. What the mesoblast of the Death's Head Moth may be, does not matter a rap in this story. But the work was far below his usual standard, and gave Hapley an opening he had coveted for years. He must have worked night and day to make the most of his advantage.

In an elaborate critique he rent Pawkins to tatters,—one can fancy the man's disordered black hair, and his queer dark eyes flashing as he went for his antagonist,—and Pawkins made a reply, halting, ineffectual, with painful gaps of silence, and yet malignant. There was no mistaking his will to wound Hapley, nor his incapacity to do it. But few of those who heard him—I was absent from that meeting—realised how ill the man was.

Hapley had got his opponent down, and meant to finish him. He followed with a simply brutal attack upon Pawkins, in the form of a paper upon the development of moths in general, a paper showing evidence of a most extraordinary amount of mental labour, and yet couched in a violently controversial tone. Violent as it was, an editorial note witnesses that it was modified. It must have covered Pawkins with shame and confusion of face. It left no loophole; it was murderous in argument, and utterly contemptuous in tone; an awful thing for the declining years of a man's career.

The world of entomologists waited breathlessly for the rejoinder from Pawkins. He would try one, for Pawkins had always been game. But when it came it surprised them. For the rejoinder of Pawkins was to catch the influenza, to proceed to pneumonia, and to die.

It was perhaps as effectual a reply as he could make under the circumstances, and largely turned the current of feeling against Hapley. The very people who had most gleefully cheered on those gladiators became serious at the consequence. There could be no reasonable doubt the fret of the defeat had contributed to the death of Pawkins. There was a limit even to scientific controversy, said serious people. Another crushing attack was already in the press and appeared on the day before the funeral. I don't think Hapley exerted himself to stop it. People remembered how Hapley had hounded down his rival, and forgot that rival's defects. Scathing satire reads ill over fresh mould. The thing provoked comment in the daily papers. This it was that made me think that you had probably heard of Hapley and this controversy. But, as I have already remarked, scientific workers live very much in a world of their own; half the people, I dare say, who go along Piccadilly to the Academy every year, could not tell you where the learned societies abide. Many even think that Research is a kind of happy-family cage in which all kinds of men lie down together in peace.

In his private thoughts Hapley could not forgive Pawkins for dying. In the first place, it was a mean dodge to escape the absolute pulverisation Hapley had in hand for him, and in the second, it left Hapley's mind with a queer gap in it. For twenty years he had worked hard, sometimes far into the night, and seven days a week, with microscope, scalpel, collecting-net, and pen, and almost entirely with reference to Pawkins. The European reputation he had won had come as an incident in that great antipathy. He had gradually worked up to a climax in this last controversy. It had killed Pawkins, but it had also thrown Hapley out of gear, so to speak, and his doctor advised him to give up work for a time, and rest. So Hapley went down into a quiet village in Kent, and thought day and night of Pawkins, and good things it was now impossible to say about him.

At last Hapley began to realise in what direction the preoccupation tended. He determined to make a fight for it, and started by trying to read novels. But he could not get his mind off Pawkins, white in the face, and making his last speech—every sentence a beautiful opening for Hapley. He turned to fiction—and found it had no grip on him. He read the "Island Nights' Entertainments" until his "sense of causation" was shocked beyond endurance by the Bottle Imp. Then he went to Kipling, and found he "proved nothing," besides being irreverent and vulgar. These scientific people have their limitations. Then, unhappily, he tried Besant's "Inner House," and the opening chapter set his mind upon learned societies and Pawkins at once.

So Hapley turned to chess, and found it a little more soothing. He soon mastered the moves and the chief gambits and commoner closing positions, and began to beat the Vicar. But then the cylindrical contours of the opposite king began to resemble Pawkins standing up and gasping ineffectually against checkmate, and Hapley decided to give up chess.

Perhaps the study of some new branch of science would after all be better diversion. The best rest is change of occupation. Hapley determined to plunge at diatoms, and had one of his smaller microscopes and Halibut's monograph sent down from London. He thought that perhaps if he could get up a vigorous quarrel with Halibut, he might be able to begin life afresh and forget Pawkins. And very soon he was hard at work, in his habitual strenuous fashion, at these microscopic denizens of the way-side pool.

It was on the third day of the diatoms that Hapley became aware of a novel addition to the local fauna. He was working late at the microscope, and the only light in the room was the brilliant little lamp with the special form of green shade. Like all experienced microscopists, he kept both eyes open. It is the only way to avoid excessive fatigue. One eye was over the instrument, and bright and distinct before that was the circular field of the microscope, across which a brown diatom was slowly moving. With the other eye Hapley saw, as it were, without seeing.[1] He was only dimly conscious of the brass side of the instrument, the illuminated part of the tablecloth, a sheet of note-paper, the foot of the lamp, and the darkened room beyond.

Suddenly his attention drifted from one eye to the other. The table-cloth was of the material called tapestry by shopmen, and rather brightly coloured. The pattern was in gold, with a small amount of crimson and pale-blue upon a greyish ground. At one point the pattern seemed displaced, and there was a vibrating movement of the colours at this point.

Hapley suddenly moved his head back and looked with both eyes. His mouth fell open with astonishment.

It was a large moth or butterfly; its wings spread in butterfly fashion!

It was strange it should be in the room at all, for the windows were closed. Strange that it should not have attracted his attention when fluttering to its present position. Strange that it should match the table-cloth. Stranger far to him,

[1]The reader unaccustomed to microscopes may easily understand this by rolling a newspaper in the form of a tube and looking through it at a book, keeping the other eye open.

Hapley, the great entomologist, it was altogether unknown. There was no delusion. It was crawling slowly towards the foot of the lamp.

"*Genus unknown*, by heavens! And in England!" said Hapley, staring.

Then he suddenly thought of Pawkins. Nothing would have maddened Pawkins more—And Pawkins was dead!

Something about the head and body of the insect became singularly suggestive of Pawkins, just as the chess king had been.

"Confound Pawkins!" said Hapley. "But I must catch this." And, looking round him for some means of capturing the moth, he rose slowly out of his chair. Suddenly the insect rose, struck the edge of the lamp-shade—Hapley heard the "ping" —and vanished into the shadow.

In a moment Hapley had whipped off the shade, so that the whole room was illuminated. The thing had disappeared, but soon his practised eye detected it upon the wall-paper near the door. He went towards it, poising the lamp-shade for capture. Before he was within striking distance, however, it had risen and was fluttering round the room. After the fashion of its kind, it flew with sudden starts and turns, seeming to vanish here and reappear there. Once Hapley struck, and missed; then again.

The third time he hit his microscope. The instrument swayed, struck and overturned the lamp, and fell noisily upon the floor. The lamp turned over on the table and, very luckily, went out. Hapley was left in the dark. With a start he felt the strange moth blunder into his face.

It was maddening. He had no lights. If he opened the door of the room the thing would get away. In the darkness he saw Pawkins quite distinctly laughing at him. Pawkins had ever an oily laugh. He swore furiously and stamped his foot on the floor.

There was a timid rapping at the door.

Then it opened, perhaps a foot, and very slowly. The alarmed face of the landlady appeared behind a pink candle flame; she wore a night-cap over her grey hair and had some purple garment over her shoulders. "What *was* that fearful smash?" she said. "Has anything—" The strange moth appeared fluttering about the chink of the door. "Shut that door!" said Hapley, and suddenly rushed at her.

The door slammed hastily. Hapley was left alone in the dark. Then in the pause he heard his landlady scuttle upstairs, lock her door and drag something heavy across the room and put against it.

It became evident to Hapley that his conduct and appearance had been strange and alarming. Confound the moth! and Pawkins! However, it was a pity to lose the moth now. He felt his way into the hall and found the matches, after sending his hat down upon the floor with a noise like a drum. With the lighted candle he returned to the sitting-room. No moth was to be seen. Yet once for a moment it seemed that the thing was fluttering round his head. Hapley very suddenly decided to give up the moth and go to bed. But he was excited. All night long his sleep was broken by dreams of the moth, Pawkins, and his landlady. Twice in the night he turned out and soused his head in cold water.

One thing was very clear to him. His landlady could not possibly understand about the strange moth, especially as he had failed to catch it. No one but an entomologist would understand quite how he felt. She was probably frightened at his behaviour, and yet he failed to see how he could explain it. He decided to say nothing further about the events of last night. After breakfast he saw her in her garden, and decided to go out to talk to her to reassure her. He talked to her about beans and potatoes, bees, caterpillars, and the price of fruit. She replied in her usual manner, but she looked at him a little suspiciously, and kept walking as he walked, so that there was always a bed of flowers, or a row of beans, or something of the sort, between them. After a while he began to feel singularly irritated at this, and to conceal his vexation went indoors and presently went out for a walk.

The moth—or butterfly, trailing an odd flavour of Pawkins with it, kept coming into that walk, though he did his best to keep his mind off it. Once he saw it quite distinctly, with its wings flattened out, upon the old stone wall that runs along the west edge of the park, but going up to it he found it was only two lumps of grey and yellow lichen. "This," said Hapley, "is the reverse of mimicry. Instead of a butterfly looking like a stone, here is a stone looking like a butterfly!" Once something hovered and fluttered round his head, but by an effort of will he drove that impression out of his mind again.

In the afternoon Hapley called upon the Vicar, and argued with him upon theological questions. They sat in the little arbour covered with briar, and smoked as they wrangled. "Look at that moth!" said Hapley, suddenly, pointing to the edge of the wooden table.

"Where?" said the Vicar.

"You don't see a moth on the edge of the table there?" said Hapley.

"Certainly not," said the Vicar.

Hapley was thunderstruck. He gasped. The Vicar was staring at him. Clearly the man saw nothing. "The eye of faith is no better than the eye of science," said Hapley, awkwardly.

"I don't see your point," said the Vicar, thinking it was part of the argument.

That night Hapley found the moth crawling over his counterpane. He sat on the edge of the bed in his shirt-sleeves and reasoned with himself. Was it pure hallucination? He knew he was slipping, and he battled for his sanity with the same silent energy he had formerly displayed against Pawkins. So persistent is mental habit, that he felt as if it were still a struggle with Pawkins. He was well versed in psychology. He knew that such visual illusions do come as a result of mental strain. But the point was, he did not only *see* the moth, he had heard it when it touched the edge of the lamp-shade, and afterwards when it hit against the wall, and he had felt it strike his face in the dark.

He looked at it. It was not at all dreamlike, but perfectly clear and solid-looking in the candlelight. He saw the hairy body, and the short, feathery antennæ, the jointed legs, even a place where the down was rubbed from the wing. He suddenly felt angry with himself for being afraid of a little insect.

His landlady had got the servant to sleep with her that night, because she was afraid to be alone. In addition she had locked the door, and put the chest of drawers against it. They listened and talked in whispers after they had gone to bed, but nothing occurred to alarm them. About eleven they had ventured to put the candle out, and had both dozed off to sleep. They woke up with a start, and sat up in bed, listening in the darkness.

Then they heard slippered feet going to and fro in Hapley's room. A chair was overturned, and there was a violent dab at the wall. Then a china mantel ornament smashed upon the fender. Suddenly the door of the room opened, and they heard him upon the landing. They clung to one another, listening. He seemed to be dancing upon the staircase. Now he would go down three or four steps quickly, then up again, then hurry down into the hall. They heard the umbrella-stand go over, and the fanlight break. Then the bolt shot and the chain rattled. He was opening the door.

They hurried to the window. It was a dim grey night; an almost unbroken sheet of watery cloud was sweeping across the moon, and the hedge and trees in front of the house were black against the pale roadway. They saw Hapley, looking like a ghost in his shirt and white trousers, running to and fro in the road, and beating the air. Now he would stop, now he would dart very rapidly at something invisible, now he would move upon it with stealthy strides. At last he went out of sight up the road towards the down. Then, while they argued who should go down and lock the door, he returned. He was walking very fast, and he came straight into the house, closed the door carefully, and went quietly up to his bedroom. Then everything was silent.

"Mrs. Colville," said Hapley, calling down the staircase next morning. "I hope I did not alarm you last night."

"You may well ask that!" said Mrs. Colville.

"The fact is, I am a sleep-walker, and the last two nights I have been without my sleeping mixture. There is nothing to be alarmed about, really. I am sorry I made such an ass of myself. I will go over the down to Shoreham, and get some stuff to make me sleep soundly. I ought to have done that yesterday."

But half-way over the down, by the chalk-pits, the moth came upon Hapley again. He went on, trying to keep his mind upon chess problems, but it was no good. The thing fluttered into his face, and he struck at it with his hat in self-defence. Then rage, the old rage—the rage he had so often felt against Pawkins—returned once more. He went on, leaping and striking at the eddying insect. Suddenly he trod on nothing, and fell headlong.

There was a gap in his sensations, and Hapley found himself sitting on the heap of flints in front of the opening of the chalk-pits, with a leg twisted back under him. The strange moth was still fluttering round his head. He struck at it with his hand, and turning his head saw two men approaching him. One was the village doctor. It occurred to Hapley that this was lucky. Then it came into his mind, with extraordinary vividness, that no one would ever be able to see the strange moth except himself, and that it behoved him to keep silent about it.

Late that night, however, after his broken leg was set, he was feverish and forgot his self-restraint. He was lying flat on his bed, and he began to run his eyes round the room to see if the moth was still about. He tried not to do this, but it was no good. He soon caught sight of the thing resting close to his hand, by the night-light, on the green table-cloth. The wings quivered. With a sudden wave of anger he smote at it with his fist, and the nurse woke up with a shriek. He had missed it.

"That moth!" he said; and then, "It was fancy. Nothing!"

All the time he could see quite clearly the insect going round the cornice and darting across the room, and he could also see that the nurse saw nothing of it and looked at him strangely. He must keep himself in hand. He knew he was a lost man if he did not keep himself in hand. But as the night waned the fever grew upon him, and the very dread he had of seeing the moth made him see it. About five, just as the dawn was grey, he tried to get out of bed and catch it, though his leg was afire with pain. The nurse had to struggle with him.

On account of this, they tied him down to the bed. At this the moth grew bolder, and once he felt it settle in his hair. Then, because he struck out violently with his arms, they tied these also. At this the moth came and crawled over his face, and Hapley wept, swore, screamed, prayed for them to take it off him, unavailingly.

The doctor was a blockhead, a half-qualified general practitioner, and quite ignorant of mental science. He simply said there was no moth. Had he possessed the wit, he might still, perhaps, have saved Hapley from his fate by entering into his delusion and covering his face with gauze, as he prayed might be done. But, as I say, the doctor was a blockhead, and until the leg was healed Hapley was kept tied to his bed, and with the imaginary moth crawling over him. It never left him while he was awake and it grew to a monster in his dreams. While he was awake he longed for sleep, and from sleep he awoke screaming.

So now Hapley is spending the remainder of his days in a padded room, worried by a moth that no one else can see. The asylum doctor calls it hallucination; but Hapley, when he is in his easier mood, and can talk, says it is the ghost of Pawkins, and consequently a unique specimen and well worth the trouble of catching.

In
the Abyss

THE LIEUTENANT STOOD in front of the steel sphere and gnawed a piece of pine splinter. "What do you think of it, Steevens?" he asked.

"It's an idea," said Steevens, in the tone of one who keeps an open mind.

"I believe it will smash—flat," said the lieutenant.

"He seems to have calculated it all out pretty well," said Steevens, still impartial.

"But think of the pressure," said the lieutenant. "At the surface of the water it's fourteen pounds to the inch, thirty feet down it's double that; sixty, treble; ninety, four times; nine hundred, forty times; five thousand three hundred—that's a mile—it's two hundred and forty times fourteen pounds; that's—let's see—thirty hundred-weight—a ton and a half, Steevens; *a ton and a half* to the square inch. And the ocean where he's going is five miles deep. That's seven and a half—"

"Sounds a lot," said Steevens, "but it's jolly thick steel."

The lieutenant made no answer, but resumed his pine splinter. The object of their conversation was a huge globe of steel, having an exterior diameter of perhaps eight feet. It looked like the shot for some Titanic piece of artillery. It was elaborately nested in a monstrous scaffolding built into the framework of the vessel, and the gigantic spars that were presently to sling it overboard gave the stern of the ship an appearance that had raised the curiosity of every decent sailor who had sighted it, from the pool of London to the Tropic of Capricorn. In two places, one above the other, the steel gave place to a couple of circular windows of enormously thick glass, and one of these, set in a steel frame of great solidity, was now partially unscrewed. Both the men had seen the interior of this globe for the first time that morning. It was elaborately padded with air cushions, with little studs sunk between bulging pillows to work the simple mechanism of the affair. Everything was elaborately padded, even the Myer's apparatus which was to absorb carbonic acid and replace the oxygen inspired by its tenant, when he had crept in by the glass manhole, and had been screwed in. It was so elaborately padded that a man might have been fired from a gun in it with perfect safety. And it had need to be, for presently a man was to crawl in through that glass manhole, to be screwed up tightly, and to be flung overboard, and to sink down—down—down, for five miles, even as the lieutenant said. It had taken the strongest hold of his imagination; it made him a bore at mess; and he found Steevens, the new arrival aboard, a godsend to talk to about it, over and over again.

"It's my opinion," said the lieutenant, "that that glass will simply bend in and bulge and smash, under a pressure of that sort. Daubrée has made rocks run like water under big pressures—and, you mark my words—"

"If the glass did break in," said Steevens, "what then?"

"The water would shoot in like a jet of iron. Have you ever felt a straight jet of high pressure water? It would hit as hard as a bullet. It would simply smash him and flatten him. It would tear down his throat, and into his lungs; it would blow in his ears—"

"What a detailed imagination you have," protested Steevens, who saw things vividly.

"It's a simple statement of the inevitable," said the lieutenant.

"And the globe?"

"Would just give out a few little bubbles, and it would settle down comfortably against the day of judgment, among the oozes and the bottom clay—with poor Elstead spread over his own smashed cushions like butter over bread."

He repeated this sentence as though he liked it very much. "Like butter over bread," he said.

"Having a look at the jigger? "said a voice behind them, and Elstead stood behind them, spick and span in white, with a cigarette between his teeth, and his eyes smiling out of the shadow of his ample hat-brim. "What's that about bread and butter, Weybridge? Grumbling as usual about the insufficient pay of naval officers? It won't be more than a day now before I start. We are to get the slings ready today. This clean sky and gentle swell is just the kind of thing for swinging off twenty tons of lead and iron; isn't it?"

"It won't affect you much," said Weybridge.

"No. Seventy or eighty feet down, and I shall be there in a dozen seconds, there's not a particle moving, though the wind shriek itself hoarse up above, and the water lifts halfway to the clouds. No. Down there—" He moved to the side of the ship and the other two followed him. All three leant forward on their elbows and stared down into the yellow-green water.

"*Peace*," said Elstead, finishing his thought aloud.

"Are you dead certain that clockwork will act?" asked Weybridge, presently.

"It has worked thirty-five times," said Elstead. "It's bound to work."

"But if it doesn't?"

"Why shouldn't it?"

"I wouldn't go down in that confounded thing," said Weybridge, "for twenty thousand pounds."

"Cheerful chap you are," said Elstead, and spat sociably at a bubble below.

"I don't understand yet how you mean to work the thing," said Steevens.

"In the first place I'm screwed into the sphere," said Elstead, "and when I've turned the electric light off and on three times to show I'm cheerful, I'm swung out over the stern by that crane, with all those big lead sinkers slung below me. The top lead weight has a roller carrying a hundred fathoms of strong cord rolled up, and that's all that joins the sinkers to the sphere, except the slings that will be cut when the affair is dropped. We use cord rather than wire rope because it's easier to cut and more buoyant—necessary points as you will see.

"Through each of these lead weights you notice there is a hole, and an iron rod will be run through that and will project six feet on the lower side. If that rod is rammed up from below it knocks up a lever and sets the clockwork in motion at the side of the cylinder on which the cord winds.

"Very well. The whole affair is lowered gently into the water, and the slings are cut. The sphere floats—with the air in it, it's lighter than water; but the lead weights go down straight and the cord runs out. When the cord is all paid out, the sphere will go down too, pulled down by the cord."

"But why the cord?" asked Steevens. "Why not fasten the weights directly to the sphere?"

"Because of the smash down below. The whole affair will go rushing down, mile after mile, at a headlong pace at last. It would be knocked to pieces on the bottom if it wasn't for that cord. But the weights will hit the bottom, and directly they do the buoyancy of the sphere will come into play. It will go on sinking slower and slower; come to a stop at last and then begin to float upward again.

"That's where the clockwork comes in. Directly the weights smash against the sea bottom, the rod will be knocked through and will kick up the clockwork, and the cord will be rewound on the reel. I shall be lugged down to the sea bottom. There I shall stay for half an hour, with the electric light on, looking about me. Then the clockwork will release a spring knife, the cord will be cut, and up I shall rush again, like a soda-water bubble. The cord itself will help the flotation."

"And if you should chance to hit a ship?" said Weybridge.

"I should come up at such a pace, I should go clean through it," said Elstead, "like a cannon ball. You needn't worry about that."

"And suppose some nimble crustacean should wriggle into your clockwork—"

"It would be a pressing sort of invitation for me to stop," said Elstead, turning his back on the water and staring at the sphere.

They had swung Elstead overboard by eleven o'clock. The day was serenely bright and calm, with the horizon lost in haze. The electric glare in the little upper compartment beamed cheerfully three times. Then they let him down slowly to the surface of the water, and a sailor in the stern chains hung ready to cut the tackle that held the lead weights and the sphere together. The globe, which had looked so large on deck, looked the smallest thing conceivable under the stern of the ship. It rolled a little, and its two dark windows, which floated uppermost, seemed like eyes turned up in round wonderment at the people who crowded the rail. A voice wondered how Elstead liked the rolling. "Are you ready?" sang out the Commander. "Aye, aye, sir!" "Then let her go!"

The rope of the tackle tightened against the blade and was cut, and an eddy rolled over the globe in a grotesquely helpless fashion. Some one waved a handkerchief, some one else tried an ineffectual cheer, a middy was counting slowly: "Eight, nine, ten!" Another roll, then with a jerk and a splash the thing righted itself.

It seemed to be stationary for a moment, to grow rapidly smaller, and then the water closed over it, and it became visible, enlarged by refraction and dimmer, below the surface. Before one could count three it had disappeared. There was a flicker of white light far down in the water, that diminished to a speck and vanished. Then there was nothing but a depth of water going down into blackness, through which a shark was swimming.

Then suddenly the screw of the cruiser began to rotate, the water was crickled, the shark disappeared in a wrinkled confusion, and a torrent of foam rushed across the crystalline clearness that had swallowed up Elstead. "What's the idee?" said one A. B. to another.

"We're going to lay off about a couple of miles, 'fear he should hit us when he comes up," said his mate.

The ship steamed slowly to her new position. Aboard her almost every one who was unoccupied remained watching the breathing swell into which the sphere had sunk. For the next half hour it is doubtful if a word was spoken that did not bear directly or indirectly on Elstead. The December sun was now high in the sky, and the heat very considerable.

"He'll be cold enough down there," said Weybridge. "They say that below a certain depth sea-water's always just about freezing."

"Where'll he come up?" asked Steevens. "I've lost my bearings."

"That's the spot," said the Commander, who prided himself on his omniscience. He extended a precise finger south-eastward. "And this, I reckon, is pretty nearly the moment," he said. "He's been thirty-five minutes."

"How long does it take to reach the bottom of the ocean?" asked Steevens.

"For a depth of five miles, and reckoning—as we did—an acceleration to two foot per second, both ways, is just about three-quarters of a minute."

"Then he's overdue," said Weybridge.

"Pretty nearly," said the Commander. "I suppose it takes a few minutes for that cord of his to wind in."

"I forgot that," said Weybridge, evidently relieved.

And then began the suspense. A minute slowly dragged itself out, and no sphere shot out of the water. Another followed, and nothing broke the low oily swell. The sailors explained to one another that little point about the winding-in of the cord. The rigging was dotted with expectant faces. "Come up, Elstead!" called one hairy-chested salt, impatiently, and the others caught it up, and shouted as though they were waiting for the curtain of a theatre to rise.

The Commander glanced irritably at them.

"Of course, if the acceleration's less than two," he said, "he'll be all the longer. We aren't absolutely certain that was the proper figure. I'm no slavish believer in calculations."

Steevens agreed concisely. No one on the quarter-deck spoke for a couple of minutes. Then Steevens's watch-case clicked.

When, twenty-one minutes after, the sun reached the zenith, they were still waiting for the globe to re-appear, and not a man aboard had dared to whisper that hope was dead. It was Weybridge who first gave expression to that realisation. He spoke while the sound of eight bells still hung in the air. "I always distrusted that window," he said quite suddenly to Steevens.

"Good God!" said Steevens, "you don't think—"

"Well!" said Weybridge, and left the rest to his imagination.

"I'm no great believer in calculations myself," said the Commander, dubiously, "so that I'm not altogether hopeless yet." And at midnight the gunboat was steaming slowly in a spiral round the spot where the globe had sunk, and the white beam of the electric light fled and halted and swept discontentedly onward again over the waste of phosphorescent waters under the little stars.

"If his window hasn't burst and smashed him," said Weybridge, "then it's a cursed sight worse, for his clockwork has gone wrong and he's alive now, five miles under our feet, down there in the cold and dark, anchored in that little bubble of his, where never a ray of light has shone or a human being lived, since the waters were gathered together. He's there without food, feeling hungry and thirsty and scared, wondering whether he'll starve or stifle. Which will it be? The Myer's apparatus is running out, I suppose. How long do they last?

"Good Heavens!" he exclaimed, "what little things we are! What daring little devils! Down there, miles and miles of water—all water, and all this empty water about us and this sky. Gulfs!" He threw his hands out, and as he did so a little white streak swept noiselessly up the sky, travelling more slowly, stopped, became a motionless dot as though a new star had fallen up into the sky. Then it went sliding back again and lost itself amidst the reflections of the stars, and the white haze of the sea's phosphorescence.

At the sight he stopped, arm extended and mouth open. He shut his mouth, opened it again and waved his arms with an impatient gesture. Then he turned, shouted, "Elstead ahoy," to the first watch, and went at a run to Lindley and the search light. "I saw him," he said. "Starboard there! His light's on and he's just shot out of the water. Bring the light round. We ought to see him drifting, when he lifts on the swell."

But they never picked up the explorer until dawn. Then they almost ran him down. The crane was swung out and a boat's crew hooked the chain to the sphere. When they had shipped the sphere they unscrewed the manhole and peered into the darkness of the interior (for the electric light chamber was intended to illuminate the water about the sphere, and was shut off entirely from its general cavity).

The air was very hot within the cavity, and the india-rubber at the lip of the manhole was soft. There was no answer to their eager questions and no sound of movement within. Elstead seemed to be lying motionless, crumpled up in the bottom of the globe. The ship's doctor crawled in and lifted him out to the men outside. For a moment or so they did not know whether Elstead was alive or dead. His face, in the yellow glow of the ship's lamps, glistened with perspiration. They carried him down to his own cabin.

He was not dead they found, but in a state of absolute nervous collapse, and besides cruelly bruised. For some days he had to lie perfectly still. It was a week before he could tell his experiences.

Almost his first words were that he was going down again. The sphere would have to be altered, he said, in order to allow him to throw off the cord if need be, and that was all. He had had the most marvellous experience. "You thought I should find nothing but ooze," he said. "You laughed at my explorations, and I've discovered a new world!" He told his story in disconnected fragments, and chiefly from the wrong end, so that it is impossible to re-tell it in his words. But what follows is the narrative of his experience.

It began atrociously, he said. Before the cord ran out the thing kept rolling over. He felt like a frog in a football. He could see nothing but the crane and the sky overhead, with an occasional glimpse of the people on the ship's rail. He couldn't tell a bit which way the thing would roll next. Suddenly he would find his feet going up and try to step, and over he went rolling, head over heels and just anyhow on the padding. Any other shape would have been more comfortable, but no other shape was to be relied upon under the huge pressure of the nethermost abyss.

Suddenly the swaying ceased; the globe righted, and when he had picked himself up, he saw the water all about him greeny-blue with an attenuated light filtering down from above, and a shoal of little floating things went rushing up past him, as it seemed to him, towards the light. And even as he looked it grew darker and darker, until the water above was as dark as the midnight sky, albeit of a greener shade, and the water below black. And little transparent things in the water developed a faint glint of luminosity, and shot past him in faint greenish streaks.

And the feeling of falling! It was just like the start of a lift, he said, only it kept on. One has to imagine what that means, that keeping on. It was then of all times that Elstead repented of his adventure. He saw the chances against him in an altogether new light. He thought of the big cuttle-fish people knew to exist in the middle waters, the kind of things they find half-digested in whales at times, or floating dead and rotten and half eaten by fish. Suppose one caught hold and wouldn't leave go. And had the clockwork really been sufficiently tested? But whether he wanted to go on or go back mattered not the slightest now.

In fifty seconds everything was as black as night outside, except where the beam from his light struck through the waters, and picked out every now and then some fish or scrap of sinking matter. They flashed by too fast for him to see what they were. Once he thought he passed a shark. And then the sphere began to get hot by friction against the water. They had under-estimated this, it seems.

The first thing he noticed was that he was perspiring, and then he heard a hissing, growing louder, under his feet, and saw a lot of little bubbles—very little bubbles they were—rushing upward like a fan through the water outside. Steam! He felt the window and it was hot. He turned on the minute glow lamp that lit his own cavity, looked at the padded watch by the studs, and saw he had been travelling now for two minutes. It came into his head that the window would crack through the conflict of temperatures, for he knew the bottom water was very near freezing.

Then suddenly the floor of the sphere seemed to press against his feet, the rush of bubbles outside grew slower and slower and the hissing diminished. The sphere rolled a little. The window had not cracked, nothing had given, and he knew that the dangers of sinking, at any rate, were over.

In another minute or so, he would be on the floor of the abyss. He thought, he said, of Steevens and Weybridge and the rest of them five miles overhead, higher to him than the very highest clouds that ever floated over land are to us, steaming slowly and staring down and wondering what had happened to him.

He peered out of the window. There were no more bubbles now, and the hissing had stopped. Outside there was a heavy blackness—as black as black velvet—except where the electric light pierced the empty water and showed the colour of it—a yellow green. Then three things like shapes of fire swam into sight, following each other through the water. Whether they were little and near, or big and far off, he could not tell.

Each was outlined in a bluish light almost as bright as the lights of a fishing-smack, a light which seemed to be smoking greatly, and all along the sides of them were specks of this, like the lighted portholes of a ship. Their phosphorescence seemed to go out as they came into the radiance of his lamp, and he saw then that they were indeed fish of some strange sort, with huge heads, vast eyes, and dwindling bodies and tails. Their eyes were turned towards him, and he judged they were following him down. He supposed they were attracted by his glare.

Presently others of the same sort joined them. As he went on down he noticed that the water became of a pallid colour, and that little specks twinkled in his ray like motes in sunbeam. This was probably due to the clouds of ooze and mud that the impact of his leaden sinkers had disturbed.

By the time he was drawn down to the lead weights he was in a dense fog of white that his electric light failed altogether to pierce for more than a few yards, and many minutes elapsed before the hanging sheets of sediment subsided to any extent. Then, lit by his light and by the transient phosphorescence of a distant shoal of fishes, he was able to see under the huge blackness of the super-incumbent water an undulating expanse of greyish-white ooze, broken here and there by tangled thickets of a growth of sea lilies, waving hungry tentacles in the air.

Farther away were the graceful translucent outlines of a group of gigantic sponges. About this floor there were scattered a number of bristling flattish tufts of rich purple and black, which he decided must be some sort of sea-urchin, and small, large-eyed or blind things, having a curious resemblance, some to woodlice, and others to lobsters, crawled sluggishly across the track of the light and vanished into the obscurity again, leaving furrowed trails behind them.

Then suddenly the hovering swarm of little fishes veered about and came towards him as a flight of starlings might do. They passed over him like a phosphorescent snow, and then he saw behind them some larger creature advancing towards the sphere.

At first he could see it only dimly, a faintly moving figure remotely suggestive of a walking man, and then it came into the spray of light that the lamp shot out. As the glare struck it, it shut its eyes, dazzled. He stared in rigid astonishment.

It was a strange, vertebrated animal. Its dark purple head was dimly suggestive of a chameleon, but it had such a high forehead and such a braincase as no reptile ever displayed before; the vertical pitch of its face gave it a most extraordinary resemblance to a human being.

Two large and protruding eyes projected from sockets in chameleon fashion, and it had a broad reptilian mouth with horny lips beneath its little nostrils. In the position of the ears were two huge gill covers, and out of these floated a branching tree of coralline filaments, almost like the tree-like gills that very young rays and sharks possess.

But the humanity of the face was not the most extraordinary thing about the creature. It was a biped, its almost globular body was poised on a tripod of two frog-like legs and a long thick tail, and its fore limbs, which grotesquely caricatured the human hand much as a frog's do, carried a long shaft of bone, tipped with copper. The colour of the creature was variegated: its head, hands, and legs were purple; but its skin, which hung loosely upon it, even as clothes might do, was a phosphorescent grey. And it stood there, blinded by the light.

At last this unknown creature of the abyss blinked its eyes open, and, shading them with its disengaged hand, opened its mouth and gave vent to a shouting noise, articulate almost as speech might be, that penetrated even the steel case and padded jacket of the sphere. How a shouting may be accomplished without lungs Elstead does not profess to explain. It then moved sideways out of the glare into the mystery of shadow that bordered it on either side, and Elstead felt rather than saw that it was coming towards him. Fancying the light had attracted it, he turned the switch that cut off the current. In another moment something soft dabbed upon the steel, and the globe swayed.

Then the shouting was repeated, and it seemed to him that a distant echo answered it. The dabbing recurred, and the globe swayed and ground against the spindle over which the wire was rolled. He stood in the blackness, and peered out into the everlasting night of the abyss. And presently he saw, very faint and remote, other phosphorescent quasi-human forms hurrying towards him.

Hardly knowing what he did, he felt about in his swaying prison for the stud of the exterior electric light, and came by accident against his own small glow lamp in its padded recess. The sphere twisted, and then threw him down; he heard shouts like shouts of surprise, and when he rose to his feet he saw two pairs of stalked eyes peering into the lower window and reflecting his light.

In another moment hands were dabbing vigorously at his steel casing, and there was a sound, horrible enough in his position, of the metal protection of the clockwork being vigorously hammered. That, indeed, sent his heart into his mouth, for if these strange creatures succeeded in stopping that his release would never occur. Scarcely had he thought as much when he felt the sphere sway violently, and the floor of it press hard against his feet. He turned off the small glow lamp that lit the interior, and sent the ray of the large light in the separate compartment out into the water. The sea floor and the man-like creatures had disappeared, and a couple of fish chasing each other dropped suddenly by the window.

He thought at once that these strange denizens of the deep sea had broken the wire rope, and that he had escaped. He drove up faster and faster, and then stopped with a jerk that sent him flying against the padded roof of his prison. For half a minute perhaps he was too astonished to think.

Then he felt that the sphere was spinning slowly, and rocking, and it seemed to him that it was also being drawn through the water. By crouching close to the window he managed to make his weight effective and roll that part of the sphere downward, but he could see nothing save the pale ray of his light striking down ineffectively into the darkness. It occurred to him that he would see more if he turned the lamp off and allowed his eyes to grow accustomed to the profound obscurity.

In this he was wise. After some minutes the velvety blackness became a translucent blackness, and then far away, and as faint as the zodiacal light of an English summer evening, he saw shapes moving below. He judged these creatures had detached his cable and were towing him along the sea bottom.

And then he saw something faint and remote across the undulations of the submarine plain, a broad horizon of pale luminosity that extended this way and that way as far as the range of his little window permitted him to see. To this he was being towed, as a balloon might be towed by men out of the open country into a town. He approached it very slowly, and very slowly the dim irradiation was gathered together into more definite shapes.

It was nearly five o'clock before he came over this luminous area, and by that time he could make out an arrangement suggestive of streets and houses grouped about a vast roofless erection that was grotesquely suggestive of a ruined abbey. It was spread out like a map below him. The houses were all roofless inclosures of walls, and their substance being, as he afterwards saw, of phosphorescent bones, gave the place an appearance as if it were built of drowned moonshine.

Among the inner caves of the place waving trees of crinoid stretched their tentacles, and tall, slender, glassy sponges shot like shining minarets and lilies of filmy light out of the general glow of the city. In the open spaces of the place he could see a stirring movement as of crowds of people, but he was too many fathoms above them to distinguish the individuals in those crowds.

Then slowly they pulled him down, and as they did so the details of the place crept slowly upon his apprehension. He saw that the courses of the cloudy buildings were marked out with beaded lines of round objects, and then he perceived that at several points below him in broad open spaces were forms like the encrusted shapes of ships.

Slowly and surely he was drawn down, and the forms below him became brighter, clearer, were more distinct. He was being pulled down, he perceived, towards the large building in the centre of the town, and he could catch a glimpse ever and again of the multitudinous forms that were lugging at his cord. He was astonished to see that the rigging of one of the ships, which formed such a prominent feature of the place, was crowded with a host of gesticulating figures regarding him, and then the walls of the great building rose about him silently, and hid the city from his eyes.

And such walls they were, of water-logged wood, and twisted wire rope and iron spars, and copper, and the bones and skulls of dead men.

The skulls ran in curious zigzag lines and spirals and fantastic curves over the building; and in and out of their eye-sockets, and over the whole surface of the place, lurked and played a multitude of silvery little fishes.

And now he was at such a level that he could see these strange people of the abyss plainly once more. To his astonishment, he perceived that they were prostrating themselves before him, all save one, dressed as it seemed in a robe of placoid scales, and crowned with a luminous diadem, who stood with his reptilian mouth opening and shutting as though he led the chanting of the worshippers.

They continued worshipping him, without rest or intermission, for the space of three hours.

Most circumstantial was Elstead's account of this astounding city and its people, these people of perpetual night, who have never seen sun or moon or stars, green vegetation, nor any living air-breathing creatures, who know nothing of fire, nor any light but the phosphorescent light of living things.

Startling as is his story, it is yet more startling to find that scientific men, of such eminence as Adams and Jenkins, find nothing incredible in it. They tell me they see no reason why intelligent, water-breathing, vertebrated creatures inured to a low temperature and enormous pressure, and of such a heavy structure, that neither alive nor dead would they float, might not live upon the bottom of the deep sea, and quite unsuspected by us, descendants like ourselves of the great Theriomorpha of the New Red Sandstone age.

We should be known to them, however, as strange meteoric creatures wont to fall catastrophically dead out of the mysterious blackness of their watery sky. And not only we ourselves, but our ships, our metals, our appliances, would come raining down out of the night. Sometimes sinking things would smite down and crush them, as if it were the judgment of some unseen power above, and sometimes would come things of the utmost rarity or utility or shapes of inspiring suggestion. One can understand, perhaps, something of their behaviour at the descent of a living man, if one thinks what a barbaric people might do, to whom an enhaloed shining creature came suddenly out of the sky.

At one time or another Elstead probably told the officers of the *Ptarmigan* every detail of his strange twelve hours in the abyss. That he also intended to write them down is certain, but he never did, and so unhappily we have to piece together the discrepant fragments of his story from the reminiscences of Commander Simmons, Weybridge, Steevens, Lindley, and the others.

We see the thing darkly in fragmentary glimpses—the huge ghostly building, the bowing, chanting people, with their dark, chameleon-like heads and faintly luminous forms, and Elstead, with his light turned on again, vainly trying to convey to their minds that the cord by which the sphere was held was to be severed. Minute after minute slipped away, and Elstead, looking at his watch, was horrified to find that he had oxygen only for four hours more. But the chant in his honour kept on as remorselessly as if it was the marching song of his approaching death.

The manner of his release he does not understand, but to judge by the end of cord that hung from the sphere, it had been cut through by rubbing against the edge of the altar.

Abruptly the sphere rolled over, and he swept up, out of their world, as an ethereal creature clothed in a vacuum would sweep through our own atmosphere back to its native ether again. He must have torn out of their sight as a hydrogen bubble hastens upwards from our air. A strange ascension it must have seemed to them.

The sphere rushed up with even greater velocity than, when weighed with the lead sinkers, it had rushed down. It became exceedingly hot. It drove up with the windows uppermost, and he remembers the torrent of bubbles frothing against the glass. Every moment he expected this to fly. Then suddenly something like a huge wheel seemed to be released in his head, the padded compartment began spinning about him, and he fainted. His next recollection was of his cabin, and of the doctor's voice.

But that is the substance of the extraordinary story that Elstead related in fragments to the officers of the *Ptarmigan*. He promised to write it all down at a later date. His mind was chiefly occupied with the improvement of his apparatus, which was effected at Rio.

It remains only to tell that on February 2d, 1896, he made his second descent into the ocean abyss, with the improvements his first experience suggested. What happened we shall probably never know. He never returned. The *Ptarmigan* beat about over the point of his submersion, seeking him in vain for thirteen days. Then she returned to Rio, and the news was telegraphed to his friends. So the matter remains for the present. But it is hardly probable that any further attempt will be made to verify his strange story of these hitherto unsuspected cities of the deep sea.

Under the Knife

"WHAT IF I die under it!" The thought recurred again and again as I walked home from Haddon's. It was a purely personal question. I was spared the deep anxieties of a married man, and I knew there were few of my intimate friends but would find my death troublesome chiefly on account of the duty of regret. I was surprised indeed, and perhaps a little humiliated, as I turned the matter over, to think how few could possibly exceed the conventional requirement. Things came before me stripped of glamour, in a clear dry light, during that walk from Haddon's house over Primrose Hill. There were the friends of my youth: I perceived now that our affection was a tradition, which we foregathered rather laboriously to maintain. There were the rivals and helpers of my later career. I suppose I had been cold-blooded or undemonstrative—one perhaps implies the other. It may be that even the capacity for friendship is a question of physique. There had been a time in my own life when I had grieved bitterly enough at the loss of a friend; but as I walked home that afternoon the emotional side of my imagination was dormant. I could not pity myself, nor feel sorry for my friends, nor conceive of them as grieving for me.

I was interested in this deadness of my emotional nature,—no doubt a concomitant of my stagnating physiology; and my thoughts wandered off along the line it suggested. Once before, in my hot youth, I had suffered a sudden loss of blood, and had been within an ace of death. I remembered now that my affections as well as my passions had drained out of me, leaving scarce anything but a tranquil resignation and the faintest dreg of self-pity. It had been weeks before the old ambitions, and tendernesses, and all the complex moral interplay of a man had reasserted themselves. It occurred to me that the real meaning of this numbness might be a gradual slipping away from the pleasure-pain guidance of the animal man. It has been proven, I take it, as thoroughly as anything can be proven in this world, that the higher emotions, the moral feelings, even the subtle tenderness of love, are evolved from the elemental desires and fears of the simple animal: they are the harness in which man's mental freedom goes. And, it may be that, as death overshadows us, as our possibility of acting diminishes, this complex growth of balanced impulse, propensity, and aversion, whose interplay inspires our acts, goes with it. Leaving what?

I was suddenly brought back to reality by an imminent collision with a butcher-boy's tray. I found that I was crossing the bridge over the Regent's Park Canal which runs parallel with the bridge in the Zoölogical Gardens. The boy in blue had been looking over his shoulder at a black barge advancing slowly, towed by a gaunt white horse. In the Gardens a nurse was leading three happy little children over the bridge. The trees were bright green; the spring hopefulness was still unstained by the dusts of summer; the sky in the water was bright and clear, but broken by long waves, by quivering bands of black, as the barge drove through. The breeze was stirring; but it did not stir me as the spring breeze used to do.

Was this dulness of feeling in itself an anticipation? It was curious that I could reason and follow out a network of suggestion as clearly as ever; so, at least, it seemed to me. It was calmness rather than dulness that was coming upon me. Was there any ground for the belief in the presentiment of death? Did a man near to death begin instinctively to withdraw himself from the meshes of matter and sense, even before the cold hand was laid upon his? I felt strangely isolated—isolated without regret— from the life and existence about me. The children playing in the sun and gathering strength and experience for the business of life, the park-keeper gossiping with a nurse-maid, the nursing mother, the young couple intent upon each other as they passed me, the trees by the wayside spreading new pleading leaves to the sunlight, the stir in their branches—I had been part of it all, but I had nearly done with it now.

Some way down the Broad Walk I perceived that I was tired, and that my feet were heavy. It was hot that afternoon, and I turned aside and sat down on one of the green chairs that line the way. In a minute I had dozed into a dream, and the tide of my thoughts washed up a vision of the Resurrection. I was still sitting in the chair, but I thought myself actually dead, withered, tattered, dried, one eye (I saw) pecked out by birds. "Awake!" cried a voice; and incontinently the dust of the path and the mould under the grass became insurgent. I had never before thought of Regent's Park as a cemetery, but now, through the trees, stretching as far as eye could see, I beheld a flat plain of writhing graves and heeling tombstones. There seemed to be some trouble, the rising dead appeared to stifle as they struggled upward, they bled in their struggles, the red flesh was tattered away from the white bones. "Awake!" cried a voice; but I determined I would not rise to such horrors. "Awake!" They would not let me alone. "Wike up!" said an angry voice. A cockney angel! The man who sells the tickets was shaking me, demanding my penny.

I paid my penny, pocketed my ticket, yawned, stretched my legs, and feeling now rather less torpid, got up and walked on towards Langham Place. I speedily lost myself again in a shifting maze of thoughts about death. Going across Marylebone Road into that crescent at the end of Langham Place, I had the narrowest escape from the shaft of a cab, and went on my way with a palpitating heart and a bruised shoulder. It struck me that it would have been curious if my meditations on my death on the morrow had led to my death that day.

But I will not weary you with more of my experiences that day and the next. I knew more and more certainly that I should die under the operation; at times I think I was inclined to pose to myself. The doctors were coming at eleven, and I did not get up. It seemed scarce worth while to trouble about washing and dressing, and, though I read my newspapers and the letters that came by the first post, I did not find them very interesting. There was a friendly note from Addison, my old school friend, calling my attention to two discrepancies and a printer's error in my new book; with one from Langridge, venting some vexation over Minton. The rest were business communications. I breakfasted in bed. The glow of pain at my side seemed more massive. I knew it was pain, and yet, if you can understand, I did not find it very painful. I had been awake and hot and thirsty in the night, but in the morning bed felt comfortable. In the night-time I had lain thinking of things that were past; in the morning I dozed over the question of immortality.

Haddon came, punctual to the minute, with a neat black bag; and Mowbray soon followed. Their arrival stirred me up a little. I began to take a more personal interest in the proceedings. Haddon moved the little octagonal table close to the bedside, and with his broad black back to me began taking things out of his bag. I heard the light click of steel upon steel. My imagination, I found, was not altogether stagnant. "Will you hurt me much?" I said, in an off-hand tone.

"Not a bit," Haddon answered over his shoulder. "We shall chloroform you. Your heart's as sound as a bell." And, as he spoke, I had a whiff of the pungent sweetness of the anaesthetic.

They stretched me out, with a convenient exposure of my side, and, almost before I realised what was happening, the chloroform was being administered. It stings the nostrils and there is a suffocating sensation, at first. I knew I should die,—that this was the end of consciousness for me. And suddenly I felt that I was not prepared for death; I had a vague sense of a duty overlooked—I knew not what. What was it I had not done? I could think of nothing more to do, nothing desirable left in life; and yet I had the strangest disinclination to death. And the physical sensation was painfully oppressive. Of course the doctors did not know they were going to kill me. Possibly I struggled. Then I fell motionless, and a great silence, a monstrous silence, and an impenetrable blackness, came upon me.

There must have been an interval of absolute unconsciousness, seconds or minutes. Then, with a chilly, unemotional clearness, I perceived that I was not yet dead. I was still in my body; but all the multitudinous sensations that come sweeping from it to make up the background of consciousness, had gone, leaving me free of it all. No, not free of it all; for as yet something still held me to the poor stark flesh upon the bed, held me, yet not so closely that I did not feel myself external to it, independent of it, straining away from it. I do not think I saw, I do not think I heard; but I perceived all that was going on, and it was as if I both heard and saw. Haddon was bending over me, Mowbray behind me; the scalpel—it was a large scalpel—was cutting my flesh at the side under the flying ribs. It was interesting to see myself cut like cheese, without a pang, without even a qualm. The interest was much of a quality with that one might feel in a game of chess between strangers. Haddon's face was firm, and his hand steady; but I was surprised to perceive (*how* I know now) that he was feeling the gravest doubt as to his own wisdom in the conduct of the operation.

Mowbray's thoughts, too, I could see. He was thinking that Haddon's manner showed too much of the specialist. New suggestions came up like bubbles through a stream of frothing meditation, and burst one after another in the little bright spot of his consciousness. He could not help noticing and admiring Haddon's swift dexterity, in spite of his envious quality and his disposition to detract. I saw my liver exposed. I was puzzled at my own condition. I did not feel that I was dead, but I was different in some way from my living self. The grey depression that had weighed on me for a year or more, and coloured all my thoughts, was gone. I perceived and thought without any emotional tint at all. I wondered if every one perceived things in this way under chloroform, and forgot it again when he came out of it. It would be inconvenient to look into some heads, and not forget.

Although I did not think that I was dead, I still perceived, quite clearly, that I was soon to die. This brought me back to the consideration of Haddon's proceedings. I looked into his mind, and saw that he was afraid of cutting a branch of the portal vein. My attention was distracted from details by the curious changes going on in his mind. His consciousness was like the quivering little spot of light which is thrown by the mirror of a galvanometer. His thoughts ran under it like a stream, some through the focus bright and distinct, some shadowy in the half-light of the edge. Just now the little glow was steady; but the least movement on Mowbray's part, the slightest sound from outside, even a faint difference in the slow movement of the living flesh he was cutting, set the light-spot shivering and spinning. A new sense-impression came rushing up through the flow of thoughts; and lo! the light-spot jerked away towards it, swifter than a frightened fish. It was wonderful to think that upon that unstable, fitful thing depended all the complex motions of the man, that for the next five minutes, therefore, my life hung upon its movements. And he was growing more and more nervous in his work. It was as if a little picture of a cut vein grew brighter, and struggled to oust from his brain another picture of a cut falling short of the mark. He was afraid: his dread of cutting too little was battling with his dread of cutting too far.

Then, suddenly, like an escape of water from under a lock gate, a great uprush of horrible realisation set all his thoughts swirling, and simultaneously I perceived that the vein was cut. He started back with a hoarse exclamation, and I saw the brown-purple blood gather in a swift bead, and run trickling. He was horrified. He pitched the red-stained scalpel on to the octagonal table; and instantly both doctors flung themselves upon me, making hasty and ill-conceived efforts to remedy the disaster. "Ice," said Mowbray, gasping. But I knew that I was killed, though my body still clung to me.

I will not describe their belated endeavours to save me, though I perceived every detail. My perceptions were sharper and swifter than they had ever been in life; my thoughts rushed through my mind with incredible swiftness, but with perfect definition. I can only compare their crowded clarity to the effects of a reasonable dose of opium. In a moment it would all be over, and I should be free. I knew I was immortal, but what would happen I did not know. Should I drift off presently, like a puff of smoke from a gun, in some kind of half-material body, an attenuated version of my material self? Should I find myself suddenly among the innumerable hosts of the dead, and know the world about me for the phantasmagoria it had always seemed? Should I drift to some spiritualistic *séance*, and there make foolish, incomprehensible attempts to affect a purblind medium? It was a state of unemotional curiosity, of colourless expectation. And then I realised a growing stress upon me, a feeling as though some huge human magnet was drawing me upward out of my body. The stress grew and grew. I seemed an atom, for which monstrous forces were fighting. For one brief, terrible moment sensation came back to me. That feeling of falling headlong which comes in nightmares, that feeling a thousand times intensified, that and a black horror swept across my thoughts in a torrent. Then the two doctors, the naked body with its cut side, the little room, swept away from under me, and vanished, as a speck of foam vanishes down an eddy.

I was in mid air. Far below was the West End of London, receding rapidly,—for I seemed to be flying swiftly upward,—and, as it receded, passing westward like a panorama. I could see through the faint haze of smoke the innumerable roofs chimney-set, the narrow roadways stippled with people and conveyances, the little specks of squares, and the church steeples like thorns sticking out of the fabric. But it spun away as the earth rotated on its axis, and in a few seconds (as it seemed) I was over the scattered clumps of town about Ealing, the little Thames a thread of blue to the south, and the Chiltern Hills and the North Downs coming up like the rim of a basin, far away and faint with haze. Up I rushed. And at first I had not the faintest conception what this headlong upward rush could mean.

Every moment the circle of scenery beneath me grew wider and wider, and the details of town and field, of hill and valley, got more and more hazy and pale and indistinct, a luminous grey was mingled more and more with the blue of the hills and the green of the open meadows; and a little patch of cloud, low and far to the west, shone ever more dazzlingly white. Above, as the veil of atmosphere between myself and outer space grew thinner, the sky, which had been a fair springtime blue at first, grew deeper and richer in colour, passing steadily through the intervening shades, until presently it was as dark as the blue sky of midnight, and presently as black as the blackness of a frosty starlight, and at last as black as no blackness I had ever beheld. And first one star, and then many, and at last an innumerable host, broke out upon the sky: more stars than any one has ever seen from the face of the earth. For the blueness of the sky is the light of the sun and stars sifted and spread abroad blindingly; there is diffused light even in the darkest skies of winter, and we do not see their light by day because of the dazzling irradiation of the sun. But now I saw things—I know not how; assuredly with no mortal eyes—and that defect of bedazzlement blinded me no longer. The sun was incredibly strange and wonderful. The body of it was a disc of blinding white light; not yellowish as it seems to those who live upon the earth, but livid white, all streaked with scarlet streaks, and rimmed about with a fringe of writhing tongues of red fire. And, shooting halfway across the heavens from either side of it, and brighter than the Milky Way, were two pinions of silver-white, making it look more like those winged globes I have seen in Egyptian sculpture, than anything else I can remember upon earth. These I knew for the solar corona, though I had never seen anything of it but a picture during the days of my earthly life.

When my attention came back to the earth again, I saw that it had fallen very far away from me. Field and town were long since indistinguishable, and all the varied hues of the country were merging into a uniform bright grey, broken only by the brilliant white of the clouds that lay scattered in flocculent masses over Ireland and the west of England. For now I could see the outlines of the north of France and Ireland, and all this island of Britain, save where Scotland passed over the horizon to the north, or where the coast was blurred or obliterated by cloud. The sea was a dull grey, and darker than the land; and the whole panorama was rotating slowly towards the east.

All this had happened so swiftly that, until I was some thousand miles or so from the earth, I had no thought for myself. But now I perceived I had neither hands nor feet, parts nor organs, and that I felt neither alarm nor pain. All about me, I perceived that the vacancy (for I had already left the air behind) was cold beyond the imagination of man; but it troubled me not. The sun's rays shot through the void, powerless to light or heat until they should strike on matter in their course. I saw things with a serene self forgetfulness, even as if I were God. And down below there, rushing away from me,—countless miles in a second,—where a little dark spot on the grey marked the position of London, two doctors were struggling to restore life to the poor hacked and outworn shell I had abandoned. I felt then such release, such serenity, as I can compare to no earthly delight I have ever known.

It was only after I had perceived all these things that the meaning of that headlong rush of the earth grew into comprehension. Yet it was so simple, so obvious, that I was amazed at my never anticipating the thing that was happening to me. I had suddenly been cut adrift from matter: all that was material of me was there upon earth, whirling away through space, held to the earth by gravitation, partaking of the earth-inertia, moving in its wreath of epicycles round the sun, and with the sun and the planets on their vast march through space. But the immaterial has no inertia, feels nothing of the pull of matter for matter: where it parts from its garment of flesh there it remains (so far as space concerns it any longer) immovable in space. *I* was not leaving the earth: the earth was leaving me, and not only the earth but the whole solar system was streaming past. And about me in space, invisible to me, scattered in the wake of the earth upon its journey, there must be an innumerable multitude of souls, stripped like myself of the material, stripped like myself of the passions of the individual and the generous emotions of the gregarious brute, naked intelligences, things of newborn wonder and thought, marvelling at the strange release that had suddenly come on them!

As I receded faster and faster from the strange white sun in the black heavens, and from the broad and shining earth upon which my being had begun, I seemed to grow, in some incredible manner, vast: vast as regards this world I had left, vast as regards the moments and periods of a human life. Very soon I saw the full circle of the earth, slightly gibbous, like the moon when she nears her full, but very great; and the silvery shape of America as now in the noonday blaze, wherein (as it seemed) little England had been basking but a few minutes ago. At first the earth was large, and shone in the heavens, filling a great part of them; but every moment she grew smaller and more distant. As she shrunk, the broad moon in its third quarter crept into view over the rim of her disc. I looked for the constellations. Only that part of Aries directly behind the sun and the Lion which the earth covered were hidden. I recognised the tortuous, tattered band of the Milky Way, with Vega very bright between sun and earth; and Sirius and Orion shone splendid against the unfathomable blackness in the opposite quarter of the heavens. The Polestar was overhead, and the Great Bear hung over the circle of the earth. And away beneath and beyond the shining corona of the sun were strange groupings of stars I had never seen in my life; notably a dagger-shaped group that I knew for the Southern Cross. All these were no larger than when they had shone on earth; but the little stars that one scarce sees shone now as brightly as the first magnitudes had done, while the larger worlds were points of indescribable glory and colour. Aldebaran was a spot of blood-red fire, and Sirius condensed to one point the light of a world of sapphires. And they shone steadily: they did not scintillate, they were calmly glorious. My impressions had an adamantine hardness and brightness; there was no blurring softness, no atmosphere, nothing but infinite darkness set with the myriads of these acute and brilliant points and specks of light. Presently, when I looked again, the little earth seemed no bigger than the sun, and it dwindled and turned as I looked, until, in a second's space (as it seemed to me), it was halved; and so it went on swiftly dwindling. Far away in the opposite direction a little pinkish pin's head of light, shining steadily, was the planet Mars. I swam motionless in vacancy, and without a trace of terror or astonishment, watched the speck of cosmic dust we call the world fall away from me.

Presently it dawned upon me that my sense of duration had changed: that my mind was moving not faster, but infinitely slower; that between each separate impression there was a period of many days. The moon spun once round the earth as I noted this; and I perceived, clearly, the motion of Mars in his orbit. Moreover it appeared as if the time between thought and thought grew steadily greater, until at last a thousand years was but a moment in my perception.

At first the constellations had shone motionless against the black background of infinite space; but presently it seemed as though the group of stars about Hercules and the Scorpion was contracting, while Orion and Aldebaran and their neighbours were scattering apart. Flashing suddenly out of the darkness, there came a flying multitude of particles of rock, glittering like dust-specks in a sunbeam and encompassed in a faintly luminous haze. They swirled all about me and vanished again in a twinkling far behind. And then I saw that a bright spot of light, that shone a little to one side of my path, was growing very rapidly larger, and perceived that it was the planet Saturn rushing towards me. Larger and larger it grew, swallowing up the heavens behind it, and hiding every moment a fresh multitude of stars. I perceived its flattened whirling body, its disc-like belt, and seven of its little satellites. It grew and grew, till it towered enormous, and then I plunged amid a streaming multitude of clashing stones and dancing dust-particles and gas-eddies, and saw for a moment the mighty triple belt like three concentric arches of moonlight above me, its shadow black on the boiling tumult below. These things happened in one tenth of the time it takes to tell of them. The planet went by like a flash of lightning; for a few seconds it blotted out the sun, and there and then became a mere black, dwindling, winged patch against the light. The earth, the mother mote of my being, I could no longer see.

So with a stately swiftness, in the profoundest silence, the solar system fell from me, as it had been a garment, until the sun was a mere star amid the multitude of stars, with its eddy of planet-specks lost in the confused glittering of the remoter light. I was no longer a denizen of the solar system: I had come to the Outer Universe, I seemed to grasp and comprehend the whole world of matter. Ever more swiftly the stars closed in about the spot where Antares and Vega had vanished in a luminous haze, until that part of the sky had the semblance of a whirling mass of nebulæ, and ever before me yawned vaster gaps of vacant blackness, and the stars shone fewer and fewer. It seemed as if I moved towards a point between Orion's belt and sword; and the void about that region opened vaster and vaster every second, an incredible gulf of nothingness into which I was falling. Faster and ever faster the universe rushed by, a hurry of whirling motes at last, speeding silently into the void. Stars, glowing brighter and brighter, with their circling planets catching the light in a ghostly fashion as I neared them, shone out and vanished again into inexistence; faint comets, clusters of meteorites, winking specks of matter, eddying light points whizzed past, some perhaps a hundred millions of miles or so from me at most, few nearer, travelling with unimaginable rapidity, shooting constellations, momentary darts of fire through the black night. More than anything else it was like a dusty draught, sunbeam-lit. Broader and wider and deeper grew the starless space, the vacant Beyond, into which I was being drawn. At last a quarter of the heavens was black and blank, and the whole headlong rush of stellar universe closed in behind me like a veil of light that is gathered together. It drove away from me like a monstrous Jack-o'-lantern driven by the wind. I had come out into the wilderness of space. Even the vacant blackness grew broader, until the hosts of the stars seemed only like a swarm of fiery specks hurrying away from me, inconceivably remote, and the darkness, the nothingness and emptiness, was about me on every side. Soon the little universe of matter, the cage of points in which I had begun to be, was dwindling, now to a whirling disc of luminous glittering, and now to one minute disc of hazy light. In a little while it would shrink to a point, and at last would vanish altogether.

Suddenly feeling came back to me: feeling in the shape of overwhelming terror,—such a dread of those dark vastitudes as no words can describe, a passionate resurgence of sympathy and social desire. Were there other souls, invisible to me as I to them, about me in the blackness? or was I indeed, even as I felt, alone? Had I passed out of being into something that was neither being nor not-being? The covering of the body, the covering of matter had been torn from me, and the hallucinations of companionship and security. Everything was black and silent. I had ceased to be. I was nothing. There was nothing, save only that infinitesimal dot of light that dwindled in the gulf. I strained myself to hear and see, and for a while there was naught but infinite silence, intolerable darkness, horror, and despair.

Then I saw that about the spot of light into which the whole world of matter had shrunk, there was a faint glow. And in a band on either side of that the darkness was not absolute. I watched it for ages, as it seemed to me, and through the long waiting the haze grew imperceptibly more distinct. And then about the band appeared an irregular cloud of the faintest, palest brown. I felt a passionate impatience; but the things grew brighter so slowly that they scarce seemed to change. What was unfolding itself? What was this strange reddish dawn in the interminable night of space?

The cloud's shape was grotesque. It seemed to be looped along its lower side into four projecting masses, and, above, it ended in a straight line. What phantom was it? I felt assured I had seen that figure before; but I could not think what, nor where, nor when it was. Then the realisation rushed upon me. *It was a clenched hand.* I was alone, in space, alone with this huge, shadowy Hand, upon which the whole Universe of Matter lay like an unconsidered speck of dust. It seemed as though I watched it through vast periods of time. On the forefinger glittered a ring; and the universe from which I had come was but a spot of light upon the ring's curvature. And the thing that the Hand gripped had the likeness of a black rod. Through a long eternity I watched the Hand, with the ring and the rod, marvelling and fearing and waiting helplessly on what might follow. It seemed as though nothing could follow: that I should watch forever, seeing only the Hand and the thing it held, and understanding nothing of its import. Was the whole universe but a refracting speck upon some greater Being? Were our worlds but the atoms of another universe, and those again of another, and so on through an endless progression? And what was I? Was I indeed immaterial? A vague persuasion of a body gathering about me came into my suspense. The abysmal darkness about the Hand filled with impalpable suggestions, with uncertain, fluctuating shapes.

Then, suddenly, came a sound, like the sound of a tolling bell: faint, as if infinitely far; muffled, as though heard through thick swathings of darkness,—a deep vibrating resonance with vast gulfs of silence between each stroke. And the Hand appeared to tighten on the rod. And I saw far above the Hand, towards the apex of the darkness, a circle of dim phosphorescence, a ghostly sphere whence these sounds came throbbing; and at the last stroke the Hand vanished, for the hour had come, and I heard a noise of many waters. But the black rod remained as a great band across the sky. And then a voice, which seemed to run to the uttermost parts of space, spoke, saying: "There will be no more pain."

At that an almost intolerable gladness and radiance rushed in upon me, and I saw the circle shining white and bright, and the rod black and shining, and many other things else distinct and clear. And the circle was the face of the clock, and the rod the rail of my bed. Haddon was standing at the foot, against the rail, with a small pair of scissors on his fingers; and the hands of my clock on the mantel over his shoulder were clasped together over the hour of twelve. Mowbray was washing something in a basin at the octagonal table, and at my side I felt a subdued feeling that could scarce be spoken of as pain.

The operation had not killed me. And I perceived suddenly that the dull melancholy of half a year was lifted from my mind.

The Reconciliation

TEMPLE HAD SCARCELY been with Findlay five minutes before he felt his old resentments, and the memory of that unforgettable wrong growing vivid again. But with the infatuation of his good resolution still upon him, he maintained the air of sham reconciliation that Findlay had welcomed so eagerly. They talked of this and that, carefully avoiding the matter of the separation. Temple at first spoke chiefly of his travels. He stood between the cabinet of minerals and the fireplace, his whiskey on the mantel-board, while Findlay sat with his chair pushed back from his writing-desk, on which were scattered the dozen little skulls of hedgehogs and shrew mice upon which he had been working.

Temple's eye fell upon them, and abruptly brought his mind round from the topic of West Africa. "And you—" said Temple. "While I have been wandering I suppose you have been going on steadily."

"Drumming along," said Findlay.

"To the Royal Society and fame and all the things we used to dream about—How long is it?"

"Five years—since our student days."

Temple glanced round the room, and his eye rested for a moment on a round greyish-drab object that lay in the corner near the door. "The same fat books and folios, only more of them, the same smell of old bones, and a dissection—is it the same one?—in the window. Fame is *your* mistress?"

"Fame," said Findlay. "But it's hardly fame. The herd outside say, 'Eminence in comparative anatomy.'"

"Eminence in comparative anatomy. No marrying—no avarice."

"None," said Findlay, glancing askance at him.

"I suppose it's the happiest way of living. But it wouldn't be the thing for me. Excitement—but, I say!"—his eye had fallen again on that fungoid shape of drabbish-grey—"there's a limit to scientific inhumanity. You really mustn't keep your door open with a human brainpan."

He went across the room as he spoke and picked the thing up. "Brainpan!" said Findlay. "Oh, *that!* Man alive, that's not a brainpan. Where's your science?"

"No. I see it's not," said Temple, carrying the object in his hand as he came back to his former position and scrutinising it curiously. "But what the devil is it?"

"Don't you know?" said Findlay.

The thing was about thrice the size of a man's hand, like a rough watch-pocket of thick bone.

Findlay laughed almost naturally. "You have a bad memory—It's a whale's ear-bone."

"Of course," said Temple, his appearance of interest vanishing. "The *bulla* of a whale. I've forgotten a lot of these things."

He half turned, and put the thing on the top of the cabinet beside Findlay's dumb-bells.

"If you are serious in your music-hall proposal," he said, reverting to a jovial suggestion of Findlay's, "I am at your service. I'm afraid—I may find myself a little old for that sort of thing—I haven't tried one for ages."

"But we are meeting to commemorate youth," said Findlay.

"And bury our early manhood," said Temple. "Well, well—yes, let us go to the music hall, by all means, if you desire it. It is trivial—and appropriate. We want no tragic issues."

When the men returned to Findlay's study the little clock in the dimness on the mantel-shelf was pointing to half-past one. After the departure the little brown room, with its books and bones, was undisturbed, save for the two visits Findlay's attentive servant paid, to see to the fire and to pull down the blinds and draw the curtains. The ticking of the clock was the only sound in the quiet. Now and then the fire flickered and stirred, sending blood-red reflections chasing the shadows across the ceiling, and bringing into ghostly transitory prominence some grotesque grouping of animals' bones or skulls upon the shelves. At last the stillness was broken by the unlatching and slamming of the heavy street door and the sound of unsteady footsteps approaching along the passage. Then the door opened, and the two men came into the warm firelight.

Temple came in first, his brown face flushed with drink, his coat unbuttoned, his hands deep in his trousers' pockets. His Christmas resolution had long since dissolved in alcohol. He was a little puzzled to find himself in Findlay's company. And his fuddled brain insisted upon inopportune reminiscence. He walked straight to the fire and stood before it, an exaggerated black figure, staring down into the red glow. "After all," he said, "we are fools to quarrel—fools to quarrel about a little thing like that. Damned fools!"

Findlay went to the writing-table and felt about for the matches with quivering hands.

"It wasn't my doing," he said.

"It wasn't your doing," said Temple. "Nothing ever was your doing. You are always in the right—Findlay the all-right."

Findlay's attention was concentrated upon the lamp. His hand was unsteady, and he had some difficulty in turning up the wicks; one got jammed down and the other flared furiously. When at last it was lit and turned up, he came up to Temple. "Take your coat off, old man, and have some more whiskey," he said. "That was a ripping little girl in the skirt dance."

"Fools to quarrel," said Temple, slowly, and then woke up to Findlay's words. "Heigh?"

"Take off your coat and sit down," said Findlay, moving up the little metal table and producing cigars and a syphon and whiskey. "That lamp gives an infernally bad light, but it is all I have. Something wrong with the oil. Did you notice the drudge of that stone-smashing trick?"

Temple remained erect and gloomy, staring into the fire. "Fools to quarrel," he said. Findlay was now half drunk, and his finesse began to leave him. Temple had been drinking heavily, and was now in a curious rambling stage. And Findlay's one idea now was to close this curious reunion.

"There's no woman worth a man's friendship," said Temple, abruptly.

He sat down in an easy chair, poured out and drank a dose of whiskey and lithia. The idea of friendship took possession of him, and he became reminiscent of student days and student adventures. For some time it was, "Do you remember" this, and "Do you remember" that. And Findlay grew cheerful again.

"They were glorious times," said Findlay, pouring whiskey into Temple's glass.

Then Temple startled him by abruptly reverting to that bitter quarrel. "No woman in the world," he said. "Curse them!"

He began to laugh stupidly. "After all—" he said, "in the end."

"Oh, damn!" said Findlay.

"All very well for you to swear," said Temple, "but you forget about me. 'Tain't your place to swear. If only you'd left things alone—"

"I thought the pass-word was forget," said Findlay.

Temple stared into the fire for a space, "Forget," he said, and then with a curious return to a clarity of speech, "Findlay, I'm getting drunk."

"Nonsense, man, take some more."

Temple rose out of his chair with the look of one awakening. "There's no reason why I should get drunk, because—"

"Drink," said Findlay, "and forget it."

"Faugh! I want to stick my head in water. I want to think. What the deuce am I doing here, with *you* of all people."

"Nonsense! *Talk* and forget it, if you won't drink. Do you remember old Jason and the boxing-gloves? I wonder whether you could put up your fives now."

Temple stood with his back to the fire, his brain spinning with drink, and the old hatred of Findlay came back in flood. He sought in his mind for some offensive thing to say, and his face grew dark. Findlay saw that a crisis was upon him and he cursed under his breath. His air of conviviality, his pose of hearty comforter, grew more and more difficult. But what else was there to do?

"Old Jason—full of science and as slow as an elephant!—but he made boxers of us. Do you remember our little set-to—at that place in Gower Street?"

To show his innocent liveliness, his freedom from preoccupation, Findlay pushed his chair aside, and stepped out into the middle of the room. There he began to pose in imitation of Jason, and to give a colourable travesty of the old prize-fighter's instructions. He picked up his boxing-gloves from the shelf in the recess, and slipped them on. Temple, lowering there, on the brink of an explosion, was almost too much for his nerves. He felt his display of high spirits was a mistake, but he must go through with it now.

"Don't stand glooming there, man. You're in just that state when the world looks black as ink. Drink yourself merry again. There's no woman in the world worth a man's friendship—that's agreed upon. Come and have a bout with these gloves of mine—four-ounce gloves. There's nothing sets the blood and spirits stirring like that."

"All right," said Temple, quite mechanically. And then, waking up to what he was doing, "Where are the other gloves?"

"Over there in the corner. On the top of the mineral cabinet. By Jove! Temple, this is like old times!"

Temple, quivering strangely, went to the corner. He meant to thrash Findlay, and knew that in spite of his lighter weight he would do it. Yet it seemed puerile and inadequate to the pitch of absurdity for the wrong Findlay had done him was great. And, putting his hand on something pale in the shadow, he touched the *bulla* of the whale. The temptation was like a lightning flash. He slipped one glove on his left hand, and thrust the fingers of his right into the cavity of the *bulla*. It took all his fingers, and covered his knuckles and all the back of his hand. And it was so oddly like a thumbless boxing-glove! Just the very shape of the padded part. His spirits rose abruptly at the sudden prospect of a savage joke,—how savage it could be, he did not know.

Meanwhile Findlay, with a nervous alacrity, moved the lamp into the corner behind the armchair, and thrust his writing-desk into the window bay.

"Come on," said Findlay, behind him, and abruptly he turned.

Findlay looked straight into his eyes, on guard, his hands half open. He did not see the strange substitute for a glove that covered Temple's right hand. Both men were gone so far towards drunkenness that their power of observation was obscured. For a moment they stood squaring at one another, the host smiling, and his guest smiling also, but with his teeth set; two dark figures swaying in the firelight and the dim lamp-light. Then Findlay struck at his opponent's face with his left hand. As he did so Temple ducked slightly to the left, and struck savagely over Findlay's shoulder at his temple with the bone-covered fist. The blow was given with such tremendous force that it sent Findlay reeling sideways, half stunned, and overcome with astonishment. The thing struck his ear, and the side of his face went white at the blow. He struggled to keep his footing, and as he did so Temple's gloved right hand took him in the chest and sent him spinning to the foot of the cigar cabinet.

Findlay's eyes were wide open with astonishment. Temple was a lighter man by a stone or more than himself, and he did not understand how he had been felled. He was not stunned, although he was so dulled by the blow as not to notice the blood running down his cheek from his ear. He laughed insincerely, and, almost pulling the cigar cabinet over, scrambled to his feet, made as if he would speak, and put up his hand instinctively as Temple struck out at him again, a feint with the left hand. Findlay was an expert boxer, and, anticipating another right-hand blow over the ear, struck sharply at once with his own left hand in

Temple's face, throwing his full weight into the blow, and dodging Temple's reply.

Temple's upper lip was cut against his teeth, and the taste of blood and the sight of it trickling down Findlay's cheek destroyed the last vestiges of restraint that drink had left him, stripped off all that education had ever done for him. There remained now only the savage man-animal, the creature that thirsts for blood. With a half bestial cry, he flung himself upon Findlay as he jumped back, and with a sudden sweep of his right arm cut down the defence, breaking Findlay's arm just above the wrist, and following with three rapid blows of the *bulla* upon the face. Findlay gave an inarticulate cry of astonishment, countered weakly once, and then went down like a felled ox. As he fell, Temple fell kneeling upon the top of him. There was a smash as the lamp went reeling.

The lamp was extinguished as it fell, and left the room red and black. Findlay struck heavily at Temple's ribs, and Temple, with his left elbow at Findlay's neck, swung up his right arm and struck down a sledge-hammer blow upon the face, and again and yet again, until the body beneath his knees had ceased to writhe.

Then suddenly his frenzy left him at the voice of a woman shrieking so that it filled the room. He looked up and crouched motionless as he heard and saw the study door closing and heard the patter of feet retreating in panic. Then he looked down and saw the thing that had once been the face of Findlay. For an awful minute he remained kneeling agape.

Then he staggered to his feet and stood over Findlay's body in the glow of the dying fire, like a man awakening from a nightmare. Suddenly he perceived the *bulla* on his hand, covered with blood and hair, and began to understand what had happened. In a sudden horror he flung the diabolical thing from him. It struck the floor near the cigar cabinet, rolled for a yard or so on its edge, and came to rest in almost the position it had occupied when he had first set eyes on it. To Temple's excited imagination it seemed to be lying at exactly the same spot, the sole and sufficient cause of Findlay's death and his own.

A Slip Under the Microscope

OUTSIDE THE LABORATORY windows was a watery grey fog, and within a close warmth and the yellow light of the green-shaded gas lamps that stood two to each table down its narrow length. On each table stood a couple of glass jars containing the mangled vestiges of the crayfish, mussels, frogs, and guinea-pigs, upon which the students had been working, and down the side of the room, facing the windows, were shelves bearing bleached dissections in spirit, surmounted by a row of beautifully executed anatomical drawings in white wood frames and overhanging a row of cubical lockers. All the doors of the laboratory were panelled with blackboard, and on these were the half-erased diagrams of the previous day's work. The laboratory was empty, save for the demonstrator, who sat near the preparation-room door, and silent, save for a low, continuous murmur, and the clicking of the rocker microtome at which he was working. But scattered about the room were traces of numerous students: hand-bags, polished boxes of instruments, in one place a large drawing covered by newspaper, and in another a prettily bound copy of "News from Nowhere," a book oddly at variance with its surroundings. These things had been put down hastily as the students had arrived and hurried at once to secure their seats in the adjacent lecture theatre. Deadened by the closed door, the measured accents of the professor sounded as a featureless muttering.

Presently, faint through the closed windows came the sound of the Oratory clock striking the hour of eleven. The clicking of the microtome ceased, and the demonstrator looked at his watch, rose, thrust his hands into his pockets, and walked slowly down the laboratory towards the lecture-theatre door. He stood listening for a moment, and then his eye fell on the little volume by William Morris. He picked it up, glanced at the title, smiled, opened it, looked at the name on the fly-leaf, ran the leaves through with his hand, and put it down. Almost immediately the even murmur of the lecturer ceased, there was a sudden burst of pencils rattling on the desks in the lecture-theatre, a stirring, a scraping of feet, and a number of voices speaking together. Then a firm footfall approached the door, which began to open, and stood ajar, as some indistinctly heard question arrested the new-comer.

The demonstrator turned, walked slowly back past the microtome and left the laboratory by the preparation-room door. As he did so, first one, and then several students carrying note-books, entered the laboratory from the lecture-theatre, and distributed themselves among the little tables, or stood in a group about the doorway. They were an exceptionally heterogeneous assembly,—for while Oxford and Cambridge still recoil from the blushing prospect of mixed classes, the College of Science anticipated America in the matter years ago,—mixed socially, too, for the prestige of the College is high, and its scholarships, free of any age limit, dredge deeper even than do those of the Scotch universities. The class numbered one and twenty, but some remained in the theatre questioning the professor, copying the blackboard diagrams before they were washed off, or examining the special specimens he had produced to illustrate the day's teaching. Of the nine who had come into the laboratory, three were girls, one of whom, a little fair woman wearing spectacles and dressed in greyish green, was peering out of the window at the fog, while the other two, both wholesome-looking, plain-faced school-girls, unrolled and put on the brown holland aprons they wore while dissecting. Of the men, two went down the laboratory and sat down in their places, one a pallid, dark-bearded man who had once been a tailor, the other a pleasant-featured, ruddy young man of twenty, dressed in a well-fitting brown suit, young Wedderburn, the son of Wedderburn the eye-specialist. The others formed a little knot near the theatre door. One of these, a dwarfed, spectacled figure with a hunch back, sat on a bent wood stool, two others, one a short, dark youngster, and the other a flaxen-haired, reddish-complexioned young man, stood leaning side by side against the slate sink, while the fourth stood facing them and maintained the larger share of the conversation.

This last person was named Hill. He was a sturdily built young fellow of the same age as Wedderburn, he had a white face, dark grey eyes, hair of an indeterminate colour, and prominent, irregular features. He talked rather louder than was needful, and thrust his hands deeply into his pockets. His collar was frayed and blue with the starch of a careless laundress, his clothes were evidently ready-made, and there was a patch on the side of his boot near the toe. And as he talked or listened to the others, he glanced now and again towards the lecture-theatre door. They were discussing the depressing peroration of the lecture they had just heard, the last lecture it was in the introductory course in Zoölogy. "From ovum to ovum is the goal of the higher vertebrata," the lecturer had said in his melancholy tones, and so had neatly rounded off the sketch of comparative anatomy he had been developing. The spectacled hunchback had repeated it, with noisy appreciation, had tossed it towards the fair-haired student with an evident provocation, and had started one of those vague, rambling discussions on generalities so unaccountably dear to the student mind all the world over.

"That is our goal, perhaps,—I admit it,—as far as science goes," said the fair-haired student, rising to the challenge. "But there are things above science."

"Science," said Hill, confidently, "is systematic knowledge. Ideas that don't come into the system must anyhow—be loose ideas." He was not quite sure whether that was a clever saying or a fatuity, until his hearers took it seriously.

"The thing I cannot understand," said the hunchback, at large, "is whether Hill is a materialist or not."

"There is one thing above matter," said Hill, promptly, feeling he had a better thing this time, aware too of some one in the doorway behind him, and raising his voice a trifle for her benefit, "and that is—the delusion that there is something above matter."

"So we have your gospel at last," said the fair-haired student. "It's all a delusion, is it? All our aspirations to lead something more than dogs' lives, all our work for anything beyond ourselves. But see how inconsistent you are! Your socialism, for instance. Why do you trouble about the interests of the race? Why do you concern yourself about the beggar in the gutter? Why are you bothering yourself to lend that book"—he indicated William Morris by a movement of the head—"to every one in the lab?"

"Girl," said the hunchback, indistinctly, and glanced guiltily over his shoulder.

The girl in brown, with the brown eyes, had come into the laboratory, and stood on the other side of the table behind him with her rolled-up apron in one hand, looking over her shoulder, listening to the discussion. She did not notice the hunchback, because she was glancing from Hill to his interlocutor. Hill's consciousness of her presence betrayed itself to her only in his studious ignorance of the fact; but she understood that and it pleased her. "I see no reason," said he, "why a man should live like a brute because he knows of nothing beyond matter, and does not expect to exist a hundred years hence."

"Why shouldn't he?" said the fair-haired student.

"Why *should* he?" said Hill.

"What inducement has he?"

"That's the way with all you religious people. It's all a business of inducements. Cannot a man seek after righteousness for righteousness' sake?"

There was a pause. The fair man answered with a kind of vocal padding, "But—you see—inducement—when I said inducement—" to gain time. And then the hunchback came to his rescue and inserted a question. He was a terrible person in the debating society with his questions, and they invariably took one form,—a demand for a definition. "What's your definition of righteousness?" said the hunchback, at this stage.

Hill experienced a sudden loss of complacency at this question, but even as it was asked, relief came in the person of Brooks, the laboratory attendant, who entered by the preparation-room door, carrying a number of freshly-killed guinea-pigs by their hind-legs. "This is the last batch of material this session," said the youngster who had not previously spoken. Brooks advanced up the laboratory, smacking down a couple of guinea-pigs at each table, and the discussion perished abruptly as the students who were not already in their places hurried to them to secure the choice of a specimen. There was a noise of keys rattling on split rings as lockers were opened, and dissecting instruments taken out. Hill was already standing by his table, and his box of scalpels was sticking out of his pocket. The girl in brown came a step towards him, and leaning over his table, said softly, "Did you see that I returned your book, Mr. Hill?"

During the whole scene, she and the book had been vividly present in his consciousness, but he made a clumsy pretence of looking at the book and seeing it for the first time. "Oh, yes," he said, taking it up. "I see. Did you like it?"

"I want to ask you some questions about it—sometime."

"Certainly," said Hill. "I shall be glad." He stopped awkwardly. "You liked it?" he said.

"It's a wonderful book. Only some things I don't understand."

Then suddenly the laboratory was hushed by a curious braying noise. It was the demonstrator. He was at the blackboard ready to begin the day's instruction, and it was his custom to demand silence by a sound midway between the "Er" of common intercourse, and the blast of a trumpet. The girl in brown slipped back to her place, it was immediately in front of Hill's, and Hill, forgetting her forthwith, took a note-book out of the drawer of his table, turned over its leaves hastily, drew a stumpy pencil from his pocket, and prepared to make a copious note of the coming demonstration. For demonstrations and lectures are the sacred text of the College students. Books, saving only the professor's own, you may—it is even expedient to—ignore.

Hill was the son of a Landport cobbler, and had been hooked by a chance blue paper the authorities had thrown out to the Landport Technical College. He kept himself in London on his allowance of a guinea a week, and found that with proper care this also covered his clothing allowance, an occasional waterproof collar, that is, and ink and needles and cotton and suchlike necessaries for a man about town. This was his first year and his first session, but the brown old man in Landport had already got himself detested in many public-houses by boasting of his son "the professor." Hill was a vigorous youngster, with a serene contempt for the clergy of all denominations, and a fine ambition to reconstruct the world. He regarded his scholarship as a brilliant opportunity. He had begun to read at seven, and had read steadily whatever came in his way, good or bad, since then. His worldly experience had been limited to the Island of Portsea, and acquired chiefly in the wholesale boot factory in which he had worked by day, after passing the seventh standard of the Board School. He had a considerable gift of speech, as the College Debating Society, which met amidst the crushing machines and mine models in the Metallurgical Theatre downstairs, already recognised, recognised by a violent battering of desks whenever he rose. And he was just at that fine emotional age when life opens at the end of a narrow pass, like a broad valley at one's feet, full of the promise of wonderful discoveries and tremendous achievements. And his own limitations, save that he knew that he knew neither Latin or French, were all unknown to him.

At first his interest had been divided pretty equally between his biological work at the College and social and theological theorising, an employment which he took in deadly earnest. Of a night, when the big museum library was not open, he would sit on the bed of his room in Chelsea with his coat and a muffler on, and write out the lecture notes and revise his dissection memoranda until Thorpe called him out by a whistle,—the landlady objected to open the door to attic visitors,—and then the two would go prowling about the shadowy, shiny, gas-lit streets, talking, very much in the fashion of the sample just given, of the God Idea and Righteousness and Carlyle and the Reorganisation of Society. And in the midst of it all, Hill, arguing not only for Thorpe but for the casual passer-by, would lose the thread of his argument, glancing at some pretty, painted face that looked meaningly at him as he passed. Science and Righteousness! But once or twice lately there had been signs that a third interest was creeping into his life, and he had found his attention wandering from the fate of the mesoblastic somites or the probable meaning of the blastopore, to the thought of the girl with the brown eyes who sat at the table before him.

She was a paying student; she descended inconceivable social altitudes to speak to him. At the thought of the education she must have had and the accomplishments she must possess, the soul of Hill became abject within him. She had spoken to him first over a difficulty about the alisphenoid of a rabbit's skull, and he had found that, in biology at least, he had no reason for self-abasement. And from that, after the manner of young people starting from any starting-point, they got to generalities, and while Hill attacked her upon the question of socialism,—some instinct told him to spare her a direct assault upon her religion,—she was gathering resolution to undertake what she told herself was his aesthetic education. She was a year or two older than he, though the thought never occurred to him. The loan of "News from Nowhere" was the beginning of a series of cross loans. Upon some absurd first principle of his, Hill had never "wasted time" upon poetry, and it seemed an appalling deficiency to her. One day in the lunch hour, when she chanced upon him alone in the little museum where the skeletons were arranged, shamefully eating the bun that constituted his midday meal, she retreated and returned, to lend him, with a slightly furtive air, a volume of Browning. He stood sideways towards her and took the book rather clumsily, because he was holding the bun in the other hand. And in the retrospect his voice lacked the cheerful clearness he could have wished.

That occurred after the examination in comparative anatomy, on the day before the College turned out its students and was carefully locked up by the officials, for the Christmas holidays. The excitement of cramming for the first trial of strength had for a little while dominated Hill to the exclusion of his other interests. In the forecasts of the result in which every one indulged, he was surprised to find that no one regarded him as a possible competitor for the Harvey Commemoration Medal, of which this and the two subsequent examinations disposed. It was about this time that Wedderburn, who so far had lived inconspicuously on the uttermost margin of Hill's perceptions, began to take on the appearance of an obstacle. By a mutual agreement the nocturnal prowlings with Thorpe ceased for the three weeks before the examination, and his landlady pointed out that she really could not supply so much lamp-oil at the price. He walked to and fro from the College with little slips of mnemonics in his hand, lists of crayfish appendages, rabbits' skull-bones, and vertebrate nerves, for example, and became a positive nuisance to foot-passengers in the opposite direction.

But by a natural reaction Poetry and the girl with the brown eyes ruled the Christmas holiday. The pending results of the examination became such a secondary consideration that Hill marvelled at his father's excitement. Even had he wished it, there was no comparative anatomy to read in Landport, and he was too poor to buy books, but the stock of poets in the library was extensive and Hill's attack was magnificently sustained. He saturated himself with the fluent numbers of Longfellow and Tennyson, and fortified himself with Shakespeare, found a kindred soul in Pope and a master in Shelley, and heard and fled the siren voices of Eliza Cook and Mrs. Hemans. But he read no more Browning, because he hoped for the loan of other volumes from Miss Haysman when he returned to London.

He walked from his lodgings to the College with that volume of Browning in his shiny black bag, and his mind teeming with the finest general propositions about poetry. Indeed he framed first this little speech and then that with which to grace the return. The morning was an exceptionally pleasant one for London, there was a clear, hard frost and undeniable blue in the sky, a thin haze softened every outline, and warm shafts of sunlight struck between the houseblocks and turned the sunny side of the street to amber and gold. In the hall of the College he pulled off his glove and signed his name with fingers so stiff with cold that the characteristic dash under the signature he cultivated became a quivering line. He imagined Miss Haysman about him everywhere. He turned at the staircase, and there, below, he saw a crowd struggling at the foot of the notice board. This, possibly, was the biology list. He forgot Browning and Miss Haysman for the moment, and joined the scrimmage. And at last with his cheek flattened against the sleeve of the man on the step above him, he read the list:

"*Class I.*

H. J. SOMERS WEDDERBURN.

WILLIAM HILL."

And thereafter followed a second class that is outside our present sympathies. It was characteristic that he did not trouble to look for Thorpe on the Physics list, but backed out of the struggle at once, and in a curious emotional state between pride over common second-class humanity and acute disappointment at Wedderburn's success, went on his way upstairs. At the top, as he was hanging up his coat in the passage, the zoölogical demonstrator, a young man from Oxford, who secretly regarded him as a blatant "mugger" of the very worst type, offered his heartiest congratulations.

At the laboratory door Hill stopped for a second to get his breath, and then entered. He looked straight up the laboratory and saw all five girl students grouped in their places, and Wedderburn, the once retiring Wedderburn, leaning rather gracefully against the window, playing with the blind tassel and talking, apparently, to the five of them. Now Hill could talk bravely enough and even overbearingly to one girl, and he could have made a speech to a roomful of girls, but this business of standing at ease and appreciating, fencing, and returning quick remarks round a group, was, he knew, altogether beyond him. Coming up the staircase his feelings for Wedderburn had been generous, a certain admiration perhaps, a willingness to shake his hand conspicuously and heartily as one who had fought but the first round. But before Christmas Wedderburn had never gone up to that end of the room to talk. In a flash Hill's mist of vague excitement condensed abruptly to a vivid dislike of Wedderburn. Possibly his expression changed. As he came up to his place Wedderburn nodded carelessly to him, and the others glanced round. Miss Haysman looked at him and away again, the faintest touch of her eyes. "I can't agree with you, Mr. Wedderburn," she said.

"I must congratulate you on your first class, Mr. Hill," said the spectacled girl in green, turning round and beaming at him.

"It's nothing," said Hill, staring at Wedderburn and Miss Haysman talking together, and eager to hear what they talked about.

"We poor folks in the second class don't think so," said the girl in spectacles.

What was it Wedderburn was saying? Something about William Morris! Hill did not answer the girl in spectacles, and the smile died out of his face. He could not hear and failed to see how he could "cut in." Confound Wedderburn! He sat down, opened his bag, hesitated whether to return the volume of Browning forthwith, in the sight of all, and instead drew out his new notebooks for the short course in elementary botany that was now beginning, and which would terminate in February. As he did so a fat heavy man with a white face and pale grey eyes, Bindon, the professor of Botany who came up from Kew for January and February, came in by the lecture-theatre door and passed, rubbing his hands together and smiling in silent affability, down the laboratory.

In the subsequent six weeks Hill experienced some very rapid and curiously complex emotional developments. For the most part he had Wedderburn in focus—a fact that Miss Haysman never suspected. She told Hill (for in the comparative privacy of the museum she talked a good deal to him of socialism and Browning and general propositions) that she had met Wedderburn at the house of some people she knew, and "He's inherited his cleverness; for his father, you know, is the great eye-specialist."

"*My* father is a cobbler," said Hill, quite irrelevantly, and perceived the want of dignity even as he said it. But the gleam of jealousy did not offend her. She conceived herself the fundamental source of it. He suffered bitterly from a sense of Wedderburn's unfairness and a realisation of his own handicap. Here was this Wedderburn had picked up a prominent man for a father, and instead of his losing so many marks on the score of that advantage, it was counted to him for righteousness! And while Hill had to introduce himself and talk to Miss Haysman clumsily over mangled guinea-pigs in the laboratory, this Wedderburn, in some backstairs way, had access to her social altitudes, and could converse in a polished argot that Hill understood perhaps, but felt incapable of speaking. Not of course that he wanted to. Then it seemed to Hill that for Wedderburn to come there day after day with cuffs unfrayed, neatly tailored, precisely barbered, quietly perfect, was in itself an ill-bred, sneering sort of proceeding. Moreover, it was a stealthy thing for Wedderburn to behave insignificantly for a space, to mock modesty, to lead Hill to fancy that he himself was beyond dispute the man of the year, and then suddenly to dart in front of him, and incontinently to swell up in this fashion. In addition to these things Wedderburn displayed an increasing disposition to join in any conversational grouping that included Miss Haysman, and would venture, and indeed seek occasion to pass opinions derogatory to Socialism and Atheism. He goaded Hill to incivilities by neat, shallow, and exceedingly effective personalities about the socialist leaders, until Hill hated Bernard Shaw's graceful egotisms, William Morris's limited editions and luxurious wall-papers, and Walter Crane's charmingly absurd ideal working-men, about as much as he hated Wedderburn. The dissertations in the laboratory that had been his glory in the previous term, became a danger, degenerated into inglorious tussles with Wedderburn, and Hill kept to them only out of an obscure perception that his honour was involved.

In the Debating Society Hill knew quite clearly that, to a thunderous accompaniment of banged desks, he could have pulverised Wedderburn. Only Wedderburn never attended the Debating Society to be pulverised, because—nauseous affectation!—he "dined late."

You must not imagine that these things presented themselves in quite such a crude form to Hill's perception. Hill was a born generaliser. Wedderburn to him was not so much an individual obstacle as a type, the salient angle of a class. The economic theories that, after infinite ferment, had shaped themselves in Hill's mind, became abruptly concrete at the contact. The world became full of easy-mannered, graceful, gracefully dressed, conversationally dexterous, finally shallow Wedderburns, Bishops Wedderburn, Wedderburns, M.P., Professors Wedderburn, Wedderburn landlords, all with finger-bowl shibboleths and epigrammatic cities of refuge from a sturdy debater. And every one ill clothed or ill dressed, from the cobbler to the cab runner, was a man and a brother, a fellow-sufferer, to Hill's imagination. So that he became, as it were, a champion of the fallen and oppressed, albeit to outward seeming only a self-assertive, ill-mannered young man, and an unsuccessful champion at that. Again and again, a skirmish over the afternoon tea that the girl-students had inaugurated, left Hill with flushed cheeks and a tattered temper, and the Debating Society noticed a new quality of sarcastic bitterness in his speeches.

You will understand now how it was necessary if only in the interests of humanity, that Hill should demolish Wedderburn in the forthcoming examination and outshine him in the eyes of Miss Haysman, and you will perceive, too, how Miss Haysman fell into some common feminine misconceptions. The Hill-Wedderburn quarrel, for in his unostentatious way Wedderburn reciprocated Hill's ill-veiled rivalry, became a tribute to her indefinable charm. She was the Queen of Beauty in a tournament of scalpels and stumpy pencils. To her confidential friend's secret annoyance, it even troubled her conscience, for she was a good girl, and painfully aware, from Ruskin and contemporary fiction, how entirely men's activities are determined by women's attitudes. And if Hill never by any chance mentioned the topic of love to her, she only credited him with the finer modesty for that omission.

So the time came on for the second examination, and Hill's increasing pallor confirmed the general rumour that he was working hard. In the Aërated Bread Shop near South Kensington Station you would see him, breaking his bun and sipping his milk, with his eyes intent upon a paper of closely written notes. In his bedroom there were propositions about buds and stems round his looking-glass, a diagram to catch his eye, if soap should chance to spare it, above his washing-basin. He missed several meetings of the Debating Society, but he found the chance encounters with Miss Haysman in the spacious ways of the adjacent Art Museum, or in the little Museum at the top of the College, or in the College corridors, more frequent and very restful. In particular they used to meet in a little gallery full of wrought-iron chests and gates, near the Art Library, and there Hill used to talk, under the gentle stimulus of her flattering attention, of Browning and his personal ambitions. A characteristic she found remarkable in him was his freedom from avarice. He contemplated quite calmly the prospect of living all his life on an income below a hundred pounds a year. But he was determined to be famous, to make, recognisably in his own proper person, the world a better place to live in. He took Bradlaugh and John Burns for his leaders and models, poor, even impecunious, Great Men. But Miss Haysman thought that such lives were deficient on the aesthetic side, by which, though she did not know it, she meant good wall-paper and upholstery, pretty books, tasteful clothes, concerts, and meals nicely cooked and respectfully served.

At last came the day of the second examination, and the professor of botany, a fussy conscientious man, rearranged all the tables in the long narrow laboratory to prevent copying, and put his demonstrator on a chair on a table (where he felt, he said, like a Hindu god) to see all the cheating, and stuck a notice outside the door, "Door Closed," for no earthly reason that any human being could discover. And all the morning from ten to one the quill of Wedderburn shrieked defiance at Hill's, and the quills of the others chased their leaders in a tireless pack. So also it was in the afternoon. Wedderburn was a little quieter than usual, and Hill's face was hot all day, and his overcoat bulged with text-books and note-books against the last moment's revision. And the next day, in the morning and in the afternoon, was the practical examination, when sections had to be cut and slides identified. In the morning Hill was depressed because he knew he had cut a thick section, and in the afternoon came the Mysterious Slip.

It was just the kind of thing that the botanical professor was always doing. Like the income tax, it offered a premium to the cheat. It was a preparation under the microscope, a little glass slip, held in its place on the stage of the instrument by light steel clips, and the inscription set forth that the slip was not to be moved. Each student was to go in turn to it, sketch it, write in his book of answers what he considered it to be, and return to his place. Now to move such a slip is a thing one can do by a chance movement of the finger, and in a fraction of a second. The professor's reason for decreeing that the slip should not be moved depended on the fact that the object he wanted identified was characteristic of a certain tree stem. In the position in which it was placed it was a difficult thing to recognise, but once the slip was moved so as to bring other parts of the preparation into view, its nature was obvious enough.

Hill came to this, flushed from a contest with staining reagents, sat down on the little stool before the microscope, turned the mirror to get the best light, and then out of sheer habit shifted the slip. At once he remembered the prohibition, and with an almost continuous motion of his hands, moved it back, and sat paralysed with astonishment at his action.

Then slowly he turned his head. The professor was out of the room, the demonstrator sat aloft on his impromptu rostrum, reading the "Q. Jour. Mi. Sci.," the rest of the examinees were busy and with their backs to him. Should he own up to the accident now? He knew quite clearly what the thing was. It was a lenticel, a characteristic preparation from the elder-tree. His eye roved over his intent fellow-students and Wedderburn suddenly glanced over his shoulder at him with a queer expression in his eyes. The mental excitement that had kept Hill at an abnormal pitch of vigour these two days gave way to a curious nervous tension. His book of answers was beside him. He did not write down what the thing was, but with one eye at the microscope he began making a hasty sketch of it. His mind was full of this grotesque puzzle in ethics that had suddenly been sprung upon him. Should he identify it? Or should he leave this question unanswered? In that case Wedderburn would probably come out first in the botanical list. How could he tell now whether he might not have identified the thing without shifting it? It was possible that Wedderburn had failed to recognise it, of course. Suppose Wedderburn, too, had shifted the slide? He looked up at the clock. There were fifteen minutes in which to make up his mind. He gathered up his book of answers and the coloured pencils he used in illustrating his replies, and walked back to his seat.

He read through his manuscript and then sat thinking and gnawing his knuckle. It would look queer now if he owned up. He *must* beat Wedderburn. He forgot the examples of those starry gentlemen, John Burns and Bradlaugh. Besides, he reflected, the glimpse of the rest of the slip he had had, was after all quite accidental, forced upon him by chance, a kind of providential revelation rather than an unfair advantage. It was not nearly so dishonest to avail himself of that as it was of Broome, who believed in the efficacy of prayer, to pray daily for a First-Class. "Five minutes more," said the demonstrator, folding up his paper and becoming observant. Hill watched the clock hands until two minutes remained, then he opened the book of answers, and with hot ears and an affectation of ease, gave his drawing of the lenticel its name.

When the second pass list appeared, the previous positions of Wedderburn and Hill were reversed, and the spectacled girl in green who knew the demonstrator in private life (where he was practically human) said that in the result of the two examinations taken together, Hill had the advantage of a mark, 167 to 166, out of a possible 200. Every one admired Hill in a way, though the suspicion of "mugging" clung to him. But Hill was to find congratulations and Miss Haysman's enhanced opinion of him, and even the decided decline in the crest of Wedderburn tainted by an unhappy memory. He felt a remarkable access of energy at first, and the note of a Democracy marching to Triumph returned to his Debating Society speeches; he worked at his comparative anatomy with tremendous zeal and effect, and he went on with his aesthetic education. But through it all, a vivid little picture was continually coming before his mind's eye, of a sneakish person manipulating a slide. . . .

No human being had witnessed the act, and he was cocksure that no Higher Power existed to see it, but for all that it worried him. Memories are not dead things, but alive; they dwindle in disuse, but they harden and develop in all sorts of queer ways if they are being continually fretted. Curiously enough, though at the time he perceived clearly that the shifting was accidental, as the days wore on his memory became confused about it, until at last he was not sure, although he assured himself that he *was* sure, whether the movement had been absolutely involuntary. Then it is possible that Hill's dietary was conducive to morbid conscientiousness,—a breakfast frequently eaten in a hurry, a midday bun, and, at such hours after five as chanced to be convenient, such meat as his means determined, usually in a chop-house in a back street off the Brompton Road. Occasionally he treated himself to threepenny and ninepenny classics, and they usually represented a suppression of potatoes or chops. It is indisputable that outbreaks of self-abasement and emotional revival have a distinct relation to periods of scarcity. But apart from this influence on the feelings, there was in Hill a distinct aversion to falsity, that the blasphemous Landport cobbler had inculcated by strap and tongue from his earliest years. Of one fact about professed Atheists I am convinced: they may be, they usually are, fools, void of subtlety, revilers of holy institutions, brutal speakers, and mischievous knaves; but they lie with difficulty. If it were not so, if they had the faintest grasp of the idea of compromise, they would simply be liberal Churchmen. And, moreover, this memory poisoned his regard for Miss Haysman. For she now preferred him to Wedderburn so evidently that he felt sure he cared for her, and began reciprocating her attentions by timid marks of personal regard,—at one time he even bought a bunch of violets, carried it about in his pocket, and produced it with a stumbling explanation, withered and dead, in the gallery of old iron. It poisoned, too, the denunciation of capitalist dishonesty that had been one of his life's pleasures. And, lastly, it poisoned his triumph over Wedderburn. Previously he had been Wedderburn's superior in his own eyes, and had raged simply at a want of recognition. Now he began to fret at the darker suspicion of a positive inferiority. He fancied he found justification for his position in Browning; but they vanished on analysis. At last, moved curiously enough by exactly the same motive forces that had resulted in his dishonesty, he went to Professor Bindon and made a clean breast of the whole affair. As Hill was a paid student, Professor Bindon did not ask him to sit down, and he stood before the Professor's desk as he made his confession.

"It's a curious story," said Professor Bindon, slowly realising how the thing reflected on himself, and then letting his anger rise. "A most remarkable story. I can't understand your doing it, and I can't understand this avowal. You're a type of student—Cambridge men would never dream—I suppose I ought to have thought—Why *did* you cheat?"

"I didn't—cheat," said Hill.

"But you have just been telling me you did."

"I thought I explained—"

"Either you cheated or you did not cheat."

"I said my motion was involuntary—"

"I am not a metaphysician, I am a servant of science—of fact. You were told not to move the slip. You did move the slip. If that is not cheating—"

"If I was a cheat," said Hill, with the note of hysterics in his voice, "should I come here and tell you?"

"Your repentance, of course, does you credit," said Professor Bindon; "but it does not alter the original facts."

"No, sir," said Hill, giving in, in utter self-abasement.

"Even now you cause an enormous amount of trouble. The examination list will have to be revised."

"I suppose so, sir."

"Suppose so! Of course it must be revised. And I don't see how I can conscientiously pass you."

"Not pass me!" said Hill. "Fail me!"

"It's the rule in all examinations. Or where should we be? What else did you expect? You don't want to shirk the consequences of your own acts?"

"I thought perhaps," said Hill. And then, "Fail me! I thought, as I told you, you would simply deduct the marks given for that slip—"

"Impossible!" said Bindon. "Besides, it would still leave you above Wedderburn. Deduct only the marks! Preposterous! The Departmental Regulations distinctly say—"

"But it's my own admission, sir."

"The Regulations say nothing whatever of the manner in which the matter comes to light. They simply provide—"

"It will ruin me. If I fail this examination, they won't renew my scholarship."

"You should have thought of that before."

"But, sir, consider all my circumstances—"

"I cannot consider anything. Professors in this College are machines. The Regulations will not even let us recommend our students for appointments. I am a machine, and you have worked me. I have to do—"

"It's very hard, sir."

"Possibly it is."

"If I am to be failed this examination I might as well go home at once."

"That is as you think proper." Bindon's voice softened a

little, he perceived he had been unjust, and, provided he did not contradict himself, he was disposed to amelioration. "As a private person," he said, "I think this confession of yours goes far to mitigate your offence. But you have set the machinery in motion, you know, and now it must take its course. I—I am really sorry you gave way."

A wave of emotion prevented Hill from answering. Suddenly very vividly he saw the heavily-lined face of the old Landport cobbler, his father. "Good God!—What a fool I have been!" he said hotly and abruptly.

"I hope," said Bindon, "that it will be a lesson to you."

But curiously enough they were not thinking of quite the same indiscretion.

There was a pause.

"I would like a day to think, sir, and then I will let you know—about going home, I mean," said Hill, moving towards the door.

The next day Hill's place was vacant. The spectacled girl in green was, as usual, first with the news. Wedderburn and Miss Haysman were talking of the Meistersingers, when she came up to them.

"Have you heard?" she said.

"Heard what?"

"There was cheating in the examination."

"Cheating!" said Wedderburn, with his face suddenly hot. "How?"

"That slide—"

"Moved? Never!"

"It was. That slide that we weren't to move—"

"Nonsense!" said Wedderburn. "Why! How could they find out? Who do they say—"

"It was Mr. Hill."

"Hill!"

"Mr. Hill!"

"Not—surely not the immaculate Hill?" said Wedderburn, recovering.

"I don't believe it," said Miss Haysman. "How do you know?"

"I *didn't*," said the girl in spectacles. "But I know it now for a fact. Mr. Hill went and confessed to Professor Bindon himself."

"By Jove!" said Wedderburn. "Hill of all people—But I am always inclined to distrust these philanthropists-on-principle—"

"Are you quite sure?" said Miss Haysman, with a catch in her breath.

"Quite. It's dreadful, isn't it? But you know, what can you expect? His father is a cobbler—"

Then Miss Haysman astonished the girl in spectacles.

"I don't care. I will not believe it," she said, flushing darkly under her warm-tinted skin. "I will not believe it until he has told me so himself—face to face. I would scarcely believe it then," and abruptly she turned her back on the girl in spectacles, and walked to her own place.

"It's true, all the same," said the girl in spectacles, peering and smiling at Wedderburn.

But Wedderburn did not answer her. She was, indeed, one of those people who are destined to make unanswered remarks.

In the Avu Observatory

THE OBSERVATORY AT Avu, in Borneo, stands on the spur of the mountain. To the north rises the old crater, black against the unfathomable blue of the sky. From the little circular building, with its mushroom dome, the slopes plunge steeply downward into the black mysteries of the tropical forest beneath. The little house in which the observer and his assistant live is about fifty yards from the observatory, and beyond this are the huts of their native attendants.

Thaddy, the chief observer, was down with a slight fever. His assistant, Woodhouse, paused for a moment in silent contemplation of the tropical night before commencing his solitary vigil. The night was very silent. Now and then voices and laughter came from the native huts, or the cry of some strange animal was heard from the midst of the mystery of the forest. Nocturnal insects appeared in ghostly fashion out of the darkness, and fluttered round his light. He thought, perhaps, of all the possibilities of discovery that still lay in the black tangle beneath him; for to the naturalist the virgin forests of Borneo are still a wonderland, full of strange questions and half-suspected discoveries. Woodhouse carried a small lantern in his hand, and its yellow glow contrasted vividly with the infinite series of tints between lavender-blue and black in which the landscape was painted. His hands and face were smeared with ointment against the attacks of the mosquitoes.

Even in these days of celestial photography, work done in a purely temporary erection, and with only the most primitive appliances in addition to the telescope, still involves a very large amount of cramped and motionless watching. He sighed as he thought of the physical fatigues before him, stretched himself, and entered the observatory.

The reader is probably familiar with the structure of an ordinary astronomical observatory. The building is usually cylindrical in shape, with a very light hemispherical roof capable of being turned round from the interior. The telescope is supported upon a stone pillar in the centre, and a clockwork arrangement compensates for the earth's rotation, and allows a star once found to be continuously observed. Besides this, there is a compact tracery of wheels and screws about its point of support, by which the astronomer adjusts it. There is, of course, a slit in the movable roof which follows the eye of the telescope in its survey of the heavens. The observer sits or lies on a sloping wooden arrangement, which he can wheel to any part of the observatory as the position of the telescope may require. Within it is advisable to have things as dark as possible, in order to enhance the brilliance of the stars observed.

The lantern flared as Woodhouse entered his circular den, and the general darkness fled into black shadows behind the big machine, from which it presently seemed to creep back over the whole place again as the light waned. The slit was a profound transparent blue, in which six stars shone with tropical brilliance, and their light lay, a pallid gleam, along the black tube of the instrument. Woodhouse shifted the roof, and then proceeding to the telescope, turned first one wheel and then another, the great cylinder slowly swinging into a new position. Then he glanced through the finder, the little companion telescope, moved the roof a little more, made some further adjustments, and set the clockwork in motion. He took off his jacket, for the night was very hot, and pushed into position the uncomfortable seat to which he was condemned for the next four hours. Then with a sigh he resigned himself to his watch upon the mysteries of space.

There was no sound now in the observatory, and the lantern waned steadily. Outside there was the occasional cry of some animal in alarm or pain, or calling to its mate, and the intermittent sounds of the Malay and Dyak servants. Presently one of the men began a queer chanting song, in which the others joined at intervals. After this it would seem that they turned in for the night, for no further sound came from their direction, and the whispering stillness became more and more profound.

The clockwork ticked steadily. The shrill hum of a mosquito explored the place and grew shriller in indignation at Woodhouse's ointment. Then the lantern went out and all the observatory was black.

Woodhouse shifted his position presently, when the slow movement of the telescope had carried it beyond the limits of his comfort.

He was watching a little group of stars in the Milky Way, in one of which his chief had seen or fancied a remarkable colour variability. It was not a part of the regular work for which the establishment existed, and for that reason perhaps Woodhouse was deeply interested. He must have forgotten things terrestrial. All his attention was concentrated upon the great blue circle of the telescope field—a circle powdered, so it seemed, with an innumerable multitude of stars, and all luminous against the blackness of its setting. As he watched he seemed to himself to become incorporeal, as if he too were floating in the ether of space. Infinitely remote was the faint red spot he was observing.

Suddenly the stars were blotted out. A flash of blackness passed, and they were visible again.

"Queer," said Woodhouse. "Must have been a bird."

The thing happened again, and immediately after the great tube shivered as though it had been struck. Then the dome of the observatory resounded with a series of thundering blows. The stars seemed to sweep aside as the telescope swung round and away from the slit in the roof.

"Great Scott!" cried Woodhouse. "What's this?"

Some huge, vague, black shape, with a flapping something like a wing, seemed to be struggling in the aperture of the roof. In another moment the slit was clear again, and the luminous haze of the Milky Way shone warm and bright.

The interior of the roof was perfectly black, and only a scraping sound marked the whereabouts of the unknown creature.

Woodhouse had scrambled from the seat to his feet. He was trembling violently and in a perspiration with the suddenness of the occurrence. Was the thing, whatever it was, inside or out? It was big, whatever else it might be. Something shot across the skylight, and the telescope swayed. He started violently and put his arm up. It was in the observatory, then, with him. It was clinging to the roof, apparently. What the devil was it? Could it see him?

He stood for perhaps a minute in a state of stupefaction. The beast, whatever it was, clawed at the interior of the dome, and then something flapped almost into his face, and he saw the momentary gleam of starlight on a skin like oiled leather. His water-bottle was knocked off his little table with a smash.

The sense of some strange bird-creature hovering a few yards from his face in the darkness was indescribably unpleasant to Woodhouse. As his thought returned he concluded that it must be some night-bird or large bat. At any risk he would see what it was, and pulling a match from his pocket, he tried to strike it on the telescope seat. There was a smoking streak of phosphorescent light, the match flared for a moment, and he saw a vast wing sweeping towards him, a gleam of grey-brown fur, and then he was struck in the face and the match knocked out of his hand. The blow was aimed at his temple, and a claw tore sideways down to his cheek. He reeled and fell, and he heard the extinguished lantern smash. Another blow followed as he fell. He was partly stunned, he felt his own warm blood stream out upon his face. Instinctively he felt his eyes had been struck at, and, turning over on his face to protect them, tried to crawl under the protection of the telescope.

He was struck again upon the back, and he heard his jacket rip, and then the thing hit the roof of the observatory. He edged as far as he could between the wooden seat and the eyepiece of the instrument, and turned his body round so that it was chiefly his feet that were exposed. With these he could at least kick. He was still in a mystified state. The strange beast banged about in the darkness, and presently clung to the telescope, making it sway and the gear rattle. Once it flapped near him, and he kicked out madly and felt a soft body with his feet. He was horribly scared now. It must be a big thing to swing the telescope like that. He saw for a moment the outline of a head black against the starlight, with sharply-pointed upstanding ears and a crest between them. It seemed to him to be as big as a mastiff's. Then he began to bawl out as loudly as he could for help.

At that the thing came down upon him again. As it did so his hand touched something beside him on the floor. He kicked out, and the next moment his ankle was gripped and held by a row of keen teeth. He yelled again, and tried to free his leg by kicking with the other. Then he realised he had the broken water-bottle at his hand, and, snatching it, he struggled into a sitting posture, and feeling in the darkness towards his foot, gripped a velvety ear, like the ear of a big cat. He had seized the water-bottle by its neck and brought it down with a shivering crash upon the head of the strange beast. He repeated the blow, and then stabbed and jobbed with the jagged end of it, in the darkness, where he judged the face might be.

The small teeth relaxed their hold, and at once Woodhouse pulled his leg free and kicked hard. He felt the sickening feel of fur and bone giving under his boot. There was a tearing bite at his arm, and he struck over it at the face, as he judged, and hit damp fur.

There was a pause; then he heard the sound of claws and the dragging of a heavy body away from him over the observatory floor. Then there was silence, broken only by his own sobbing breathing, and a sound like licking. Everything was black except the parallelogram of the blue skylight with the luminous dust of stars, against which the end of the telescope now appeared in silhouette. He waited, as it seemed, an interminable time.

Was the thing coming on again? He felt in his trouser-pocket for some matches, and found one remaining. He tried to strike this, but the floor was wet, and it spat and went out. He cursed. He could not see where the door was situated. In his struggle he had quite lost his bearings. The strange beast, disturbed by the splutter of the match, began to move again. "Time!" called Woodhouse, with a sudden gleam of mirth, but the thing was not coming at him again. He must have hurt it, he thought, with the broken bottle. He felt a dull pain in his ankle. Probably he was bleeding there. He wondered if it would support him if he tried to stand up. The night outside was very still. There was no sound of any one moving. The sleepy fools had not heard those wings battering upon the dome, nor his shouts. It was no good wasting strength in shouting. The monster flapped its wings and startled him into a defensive attitude. He hit his elbow against the seat, and it fell over with a crash. He cursed this, and then he cursed the darkness.

Suddenly the oblong patch of starlight seemed to sway to and fro. Was he going to faint? It would never do to faint. He clenched his fists and set his teeth to hold himself together. Where had the door got to? It occurred to him he could get his bearings by the stars visible through the skylight. The patch of stars he saw was in Sagittarius and south-eastward; the door was north—or was it north by west? He tried to think. If he could get the door open he might retreat. It might be the thing was wounded. The suspense was beastly. "Look here!" he said, "if you don't come on, I shall come at you."

Then the thing began clambering up the side of the observatory, and he saw its black outline gradually blot out the skylight. Was it in retreat? He forgot about the door, and watched as the dome shifted and creaked. Somehow he did not feel very frightened or excited now. He felt a curious sinking sensation inside him. The sharply-defined patch of light, with the black form moving across it, seemed to be growing smaller and smaller. That was curious. He began to feel very thirsty, and yet he did not feel inclined to get anything to drink. He seemed to be sliding down a long funnel.

He felt a burning sensation in his throat, and then he perceived it was broad daylight, and that one of the Dyak servants was looking at him with a curious expression. Then there was the top of Thaddy's face upside down. Funny fellow Thaddy, to go about like that! Then he grasped the situation better, and perceived that his head was on Thaddy's knee, and Thaddy was giving him brandy. And then he saw the eyepiece of the telescope with a lot of red smears on it. He began to remember.

"You've made this observatory in a pretty mess," said Thaddy.

The Dyak boy was beating up an egg in brandy. Woodhouse took this and sat up. He felt a sharp twinge of pain. His ankle was tied up, so were his arm and the side of his face. The smashed glass, red-stained, lay about the floor, the telescope seat was overturned, and by the opposite wall was a dark pool. The door was open, and he saw the grey summit of the mountain against a brilliant background of blue sky.

"Pah!" said Woodhouse. "Who's been killing calves here? Take me out of it."

Then he remembered the Thing, and the fight he had had with it.

"What *was* it?" he said to Thaddy—"the Thing I fought with?"

"*You* know that best," said Thaddy. "But, anyhow, don't worry yourself now about it. Have some more to drink."

Thaddy, however, was curious enough, and it was a hard struggle between duty and inclination to keep Woodhouse quiet until he was decently put away in bed, and had slept upon the copious dose of meat-extract Thaddy considered advisable. They then talked it over together.

"It was," said Woodhouse, "more like a big bat than anything else in the world. It had sharp, short ears, and soft fur, and its wings were leathery. Its teeth were little, but devilish sharp, and its jaw could not have been very strong or else it would have bitten through my ankle."

"It has pretty nearly," said Thaddy.

"It seemed to me to hit out with its claws pretty freely. That is about as much as I know about the beast. Our conversation was intimate, so to speak, and yet not confidential."

"The Dyak chaps talk about a Big Colugo, a Klang-utang—whatever that may be. It does not often attack man, but I suppose you made it nervous. They say there is a Big Colugo and a Little Colugo, and a something else that sounds like gobble. They all fly about at night. For my own part I know there are flying foxes and flying lemurs about here; but they are none of them very big beasts."

"There are more things in heaven and earth," said Woodhouse,—and Thaddy groaned at the quotation,—"and more particularly in the forests of Borneo, than are dreamt of in our philosophies. On the whole, if the Borneo fauna is going to disgorge any more of its novelties upon me, I should prefer that it did so when I was not occupied in the observatory at night and alone."

The Triumphs of a Taxidermist

HERE ARE SOME of the secrets of taxidermy. They were told me by the taxidermist in a mood of elation. He told me them in the time between the first glass of whiskey and the fourth, when a man is no longer cautious and yet not drunk. We sat in his den together; his library it was, his sitting and his eating room—separated by a bead curtain, so far as the sense of sight went, from the noisome den where he plied his trade.

He sat on a deck chair, and when he was not tapping refractory bits of coal with them, he kept his feet—on which he wore, after the manner of sandals, the holey relics of a pair of carpet slippers—out of the way upon the mantel-piece, among the glass eyes. And his trousers, by-the-by—though they have nothing to do with his triumphs—were a most horrible yellow plaid, such as they made when our fathers wore side-whiskers and there were crinolines in the land. Further, his hair was black, his face rosy, and his eye a fiery brown; and his coat was chiefly of grease upon a basis of velveteen. And his pipe had a bowl of china showing the Graces, and his spectacles were always askew, the left eye glaring nakedly at you, small and penetrating; the right, seen through a glass darkly, magnified and mild. Thus his discourse ran: "There never was a man who could stuff like me, Bellows, never. I have stuffed elephants and I have stuffed moths, and the things have looked all the livelier and better for it. And I have stuffed human beings—chiefly amateur ornithologists. But I stuffed a nigger once.

"No, there is no law against it. I made him with all his fingers out and used him as a hat-rack, but that fool Homersby got up a quarrel with him late one night and spoilt him. That was before your time. It is hard to get skins, or I would have another.

"Unpleasant? I don't see it. Seems to me taxidermy is a promising third course to burial or cremation. You could keep all your dear ones by you. Bric-à-brac of that sort stuck about the house would be as good as most company, and much less expensive. You might have them fitted up with clockwork to do things.

"Of course they would have to be varnished, but they need not shine more than lots of people do naturally. Old Manningtree's bald head—Anyhow, you could talk to them without interruption. Even aunts. There is a great future before taxidermy, depend upon it. There is fossils again—"

He suddenly became silent.

"No, I don't think I ought to tell you that." He sucked at his pipe thoughtfully. "Thanks, yes. Not too much water."

"Of course, what I tell you now will go no further. You know I have made some dodos and a great auk? No! Evidently you are an amateur at taxidermy. My dear fellow, half the great auks in the world are about as genuine as the handkerchief of Saint Veronica, as the Holy Coat of Treves. We make 'em of grebes' feathers and the like. And the great auk's eggs too!"

"Good heavens!"

"Yes, we make them out of fine porcelain. I tell you it is worth while. They fetch—one fetched £300 only the other day. That one was really genuine, I believe, but of course one is never certain. It is very fine work, and afterwards you have to get them dusty, for no one who owns one of these precious eggs has ever the temerity to clean the thing. That's the beauty of the business. Even if they suspect an egg they do not like to examine it too closely. It's such brittle capital at the best.

"You did not know that taxidermy rose to heights like that. My boy, it has risen higher. I have rivalled the hands of Nature herself. One of the *genuine* great auks—" his voice fell to a whisper—"one of the *genuine* great auks *was made by me.*

"No. You must study ornithology, and find out which it is yourself. And what is more, I have been approached by a syndicate of dealers to stock one of the unexplored skerries to the north of Iceland with specimens. I may—someday. But I have another little thing in hand just now. Ever heard of the dinornis?

"It is one of those big birds recently extinct in New Zealand. 'Moa' is its common name, so-called because extinct; there is no moa now. See? Well, they have got bones of it, and from some of the marshes even feathers and dried bits of skin. Now, I am going to—well, there is no need to make any bones about it—going to *forge* a complete stuffed moa. I know a chap out there who will pretend to make the find in a kind of antiseptic swamp, and say he stuffed it at once, as it threatened to fall to pieces. The feathers are peculiar, but I have got a simply lovely way of dodging up singed bits of ostrich plume. Yes, that is the new smell you noticed. They can only discover the fraud with a microscope, and they will hardly care to pull a nice specimen to bits for that.

"In this way, you see, I give my little push in the advancement of science."

"But all this is merely imitating Nature. I have done more than that in my time. I have—beaten her."

He took his feet down from the mantel-board, and leant over confidentially towards me. "I have *created* birds," he said in a low voice. "*New* birds. Improvements. Like no birds that was ever seen before."

He resumed his attitude during an impressive silence.

"Enrich the universe; *rath*-er. Some of the birds I made were new kinds of humming-birds, and very beautiful little things, but some of them were simply rum. The rummest, I think, was the *Anomalopteryx Jejuna. Jejunus-a-um*—empty — so-called because there was really nothing in it; a thoroughly empty bird—except for stuffing. Old Javvers has the thing now, and I suppose he is almost as proud of it as I am. It is a masterpiece, Bellows. It has all the silly clumsiness of your pelican, all the solemn want of dignity of your parrot, all the gaunt ungainliness of a flamingo, with all the extravagant chromatic conflict of a mandarin duck. *Such* a bird. I made it out of the skeletons of a stork and a toucan and a job lot of feathers. Taxidermy of that kind is just pure joy, Bellows, to a real artist in the art.

"How did I come to make it? Simple enough, as all great inventions are. One of those young genii who write us Science Notes in the papers got hold of a German pamphlet about the birds of New Zealand, and translated some of it by means of a dictionary and his mother-wit—he must have been one of a very large family with a small mother—and he got mixed between the living apteryx and the extinct anomalopteryx; talked about a bird five feet high, living in the jungles of the North Island, rare, shy, specimens difficult to obtain, and so on. Javvers, who even for a collector, is a miraculously ignorant man, read these paragraphs, and swore he would have the thing at any price. Raided the dealers with inquiries. It shows what a man can do by persistence—will-power. Here was a bird-collector swearing he would have a specimen of a bird that did not exist, that never had existed, and which for very shame of its own profane ungainliness, probably would not exist now if it could help itself. And he got it. *He got it.*

"Have some more whiskey, Bellows?" said the taxidermist, rousing himself from a transient contemplation of the mysteries of will-power and the collecting turn of mind. And, replenished, he proceeded to tell me of how he concocted a most attractive mermaid, and how an itinerant preacher, who could not get an audience because of it, smashed it because it was idolatry, or worse, at Burslem Wakes. But as the conversation of all the parties to this transaction, creator, would-be preserver, and destroyer, was uniformly unfit for publication, this cheerful incident must still remain unprinted.

The reader, unacquainted with the dark ways of the collector, may perhaps be inclined to doubt my taxidermist; but so far as great auks' eggs, and the bogus stuffed birds are concerned, I find that he has the confirmation of distinguished ornithological writers. And the note about the New Zealand bird certainly appeared in a morning paper of unblemished reputation, for the taxidermist keeps a copy and has shown it to me.

A Deal in Ostriches

"TALKING OF THE prices of birds, I've seen an ostrich that cost three hundred pounds," said the taxidermist, recalling his youth of travel. "Three hundred pounds!"

He looked at me over his spectacles. "I've seen another that was refused at four.

"No," he said, "it wasn't any fancy points. They was just plain ostriches. A little off colour, too—owing to dietary. And there wasn't any particular restriction of the demand either. You'd have thought five ostriches would have ruled cheap on an East Indiaman. But the point was, one of 'em had swallowed a diamond.

"The chap it got it off was Sir Mohini Padishah, a tremendous swell, a Piccadilly swell you might say up to the neck of him, and then an ugly black head and a whopping turban, with this diamond in it. The blessed bird pecked suddenly and had it, and when the chap made a fuss it realised it had done wrong, I suppose, and went and mixed itself with the others to preserve its *incog.* It all happened in a minute. I was among the first to arrive, and there was this heathen going over his gods, and two sailors and the man who had charge of the birds laughing fit to split. It was a rummy way of losing a jewel, come to think of it. The man in charge hadn't been about just at the moment, so that he didn't know which bird it was. Clean lost, you see. I didn't feel half sorry, to tell you the truth. The beggar had been swaggering over his blessed diamond ever since he came aboard.

"A thing like that goes from stem to stern of a ship in no time. Every one was talking about it. Padishah went below to hide his feelings. At dinner—he pigged at a table by himself, him and two other Hindoos—the captain kind of jeered at him about it, and he got very excited. He turned round and talked into my ear. He would not buy the birds; he would have his diamond. He demanded his rights as a British subject. His diamond must be found. He was firm upon that. He would appeal to the House of Lords. The man in charge of the birds was one of those wooden-headed chaps you can't get a new idea into anyhow. He refused any proposal to interfere with the birds by way of medicine. His instructions were to feed them so-and-so and treat them so-and-so, and it was as much as his place was worth not to feed them so-and-so, and treat them so-and-so. Padishah had wanted a stomach-pump—though you can't do that to a bird, you know. This Padishah was full of bad law, like most of these blessed Bengalis, and talked of having a lien on the birds, and so forth. But an old boy, who said his son was a London barrister, argued that what a bird swallowed became *ipso facto* part of the bird, and that Padishah's only remedy lay in an action for damages, and even then it might be possible to show contributory negligence. He hadn't any right of way about an ostrich that didn't belong to him. That upset Padishah extremely, the more so as most of us expressed an opinion that that was the reasonable view.

There wasn't any lawyer aboard to settle the matter, so we all talked pretty free. At last, after Aden, it appears that he came round to the general opinion, and went privately to the man in charge and made an offer for all five ostriches.

"The next morning there was a fine shindy at breakfast. The man hadn't any authority to deal with the birds, and nothing on earth would induce him to sell; but it seems he told Padishah that a Eurasian named Potter had already made him an offer, and on that Padishah denounced Potter before us all. But I think the most of us thought it rather smart of Potter, and I know that when Potter said that he'd wired at Aden to London to buy the birds, and would have an answer at Suez, I cursed pretty richly at a lost opportunity.

"At Suez, Padishah gave way to tears—actual wet tears—when Potter became the owner of the birds, and offered him two hundred and fifty right off for the five, being more than two hundred per cent. on what Potter had given. Potter said he'd be hanged if he parted with a feather of them—that he meant to kill them off one by one, and find the diamond; but afterwards, thinking it over, he relented a little. He was a gambling hound, was this Potter, a little queer at cards, and this kind of prize-packet business must have suited him down to the ground. Anyhow, he offered, for a lark, to sell the birds separately to separate people by auction at a starting price of £80 for a bird. But one of them, he said, he meant to keep for luck.

"You must understand this diamond was a valuable one—a little Jew chap, a diamond merchant, who was with us, had put it at three or four thousand when Padishah had shown it to him—and this idea of an ostrich gamble caught on. Now it happened that I'd been having a few talks on general subjects with the man who looked after these ostriches, and quite incidentally he'd said one of the birds was ailing, and he fancied it had indigestion. It had one feather in its tail almost all white, by which I knew it, and so when, next day, the auction started with it, I capped Padishah's eighty-five by ninety. I fancy I was a bit too sure and eager with my bid, and some of the others spotted the fact that I was in the know. And Padishah went for that particular bird like an irresponsible lunatic. At last the Jew diamond merchant got it for £175, and Padishah said £180 just after the hammer came down—so Potter declared. At any rate, the Jew merchant secured it, and there and then he got a gun and shot it. Potter made a Hades of a fuss because he said it would injure the sale of the other three, and Padishah, of course, behaved like an idiot; but all of us were very much excited. I can tell you I was precious glad when that dissection was over, and no diamond had turned up—precious glad. I'd gone to one-forty on that particular bird myself.

"The little Jew was like most Jews—he didn't make any great fuss over bad luck; but Potter declined to go on with the auction until it was understood that the goods could not be delivered until the sale was over. The little Jew wanted to argue that the case was exceptional, and as the discussion ran pretty even, the thing was postponed until the next morning. We had a lively dinner-table that evening, I can tell you, but in the end Potter got his way, since it would stand to reason he would be safer if he stuck to all the birds, and that we owed him some consideration for his sportsman-like behaviour. And the old gentleman whose son was a lawyer said he'd been thinking the thing over and that it was very doubtful if, when a bird had been opened and the diamond recovered, it ought not to be handed back to the proper owner. I remember I suggested it came under the laws of treasure-trove—which was really the truth of the matter. There was a hot argument, and we settled it was certainly foolish to kill the bird on board the ship. Then the old gentleman, going at large through his legal talk, tried to make out the sale was a lottery and illegal, and appealed to the captain; but Potter said he sold the birds *as* ostriches. He didn't want to sell any diamonds, he said, and didn't offer that as an inducement. The three birds he put up, to the best of his knowledge and belief, did *not* contain a diamond. It was in the one he kept—so he hoped.

"Prices ruled high next day all the same. The fact that now there were four chances instead of five of course caused a rise. The blessed birds averaged 227, and, oddly enough, this Padishah didn't secure one of 'em—not one. He made too much shindy, and when he ought to have been bidding he was talking about liens, and, besides, Potter was a bit down on him. One fell to a quiet little officer chap, another to the little Jew, and the third was syndicated by the engineers. And then Potter seemed suddenly sorry for having sold them, and said he'd flung away a clear thousand pounds, and that very likely he'd draw a blank, and that he always had been a fool, but when I went and had a bit of a talk to him, with the idea of getting him to hedge on his last chance, I found he'd already sold the bird he'd reserved to a political chap that was on board, a chap who'd been studying Indian morals and social questions in his vacation. That last was the three hundred pounds bird. Well, they landed three of the blessed creatures at Brindisi—though the old gentleman said it was a breach of the Customs regulations—and Potter and Padishah landed too. The Hindoo seemed half mad as he saw his blessed diamond going this way and that, so to speak. He kept on saying he'd get an injunction—he had injunction on the brain—and giving his name and address to the chaps who'd bought the birds, so that they'd know where to send the diamond. None of them wanted his name and address, and none of them would give their own. It was a fine row I can tell you—on the platform. They all went off by different trains. I came on to Southampton, and there I saw the last of the birds, as I came ashore; it was the one the engineers bought, and it was standing up near the bridge, in a kind of crate, and looking as leggy and silly a setting for a valuable diamond as ever you saw—if it *was* a setting for a valuable diamond.

"*How did it end?* Oh! like that. Well—perhaps. Yes, there's one more thing that may throw light on it. A week or so after landing I was down Regent Street doing a bit of shopping, and who should I see arm-in-arm and having a purple time of it but Padishah and Potter. If you come to think of it—

"Yes. *I've* thought that. Only, you see, there's no doubt the diamond was real. And Padishah was an eminent Hindoo. I've seen his name in the papers—often. But whether the bird swallowed the diamond certainly is another matter, as you say."

The Rajah's Treasure

BETWEEN JEHUN AND Bimabur on the Himalayan slopes, and between the jungles and the higher country where the pines and deodars are gathered together, ruled the petty Rajah, of whose wonderful treasure I am telling. Very great was the treasure, people said, for the Rajah had prospered all his days. He had found Mindapore a village, and, behold! it was a city. Below his fort of unhewn stone the flat-roofed huts of mud had multiplied; and now there sprang up houses with upstairs rooms, and the place which had once boasted no more than one buniah man, engendered a bazaar in the midst of it, as a fat oyster secretes a pearl. And the Holy Place up the river prospered, and the road up the passes was made safe. Merchants and fakirs multiplied about the wells, men came and went, twice even white men from the plain on missions to the people over beyond the deodars, and the streets of the town were ever denser with poultry and children, and little dogs dyed yellow, and with all the multitudinous rich odours of human increase. As at last, at the crown of his prosperity, this legend of his treasures began.

He was a portly, yellow-faced man, with a long black beard, now steadily growing grey, thick lips, and shifty eyes. He was pious, very pious in his daily routine, and swift and unaccountable in his actions. None dared withstand him to his face, even in little things. Golam Shah, his vizier, was but a servant, a carrier of orders; and Samud Singh, his master of horse, but a driller of soldiers. They were tools, he would tell them outright in his pride of power, staves in his hand that he could break at his will. He was childless. And his cousin, the youth Azim Khan, feared him, and only in the remotest recesses of his heart dared to wish the Rajah would presently die and make a way for the cyons.

It would be hard to say when first the rumour spread that the Rajah of little Mindapore was making a hoard. None knew how it began or where. Perhaps from merchants of whom he had bought. It began long before the days of the safe. It was said that rubies had been bought and hidden away; and then not only rubies, but ornaments of gold, and then pearls, and diamonds from Golconda, and all manner of precious stones. Even the Deputy-Commissioner at Allapore heard of it. At last the story re-entered the palace at Mindapore itself, and Azim Khan, who was the Rajah's cousin and his heir, and nominally his commander-in-chief, and Golam Shah, the chief minister, talked it over one with another in a tentative way.

"He has something new," said Golam Shah, querulously; "he has something new, and he is keeping it from me."

Azim Khan watched him cunningly. "I have told you what I have heard," he said. "For my own part I know nothing."

"He goes to and fro musing and humming to himself," said Golam, meditatively, "as one who thinks of a pleasure."

"More rubies, they are saying," said Azim, dreamily, and repeated, as if for his own pleasure, "Rubies." For Azim was the heir.

"Especially is it since that Englishman came," said Golam, "three months ago. A big old man, not wrinkled as an old man should be, but red, and with red hair streaking his grey, and with a tight skin and a big body sticking out before. So. An elephant of a man, a great quivering mud-bank of a man, who laughed mightily, so that the people stopped and listened in the street. He came, he laughed, and as he went away we heard them laugh together—"

"Well?" said Azim.

"He was a diamond merchant, perhaps—or a dealer in rubies. Do Englishmen deal in such things?"

"Would I had seen him!" said Azim.

"He took gold away," said Golam.

Both were silent for a space, and the purring noise of the wheel of the upper well, and the chatter of voices about it rising and falling, made a pleasant sound in the air. "Since the Englishman went," said Golam, "he has been different. He hides something from me—something in his robe. Rubies! What else can it be?"

"He has not buried it?" said Azim.

"He will. Then he will want to dig it up again and look at it," said Golam, for he was a man of experience. "I go softly. Sometimes almost I come upon him. Then he starts—"

"He grows old and nervous," said Azim, and there was a pause.

"Before the English came," said Golam, looking at the rings upon his fingers, as he recurred to his constant preoccupation; "there were no Rajahs nervous and old."

That, I say, was even before the coming of the safe. It came in a packing case. Such a case it was as had never been seen before on all the slopes of the Himalayan mountains, it was an elephant's burden even on the plain. It was days drawing nearer and nearer. At Allapore crowds went to see it pass upon the railway. Afterwards elephants and then a great multitude of men dragged it up the hills. And this great case being opened in the Hall of Audience revealed within itself a monstrous iron box, like no other box that had ever come to the city. It had been made, so the story went, by necromancers in England, expressly to the order of the Rajah, that he might keep his treasure therein and sleep in peace. It was so hard that the hardest files powdered upon its corners, and so strong that cannon fired point-blank at it would have produced no effect upon it. And it locked with a magic lock. There was a word, and none knew the word but the Rajah. With that word, and a little key that hung about his neck, one could open the lock; but without it none could do so.

The Rajah caused this safe to be built into the wall of his palace in a little room beyond the Hall of Audience. He superintended the building up of it with jealous eyes. And thereafter he would go thither day by day, once at least every day, coming back with brighter eyes. "He goes to count his treasure," said Golam Shah, standing beside the empty daïs.

And in those days it was that the Rajah began to change. He who had been cunning and subtle became choleric and outspoken. His judgment grew harsh, and a taint that seemed to all about him to be assuredly the taint of avarice crept into his acts. Moreover, which inclined Golam Shah to hopefulness, he seemed to take a dislike to Azim Khan. Once indeed he made a kind of speech in the Hall of Audience. Therein he declared many times over in a peculiarly husky voice, husky yet full of conviction, that Azim Khan was not worth a half anna, not worth a half anna to any human soul.

In these latter days of the Rajah's decline, moreover, when merchants came, he would go aside with them secretly into the little room, and speak low, so that those in the Hall of Audience, howsoever they strained their ears, could hear nothing of his speech. These things Golam Shah and Azim Khan and Samud Singh, who had joined their councils, treasured in their hearts.

"It is true about the treasure," said Azim; "they talked of it round the well of the travellers, even the merchants from Tibet had heard the tale, and had come this way with jewels of price, and afterwards they went secretly telling no one." And ever and again, it was said, came a negro mute from the plains, with secret parcels for the Rajah. "Another stone," was the rumour that went the round of the city.

"The bee makes hoards," said Azim Khan, the Rajah's heir, sitting in the upper chamber of Golam Shah. "Therefore, we will wait awhile." For Azim was more coward than traitor.

At last there were men in the Deccan even who could tell you particulars of the rubies and precious stones that the Rajah had gathered together. But so circumspect was the Rajah that Azim Khan and Golam Shah had never even set eyes on the glittering heaps that they knew were accumulating in the safe.

The Rajah always went into the little room alone, and even then he locked the door of the little room—it had a couple of locks—before he went to the safe and used the magic word. How all the ministers and officers and guards listened and looked at one another as the door of the room behind the curtain closed!

The Rajah changed indeed, in these days, not only in the particulars of his rule, but in his appearance. "He is growing old. How fast he grows old! The time is almost ripe," whispered Samud Singh. The Rajah's hand became tremulous, his step was now sometimes unsteady, and his memory curiously defective. He would come back out from the treasure-room, and his hand would tighten fiercely on the curtain, and he would stumble on the steps of the daïs. "His eyesight fails," said Golam. "See!—His turban is askew. He is sleepy even in the forenoon, before the heat of the day. His judgments are those of a child."

It was a painful sight to see a man so suddenly old and enfeebled still ruling men.

"He may go on yet, a score of years," said Golam Shah.

"Should a ruler hoard riches," said Shere Ali, in the guardroom, "and leave his soldiers unpaid?" That was the beginning of the end.

It was the thought of the treasure won over the soldiers, even as it did the mollahs and the eunuchs. Why had the Rajah not buried it in some unthinkable place, as his father had done before him, and killed the diggers with his hand? "He has hoarded," said Samud, with a chuckle,—for the old Rajah had once pulled his beard,—"only to pay for his own undoing." And in order to insure confidence, Golam Shah went beyond the truth perhaps, and gave a sketchy account of the treasures to this man and that, even as a casual eyewitness might do.

Then, suddenly and swiftly, the palace revolution was accomplished. When the lonely old Rajah was killed, a shot was to be fired from the harem lattice, bugles were to be blown, and the sepoys were to turn out in the square before the palace, and fire a volley in the air. The murder was done in the dark save for a little red lamp that burnt in the corner. Azim knelt on the body and held up the wet beard, and cut the throat wide and deep to make sure. It was so easy! Why had he waited so long? And then, with his hands covered with warm blood, he sprang up eagerly—Rajah at last! —and followed Golam and Samud and the eunuchs down the long, faintly moonlit passage, towards the Hall of Audience.

As they did so, the crack of a rifle sounded far away, and after a pause came the first awakening noises of the town. One of the eunuchs had an iron bar, and Samud carried a pistol in his hand. He fired into the locks of the treasure-room, and wrecked them, and the eunuch smashed the door in. Then they all rushed in together, none standing aside for Azim. It was dark, and the second eunuch went reluctantly to get a torch, in fear lest his fellow murderers should open the safe in his absence.

But he need have had no fear. The cardinal event of that night is the triumphant vindication of the advertised merits of Chobbs' unrivalled safes. The tumult that occurred between the Mindapore sepoys and the people need not concern us. The people loved not the new Rajah—let that suffice. The conspirators got the key from round the dead Rajah's neck, and tried a multitude of the magic words of the English that Samud Singh knew, even such words as "Kemup" and "Gorblimey"—in vain.

In the morning, the safe in the treasure-room remained intact and defiant, the woodwork about it smashed to splinters, and great chunks of stone knocked out of the wall, dents abundantly scattered over its impregnable door, and a dust of files below. And the shifty Golam had to explain the matter to the soldiers and mollahs as best he could. This was an extremely difficult thing to do, because in no kind of business is prompt cash so necessary as in the revolutionary line.

The state of affairs for the next few days in Mindapore was exceedingly strained. One fact stands out prominently, that Azim Khan was hopelessly feeble. The soldiers would not at first believe in the exemplary integrity of the safe, and a deputation insisted in the most occidental manner in verifying the new Rajah's statements. Moreover, the populace clamoured, and then by a naked man running, came the alarming intelligence that the new Deputy-Commissioner at Allapore was coming headlong and with soldiers to verify the account of the revolution Golam Shah and Samud Singh had sent him in the name of Azim.

The new Deputy-Commissioner was a raw young man, partly obscured by a pith helmet, and chock full of zeal and the desire for distinction; and he had heard of the treasure. He was going, he said, to sift the matter thoroughly. On the arrival of this distressing intelligence there was a hasty and informal council of state (at which Azim was not present), a counter-revolution was arranged, and all that Azim ever learnt of it was the sound of a footfall behind him, and the cold touch of a pistol barrel on the neck.

When the Commissioner arrived, that dexterous statesman, Golam Shah, and that honest soldier, Samud Singh, were ready to receive him, and they had two corpses, several witnesses, and a neat little story. In addition to Azim they had shot an unpopular officer of the Mindapore sepoys. They told the Commissioner how Azim had plotted against the Rajah and raised a military revolt, and how the people, who loved the old Rajah, even as Golam Shah and Samud Singh loved him, had quelled the revolt, and how peace was restored again. And Golam explained how Azim had fought for life even in the Hall of Audience, and how he, Golam, had been wounded in the struggle, and how Samud had shot Azim with his own hand.

And the Deputy-Commissioner, being weak in his dialect, had swallowed it all. All round the Deputy-Commissioner, in the minds of the people, the palace, and the city, hung the true story of the case, as it seemed to Golam Shah, like an avalanche ready to fall; and yet the Deputy-Commissioner did not learn of it for four days. And Golam and Samud went to and fro, whispering and pacifying, promising to get at the treasure as soon as the Deputy-Commissioner could be got out of the way. And as they went to and fro so also the report went to and fro—that Golam and Samud had opened the safe and hidden the treasure, and closed and locked it again; and bright eyes watched them curiously and hungrily even as they had watched the Rajah in the days that were gone.

"This city is no longer an abiding place for you and me," said Golam Shah, in a moment of clear insight. "They are mad about this treasure. Golconda would not satisfy them."

The Deputy-Commissioner, when he heard their story, did indeed make knowing inquiries (as knowing as the knowingness of the English goes) in order to show himself not too credulous; but he elicited nothing. He had heard tales of treasure, had the Commissioner, and of a great box? So had Golam and Samud, but where it was they could not tell. They too had certainly heard tales of treasure—many tales indeed. Perhaps there *was* treasure.

Had the Deputy-Commissioner had the scientific turn of mind, he would have observed that a strong smell of gunpowder still hung about the Audience Chamber, more than was explained by the narrative told him; and had he explored the adjacent apartments, he would presently have discovered the small treasure-room with its smashed locks, and the ceiling now dependent ruins, and amid the ruins the safe, bulging perilously from the partly collapsed walls, but still unconquered, and with its treasures unexplored. Also it is a fact that Golam Shah's bandaged hand was not the consequence of heroism in combat, but of certain private blasting operations too amateurishly prosecuted.

So you have the situation: Deputy-Commissioner installed in the palace, sending incorrect information to headquarters and awaiting instructions, the safe as safe as ever; assistant conspirators grumbling louder and louder; and Golam and Samud getting more and more desperate lest this voice should reach the Deputy's ears.

Then came the night when the Commissioner heard a filing and a tapping, and being a brave man, rose and went forthwith, alone and very quietly, across the Hall of Audience, pistol in hand, in search of the sound. Across the Hall a light came from an open door that had been hidden in the day by a curtain. Stopping silently in the darkness of the outer apartment, he looked into the treasure-room. And there stood Golam with his arm in a sling, holding a lantern, while Samud fumbled with pieces of wire and some little keys. They were without boots, but otherwise they were dressed ready for a journey.

The Deputy-Commissioner was, for a Government official, an exceedingly quick-witted man. He slipped back in the darkness again, and within five minutes, Golam and Samud, still fumbling, heard footsteps hurrying across the Hall of Audience, and saw a flicker of light. Out went their lantern, with a groan because of a bandaged arm, but it was too late. In another moment Lieutenant Earl, in pyjamas and boots, but with a brace of revolvers and a couple of rifles behind him, stood in the doorway of the treasure-room, and Golam and Samud were caught. Samud clicked his pistol and then threw it down, for it was three to one—Golam being not only a bandaged man, but fundamentally a man of peace.

When the intelligence of this treachery filtered from the palace into the town, there was an outbreak of popular feeling, and a dozen officious persons set out to tell the Deputy-Commissioner the true connection between Golam, Samud, and the death of the Rajah. The first to penetrate to the Deputy-Commissioner's presence was an angry fakir, from the colony that dwelt about the Holy place. And after a patient hearing the Deputy-Commissioner extracted the thread of the narrative from the fabric of curses in which the holy man presented it.

"This is most singular," said the Deputy-Commissioner to the Lieutenant, standing in the treasure-room (which looked as though the palace had been bombarded), and regarding the battered but still inviolable safe. "Here we seem to have the key of the whole position."

"Key!" said the Lieutenant. "It's the key they haven't got."

"Curious mingling of the new and the old," said the Deputy-Commissioner. "Patent safe—and a hoard."

"Send to Allapore and wire Chobbs, I suppose?" said the Lieutenant.

The Deputy-Commissioner signified that was his intention, and they set guards before and behind and all about the treasure-room, until the proper instructions about the lock should come.

So it was that the *Pax Britannica* solemnly took possession of the Rajah's hoard, and men in Simla heard the news, and envied that Deputy-Commissioner his adventure with all their hearts. For his promptitude and decision was a matter of praise, and they said that Mindapore would certainly be annexed and added to the district over which he ruled. Only a fat old man named MacTurk, living in Allapore, a big man with a noisy quivering laugh, and a secret trade with certain native potentates, did not hear the news, excepting only the news of the murder of the Rajah and the departure of the Deputy-Commissioner, for several days. He heard nothing of the disposition of the treasure—an unfortunate thing, since, among other things, he had sold the Rajah his safe, and may even have known the word by which the lock was opened.

The Deputy-Commissioner had theatrical tastes. These he gratified under the excuse that display was above all things necessary in dealing with Orientals. He imprisoned his four malefactors theatrically, and when the instructions came from Chobbs he had the safe lugged into the Hall of Audience, in order to open it with more effect. The Commissioner sat on the daïs, while the engineer worked at the safe on the crimson steps.

In the central space was stretched a large white cloth. It reminded the Deputy-Commissioner of a picture he had seen of Alexander at Damascus receiving the treasures of Darius.

"It is gold," said one bystander to another. "There was a sound of chinking as they brought the safe in. My brother was among those who hauled."

The engineer clicked the lock. Every eye in the Hall of Audience grew brighter and keener, excepting the eyes of the Deputy-Commissioner. He felt the dignity of his responsibilities, and sat upon the daïs looking as much like the *Pax Britannica* as possible.

"Holy Smoke!" said the engineer, and slammed the safe again. A murmur of exclamations ran round the hall. Every one was asking every one else what they had seen.

"An asp!" said some one.

The Deputy-Commissioner lost his imperturbability. "What is it?" he said, springing to his feet. The engineer leant across the safe and whispered two words, something indistinct and with a blasphemous adjective in front.

"*What?*" said the Deputy-Commissioner, sharply.

"Glass!" said the engineer, in a bitter whisper. "Broken bottles. 'Undreds!"

"Let me see!" said the Deputy-Commissioner, losing all his dignity.

"Scotch, if I'm not mistaken," said the engineer, sniffing curiously.

"Curse it!" said the Deputy-Commissioner, and looked up to meet a multitude of ironical eyes. "Er—

"The assembly is dismissed," said the Deputy-Commissioner.

"What a *fool* he must have looked!" wheezed MacTurk, who did not like the Deputy-Commissioner. "What a *fool* he must have looked!

"Simple enough," said MacTurk, "when you know how it came about."

"But how did it come about?" asked the station-master.

"Secret drinking," said MacTurk. "Bourbon whiskey. I taught him how to take it myself. But he didn't dare let on that he was doing it, poor old chap! Mindapore's one of the most fanatically Mahometan states in the hills you see. And he always was a secretive kind of chap, and given to doing things by himself. So he got that safe to hide it in, and keep the bottles. Broke 'em up to pack, I s'pose, when it got too full. Lord! I might ha' known. When people spoke of his treasure—I never thought of putting that and the safe and the Bourbon together! But how plain it is! And *what* a sell for Parkinson. Pounded glass! The accumulation of years! Lord!—I'd 'a' given a couple of stone off my weight to see him open that safe!"

The Story of Davidson's Eyes

I

The transitory mental aberration of Sidney Davidson, remarkable enough in itself, is still more remarkable if Wade's explanation is to be credited. It sets one dreaming of the oddest possibilities of intercommunication in the future, of spending an intercalary five minutes on the other side of the world, or being watched in our most secret operations by unsuspected eyes. It happened that I was the immediate witness of Davidson's seizure, and so it falls naturally to me to put the story upon paper.

When I say that I was the immediate witness of his seizure, I mean that I was the first on the scene. The thing happened at the Harlow Technical College just beyond the Highgate Archway. He was alone in the larger laboratory when the thing happened. I was in the smaller room, where the balances are, writing up some notes. The thunderstorm had completely upset my work, of course. It was just after one of the louder peals that I thought I heard some glass smash in the other room. I stopped writing, and turned round to listen. For a moment I heard nothing; the hail was playing the devil's tattoo on the corrugated zinc of the roof. Then came another sound, a smash—no doubt of it this time. Something heavy had been knocked off the bench. I jumped up at once and went and opened the door leading into the big laboratory.

I was surprised to hear a queer sort of laugh, and saw Davidson standing unsteadily in the middle of the room, with a dazzled look on his face. My first impression was that he was drunk. He did not notice me. He was clawing out at something invisible a yard in front of his face. He put out his hand, slowly, rather hesitatingly, and then clutched nothing. "What's come to it?" he said. He held up his hands to his face, fingers spread out. "Great Scott!" he said. The thing happened three or four years ago, when every one swore by that personage. Then he began raising his feet clumsily, as though he had expected to find them glued to the floor.

"Davidson!" cried I. "What's the matter with you?" He turned round in my direction and looked about for me. He looked over me and at me and on either side of me, without the slightest sign of seeing me. "Waves," he said; "and a remarkably neat schooner. I'd swear that was Bellows's voice. *Hullo!*" He shouted suddenly at the top of his voice.

I thought he was up to some foolery. Then I saw littered about his feet the shattered remains of the best of our electrometers. "What's up, man?" said I. "You've smashed the electrometer!"

"Bellows again!" said he. "Friends left, if my hands are gone. Something about electrometers. Which way *are* you, Bellows?" He suddenly came staggering towards me. "The damned stuff cuts like butter," he said. He walked straight into the bench and recoiled. "None so buttery, that!" he said, and stood swaying.

I felt scared. "Davidson," said I, "what on earth's come over you?"

He looked round him in every direction. "I could swear that was Bellows. Why don't you show yourself like a man, Bellows?"

It occurred to me that he must be suddenly struck blind. I walked round the table and laid my hand upon his arm. I never saw a man more startled in my life. He jumped away from me, and came round into an attitude of self-defence, his face fairly distorted with terror. "Good God!" he cried. "What was that?"

"It's I—Bellows. Confound it, Davidson!"

He jumped when I answered him and stared—how can I express it?—right through me. He began talking, not to me, but to himself. "Here in broad daylight on a clear beach. Not a place to hide in." He looked about him wildly. "Here! I'm *off*." He suddenly turned and ran headlong into the big electro-magnet—so violently that, as we found afterwards, he bruised his shoulder and jawbone cruelly. At that he stepped back a pace, and cried out with almost a whimper, "What, in Heaven's name, has come over me?" He stood, blanched with terror and trembling violently, with his right arm clutching his left, where that had collided with the magnet.

By that time I was excited, and fairly excited. "Davidson," said I, "don't be afraid."

He was startled at my voice, but not so excessively as before. I repeated my words in as clear and firm a tone as I could assume. "Bellows," he said, "is that you?"

"Can't you see it's me?"

He laughed. "I can't even see it's myself. Where the devil are we?"

"Here," said I, "in the laboratory."

"The laboratory!" he answered, in a puzzled tone, and put his hand to his forehead. "I *was* in the laboratory—till that flash came, but I'm hanged if I'm there now. What ship is that?"

"There's no ship," said I. "Do be sensible, old chap."

"No ship!" he repeated, and seemed to forget my denial forthwith. "I suppose," said he, slowly, "we're both dead. But the rummy part is I feel just as though I still had a body. Don't get used to it all at once, I suppose. The old shop was struck by lightning, I suppose. Jolly quick thing, Bellows—eigh?"

"Don't talk nonsense. You're very much alive. You are in the laboratory, blundering about. You've just smashed a new electrometer. I don't envy you when Boyce arrives."

He stared away from me towards the diagrams of cryohydrates. "I must be deaf," said he. "They've fired a gun, for there goes the puff of smoke, and I never heard a sound."

I put my hand on his arm again, and this time he was less alarmed. "We seem to have a sort of invisible bodies," said he. "By Jove! there's a boat coming round the headland! It's very much like the old life after all—in a different climate."

I shook his arm. "Davidson," I cried, "wake up!"

II

It was just then that Boyce came in. So soon as he spoke Davidson exclaimed: "Old Boyce! Dead too! What a lark!" I hastened to explain that Davidson was in a kind of somnambulistic trance. Boyce was interested at once. We both did all we could to rouse the fellow out of his extraordinary state. He answered our questions, and asked us some of his own, but his attention seemed distracted by his hallucination about a beach and a ship. He kept interpolating observations concerning some boat and the davits and sails filling with the wind. It made one feel queer, in the dusky laboratory, to hear him saying such things.

He was blind and helpless. We had to walk him down the passage, one at each elbow, to Boyce's private room, and while Boyce talked to him there, and humoured him about this ship idea, I went along the corridor and asked old Wade to come and look at him. The voice of our Dean sobered him a little, but not very much. He asked where his hands were, and why he had to walk about up to his waist in the ground. Wade thought over him a long time—you know how he knits his brows—and then made him feel the couch, guiding his hands to it. "That's a couch," said Wade. "The couch in the private room of Professor Boyce. Horsehair stuffing."

Davidson felt about, and puzzled over it, and answered presently that he could feel it all right, but he couldn't see it.

"What *do* you see?" asked Wade. Davidson said he could see nothing but a lot of sand and broken-up shells. Wade gave him some other things to feel, telling him what they were, and watching him keenly.

"The ship is almost hull down," said Davidson, presently, *apropos* of nothing.

"Never mind the ship," said Wade. "Listen to me, Davidson. Do you know what hallucination means?"

"Rather," said Davidson.

"Well, everything you see is hallucinatory."

"Bishop Berkeley," said Davidson.

"Don't mistake me," said Wade. "You are alive, and in this room of Boyce's. But something has happened to your eyes. You cannot see; you can feel and hear, but not see. Do you follow me?"

"It seems to me that I see too much." Davidson rubbed his knuckles into his eyes. "Well?" he said.

"That's all. Don't let it perplex you. Bellows, here, and I will take you home in a cab."

"Wait a bit." Davidson thought. "Help me to sit down," said he, presently; "and now—I'm sorry to trouble you—but will you tell me all that over again?"

Wade repeated it very patiently. Davidson shut his eyes, and pressed his hands upon his forehead. "Yes," said he. "It's quite right. Now my eyes are shut I know you're right. That's you, Bellows, sitting by me on the couch. I'm in England again. And we're in the dark."

Then he opened his eyes. "And there," said he, "is the sun just rising, and the yards of the ship, and a tumbled sea, and a couple of birds flying. I never saw anything so real. And I'm sitting up to my neck in a bank of sand."

He bent forward and covered his face with his hands. Then he opened his eyes again. "Dark sea and sunrise! And yet I'm sitting on a sofa in old Boyce's room!—God help me!"

III

That was the beginning. For three weeks this strange affection of Davidson's eyes continued unabated. It was far worse than being blind. He was absolutely helpless, and had to be fed like a newly-hatched bird, and led about and undressed. If he attempted to move he fell over things or struck himself against walls or doors. After a day or so he got used to hearing our voices without seeing us, and willingly admitted he was at home, and that Wade was right in what he told him. My sister, to whom he was engaged, insisted on coming to see him, and would sit for hours every day while he talked about this beach of his. Holding her hand seemed to comfort him immensely. He explained that when we left the College and drove home,—he lived in Hampstead Village,—it appeared to him as if we drove right through a sandhill—it was perfectly black until he emerged again—and through rocks and trees and solid obstacles, and when he was taken to his own room it made him giddy and almost frantic with the fear of falling, because going upstairs seemed to lift him thirty or forty feet above the rocks of his imaginary island. He kept saying he should smash all the eggs. The end was that he had to be taken down into his father's consulting room and laid upon a couch that stood there.

He described the island as being a bleak kind of place on the whole, with very little vegetation, except some peaty stuff, and a lot of bare rock. There were multitudes of penguins, and they made the rocks white and disagreeable to see. The sea was often rough, and once there was a thunderstorm, and he lay and shouted at the silent flashes. Once or twice seals pulled up on the beach, but only on the first two or three days. He said it was very funny the way in which the penguins used to waddle right through him, and how he seemed to lie among them without disturbing them.

I remember one odd thing, and that was when he wanted very badly to smoke. We put a pipe in his hands—he almost poked his eye out with it—and lit it. But he couldn't taste anything. I've since found it's the same with me—I don't know if it's the usual case—that I cannot enjoy tobacco at all unless I can see the smoke.

But the queerest part of his vision came when Wade sent him out in a bath-chair to get fresh air. The Davidsons hired a chair, and got that deaf and obstinate dependent of theirs, Widgery, to attend to it. Widgery's ideas of healthy expeditions were peculiar. My sister, who had been to the Dog's

Home, met them in Camden Town, towards King's Cross. Widgery trotting along complacently, and Davidson evidently most distressed, trying in his feeble, blind way to attract Widgery's attention.

He positively wept when my sister spoke to him. "Oh, get me out of this horrible darkness!" he said, feeling for her hand. "I must get out of it, or I shall die." He was quite incapable of explaining what was the matter, but my sister decided he must go home, and presently, as they went up the hill towards Hampstead, the horror seemed to drop from him. He said it was good to see the stars again, though it was then about noon and a blazing day.

"It seemed," he told me afterwards, "as if I was being carried irresistibly towards the water. I was not very much alarmed at first. Of course it was night there—a lovely night."

"Of course?" I asked, for that struck me as odd.

"Of course," said he. "It's always night there when it is day here—Well, we went right into the water, which was calm and shining under the moonlight—just a broad swell that seemed to grow broader and flatter as I came down into it. The surface glistened just like a skin—it might have been empty space underneath for all I could tell to the contrary. Very slowly, for I rode slanting into it, the water crept up to my eyes. Then I went under, and the skin seemed to break and heal again about my eyes. The moon gave a jump up in the sky and grew green and dim, and fish, faintly glowing, came darting round me—and things that seemed made of luminous glass, and I passed through a tangle of seaweeds that shone with an oily lustre. And so I drove down into the sea, and the stars went out one by one, and the moon grew greener and darker, and the seaweed became a luminous purple-red. It was all very faint and mysterious, and everything seemed to quiver. And all the while I could hear the wheels of the bath-chair creaking, and the footsteps of people going by, and a man with a bell crying coals.

"I kept sinking down deeper and deeper into the water. It became inky black about me, not a ray from above came down into that darkness, and the phosphorescent things grew brighter and brighter. The snaky branches of the deeper weeds flickered like the flames of spirit lamps; but, after a time, there were no more weeds. The fishes came staring and gaping towards me, and into me and through me. I never imagined such fishes before. They had lines of fire along the sides of them as though they had been outlined with a luminous pencil. And there was a ghastly thing swimming backwards with a lot of twining arms. And then I saw, coming very slowly towards me through the gloom, a hazy mass of light that resolved itself as it drew nearer into multitudes of fishes, struggling and darting round something that drifted. I drove on straight towards it, and presently I saw in the midst of the tumult, and by the light of the fish, a bit of splintered spar looming over me, and a dark hull tilting over, and some glowing phosphorescent forms that were shaken and writhed as the fish bit at them. Then it was I began to try to attract Widgery's attention. A horror came upon me. Ugh! I should have driven right into those half-eaten—things. If your sister had not come! They had great holes in them, Bellows, and—Never mind. But it was ghastly!"

IV

For three weeks Davidson remained in this singular state, seeing what at the time we imagined was an altogether phantasmal world, and stone blind to the world around him. Then, one Tuesday, when I called, I met old Davidson in the passage. "He can see his thumb!" the old gentleman said, in a perfect transport. He was struggling into his overcoat. "He can see his thumb, Bellows!" he said, with the tears in his eyes. "The lad will be all right yet."

I rushed in to Davidson. He was holding up a little book before his face, and looking at it and laughing in a weak kind of way.

"It's amazing," said he. "There's a kind of patch come there." He pointed with his finger. "I'm on the rocks as usual, and the penguins are staggering and flapping about as usual, and there's been a whale showing every now and then, but it's got too dark now to make him out. But put something *there,* and I see it—I do see it. It's very dim and broken in places, but I see it all the same, like a faint spectre of itself. I found it out this morning while they were dressing me. It's like a hole in this infernal phantom world. Just put your hand by mine. No—not there. Ah! Yes! I see it. The base of your thumb and a bit of cuff! It looks like the ghost of a bit of your hand sticking out of the darkening sky. Just by it there's a group of stars like a cross coming out."

From that time Davidson began to mend. His account of the change, like his account of the vision, was oddly convincing. Over patches of his field of vision the phantom world grew fainter, grew transparent, as it were, and through these translucent gaps he began to see dimly the real world about him. The patches grew in size and number, ran together and spread until only here and there were blind spots left upon his eyes. He was able to get up and steer himself about, feed himself once more, read, smoke, and behave like an ordinary citizen again. At first it was very confusing to him to have these two pictures overlapping each other like the changing views of a lantern, but in a little while he began to distinguish the real from the illusory.

At first he was unfeignedly glad, and seemed only too anxious to complete his cure by taking exercise and tonics. But as that odd island of his began to fade away from him, he became queerly interested in it. He wanted particularly to go down into the deep sea again, and would spend half his time wandering about the low-lying parts of London, trying to find the water-logged wreck he had seen drifting. The glare of real daylight very soon impressed him so vividly as to blot out everything of his shadowy world, but of a night-time, in a darkened room, he could still see the white-splashed rocks of the island, and the clumsy penguins staggering to and fro. But even these grew fainter and fainter, and, at last, soon after he married my sister, he saw them for the last time.

V

And now to tell of the queerest thing of all. About two years after his cure, I dined with the Davidsons, and after dinner a man named Atkins called in. He is a lieutenant in the Royal Navy, and a pleasant, talkative man. He was on friendly terms with my brother-in-law, and was soon on friendly terms with me. It came out that he was engaged to Davidson's cousin, and incidentally he took out a kind of pocket photograph case to show us a new rendering of his *fiancée.* "And, by-the-by," said he, "here's the old *Fulmar.*"

Davidson looked at it casually. Then suddenly his face lit up. "Good heavens!" said he. "I could almost swear—"

"What?" said Atkins.

"That I had seen that ship before."

"Don't see how you can have. She hasn't been out of the South Seas for six years, and before then—"

"But," began Davidson, and then, "Yes—that's the ship I dreamt of. I'm sure that's the ship I dreamt of. She was standing off an island that swarmed with penguins, and she fired a gun."

"Good Lord!" said Atkins, who had never heard the particulars of the seizure. "How the deuce could you dream that?"

And then, bit by bit, it came out that on the very day Davidson was seized, H.M.S. *Fulmar* had actually been off a little rock to the south of Antipodes Island. A boat had landed overnight to get penguins' eggs, had been delayed, and a thunderstorm drifting up, the boat's crew had waited until the morning before rejoining the ship. Atkins had been one of them, and he corroborated, word for word, the descriptions Davidson had given of the island and the boat. There is not the slightest doubt in any of our minds that Davidson has really seen the place. In some unaccountable way, while he moved hither and thither in London, his sight moved hither and thither in a manner that corresponded, about this distant island. *How* is absolutely a mystery.

That completes the remarkable story of Davidson's eyes. It is perhaps the best authenticated case in existence of a real vision at a distance. Explanation there is none forthcoming, except what Professor Wade has thrown out. But his explanation invokes the Fourth Dimension, and a dissertation on theoretical kinds of space. To talk of there being "a kink in space" seems mere nonsense to me; it may be because I am no mathematician. When I said that nothing would alter the fact that the place is eight thousand miles away, he answered that two points might be a yard away on a sheet of paper and yet be brought together by bending the paper round. The reader may grasp his argument, but I certainly do not. His idea seems to be that Davidson, stooping between the poles of the big electro-magnet, had some extraordinary twist given to his retinal elements through the sudden change in the field of force due to the lightning.

He thinks, as a consequence of this, that it may be possible to live visually in one part of the world, while one lives bodily in another. He has even made some experiments in support of his views; but, so far, he has simply succeeded in blinding a few dogs. I believe that is the net result of his work, though I have not seen him for some weeks. Latterly, I have been so busy with my work in connection with the Saint Pancras installation that I have had little opportunity of calling to see him. But the whole of his theory seems fantastic to me. The facts concerning Davidson stand on an altogether different footing, and I can testify personally to the accuracy of every detail I have given.

The Cone

THE NIGHT WAS hot and overcast, the sky red-rimmed with the lingering sunset of midsummer. They sat at the open window trying to fancy the air was fresher there. The trees and shrubs of the garden stood stiff and dark; beyond in the roadway a gas lamp burnt, bright orange against the hazy blue of the evening. Further were the three lights of the railway signal against the lowering sky. The man and woman spoke to one another in low tones.

"He does not suspect?" said the man, a little nervously.

"Not he," she said peevishly, as though that too irritated her. "He thinks of nothing but the works and the prices of fuel. He has no imagination, no poetry—"

"None of these men of iron have," he said sententiously. "They have no hearts."

"*He* has not," she said. She turned her discontented face towards the window. The distant sound of a roaring and rushing drew nearer and grew in volume; the house quivered; one heard the metallic rattle of the tender. As the train passed there was a glare of light above the cutting and a driving tumult of smoke; one, two, three, four, five, six, seven, eight black oblongs—eight trucks—passed across the dim grey of the embankment, and were suddenly extinguished one by one in the throat of the tunnel, which, with the last, seemed to swallow down train, smoke, and sound in one abrupt gulp.

"This country was all fresh and beautiful once," he said; "and now—it is Gehenna. Down that way—nothing but pot-banks and chimneys belching fire and dust into the face of heaven—But what does it matter? An end comes, an end to all this cruelty—*to-morrow.*" He spoke the last word in a whisper."

"To-morrow," she said, speaking in a whisper too, and still staring out of the window.

"Dear!" he said, putting his hand on hers.

She turned with a start, and their eyes searched one another's. Hers softened to his gaze. "My dear one," she said, and then: "It seems so strange—that you should have come into my life like this—to open—" She paused.

"To open?" he said.

"All this wonderful world—" she hesitated and spoke still more softly—"this world of *love* to me."

Then suddenly the door clicked and closed. They turned their heads, and he started violently back. In the shadow of the room stood a great shadowy figure—silent. They saw the face dimly in the half-light, with unexpressive dark patches under the pent-house brows. Every muscle in Raut's body suddenly became tense. When could the door have opened? What had he heard? Had he heard all? What had he seen? A tumult of questions.

The new-comer's voice came at last, after a pause that seemed interminable. "Well?" he said.

"I was afraid I had missed you, Horrocks," said the man at the window, gripping the window-ledge with his hand. His voice was unsteady.

The clumsy figure of Horrocks came forward out of the shadow. He made no answer to Raut's remark. For a moment he stood above them.

The woman's heart was cold within her. "I told Mr. Raut it was just possible you might come back," she said, in a voice that never quivered.

Horrocks, still silent, sat down abruptly in the chair by her little work-table. His big hands were clenched; one saw now the fire of his eyes under the shadow of his brows. He was trying to get his breath. His eyes went from the woman he had trusted to the friend he had trusted, and then back to the woman.

By this time and for the moment all three half understood one another. Yet none dared say a word to ease the pent-up things that choked them.

It was the husband's voice that broke the silence at last.

"You wanted to see me?" he said to Raut.

Raut started as he spoke. "I came to see you," he said, resolved to lie to the last.

"Yes?" said Horrocks.

"You promised," said Raut, "to show me some fine effects of moonlight and smoke."

"I promised to show you some fine effects of moonlight and smoke," repeated Horrocks, in a colourless voice.

"And I thought I might catch you to-night before you went down to the works," proceeded Raut, "and come with you."

There was another pause. Did the man mean to take the thing coolly? Did he after all know? How long had he been in the room? Yet even at the moment when they heard the door, their attitudes—Horrocks glanced at the profile of the woman, shadowy pallid in the half-light. Then he glanced at Raut, and seemed to recover himself suddenly. "Of course," he said, "I promised to show you the works under their proper dramatic conditions. It's odd how I could have forgotten."

"If I'm troubling you—" began Raut.

Horrocks started again. A new light had suddenly come into the sultry gloom of his eyes. "Not in the least," he said.

"Have you been telling Mr. Raut of all these contrasts of flame and shadow you think so splendid?" said the woman, turning now to her husband for the first time, her confidence creeping back again, her voice just one half-note too high. "That dreadful theory of yours that machinery is beautiful and everything else in the world ugly. I thought he would not spare you, Mr. Raut. It's his great Theory, his one discovery in Art—"

"I am slow to make discoveries," said Horrocks, grimly, damping her suddenly. "But what I discover—" He stopped.

"Well?" she said.

"Nothing," and suddenly he rose to his feet.

"I promised to show you the works," he said to Raut, and put his big, clumsy hand on his friend's shoulder. "And you are ready to go?"

"Quite," said Raut, and stood up also.

There was another pause. Each of them peered through the indistinctness of the dusk at the other two. Horrocks's hand still rested on Raut's shoulder. Raut half fancied still that the incident was trivial after all. But Mrs. Horrocks knew her husband better, knew that grim quiet in his voice, and the confusion in her mind took a vague shape of physical evil. "Very well," said Horrocks, and, dropping his hand, turned towards the door.

"My hat?" Raut looked round in the halflight.

"That's my work-basket," said Mrs. Horrocks, with a gust of hysterical laughter. The hands came together on the back of the chair. "Here it is!" he said. She had an impulse to warn him in an undertone, but she could not frame a word. "Don't go!" and "Beware of him!" struggled in her mind, and the swift moment passed.

"Got it?" said Horrocks, standing with door half open.

Raut stepped towards him. "Better say goodbye to Mrs. Horrocks," said the ironmaster, even more grimly quiet in his tone than before.

Raut started and turned. "Good-evening, Mrs. Horrocks," he said, and their hands touched.

Horrocks held the door open with a ceremonial politeness unusual in him towards men. Raut went out and then, after a wordless look at her, her husband followed. She stood motionless while Raut's light footfall and her husband's heavy tread, like bass and treble, passed down the passage together. The front door slammed heavily. She went to the window, moving slowly, and stood watching—leaning forward. The two men appeared for a moment at the gateway in the road, passed under the street lamp, and were hidden by the black masses of the shrubbery. The lamplight fell for a moment on their faces, showing only unmeaning pale patches, telling nothing of what she still feared, and doubted, and craved vainly to know. Then she sank down into a crouching attitude in the big arm-chair, her eyes wide open and staring out at the red lights from the furnaces that flickered in the sky. An hour after she was still there, her attitude scarcely changed.

The oppressive stillness of the evening weighed heavily upon Raut. They went side by side down the road in silence, and in silence turned into the cinder-made by-way that presently opened out the prospect of the valley.

A blue haze, half dust, half mist, touched the long valley with mystery. Beyond were Hanley and Etruria, grey and dark masses, outlined thinly by the rare golden dots of the street lamps, and here and there a gaslit window, or the yellow glare of some late-working factory or crowded public-house. Out of the masses, clear and slender against the evening sky, rose a multitude of tall chimneys, many of them reeking, a few smokeless during a season of "play." Here and there a pallid patch and ghostly stunted beehive shapes showed the position of a pot-bank, or a wheel, black and sharp against the hot lower sky, marked some colliery where they raise the iridescent coal of the place. Nearer at hand was the broad stretch of railway, and half invisible trains shunted—a steady puffing and rumbling, with every run a ringing concussion and a rhythmic series of impacts, and a passage of intermittent puffs of white steam across the further view. And to the left, between the railway and the dark mass of the low hill beyond, dominating the whole view, colossal, inky black, and crowned with smoke and fitful flames, stood the great cylinders of the Jeddah Company Blast Furnaces, the central edifices of the big ironworks of which Horrocks was the manager. They stood heavy and threatening, full of an incessant turmoil of flames and seething molten iron, and about the feet of them rattled the rolling mills, and the steam hammer beat heavily and splashed the white iron sparks hither and thither. Even as they looked, a truckful of fuel was shot into one of the giants, and the red flames gleamed out, and a confusion of smoke and black dust came boiling upwards towards the sky.

"Certainly you get some fine effects of colour with your furnaces," said Raut, breaking a silence that had become apprehensive.

Horrocks grunted. He stood with his hands in his pockets, frowning down at the dim steaming railway and the busy ironworks beyond, frowning as if he were thinking out some knotty problem.

Raut glanced at him and away again. "At present your moonlight effect is hardly ripe," he continued, looking upward; "the moon is still smothered by the vestiges of daylight."

Horrocks stared at him with the expression of a man who has suddenly awakened. "Vestiges of daylight! Of course, of course." He too looked up at the moon, pale still in the midsummer sky. "Come along," he said suddenly, and, gripping Raut's arm in his hand, made a move towards the path that dropped from them towards the railway.

Raut hung back. Their eyes met and saw a thousand things in a moment that their lips came near to say. Horrocks's hand tightened and then relaxed. He left go, and before Raut was aware, they were arm in arm, and walking, one unwillingly enough, down the path.

"You see the fine effect of the railway signals towards Burslem," said Horrocks, suddenly breaking into loquacity, striding fast and tightening the grip of his elbow the while. "Little green lights and red and white lights, all against the haze. You have an eye for effect, Raut. It's a fine effect. And look at those furnaces of mine, how they rise upon us as we come down the hill. That to the right is my pet—seventy feet of him. I packed him myself, and he's boiled away cheerfully with iron in his guts for five long years. I've a particular fancy for *him*. That line of red there,—a lovely bit of warm orange you'd call it, Raut,—that's the puddler's furnaces, and there, in the hot light, three black figures—did you see the white splash of the steam hammer then?—that's the rolling mills. Come along! Clang, clatter, how it goes rattling across the floor! Sheet tin, Raut,—amazing stuff. Glass mirrors are not in it when that stuff comes from the mill. And, squelch!—there goes the hammer again. Come along!"

He had to stop talking to catch at his breath. His arm twisted into Raut's with benumbing tightness. He had come striding down the black path towards the railway as though he was possessed. Raut had not spoken a word, had simply hung back against Horrocks's pull with all his strength.

"I say," he said now, laughing nervously, but with an undernote of snarl in his voice, "why on earth are you nipping my arm off, Horrocks, and dragging me along like this?"

At length Horrocks released him. His manner changed again. "Nipping your arm off!" he said. "Sorry. But it's you taught me the trick of walking in that friendly way."

"You haven't learnt the refinements of it yet then," said Raut, laughing artificially again. "By Jove! I'm black and blue." Horrocks offered no apology. They stood now near the bottom of the hill, close to the fence that bordered the railway. The ironworks had grown larger and spread out with their approach. They looked up to the blast furnaces now instead of down; the further view of Etruria and Hanley had dropped out of sight with their descent. Before them, by the stile, rose a notice board, bearing, still dimly visible, the words "BEWARE OF THE TRAINS," half hidden by splashes of coaly mud.

"Fine effects," said Horrocks, waving his arm. "Here comes a train. The puffs of smoke, the orange glare, the round eye of light in front of it, the melodious rattle. Fine effects! But these furnaces of mine used to be finer, before we shoved cones in their throats and saved the gas."

"How?" said Raut. "Cones?"

"Cones, my man, cones. I'll show you one nearer. The flames used to flare out of the open throats, great—what is it?—pillars of cloud by day, red and black smoke, and pillars of fire by night. Now we run it off in pipes and burn it to heat the blast, and the top is shut by a cone. You'll be interested in that cone."

"But every now and then," said Raut, "you get a burst of fire and smoke up there."

"The cone's not fixed, it's hung by a chain from a lever and balanced by an equipoise. You shall see it nearer. Else, of course, there'd be no way of getting fuel into the thing. Every now and then the cone dips and out comes the flare."

"I see," said Raut. He looked over his shoulder. "The moon gets brighter," he said.

"Come along," said Horrocks, abruptly, gripping his shoulder again, and moving him suddenly towards the railway crossing. And then came one of those swift incidents, vivid, but so rapid that they leave one doubtful and reeling. Half way across, Horrocks's hand suddenly clenched upon him like a vice, and swung him backward and through a half turn, so that he looked up the line. And there a chain of lamp-lit carriage-windows telescoped swiftly as it came towards them, and the red and yellow lights of an engine grew larger and larger rushing down upon them. As he grasped what this meant, he turned his face to Horrocks and pushed with all his strength against the arm that held him back between the rails. The struggle did not last a moment. Just as certain as it was that Horrocks held him there, so certain was it that he had been violently lugged out of danger.

"Out of the way!" said Horrocks, with a gasp, as the train came rattling by, and they stood panting by the gate into the ironworks.

"I did not see it coming," said Raut, still, even in spite of his own apprehensions, trying to keep up an appearance of ordinary intercourse.

Horrocks answered with a grunt. "The cone," he said, and then as one who recovers himself—"I thought you did not hear."

"I didn't," said Raut.

"I wouldn't have had you run over then for the world," said Horrocks.

"For a moment I lost my nerve," said Raut.

Horrocks stood for half a minute, then turned abruptly towards the ironworks again. "See how fine these great mounds of mine, these clinker heaps, look in the night! That truck yonder, up above there! Up it goes, and out-tilts the slag. See the palpitating red stuff go sliding down the slope. As we get nearer, the heap rises up and cuts the blast furnaces. See the quiver up above the big one. Not that way! This way, between the block heaps. That goes to the puddling furnaces, but I want to show you the canal first." He came and took Raut by the elbow, and so they went along side by side. Raut answered Horrocks vaguely. What, he asked himself, had really happened on the line? Was he deluding himself with his own fancies, or had Horrocks actually held him back in the way of the train? Had he just been within an ace of being murdered?

Suppose this slouching, scowling monster *did* know anything? For a minute or two then Raut was really afraid for his life, but the mood passed as he reasoned with himself. After all, Horrocks might have heard nothing. At any rate, he had pulled him out of the way in time. His odd manner might be due to the mere vague jealousy he had shown once before. He was talking now of the ash-heaps and the canal. "Eigh?" said Horrocks.

"What?" said Raut. "Rather! The haze in the moonlight. Fine!"

"Our canal," said Horrocks, stopping suddenly. "Our canal by moonlight and firelight is an immense effect. You've never seen it? Fancy that! You've spent too many of your evenings philandering up in Newcastle there. I tell you, for real florid effects—But you shall see. Boiling water—"

As they came out of the labyrinth of clinker heaps and mounds of coal and ore, the noises of the rolling mill sprang upon them suddenly, loud, near, and distinct. Three shadowy workmen went by and touched their caps to Horrocks. Their faces were vague in the darkness. Raut felt a futile impulse to address them, and before he could frame his words they passed into the shadows. Horrocks pointed to the canal close before them now: a weird-looking place it seemed, in the blood-red reflections of the furnaces. The hot water that cooled the tuyeres came into it, some fifty yards up—a tumultuous, almost boiling affluent, and the steam rose up from the water in silent white whisps and streaks, wrapping damply about them, an incessant succession of ghosts coming up from the black and red eddies, a white uprising that made the head swim. The shining black tower of the larger blast-furnace rose overhead out of the mist, and its tumultuous riot filled their ears. Raut kept away from the edge of the water and watched Horrocks.

"Here it is red," said Horrocks, "blood-red vapour as red and hot as sin; but yonder there, where the moonlight falls on it and it drives across the clinker heaps, it is as white as death."

Raut turned his head for a moment, and then came back hastily to his watch on Horrocks. "Come along to the rolling mills," said Horrocks. The threatening hold was not so evident that time, and Raut felt a little reassured. But all the same, what on earth did Horrocks mean about "white as death" and "red as sin"? Coincidence, perhaps?

They went and stood behind the puddlers for a little while, and then through the rolling mills, where amidst an incessant din the deliberate steam hammer beat the juice out of the succulent iron, and black, half-naked Titans rushed the plastic bars, like hot sealing-wax, between the wheels. "Come on," said Horrocks in Raut's ear, and they went and peeped through the little glass hole behind the tuyeres, and saw the tumbled fire writhing in the pit of the blast-furnace. It left one eye blinded for a while. Then with green and blue patches dancing across the dark they went to the lift by which the trucks of ore and fuel and lime were raised to the top of the big cylinder.

And out upon the narrow rail that overhung the furnace Raut's doubts came upon him again. Was it wise to be here? If Horrocks did know—everything! Do what he would, he could not resist a violent trembling. Right underfoot was a sheer depth of seventy feet. It was a dangerous place. They pushed by a truck of fuel to get to the railing that crowned the place. The reek of the furnace, a sulphurous vapour streaked with pungent bitterness, seemed to make the distant hillside of Hanley quiver. The moon was riding out now from among a drift of clouds, half way up the sky above the undulating wooded outlines of Newcastle. The steaming canal ran away from below them under an indistinct bridge, and vanished into the dim haze of the flat fields towards Burslem.

"That's the cone I've been telling you of," shouted Horrocks, "and, below that, sixty feet of fire and molten metal, with the air of the blast frothing through it like gas in soda-water."

Raut gripped the handrail tightly, and stared down at the cone. The heat was intense. The boiling of the iron and the tumult of the blast made a thunderous accompaniment to Horrocks's voice. But the thing had to be gone through now. Perhaps, after all—

"In the middle," bawled Horrocks, "temperature near a thousand degrees. If *you* were dropped into it—flash into flame like a pinch of gunpowder in a candle. Put your hand out and feel the heat of his breath. Why even up here I've seen the rain-water boiling off the trucks. And that cone there. It's a damned sight too hot for roasting cakes. The top side of it's three hundred degrees."

"Three hundred degrees!" said Raut.

"Three hundred centigrade, mind!" said Horrocks. "It will boil the blood out of you in no time."

"Eigh?" said Raut, and turned.

"Boil the blood out of you in—No you don't!"

"Let me go!" screamed Raut. "Let go my arm."

With one hand he clutched at the handrail, then with both. For a moment the two men stood swaying. Then suddenly, with a violent jerk, Horrocks had twisted him from his hold. He clutched at Horrocks and missed, his foot went back into empty air; in mid-air he twisted himself, and then cheek and shoulder and knee struck the hot cone together.

He clutched the chain by which the cone hung, and the thing sank an infinitesimal amount as he struck it. A circle of glowing red appeared about him, and a tongue of flame, released from the chaos within, flickered up towards him. An intense pain assailed him at the knees, and he could smell the singeing of his hands. He raised himself to his feet and tried to climb up the chain, and then something struck his head. Black and shining with the moonlight the throat of the furnace rose about him.

Horrocks he saw stood above him by one of the trucks of fuel on the rail. The gesticulating figure was bright and white in the moonlight, and shouting, "Fizzle, you fool! Fizzle, you hunter of women! You hot-blooded hound! Boil! boil! boil!"

Suddenly he caught up a handful of coal out of the truck and flung it deliberately, lump after lump, at Raut.

"Horrocks!" cried Raut, "Horrocks!"

He clung crying to the chain, pulling himself up from the burning of the cone. Each missile Horrocks flung hit him.

His clothes charred and glowed, and as he struggled the cone dropped and a rush of hot suffocating gas whooped out and burned round him in a swift breath of flame.

His human likeness departed from him. When the momentary red had passed Horrocks saw a charred, blackened figure, its head streaked with blood, still clutching and fumbling with the chain and writhing in agony—a cindery animal, an inhuman, monstrous creature that began a sobbing, intermittent shriek.

Abruptly at the sight the ironmaster's anger passed. A deadly sickness came upon him. The heavy odour of burning flesh came drifting up to his nostrils. His sanity returned to him.

"God have mercy upon me!" he cried. "Oh, God! what have I done?"

He knew the thing below him, save that it still moved and felt, was already a dead man—that the blood of the poor wretch must be boiling in his veins. An intense realisation of that agony came to his mind and overcame every other feeling. For a moment he stood irresolute, and then, turning to the truck, he hastily tilted its contents upon the struggling thing that had once been a man. The mass fell with a thud and went radiating over the cone. With the thud the shriek ended, and a boiling confusion of smoke, dust, and flame came rushing up towards him. As it passed he saw the cone clear again.

Then he staggered back and stood trembling, clinging to the rail with both hands. His lips moved, but no words came to them.

Down below was the sound of voices and running steps. The clangour of rolling in the shed ceased abruptly.

The Purple Pileus

MR. COOMBES WAS sick of life. He walked away from his unhappy home, and, sick not only of his own existence, but of everybody else's, turned aside down Gaswork Lane to avoid the town, and, crossing the wooden bridge that goes over the canal to Starling's Cottages, was presently alone in the damp pinewoods and out of sight and sound of human habitation. He would stand it no longer. He repeated aloud with blasphemies unusual to him that he would stand it no longer.

He was a pale-faced little man, with dark eyes and a fine and very black moustache. He had a very stiff, upright collar slightly frayed, that gave him an illusory double chin, and his overcoat (albeit shabby) was trimmed with astrachan. His gloves were a bright brown with black stripes over the knuckles, and split at the finger-ends. His appearance, his wife had said once in the dear, dead days beyond recall,—before he married her, that is,—was military. But now she called him—It seems a dreadful thing to tell of between husband and wife, but she called him "a little grub." It wasn't the only thing she had called him, either.

The row had arisen about that beastly Jennie again. Jennie was his wife's friend, and, by no invitation of Mr. Coombes, she came in every blessed Sunday to dinner, and made a shindy all the afternoon. She was a big, noisy girl, with a taste for loud colours and a strident laugh; and this Sunday she had outdone all her previous intrusions by bringing in a fellow with her, a chap as showy as herself. And Mr. Coombes, in a starchy, clean collar and his Sunday frock-coat, had sat dumb and wrathful at his own table, while his wife and her guests talked foolishly and undesirably, and laughed aloud. Well, he stood that, and after dinner (which, "as usual," was late), what must Miss Jennie do but go to the piano and play banjo tunes, for all the world as if it were a week-day! Flesh and blood could not endure such goings-on. They would hear next door; they would hear in the road; it was a public announcement of their disrepute. He had to speak.

He had felt himself go pale, and a kind of rigour had affected his respiration as he delivered himself. He had been sitting on one of the chairs by the window—the new guest had taken possession of the arm-chair. He turned his head. "Sun Day!" he said over the collar, in the voice of one who warns. "Sun Day!" What people call a "nasty" tone it was.

Jennie had kept on playing; but his wife, who was looking through some music that was piled on the top of the piano, had stared at him. "What's wrong now?" she said; "can't people enjoy themselves?"

"I don't mind rational 'njoyment, at all," said little Coombes; "but I ain't a-going to have week-day tunes playing on a Sunday in this house."

"What's wrong with my playing now?" said Jennie, stopping and twirling round on the music-stool with a monstrous rustle of flounces.

Coombes saw it was going to be a row, and opened too vigorously, as is common with your timid, nervous men all the world over. "Steady on with that music-stool!" said he; "it ain't made for 'eavy weights."

"Never you mind about weights," said Jennie, incensed. "What was you saying behind my back about my playing?"

"Surely you don't 'old with not having a bit of music on a Sunday, Mr. Coombes?" said the new guest, leaning back in the arm-chair, blowing a cloud of cigarette smoke and smiling in a kind of pitying way. And simultaneously his wife said something to Jennie about "Never mind 'im. You go on, Jinny."

"I do," said Mr. Coombes, addressing the new guest.

"May I arst why?" said the new guest, evidently enjoying both his cigarette and the prospect of an argument. He was, by-the-by, a lank young man, very stylishly dressed in bright drab, with a white cravat and a pearl and silver pin. It had been better taste to come in a black coat, Mr. Coombes thought.

"Because," began Mr. Coombes, "it don't suit me. I'm a business man. I 'ave to study my connection. Rational 'njoyment—"

"His connection!" said Mrs. Coombes, scornfully. "That's what he's always a-saying. We got to do this, and we got to do that—"

"If you don't mean to study my connection," said Mr. Coombes, "what did you marry me for?"

"I wonder," said Jennie, and turned back to the piano.

"I never saw such a man as you," said Mrs. Coombes. "You've altered all round since we were married. Before—"

Then Jennie began at the tum, tum, tum again.

"Look here!" said Mr. Coombes, driven at last to revolt, standing up and raising his voice. "I tell you I won't have that." The frock-coat heaved with his indignation.

"No vi'lence, now," said the long young man in drab, sitting up.

"Who the juice are you?" said Mr. Coombes, fiercely.

Whereupon they all began talking at once. The new guest said he was Jennie's "intended," and meant to protect her, and Mr. Coombes said he was welcome to do so anywhere but in his (Mr. Coombes') house; and Mrs. Coombes said he ought to be ashamed of insulting his guests, and (as I have already mentioned) that he was getting a regular little grub; and the end was, that Mr. Coombes ordered his visitors out of the house, and they wouldn't go, and so he said he would go himself. With his face burning and tears of excitement in his eyes, he went into the passage, and as he struggled with his overcoat—his frock-coat sleeves got concertinaed up his arm—and gave a brush at his silk hat, Jennie began again at the piano, and strummed him insultingly out of the house. Tum, tum, tum. He slammed the shop-door so that the house quivered. That, briefly, was the immediate making of his mood. You will perhaps begin to understand his disgust with existence.

As he walked along the muddy path under the firs,—it was late October, and the ditches and heaps of fir-needles were gorgeous with clumps of fungi,—he recapitulated the melancholy history of his marriage. It was brief and commonplace enough. He now perceived with sufficient clearness that his wife had married him out of a natural curiosity and in order to escape from her worrying, laborious, and uncertain life in the workroom; and, like the majority of her class, she was far too stupid to realise that it was her duty to co-operate with him in his business. She was greedy of enjoyment, loquacious, and socially-minded, and evidently disappointed to find the restraints of poverty still hanging about her. His worries exasperated her, and the slightest attempt to control her proceedings resulted in a charge of "grumbling." Why couldn't he be nice—as he used to be? And Coombes was such a harmless little man, too, nourished mentally on "Self-Help," and with a meagre ambition of self-denial and competition, that was to end in a "sufficiency." Then Jennie came in as a female Mephistopheles, a gabbling chronicle of "fellers," and was always wanting his wife to go to theatres, and "all that." And in addition were aunts of his wife, and cousins (male and female), to eat up capital, insult him personally, upset business arrangements, annoy good customers, and generally blight his life. It was not the first occasion by many that Mr. Coombes had fled his home in wrath and indignation, and something like fear, vowing furiously and even aloud that he wouldn't stand it, and so frothing away his energy along the line of least resistance. But never before had he been quite so sick of life as on this particular Sunday afternoon. The Sunday dinner may have had its share in his despair—and the greyness of the sky. Perhaps, too, he was beginning to realise his unendurable frustration as a business man as the consequence of his marriage. Presently bankruptcy, and after that—Perhaps she might have reason to repent when it was too late. And destiny, as I have already intimated, had planted the path through the wood with evil-smelling fungi, thickly and variously planted it, not only on the right side, but on the left.

A small shopman is in such a melancholy position, if his wife turns out a disloyal partner. His capital is all tied up in his business, and to leave her, means to join the unemployed in some strange part of the earth. The luxuries of divorce are beyond him altogether. So that the good old tradition of marriage for better or worse holds inexorably for him, and things work up to tragic culminations. Bricklayers kick their wives to death, and dukes betray theirs; but it is among the small clerks and shopkeepers nowadays that it comes most often to a cutting of throats. Under the circumstances it is not so very remarkable—and you must take it as charitably as you can—that the mind of Mr. Coombes ran for awhile on some such glorious close to his disappointed hopes, and that he thought of razors, pistols, breadknives, and touching letters to the coroner denouncing his enemies by name, and praying piously for forgiveness. After a time his fierceness gave way to melancholia. He had been married in this very overcoat, in his first and only frock-coat that was buttoned up beneath it. He began to recall their courting along this very walk, his years of penurious saving to get capital, and the bright hopefulness of his marrying days. For it all to work out like this! Was there no sympathetic ruler anywhere in the world? He reverted to death as a topic.

He thought of the canal he had just crossed, and doubted whether he shouldn't stand with his head out, even in the middle, and it was while drowning was in his mind that the purple pileus caught his eye. He looked at it mechanically for a moment, and stopped and stooped towards it to pick it up, under the impression that it was some such small leather object as a purse. Then he saw that it was the purple top of a fungus, a peculiarly poisonous-looking purple: slimy, shiny, and emitting a sour odour. He hesitated with his hand an inch or so from it, and the thought of poison crossed his mind. With that he picked the thing, and stood up again with it in his hand.

The odour was certainly strong—acrid, but by no means disgusting. He broke off a piece, and the fresh surface was a creamy white, that changed like magic in the space of ten seconds to a yellowish-green colour. It was even an inviting-looking change. He broke off two other pieces to see it repeated. They were wonderful things, these fungi, thought Mr. Coombes, and all of them the deadliest poisons, as his father had often told him. Deadly poisons!

There is no time like the present for a rash resolve. Why not here and now? thought Mr. Coombes. He tasted a little piece, a very little piece indeed—a mere crumb. It was so pungent that he almost spat it out again, then merely hot and full-flavoured,—a kind of German mustard with a touch of horse-radish and—well, mushroom. He swallowed it in the excitement of the moment. Did he like it or did he not? His mind was curiously careless. He would try another bit. It really wasn't bad—it was good. He forgot his troubles in the interest of the immediate moment. Playing with death it was. He took another bite, and then deliberately finished a mouthful. A curious tingling sensation began in his finger-tips and toes. His pulse began to move faster. The blood in his ears sounded like a mill-race. "Try bi' more," said Mr. Coombes. He turned and looked about him, and found his feet unsteady. He saw and struggled towards a little patch of purple a dozen yards away. "Jol' goo' stuff," said Mr. Coombes. "E—lomore ye'." He pitched forward and fell on his face, his hands outstretched towards the cluster of pilei. But he did not eat any more of them. He forgot forthwith.

He rolled over and sat up with a look of astonishment on his face. His carefully brushed silk hat had rolled away towards the ditch. He pressed his hand to his brow. Something had happened, but he could not rightly determine what it was. Anyhow, he was no longer dull—he felt bright, cheerful. And his throat was afire. He laughed in the sudden gaiety of his heart. Had he been dull? He did not know; but at any rate he would be dull no longer. He got up and stood unsteadily, regarding the universe with an agreeable smile. He began to remember. He could not remember very well, because of a steam roundabout that was beginning in his head. And he knew he had been disagreeable at home, just because they wanted to be happy. They were quite right; life should be as gay as possible. He would go home and make it up, and reassure them. And why not take some of this delightful toadstool with him, for them to eat? A hatful, no less. Some of those red ones with white spots as well, and a few yellow. He had been a dull dog, an enemy to merriment; he would make up for it. It would be gay to turn his coat-sleeves inside out, and stick some yellow gorse into his waist-coat pockets. Then home—singing—for a jolly evening.

After the departure of Mr. Coombes, Jennie discontinued playing, and turned round on the music-stool again. "What a fuss about nothing," said Jennie.

"You see, Mr. Clarence, what I've got to put up with," said Mrs. Coombes.

"He is a bit hasty," said Mr. Clarence, judicially.

"He ain't got the slightest sense of our position," said Mrs. Coombes; "that's what I complain of. He cares for nothing but his old shop; and if I have a bit of company, or buy anything to keep myself decent, or get any little thing I want out of the housekeeping money, there's disagreeables. 'Economy,' he says; 'struggle for life,' and all that. He lies awake of nights about it, worrying how he can screw me out of a shilling. He wanted us to eat Dorset butter once. If once I was to give in to him—there!"

"Of course," said Jennie.

"If a man values a woman," said Mr. Clarence, lounging back in the arm-chair, "he must be prepared to make sacrifices for her. For my own part," said Mr. Clarence, with his eye on Jennie, "I shouldn't think of marrying till I was in a position to do the thing in style. It's downright selfishness. A man ought to go through the rough-and-tumble by himself, and not drag her—"

"I don't agree altogether with that," said Jennie. "I don't see why a man shouldn't have a woman's help, provided he doesn't treat her meanly, you know. It's meanness—"

"You wouldn't believe," said Mrs. Coombes. "But I was a fool to 'ave 'im. I might 'ave known. If it 'adn't been for my father, we shouldn't have had not a carriage to our wedding."

"Lord! he didn't stick out at that?" said Mr. Clarence, quite shocked.

"Said he wanted the money for his stock, or some such rubbish. Why, he wouldn't have a woman in to help me once a week if it wasn't for my standing out plucky. And the fusses he makes about money—comes to me, well, pretty near crying, with sheets of paper and figgers. 'If only we can tide over this year,' he says, 'the business is bound to go.' 'If only we can tide over this year,' I says; 'then it 'll be, if only we can tide over next year. I know you,' I says. 'And you don't catch me screwing myself lean and ugly. Why didn't you marry a slavey,' I says, 'if you wanted one—instead of a respectable girl?' I says."

So Mrs. Coombes. But we will not follow this unedifying conversation further. Suffice it that Mr. Coombes was very satisfactorily disposed of, and they had a snug little time round the fire. Then Mrs. Coombes went to get the tea, and Jennie sat coquettishly on the arm of Mr. Clarence's chair until the tea-things clattered outside. "What was that I heard?" asked Mrs. Coombes, playfully, as she entered, and there was badinage about kissing. They were just sitting down to the little circular table when the first intimation of Mr. Coombes' return was heard.

This was a fumbling at the latch of the front door.

"'Ere's my lord," said Mrs. Coombes. "Went out like a lion and comes back like a lamb, I'll lay."

Something fell over in the shop: a chair, it sounded like. Then there was a sound as of some complicated step exercise in the passage. Then the door opened and Coombes appeared. But it was Coombes transfigured. The immaculate collar had been torn carelessly from his throat. His carefully-brushed silk hat, half-full of a crush of fungi, was under one arm; his coat was inside out, and his waistcoat adorned with bunches of yellow-blossomed furze. These little eccentricities of Sunday costume, however, were quite overshadowed by the change in his face; it was livid white, his eyes were unnaturally large and bright, and his pale blue lips were drawn back in a cheerless grin. "Merry!" he said. He had stopped dancing to open the door. "Rational 'njoyment. Dance." He made three fantastic steps into the room, and stood bowing.

"Jim!" shrieked Mrs. Coombes, and Mr. Clarence sat petrified, with a dropping lower jaw.

"Tea," said Mr. Coombes. "Jol' thing, tea. Tose-stools, too. Brosher."

"He's drunk," said Jennie, in a weak voice. Never before had she seen this intense pallor in a drunken man, or such shining, dilated eyes.

Mr. Coombes held out a handful of scarlet agaric to Mr. Clarence. "Jo' stuff," said he; "ta' some."

At that moment he was genial. Then at the sight of their startled faces he changed, with the swift transition of insanity, into overbearing fury. And it seemed as if he had suddenly recalled the quarrel of his departure. In such a huge voice as Mrs. Coombes had never heard before, he shouted, "My house. I'm master 'ere. Eat what I give yer!" He bawled this, as it seemed, without an effort, without a violent gesture, standing there as motionless as one who whispers, holding out a handful of fungus.

Clarence approved himself a coward. He could not meet the mad fury in Coombes' eyes; he rose to his feet, pushing back his chair, and turned, stooping. At that Coombes rushed at him. Jennie saw her opportunity, and, with the ghost of a shriek, made for the door. Mrs. Coombes followed her. Clarence tried to dodge. Over went the tea-table with a smash as Coombes clutched him by the collar and tried to thrust the fungus into his mouth. Clarence was content to leave his collar behind him, and shot out into the passage with red patches of fly agaric still adherent to his face. "Shut 'im in!" cried Mrs. Coombes, and would have closed the door, but her supports deserted her; Jennie saw the shop-door open, and vanished thereby, locking it behind her, while Clarence went on hastily into the kitchen. Mr. Coombes came heavily against the door, and Mrs. Coombes, finding the key was inside, fled upstairs and locked herself in the spare bedroom.

So the new convert to *joie de vivre* emerged upon the passage, his decorations a little scattered, but that respectable hatful of fungi still under his arm. He hesitated at the three ways, and decided on the kitchen. Whereupon Clarence, who was fumbling with the key, gave up the attempt to imprison his host, and fled into the scullery, only to be captured before he could open the door into the yard. Mr. Clarence is singularly reticent of the details of what occurred. It seems that Mr. Coombes' transitory irritation had vanished again, and he was once more a genial playfellow. And as there were knives and meat-choppers about, Clarence very generously resolved to humour him and so avoid anything tragic. It is beyond dispute that Mr. Coombes played with Mr. Clarence to his heart's content;

they could not have been more playful and familiar if they had known each other for years. He insisted gaily on Clarence trying the fungi, and after a friendly tussle, was smitten with remorse at the mess he was making of his guest's face. It also appears that Clarence was dragged under the sink and his face scrubbed with the blacking-brush,—he being still resolved to humour the lunatic at any cost,—and that finally, in a somewhat dishevelled, chipped, and discoloured condition, he was assisted to his coat and shown out by the back door, the shopway being barred by Jennie. Mr. Coombes' wandering thoughts then turned to Jennie. Jennie had been unable to unfasten the shop-door, but she shot the bolts against Mr. Coombes' latch-key, and remained in possession of the shop for the rest of the evening.

It would appear that Mr. Coombes then returned to the kitchen, still in pursuit of gaiety, and, albeit a strict Good Templar, drank (or spilt down the front of the first and only frock-coat) no less than five bottles of the stout Mrs. Coombes insisted upon having for her health's sake. He made cheerful noises by breaking off the necks of the bottles with several of his wife's wedding-present dinner-plates, and during the earlier part of this great drunk he sang divers merry ballads. He cut his finger rather badly with one of the bottles,—the only bloodshed in this story,—and what with that, and the systematic convulsion of his inexperienced physiology by the liquorish brand of Mrs. Coombes' stout, it may be the evil of the fungus poison was somehow allayed. But we prefer to draw a veil over the concluding incidents of this Sunday afternoon. They ended in the coal cellar, in a deep and healing sleep.

An interval of five years elapsed. Again it was a Sunday afternoon in October, and again Mr. Coombes walked through the pinewood beyond the canal. He was still the same dark-eyed, black-moustached little man that he was at the outset of the story, but his double chin was now scarcely so illusory as it had been. His overcoat was new, with a velvet lapel, and a stylish collar with turn-down corners, free of any coarse starchiness, had replaced the original all-round article. His hat was glossy, his gloves newish—though one finger had split and been carefully mended. And a casual observer would have noticed about him a certain rectitude of bearing, a certain erectness of head that marks the man who thinks well of himself. He was a master now, with three assistants. Beside him walked a larger sunburnt parody of himself, his brother Tom, just back from Australia. They were recapitulating their early struggles, and Mr. Coombes had just been making a financial statement.

"It's a very nice little business, Jim," said brother Tom. "In these days of competition you're jolly lucky to have worked it up so. And you're jolly lucky, too, to have a wife who's willing to help like yours does."

"Between ourselves," said Mr. Coombes, "it wasn't always so. It wasn't always like this. To begin with, the missus was a bit giddy. Girls are funny creatures."

"Dear me!"

"Yes. You'd hardly think it, but she was downright extravagant, and always having slaps at me. I was a bit too easy and loving, and all that, and she thought the whole blessed show was run for her. Turned the 'ouse into a regular caravansary, always having her relations and girls from business in, and their chaps. Comic songs a' Sunday, it was getting to, and driving trade away. And she was making eyes at the chaps, too! I tell you, Tom, the place wasn't my own."

"Shouldn't 'a' thought it."

"It was so. Well—I reasoned with her. I said, 'I ain't a duke, to keep a wife like a pet animal. I married you for 'elp and company.' I said, 'You got to 'elp and pull the business through.' She wouldn't 'ear of it. 'Very well,' I says; 'I'm a mild man till I'm roused,' I says, 'and it's getting to that.' But she wouldn't 'ear of no warnings."

"Well?"

"It's the way with women. She didn't think I 'ad it in me to be roused. Women of her sort (between ourselves, Tom) don't respect a man until they're a bit afraid of him. So I just broke out to show her. In comes a girl named Jennie, that used to work with her, and her chap. We 'ad a bit of a row, and I came out 'ere—it was just such another day as this—and I thought it all out. Then I went back and pitched into them."

"You did?"

"I did. I was mad, I can tell you. I wasn't going to 'it 'er, if I could 'elp it, so I went back and licked into this chap, just to show 'er what I could do. 'E was a big chap, too. Well, I chucked him, and smashed things about, and gave 'er a scaring, and she ran up and locked 'erself into the spare room."

"Well?"

"That's all. I says to 'er the next morning, 'Now you know,' I says, 'what I'm like when I'm roused.' And I didn't 'ave to say anything more."

"And you've been happy ever after, eh?"

"So to speak. There's nothing like putting your foot down with them. If it 'adn't been for that afternoon I should 'a' been tramping the roads now, and she'd 'a' been grumbling at me, and all her family grumbling for bringing her to poverty—I know their little ways. But we're all right now. And it's a very decent little business, as you say."

They proceed on their way meditatively. "Women are funny creatures," said brother Tom.

"They want a firm hand," says Coombes.

"What a lot of these funguses there are about here!" remarked brother Tom, presently. "I can't see what use they are in the world."

Mr. Coombes looked. " I dessay they're sent for some wise purpose," said Mr. Coombes.

And that was as much thanks as the purple pileus ever got for maddening this absurd little man to the pitch of decisive action, and so altering the whole course of his life.

A
Catastrophe

THE LITTLE SHOP was not paying. The realisation came insensibly. Winslow was not the man for definite addition and subtraction and sudden discovery. He became aware of the truth in his mind gradually, as though it had always been there. A lot of facts had converged and led him to conviction. There was that line of cretonnes—four half pieces—untouched, save for half-a-yard sold to cover a stool. There were those shirtings at 4¾*d.*—Bandersnatch, in the Broadway, was selling them at 2¾*d.*—under cost, in fact. (Surely Bandersnatch might let a man live!) Those servants' caps, a selling line, needed replenishing, and that brought back the memory of Winslow's sole wholesale dealers, Helter, Skelter, & Grab. Why! How about their account?

Winslow stood with a big green box open on the counter before him when he thought of it. His pale grey eyes grew a little rounder, his pale straggling moustache twitched. He had been drifting along, day after day. He went round to the ramshackle cash desk in the corner—it was Winslow's weakness to sell his goods over the counter, give his customers a duplicate bill, and then dodge into the desk to receive the money, as though he doubted his own honesty. His lank forefinger with the prominent joints ran down the bright little calendar ("Clack's Cottons last for All Time"). "One—two—three; three weeks an' a day!" said Winslow, staring. "March! Only three weeks and a day. It *can't* be."

"Tea, dear," said Mrs. Winslow, opening the door with the glass window and the white blind that communicated with the parlour.

"One minute," said Winslow, and began unlocking the desk.

An irritable old gentleman, very hot and red about the face, and in a heavy fur-lined cloak, came in noisily. Mrs. Winslow vanished.

"Ugh!" said the old gentleman. "Pocket-handkerchief."

"Yes, sir," said Winslow. "About what price—"

"Ugh!" said the old gentleman. "Poggit handkerchief, quig!"

Winslow began to feel flustered. He produced two boxes.

"These, sir," began Winslow.

"Sheed tin!" said the old gentleman, clutching the stiffness of the linen. "Wad to blow my nose—not haggit about."

"A cotton one, p'raps, sir?" said Winslow.

"How much?" said the old gentleman, over the handkerchief.

"Sevenpence, sir. There's nothing more I can show you? No ties, braces—"

"Damn!" said the old gentleman, fumbling in his ticket-pocket, and finally producing half-a-crown. Winslow looked round for his little metallic duplicate book which he kept in various fixtures, according to circumstances, and then he caught the old gentleman's eye. He went straight to the desk at once and got the change, with an entire disregard of the routine of the shop.

Winslow was always more or less excited by a customer. But the open desk reminded him of his trouble. It did not come back to him all at once. He heard a finger-nail softly tapping on the glass, and, looking up, saw Minnie's eyes over the blind. It seemed like retreat opening. He shut and locked the desk, and went into the little room to tea.

But he was preoccupied. Three weeks and a day. He took unusually large bites of his bread and butter, and stared hard at the little pot of jam. He answered Minnie's conversational advances distractedly. The shadow of Helter, Skelter, & Grab lay upon the tea-table. He was struggling with this new idea of failure, the tangible realisation, that was taking shape and substance, condensing, as it were, out of the misty uneasiness of many days. At present it was simply one concrete fact; there were thirty-nine pounds left in the bank, and that day three weeks Messrs. Helter, Skelter, & Grab, those enterprising outfitters of young men, would demand their eighty pounds.

After tea there was a customer or so—little purchases: some muslin and buckram, dress-protectors, tape, and a pair of Lisle hose. Then, knowing that Black Care was lurking in the dusky corners of the shop, he lit the three lamps early and set to refolding his cotton prints, the most vigorous and least meditative proceeding of which he could think. He could see Minnie's shadow in the other room as she moved about the table. She was busy turning an old dress. He had a walk after supper, looked in at the Y. M. C. A., but found no one to talk to, and finally went to bed. Minnie was already there. And there, too, waiting for him, nudging him gently, until about midnight he was hopelessly awake, sat Black Care.

He had had one or two nights lately in that company, but this was much worse. First came Messrs. Helter, Skelter, & Grab, and their demand for eighty pounds—an enormous sum when your original capital was only a hundred and seventy. They camped, as it were, before him, sat down and beleaguered him. He clutched feebly at the circumambient darkness for expedients. Suppose he had a sale, sold things for almost anything? He tried to imagine a sale miraculously successful in some unexpected manner, and mildly profitable in spite of reductions below cost. Then Bandersnatch, Limited, 101, 102, 103, 105, 106, 107, Broadway, joined the siege, a long caterpillar of frontage, a battery of shop fronts, wherein things were sold at a farthing above cost. How could he fight such an establishment? Besides, what had he to sell? He began to review his resources. What taking line was there to bait the sale? Then straightway came those pieces of cretonne, yellow and black with a bluish-green flower; those discredited shirtings, prints without buoyancy, skirmishing haberdashery, some despairful four-button gloves by an inferior maker—a hopeless crew. And that was his force against Bandersnatch, Helter, Skelter, & Grab, and the pitiless world behind them. What ever had made him think a mortal would buy such things? Why had he bought this and neglected that? He suddenly realised the intensity of his hatred for Helter, Skelter, & Grab's salesman. Then he drove towards an agony of self-reproach. He had spent too much on that cash desk. What real need was there of a desk? He saw his vanity of that desk in a lurid glow of self-discovery. And the lamps? Five pounds! Then suddenly, with what was almost physical pain, he remembered the rent.

He groaned and turned over. And there, dim in the darkness, was the hummock of Mrs. Winslow's shoulders. That set him off in another direction. He became acutely sensible of Minnie's want of feeling. Here he was, worried to death about business, and she sleeping like a little child. He regretted having married, with that infinite bitterness that only comes to the human heart in the small hours of the morning. That hummock of white seemed absolutely without helpfulness, a burden, a responsibility. What fools men were to marry! Minnie's inert repose irritated him so much that he was almost provoked to wake her up and tell her that they were "Ruined." She would have to go back to her uncle; her uncle had always been against him; and as for his own future, Winslow was exceedingly uncertain. A shop assistant who has once set up for himself finds the utmost difficulty in getting into a situation again. He began to figure himself "crib-hunting" again, going from this wholesale house to that, writing innumerable letters. How he hated writing letters! "Sir, referring to your advertisement in the 'Christian World.'" He beheld an infinite vista of discomfort and disappointment, ending—in a gulf.

He dressed, yawning, and went down to open the shop. He felt tired before the day began. As he carried the shutters in he kept asking himself what good he was doing. The end was inevitable, whether he bothered or not. The clear daylight smote into the place and showed how old, and rough, and splintered was the floor, how shabby the second-hand counter, how hopeless the whole enterprise. He had been dreaming these past six months of a bright little shop, of a happy couple, of a modest but comely profit flowing in. He had suddenly awakened from his dream. The braid that bound his decent black coat—it was a little loose—caught against the catch of the shop-door, and was torn loose. This suddenly turned his wretchedness to wrath. He stood quivering for a moment, then, with a spiteful clutch, tore the braid looser, and went in to Minnie.

"Here," he said, with infinite reproach, "look here! You might look after a chap a bit."

"I didn't see it was torn," said Minnie.

"You never do," said Winslow, with gross injustice, "until things are too late."

Minnie looked suddenly at his face. "I'll sew it now, Sid, if you like."

"Let's have breakfast first," said Winslow, "and do things at their proper time."

He was preoccupied at breakfast, and Minnie watched him anxiously. His only remark was to declare his egg a bad one. It wasn't; it was a little flavoury—being one of those at fifteen a shilling—but quite nice. He pushed it away from him, and then, having eaten a slice of bread and butter, admitted himself in the wrong by resuming the egg.

"Sid!" said Minnie, as he stood up to go into the shop again, "you're not well."

"I'm *well* enough." He looked at her as though he hated her.

"Then there's something else the matter. You aren't angry with me, Sid, are you?—about that braid. *Do* tell me what's the matter. You were just like this at tea yesterday, and at supper-time. It wasn't the braid then."

"And I'm likely to be."

She looked interrogation. "Oh! what *is* the matter?" she said.

It was too good a chance to miss, and he brought the evil news out with dramatic force. "Matter!" he said. "I done my best, and here we are. That's the matter! If I can't pay Helter, Skelter, & Grab eighty pounds, this day three weeks—" Pause. "We shall be sold Up! Sold Up! That's the matter, Min! SOLD UP!"

"Oh, Sid!" began Minnie.

He slammed the door. For the moment he felt relieved of at least half his misery. He began dusting boxes that did not require dusting, and then re-blocked a cretonne already faultlessly blocked. He was in a state of grim wretchedness,—a martyr under the harrow of fate. At any rate, it should not be said he failed for want of industry. And how he had planned and contrived and worked! All to this end! He felt horrible doubts. Providence and Bandersnatch—surely they were incompatible! Perhaps he was being "tried"? That sent him off upon a new tack, a very comforting one. That martyr pose, the gold-in-the-furnace attitude, lasted all the morning.

At dinner—"potato pie"—he looked up suddenly, and saw Minnie regarding him. Pale she looked, and a little red about the eyes. Something caught him suddenly with a queer effect upon his throat. All his thoughts seemed to wheel round into quite a new direction.

He pushed back his plate, and stared at her blankly. Then he got up, went round the table to her—she staring at him. He dropped on his knees beside her without a word. "Oh, Minnie!" he said, and suddenly she knew it was peace, and put her arms about him, as he began to sob and weep.

He cried like a little boy, slobbering on her shoulder that he was a knave to have married her and brought her to this, that he hadn't the wits to be trusted with a penny, that it was all his fault, that he "*had* hoped *so*"—ending in a howl. And she, crying gently herself, patting his shoulders, said, "*Ssh!*" softly to his noisy weeping, and so soothed the outbreak. Then suddenly the crazy little bell upon the shop-door began, and Winslow had to jump to his feet, and be a man again.

After that scene they "talked it over" at tea, at supper, in bed, at every possible interval in between, solemnly—quite inconclusively—with set faces and eyes for the most part staring in front of them—and yet with a certain mutual comfort. "What to do I don't know," was Winslow's main proposition. Minnie tried to take a cheerful view of service—

with a probable baby. But she found she needed all her courage. And her uncle would help her again, perhaps, just at the critical time. It didn't do for folks to be too proud. Besides, "something might happen," a favourite formula with her.

One hopeful line was to anticipate a sudden afflux of customers. "Perhaps," said Minnie, "you might get together fifty. They know you well enough to trust you a bit." They debated that point. Once the possibility of Helter, Skelter, & Grab giving credit was admitted, it was pleasant to begin sweating the acceptable minimum. For some half hour over tea the second day after Winslow's discoveries they were quite cheerful again, laughing even at their terrific fears. Even twenty pounds, to go on with, might be considered enough. Then in some mysterious way the pleasant prospect of Messrs. Helter, Skelter, & Grab tempering the wind to the shorn retailer vanished—vanished absolutely, and Winslow found himself again in the pit of despair.

He began looking about at the furniture, and wondering idly what it would fetch. The chiffonier was good, anyhow, and there were Minnie's old plates that her mother used to have. Then he began to think of desperate expedients for putting off the evil day. He had heard somewhere of Bills of Sale—there was to his ears something comfortingly substantial in the phrase. Then why not "Go to the Money Lenders?"

One cheering thing happened on Thursday afternoon; a little girl came in with a pattern of "print" and he was able to match it. He had not been able to match anything out of his meagre stock before. He went in and told Minnie. The incident is mentioned lest the reader should imagine it was uniform despair with him.

The next morning, and the next, after the discovery, Winslow opened shop late. When one has been awake most of the night, and has no hope, what *is* the good of getting up punctually? But as he went into the dark shop on Friday a strange event happened. He saw something lying on the floor, something lit by the bright light that came under the ill-fitting door—a black oblong. He stooped and picked up an envelope with a deep mourning edge. It was addressed to his wife. Clearly a death in her family—perhaps her uncle. He knew the man too well to have expectations. And they would have to get mourning and go to the funeral. The brutal cruelty of people dying! He saw it all in a flash—he always visualised his thoughts. Black trousers to get, black crape, black gloves,—none in stock,—the railway fares, the shop closed for the day.

"I'm afraid there's bad news, Minnie," he said.

She was kneeling before the fireplace, blowing the fire. She had her housemaid's gloves on and the old country sunbonnet she wore of a morning, to keep the dust out of her hair. She turned, saw the envelope, gave a gasp, and pressed two bloodless lips together.

"I'm afraid it's uncle," she said, holding the letter and staring with eyes wide open into Winslow's face. *"It's a strange hand!"*

"The postmark's Hull," said Winslow.

"The postmark's Hull."

Minnie opened the letter slowly, drew it out, hesitated, turned it over, saw the signature. "It's Mr. Speight!"

"What does he say?" said Winslow.

Minnie began to read. *"Oh!"* she screamed. She dropped the letter, collapsed into a crouching heap, her hands covering her eyes. Winslow snatched at it. "A most terrible accident has occurred," he read; "Melchior's chimney fell down yesterday evening right on the top of your uncle's house, and every living soul was killed—your uncle, your cousin Mary, Will, and Ned, and the girl—every one of them, and smashed—you would hardly know them. I'm writing to you to break the news before you see it in the papers—" The letter fluttered from Winslow's fingers. He put out his hand against the mantel to steady himself.

All of them dead! Then he saw, as in a vision, a row of seven cottages, each let at seven shillings a week, a timber yard, two villas, and the ruins—still marketable—of the avuncular residence. He tried to feel a sense of loss and could not. They were sure to have been left to Minnie's aunt. All dead! 7 X 7 X 52 ÷ 20 began insensibly to work itself out in his mind, but discipline was ever weak in his mental arithmetic; figures kept moving from one line to another, like children playing at Widdy, Widdy Way. Was it two hundred pounds about—or one hundred pounds? Presently he picked up the letter again, and finished reading it. "You being the next of kin," said Mr. Speight.

"How *awful!*" said Minnie, in a horror-struck whisper, and looking up at last. Winslow stared back at her, shaking his head solemnly. There were a thousand things running through his mind, but none that, even to his dull sense, seemed appropriate as a remark. "It was the Lord's will," he said at last.

"It seems so very, very terrible," said Minnie; "auntie, dear auntie—Ted—poor, dear uncle—"

"It was the Lord's will, Minnie," said Winslow, with infinite feeling. A long silence.

"Yes," said Minnie, very slowly, staring thoughtfully at the crackling black paper in the grate. The fire had gone out. "Yes, perhaps it was the Lord's will."

They looked gravely at one another. Each would have been terribly shocked at any mention of the property by the other. She turned to the dark fireplace and began tearing up an old newspaper slowly. Whatever our losses may be, the world's work still waits for us. Winslow gave a deep sigh and walked in a hushed manner towards the front door. As he opened it a flood of sunlight came streaming into the dark shadows of the closed shop. Brandersnatch, Helter, Skelter, & Grab, had vanished out of his mind like the mists before the rising sun.

Presently he was carrying in the shutters, and in the briskest way; the fire in the kitchen was crackling exhilaratingly with a little saucepan walloping above it, for Minnie was boiling two eggs—one for herself this morning, as well as one for him—and Minnie herself was audible, laying breakfast with the greatest *éclat*. The blow was a sudden and terrible one—but it behoves us to face such things bravely in this sad, unaccountable world. It was quite midday before either of them mentioned the cottages.

Le Mari Terrible

"YOU ARE ALWAYS so sympathetic," she said; and added, reflectively, "and one can talk of one's troubles to you without any nonsense."

I wondered dimly if she meant that as a challenge. I helped myself to a biscuit thing that looked neither poisonous nor sandy. "You are one of the most puzzling human beings I ever met," I said,—a perfectly safe remark to any woman under any circumstances.

"Do you find me so hard to understand?" she said.

"You are dreadfully complex." I bit at the biscuit thing, and found it full of a kind of creamy bird-lime. (I wonder why women *will* arrange these unpleasant surprises for me—I sickened of sweets twenty years ago.)

"How so?" she was saying, and smiling her most brilliant smile.

I have no doubt she thought we were talking rather nicely. "Oh!" said I, and waved the cream biscuit thing. "You challenge me to dissect you."

"Well?"

"And that is precisely what I cannot do."

"I'm afraid you are very satirical," she said, with a touch of disappointment. She is always saying that when our conversation has become absolutely idiotic—as it invariably does. I felt an inevitable desire to quote bogus Latin to her. It seemed the very language for her.

"Malorum fiducia pars quosque libet," I said, in a low voice, looking meaningly into her eyes.

"Ah!" she said, colouring a little, and turned to pour hot water into the teapot, looking very prettily at me over her arm as she did so.

"That is one of the truest things that has ever been said of sympathy," I remarked. "Don't you think so?"

"Sympathy," she said, "is a very wonderful thing, and a very precious thing."

"You speak," said I (with a cough behind my hand), "as though you knew what it was to be lonely."

"There is solitude even in a crowd," she said, and looked round at the six other people—three discreet pairs—who were in the room.

"I, too," I was beginning, but Hopdangle came with a teacup, and seemed inclined to linger. He belongs to the "Nice Boy" class, and gives himself ridiculous airs of familiarity with grown-up people. Then the Giffens went.

"Do you know, I always take such an interest in your work," she was saying to me, when her husband (confound him!) came into the room.

He was a violent discord. He wore a short brown jacket and carpet slippers, and three of his waistcoat buttons were (as usual) undone. "Got any tea left, Millie?" he said, and came and sat down in the arm-chair beside the table.

"How do, Delalune?" he said to the man in the corner. "Damned hot, Bellows," he remarked to me, subsiding creakily.

She poured some more hot water into the teapot. (Why must charming married women always have these husbands?)

"It *is* very hot," I said.

There was a perceptible pause. He is one of those rather adipose people, who are not disconcerted by conversational gaps. "Are *you*, too, working at Argon?" I said. He is some kind of chemical investigator, I know.

He began at once to explain the most horribly complex things about elements to me. She gave him his tea, and rose and went and talked to the other people about autotypes. "Yes," I said, not hearing what he was saying.

"'No' would be more appropriate," he said. "You are absent-minded, Bellows. Not in love, I hope—at your age?"

Really, I am not thirty, but a certain perceptible thinness in my hair may account for his invariably regarding me as a contemporary. But he should understand that nowadays the beginnings of baldness merely mark the virile epoch. "I say, Millie," he said, out loud and across the room, "you haven't been collecting Bellows here—have you?"

She looked round startled, and I saw a pained look come into her eyes. "For the bazaar?" she said. "Not yet, dear." It seemed to me that she shot a glance of entreaty at him. Then she turned to the others again.

"My wife," he said, "has two distinctive traits. She is a born poetess and a born collector. I ought to warn you."

"I did not know," said I, "that she rhymed."

"I was speaking more of the imaginative quality, the temperament that finds a splendour in the grass, a glory in the flower, that clothes the whole world in a vestiture of interpretation."

"Indeed!" I said. I felt she was watching us anxiously. He could not, of course, suspect. But I was relieved to fancy he was simply talking nonsense.

"The magnificent figures of heroic, worshipful, and mysterious womanhood naturally appeal to her—Cleopatra, Messalina, Beatrice, the Madonna, and so forth."

"And she is writing—"

"No, she is acting. That is the real poetry of women and children. A platonic Cleopatra of infinite variety, spotless reputation, and a large following. Her make-believe is wonderful. She would use Falstaff for Romeo without a twinge, if no one else was at hand. She could exert herself to break the heart of a soldier. I assure you, Bellows—"

I heard her dress rustle behind me.

"I want some more tea," he said to her. "You misunderstood me about the collecting, Millie."

"What were you saying about Cleopatra?" she said, trying, I think, to look sternly at him.

"Scandal," he said. "But about the collecting, Bellows—"

"You must come to this bazaar," she interrupted.

"I shall be delighted," I said, boldly. "Where is it, and when?"

"About this collecting," he began.

"It is in aid of that delightful orphanage at Wimblingham," she explained, and gave me an animated account of the charity. He emptied his second cup of tea. "May I have a third cup?" he said.

The two girls signalled departure, and her attention was distracted. "She collects—and I will confess she does it with extraordinary skill—the surreptitious addresses—"

"John," she said over her shoulder, "I wish you would tell Miss Smithers all those interesting things about Argon." He gulped down his third cup, and rose with the easy obedience of the trained husband. Presently she returned to the tea-things. "Cannot I fill your cup?" she asked. "I really hope John was not telling you his queer notions about me.

He says the most remarkable things. Quite lately he has got it into his head that he has a formula for my character."

"I wish *I* had," I said, with a sigh.

"And he goes about explaining me to people, as though I was a mechanism. 'Scalp collector,' I think is the favourite phrase. Did he tell you? Don't you think it perfectly horrid of him?"

"But he doesn't understand you," I said, not grasping his meaning quite at the minute.

She sighed.

"You have," I said, with infinite meaning, "my sincere sympathy—" I hesitated—"my whole sympathy."

"Thank you *so much,*" she said, quite as meaningly. I rose forthwith, and we clasped hands, like souls who strike a compact.

Yet, thinking over what he said afterwards, I was troubled by a fancy that there was the faintest suggestion of a smile of triumph about her lips and mouth. Possibly it was only an honourable pride. I suppose he has poisoned my mind a little. Of course, I should not like to think of myself as one of a fortuitously selected multitude strung neatly together (if one may use the vulgarism) on a piece of string,—a stringful like a boy's string of chestnuts,—nice old gentlemen, nice boys, sympathetic and humorous men of thirty, kind fellows, gifted dreamers, and dashing blades, all trailing after her. It is confoundedly bad form of him, anyhow, to guy her visitors. She certainly took it like a saint. Of course, I shall see her again soon, and we shall talk to one another about one another. Something or other cropped up and prevented my going there on her last Tuesday.

The Apple

"I MUST GET rid of it," said the man in the corner of the carriage, abruptly breaking the silence.

Mr. Hinchcliff looked up, hearing imperfectly. He had been lost in the rapt contemplation of the college cap tied by a string to his portmanteau handles—the outward and visible sign of his newly-gained pedagogic position—in the rapt appreciation of the college cap and the pleasant anticipations it excited. For Mr. Hinchcliff had just matriculated at London University, and was going to be junior assistant at the Holmwood Grammar School—a very enviable position. He stared across the carriage at his fellow-traveller.

"'Why not give it away?" said this person. "Give it away! Why not?"

He was a tall, dark, sunburnt man with a pale face. His arms were folded tightly, and his feet were on the seat in front of him. He was pulling at a lank, black moustache. He stared hard at his toes.

"Why not?" he said.

Mr. Hinchcliff coughed.

The stranger lifted his eyes—they were curious, dark-grey eyes—and stared blankly at Mr. Hinchcliff for the best part of a minute, perhaps. His expression grew to interest.

"Yes," he said slowly. "Why not? And end it."

"I don't quite follow you, I'm afraid," said Mr. Hinchcliff, with another cough.

"You don't quite follow me?" said the stranger, quite mechanically, his singular eyes wandering from Mr. Hinchcliff to the bag with its ostentatiously displayed cap, and back to Mr. Hinchcliff's downy face.

"You're so abrupt, you know," apologised Mr. Hinchcliff.

"Why shouldn't I?" said the stranger, following his thoughts. "You are a student?" he said, addressing Mr. Hinchcliff.

"I am—by Correspondence—of the London University," said Mr. Hinchcliff, with irrepressible pride, and feeling nervously at his tie.

"In pursuit of knowledge," said the stranger, and suddenly took his feet off the seat, put his fist on his knees, and stared at Mr. Hinchcliff as though he had never seen a student before. "Yes," he said, and flung out an index finger. Then he rose, took a bag from the hat-rack, and unlocked it. Quite silently, he drew out something round and wrapped in a quantity of silver-paper, and unfolded this carefully. He held it out towards Mr. Hinchcliff,—a small, very smooth, golden-yellow fruit.

Mr. Hinchcliff's eyes and mouth were open. He did not offer to take this object—if he was intended to take it.

"That," said this fantastic stranger, speaking very slowly, "is the Apple of the Tree of Knowledge. Look at it—small, and bright, and wonderful—Knowledge—and I am going to give it to you."

Mr. Hinchcliff's mind worked painfully for a minute, and then the sufficient explanation, "Mad!" flashed across his brain, and illuminated the whole situation. One humoured madmen. He put his head a little on one side.

"The Apple of the Tree of Knowledge, eigh!" said Mr. Hinchcliff, regarding it with a finely assumed air of interest, and then looking at the interlocutor. "But don't you want to eat it yourself? And besides—how did you come by it?"

"It never fades. I have had it now three months. And it is ever bright and smooth and ripe and desirable, as you see it." He laid his hand on his knee and regarded the fruit musingly. Then he began to wrap it again in the papers, as though he had abandoned his intention of giving it away.

"But how did you come by it?" said Mr. Hinchcliff, who had his argumentative side. "And how do you know that it *is* the Fruit of the Tree?"

"I bought this fruit," said the stranger, "three months ago—for a drink of water and a crust of bread. The man who gave it to me—because I kept the life in him—was an Armenian. Armenia! that wonderful country, the first of all countries, where the ark of the Flood remains to this day, buried in the glaciers of Mount Ararat. This man, I say, fleeing with others from the Kurds who had come upon them, went up into desolate places among the mountains—places beyond the common knowledge of men. And fleeing from imminent pursuit, they came to a slope high among the mountain-peaks, green with a grass like knife-blades, that cut and slashed most pitilessly at any one who went into it. The Kurds were close behind, and there was nothing for it but to plunge in, and the worst of it was that the paths they made through it at the price of their blood served for the Kurds to follow. Every one of the fugitives was killed save this Armenian and another. He heard the screams and cries of his friends, and the swish of the grass about those who were pursuing them—it was tall grass rising overhead. And then a shouting and answers, and when presently he paused, everything was still. He pushed out again, not understanding, cut and bleeding, until he came out on a steep slope of rocks below a precipice, and then he saw the grass was all on fire, and the smoke of it rose like a veil between him and his enemies."

The stranger paused. "Yes?" said Mr. Hinchcliff. "Yes?"

"There he was, all torn and bloody from the knife-blades of the grass, the rocks blazing under the afternoon sun,—the sky molten brass,—and the smoke of the fire driving towards him. He dared not stay there. Death he did not mind, but torture! Far away beyond the smoke he heard shouts and cries. Women screaming. So he went clambering up a gorge in the rocks—everywhere were bushes with dry branches that stuck out like thorns among the leaves—until he clambered over the brow of a ridge that hid him. And then he met his companion, a shepherd, who had also escaped. And, counting cold and famine and thirst as nothing against the Kurds, they went on into the heights, and among the snow and ice. They wandered three whole days.

"The third day came the vision. I suppose hungry men often do see visions, but then there is this fruit." He lifted the wrapped globe in his hand. "And I have heard it, too, from other mountaineers who have known something of the legend. It was in the evening time, when the stars were increasing, that they came down a slope of polished rock into a huge, dark valley all set about with strange, contorted trees, and in these trees hung little globes like glow-worm spheres, strange, round, yellow lights.

"Suddenly this valley was lit far away, many miles away, far down it, with a golden flame marching slowly athwart it, that made the stunted trees against it black as night, and turned the slopes all about them and their figures to the likeness of fiery gold. And at the vision they, knowing the legends of the mountains, instantly knew that it was Eden they saw, or the sentinel of Eden, and they fell upon their faces like men struck dead.

"When they dared to look again, the valley was dark for a space, and then the light came again—returning, a burning amber.

"At that the shepherd sprang to his feet, and with a shout began to run down towards the light; but the other man was too fearful to follow him. He stood stunned, amazed, and terrified, watching his companion recede towards the marching glare. And hardly had the shepherd set out when there came a noise like thunder, the beating of invisible wings hurrying up the valley, and a great and terrible fear; and at that the man who gave me the fruit turned—if he might still escape. And hurrying headlong up the slope again, with that tumult sweeping after him, he stumbled against one of these stunted bushes, and a ripe fruit came off it into his hand. This fruit. Forthwith, the wings and the thunder rolled all about him. He fell and fainted, and when he came to his senses, he was back among the blackened ruins of his own village, and I and the others were attending to the wounded. A vision? But the golden fruit of the tree was still clutched in his hand. There were others there who knew the legend, knew what that strange fruit might be." He paused. "And this is it," he said.

It was a most extraordinary story to be told in a third-class carriage on a Sussex railway. It was as if the real was a mere veil to the fantastic, and here was the fantastic poking through. "Is it?" was all Mr. Hinchcliff could say.

"The legend," said the stranger, "tells that those thickets of dwarfed trees growing about the garden sprang from the apple that Adam carried in his hand when he and Eve were driven forth. He felt something in his hand, saw the half-eaten apple, and flung it petulantly aside. And there they grow, in that desolate valley, girdled round with the everlasting snows; and there the fiery swords keep ward against the Judgment Day."

"But I thought these things were—" Mr. Hinchcliff paused—"fables—parables rather. Do you mean to tell me that there in Armenia—"

The stranger answered the unfinished question with the fruit in his open hand.

"But you don't know," said Mr. Hinchcliff, "that that *is* the fruit of the Tree of Knowledge. The man may have had—a sort of mirage, say. Suppose—"

"Look at it," said the stranger.

It was certainly a strange-looking globe, not really an apple, Mr. Hinchcliff saw, and a curious glowing golden colour, almost as though light itself was wrought into its substance. As he looked at it, he began to see more vividly the desolate valley among the mountains, the guarding swords of fire, the strange antiquities of the story he had just heard. He rubbed a knuckle into his eye. "But—" said he.

"It has kept like that, smooth and full, three months. Longer than that it is now by some days. No drying, no withering, no decay."

"And you yourself," said Mr. Hinchcliff, "really believe that—"

"Is the Forbidden Fruit."

There was no mistaking the earnestness of the man's manner and his perfect sanity. "The Fruit of Knowledge," he said.

"Suppose it was?" said Mr. Hinchcliff, after a pause, still staring at it. "But after all," said Mr. Hinchcliff, "it's not my kind of knowledge—not the sort of knowledge. I mean, Adam and Eve have eaten it already."

"We inherit their sins—not their knowledge," said the stranger. "That would make it all clear and bright again. We should see into everything, through everything, into the deepest meaning of everything—"

"Why don't you eat it, then?" said Mr. Hinchcliff, with an inspiration.

"I took it intending to eat it," said the stranger.

"Man has fallen. Merely to eat again could scarcely—"

"Knowledge is power," said Mr. Hinchcliff.

"But is it happiness? I am older than you—more than twice as old. Time after time I have held this in my hand, and my heart has failed me at the thought of all that one might know, that terrible lucidity—Suppose suddenly all the world became pitilessly clear?"

"That, I think, would be a great advantage," said Mr. Hinchcliff, "on the whole."

"Suppose you saw into the hearts and minds of every one about you, into their most secret recesses—people you loved, whose love you valued?"

"You'd soon find out the humbugs," said Mr. Hinchcliff, greatly struck by the idea.

"And worse—to know yourself, bare of your most intimate illusions. To see yourself in your place. All that your lusts and weaknesses prevented your doing. No merciful perspective."

"That might be an excellent thing too. 'Know thyself,' you know."

"You are young," said the stranger.

"If you don't care to eat it, and it bothers you, why don't you throw it away?"

"There again, perhaps, you will not understand me. To me, how could one throw away a thing like that, glowing, wonderful? Once one has it, one is bound. But, on the other hand, to *give* it away! To give it away to some one who thirsted after knowledge, who found no terror in the thought of that clear perception—"

"Of course," said Mr. Hinchcliff, thoughtfully, "it might be some sort of poisonous fruit."

And then his eye caught something motionless, the end of a white board black-lettered outside the carriage-window. "—MWOOD," he saw. He started convulsively. "Gracious!" said Mr. Hinchcliff. "Holmwood!"—and the practical present blotted out the mystic realisations that had been stealing upon him.

In another moment he was opening the carriage-door, portmanteau in hand. The guard was already fluttering his green flag. Mr. Hinchcliff jumped out. "Here!" said a voice behind him, and he saw the dark eyes of the stranger shining and the golden fruit, bright and bare, held out of the open carriage-door. He took it instinctively, the train was already moving.

"No!" shouted the stranger, and made a snatch at it as if to take it back.

"Stand away," cried a country porter, thrusting forward to close the door. The stranger shouted something Mr. Hinchcliff did not catch, head and arm thrust excitedly out of the window, and then the shadow of the bridge fell on him, and in a trice he was hidden. Mr. Hinchcliff stood astonished, staring at the end of the last waggon receding round the bend, and with the wonderful fruit in his hand. For the fraction of a minute his mind was confused, and then he became aware that two or three people on the platform were regarding him with interest. Was he not the new Grammar School master making his début? It occurred to him that, so far as they could tell, the fruit might very well be the naïve refreshment of an orange. He flushed at the thought, and thrust the fruit into his side pocket, where it bulged undesirably. But there was no help for it, so he went towards them, awkwardly concealing his sense of awkwardness, to ask the way to the Grammar School, and the means of getting his portmanteau and the two tin boxes which lay up the platform thither. Of all the odd and fantastic yarns to tell a fellow!

His luggage could be taken on a truck for sixpence, he found, and he could precede it on foot. He fancied an ironical note in the voices. He was painfully aware of his contour.

The curious earnestness of the man in the train, and the glamour of the story he told, had, for a time, diverted the current of Mr. Hinchcliff's thoughts. It drove like a mist before his immediate concerns. Fires that went to and fro! But the preoccupation of his new position, and the impression he was to produce upon Holmwood generally, and the school people in particular, returned upon him with reinvigorating power before he left the station and cleared his mental atmosphere. But it is extraordinary what an inconvenient thing the addition of a soft and rather brightly-golden fruit, not three inches in diameter, may prove to a sensitive youth on his best appearance. In the pocket of his black jacket it bulged dreadfully, spoilt the lines altogether. He passed a little old lady in black, and he felt her eye drop upon the excrescence at once. He was wearing one glove and carrying the other, together with his stick, so that to bear the fruit openly was impossible. In one place, where the road into the town seemed suitably secluded, he took his encumbrance out of his pocket and tried it in his hat. It was just too large, the hat wobbled ludicrously, and just as he was taking it out again, a butcher's boy came driving round the corner.

"Confound it!" said Mr. Hinchcliff.

He would have eaten the thing, and attained omniscience there and then, but it would seem so silly to go into the town sucking a juicy fruit—and it certainly felt juicy. If one of the boys should come by, it might do him a serious injury with his discipline so to be seen. And the juice might make his face sticky and get upon his cuffs—or it might be an acid juice as potent as lemon, and take all the colour out of his clothes.

Then round a bend in the lane came two pleasant, sunlit, girlish figures. They were walking slowly towards the town and chattering—at any moment they might look round and see a hot-faced young man behind them carrying a kind of phosphorescent yellow tomato! They would be sure to laugh.

"Hang!" said Mr. Hinchcliff, and with a swift jerk sent the encumbrance flying over the stone wall of an orchard that there abutted on the road. As it vanished, he felt a faint twinge of loss that lasted scarcely a moment. He adjusted the stick and glove in his hand, and walked on, erect and self-conscious, to pass the girls.

But in the darkness of the night Mr. Hinchcliff had a dream, and saw the valley, and the flaming swords, and the contorted trees, and knew that it really was the Apple of the Tree of Knowledge that he had thrown regardlessly away. And he awoke very unhappy.

In the morning his regret had passed, but afterwards it returned and troubled him; never, however, when he was happy or busily occupied. At last, one moonlight night about eleven, when all Holmwood was quiet, his regrets returned with redoubled force, and therewith an impulse to adventure. He slipped out of the house and over the playground wall, went through the silent town to Station Lane, and climbed into the orchard where he had thrown the fruit. But nothing was to be found of it there among the dewy grass and the faint intangible globes of dandelion down.

The Sad Story of a Dramatic Critic

I WAS—YOU shall hear immediately why I am not now—Egbert Craddock Cummins. The name remains. I am still (Heaven help me!) Dramatic Critic to the "Fiery Cross." What I shall be in a little while I do not know. I write in great trouble and confusion of mind. I will do what I can to make myself clear in the face of terrible difficulties. You must bear with me a little. When a man is rapidly losing his own identity, he naturally finds a difficulty in expressing himself. I will make it perfectly plain in a minute, when once I get my grip upon the story. Let me see—where *am* I? I wish I knew. Ah, I have it! Dead self! Egbert Craddock Cummins!

In the past I should have disliked writing anything quite so full of "I" as this story must be. It is full of "I's" before and behind, like the beast in Revelation—the one with a head like a calf, I am afraid. But my tastes have changed since I became a Dramatic Critic and studied the masters—G.R.S., G.B.S., G.A.S., and the others. Everything has changed since then. At least the story is about myself—so that there is some excuse for me. And it is really not egotism, because, as I say, since those days my identity has undergone an entire alteration.

That past!—I was—in those days—rather a nice fellow, rather shy—taste for grey in my clothes, weedy little moustache, face "interesting," slight stutter which I had caught in early life from a schoolfellow. Engaged to a very nice girl, named Delia. Fairly new, she was—cigarettes—liked me because I was human and original. Considered I was like Lamb—on the strength of the stutter, I believe. Father, an eminent authority on postage stamps. She read a great deal in the British Museum. (A perfect pairing ground for literary people, that British Museum—you should read George Egerton and Justin Huntly M'Carthy and Gissing and the rest of them.) We loved in our intellectual way, and shared the brightest hopes. (All gone now.) And her father liked me because I seemed honestly eager to hear about stamps. She had no mother. Indeed, I had the happiest prospects a young man could have. I never went to the theatres in those days. My Aunt Charlotte before she died had told me not to.

Then Barnaby, the editor of the "Fiery Cross," made me—in spite of my spasmodic efforts to escape—Dramatic Critic. He is a fine, healthy man, Barnaby, with an enormous head of frizzy black hair and a convincing manner; and he caught me on the staircase going to see Wembly. He had been dining, and was more than usually buoyant. "Hullo, Cummins!" he said. "The very man I want!" He caught me by the shoulder or the collar or something, ran me up the little passage, and flung me over the wastepaper basket into the arm-chair in his office. "Pray be seated," he said, as he did so. Then he ran across the room and came back with some pink and yellow tickets and pushed them into my hand. "Opera

Comique," he said, "Thursday; Friday, the Surrey; Saturday, the Frivolity. That's all, I think."

"But—" I began.

"Glad you're free," he said, snatching some proofs off the desk and beginning to read.

"I don't quite understand," I said.

"Eigh?" he said, at the top of his voice, as though he thought I had gone, and was startled at my remark.

"Do you want me to criticise these plays?"

"Do something with 'em—Did you think it was a treat?"

"But I can't."

"Did you call me a fool?"

"Well, I've never been to a theatre in my life."

"Virgin soil."

"But I don't know anything about it, you know."

"That's just it. New view. No habits. No *clichés* in stock. Ours is a live paper, not a bag of tricks. None of your clock-work, professional journalism in this office. And I can rely on your integrity—"

"But I've conscientious scruples—"

He caught me up suddenly and put me outside his door. "Go and talk to Wembly about that," he said. "He'll explain."

As I stood perplexed, he opened the door again, said, "I forgot this," thrust a fourth ticket into my hand (it was for that night—in twenty minutes' time), and slammed the door upon me. His expression was quite calm, but I caught his eye.

I hate arguments. I decided that I would take his hint and become (to my own destruction) a Dramatic Critic. I walked slowly down the passage to Wembly. That Barnaby has a remarkably persuasive way. He has made few suggestions during our very pleasant intercourse of four years that he has not ultimately won me round to adopting. It may be, of course, that I am of a yielding disposition; certainly I am too apt to take my colour from my circumstances. It is, indeed, to my unfortunate susceptibility to vivid impressions that all my misfortunes are due. I have already alluded to the slight stammer I had acquired from a schoolfellow in my youth. However, this is a digression—I went home in a cab to dress.

I will not trouble the reader with my thoughts about the first-night audience, strange assembly as it is,—those I reserve for my Memoirs,—nor the humiliating story of how I got lost during the *entr'acte* in a lot of red plush passages, and saw the third act from the gallery. The only point upon which I wish to lay stress was the remarkable effect of the acting upon me. You must remember I had lived a quiet and retired life, and had never been to the theatre before, and that I am extremely sensitive to vivid impressions. At the risk of repetition I must insist upon these points.

The first effect was a profound amazement, not untinctured by alarm. The phenomenal unnaturalness of acting is a thing discounted in the minds of most people by early visits to the theatre. They get used to the fantastic gestures, the flamboyant emotions, the weird mouthings, melodious snortings, agonising yelps, lip-gnawings, glaring horrors, and other emotional symbolism of the stage. It becomes at last a mere deaf-and-dumb language to them, which they read intelligently *pari passu* with the hearing of the dialogue. But all this was new to me. The thing was called a modern comedy; the people were supposed to be English and were dressed like fashionable Americans of the current epoch, and I fell into the natural error of supposing that the actors were trying to represent human beings. I looked round on my first-night audience with a kind of wonder, discovered—as all new Dramatic Critics do—that it rested with me to reform the Drama, and, after a supper choked with emotion, went off to the office to write a column, piebald with "new paragraphs" (as all my stuff is—it fills out so) and purple with indignation. Barnaby was delighted.

But I could not sleep that night. I dreamt of actors,—actors glaring, actors smiting their chests, actors flinging out a handful of extended fingers, actors smiling bitterly, laughing despairingly, falling hopelessly, dying idiotically. I got up at eleven with a slight headache, read my notice in the "Fiery Cross," breakfasted, and went back to my room to shave. (It's my habit to do so.) Then an odd thing happened. I could not find my razor. Suddenly it occurred to me that I had not unpacked it the day before.

"Ah!" said I, in front of the looking-glass. Then "Hullo!"

Quite involuntarily, when I had thought of my portmanteau, I had flung up the left arm (fingers fully extended) and clutched at my diaphragm with my right hand. I am an acutely self-conscious man at all times. The gesture struck me as absolutely novel for me. I repeated it, for my own satisfaction. "Odd!" Then (rather puzzled) I turned to my portmanteau.

After shaving, my mind reverted to the acting I had seen, and I entertained myself before the cheval glass with some imitations of Jafferay's more exaggerated gestures. "Really, one might think it a disease,"—I said,—"Stage-Walkitis!" (There's many a truth spoken in jest.) Then, if I remember rightly, I went off to see Wembly, and afterwards lunched at the British Museum with Delia. We actually spoke about our prospects, in the light of my new appointment.

But that appointment was the beginning of my downfall. From that day I necessarily became a persistent theatre-goer, and almost insensibly I began to change. The next thing I noticed after the gesture about the razor, was to catch myself bowing ineffably when I met Delia, and stooping in an old-fashioned, courtly way over her hand. Directly I caught myself, I straightened myself up and became very uncomfortable. I remember she looked at me curiously. Then, in the office, I found myself doing "nervous business," fingers on teeth, when Barnaby asked me a question I could not very well answer. Then, in some trifling difference with Delia, I clasped my hand to my brow. And I pranced through my social transactions at times singularly like an actor! I tried not to—no one could be more keenly alive to the arrant absurdity of the histrionic bearing. And I did!

It began to dawn on me what it all meant. The acting, I saw, was too much for my delicately-strung nervous system. I have always, I know, been too amenable to the suggestions of my circumstances. Night after night of concentrated attention to the conventional attitudes and intonation of the English stage was gradually affecting my speech and carriage. I was giving way to the infection of sympathetic imitation. Night after night my plastic nervous system took the print of some new amazing gesture, some new emotional exaggeration—and retained it. A kind of theatrical veneer threatened to plate over and obliterate my private individuality altogether. I saw myself in a kind of vision. Sitting by myself one night, my new self seemed to me to glide, posing and gesticulating, across the room. He clutched his throat, he opened his fingers, he opened his legs in walking like a high-class marionette. He went from attitude to attitude. He might have been clockwork. Directly after this I made an ineffectual attempt to resign my theatrical work. But Barnaby persisted in talking about the Polywhiddle Divorce all the time I was with him, and I could get no opportunity of saying what I wished.

And then Delia's manner began to change towards me. The ease of our intercourse vanished. I felt she was learning to dislike me. I grinned, and capered, and scowled, and posed at her in a thousand ways, and knew—with what a voiceless agony!—that I did it all the time. I tried to resign again; and Barnaby talked about "X" and "Z" and "Y" in the "New Review," and gave me a strong cigar to smoke, and so routed me. And then I walked up the Assyrian Gallery in the manner of Irving to meet Delia, and so precipitated the crisis.

"Ah!—*Dear!*" I said, with more sprightliness and emotion in my voice than had ever been in all my life before I became (to my own undoing) a Dramatic Critic.

She held out her hand rather coldly, scrutinising my face as she did so. I prepared, with a new-won grace, to walk by her side.

"Egbert," she said, standing still, and thought. Then she looked at me.

I said nothing. I felt what was coming. I tried to be the old Egbert Craddock Cummins of shambling gait and stammering sincerity, whom she loved; but I felt, even as I did so, that I was a new thing, a thing of surging emotions and mysterious fixity—like no human being that ever lived, except upon the stage. "Egbert," she said, "you are not yourself."

"Ah!" Involuntarily I clutched my diaphragm and averted my head (as is the way with them).

"There!" she said.

"What do you mean?" I said, whispering in vocal italics,—you know how they do it,—turning on her, perplexity on face, right hand down, left on brow. I knew quite well what she meant. I knew quite well the dramatic unreality of my behaviour. But I struggled against it in vain. "What do you mean?" I said, and, in a kind of hoarse whisper, "I don't understand!"

She really looked as though she disliked me. "What do you keep on posing for?" she said. "I don't like it. You didn't use to."

"Didn't use to!" I said slowly, repeating this twice. I glared up and down the gallery, with short, sharp glances. "We are alone," I said swiftly. "*Listen!*" I poked my forefinger towards her, and glared at her. "I am under a curse."

I saw her hand tighten upon her sunshade. "You are under some bad influence or other," said Delia. "You should give it up. I never knew any one change as you have done."

"Delia!" I said, lapsing into the pathetic. "Pity me. Augh! Delia! *Pit*—y me!"

She eyed me critically. "*Why* you keep playing the fool like this I don't know," she said. "Anyhow, I really cannot go about with a man who behaves as you do. You made us both ridiculous on Wednesday. Frankly, I dislike you, as you are now. I met you here to tell you so—as it's about the only place where we can be sure of being alone together—"

"Delia!" said I, with intensity, knuckles of clenched hands white. "You don't mean—"

"I do," said Delia. "A woman's lot is sad enough at the best of times. But with you—"

I clapped my hand on my brow.

"So, good-bye," said Delia, without emotion.

"Oh, Delia!" I said. "Not *this?*"

"Good-bye, Mr. Cummins," she said.

By a violent effort I controlled myself and touched her hand. I tried to say some word of explanation to her. She looked into my working face and winced. "I *must* do it," she said hopelessly. Then she turned from me and began walking rapidly down the gallery.

Heavens! How the human agony cried within me! I loved Delia. But nothing found expression—I was already too deeply crusted with my acquired self.

"Good-baye!" I said at last, watching her retreating figure. How I hated myself for doing it! After she had vanished, I repeated in a dreamy way, "Good-baye!" looking hopelessly round me. Then, with a kind of heart-broken cry, I shook my clenched fists in the air, staggered to the pedestal of a winged figure, buried my face in my arms, and made my shoulders heave. Something within me said, "Ass!" as I did so. (I had the greatest difficulty in persuading the Museum policeman, who was attracted by my cry of agony, that I was not intoxicated, but merely suffering from a transient indisposition.)

But even this great sorrow has not availed to save me from my fate. I see it, every one sees it; I grow more "theatrical" every day. And no one could be more painfully aware of the pungent silliness of theatrical ways. The quiet, nervous, but pleasing E. C. Cummins vanishes. I cannot save him. I am driven like a dead leaf before the winds of March. My tailor even enters into the spirit of my disorder. He has a peculiar sense of what is fitting. I tried to get a dull grey suit from him this spring, and he foisted a brilliant blue upon me, and I see he has put braid down the sides of my new dress trousers. My hairdresser insists upon giving me a "wave."

I am beginning to associate with actors. I detest them, but it is only in their company that I can feel I am not glaringly conspicuous. Their talk infects me. I notice a growing tendency to dramatic brevity, to dashes and pauses in my style, to a punctuation of bows and attitudes. Barnaby has remarked it too. I offended Wembly by calling him "Dear Boy" yesterday. I dread the end, but I cannot escape from it.

The fact is, I am being obliterated. Living a grey, retired life all my youth, I came to the theatre a delicate sketch of a man, a thing of tints and faint lines. Their gorgeous colouring has effaced me altogether. People forget how much mode of expression, method of movement, are a matter of contagion. I have heard of stage-struck people before, and thought it a figure of speech. I spoke of it jestingly, as a disease. It is no jest. It *is* a disease. And I have got it bad! Deep down within me I protest against the wrong done to my personality—unavailingly. For three hours or more a week I have to go and concentrate my attention on some fresh play, and the suggestions of the drama strengthen their awful hold upon me. My manners grow so flamboyant, my passions so professional, that I doubt, as I said at the outset, whether it is really myself that behaves in such a manner. I feel merely the core to this dramatic casing, that grows thicker and presses upon me—me and mine. I feel like King John's abbot in his cope of lead.

I doubt, indeed, whether I should not abandon the struggle altogether—leave this sad world of ordinary life for which I am so ill-fitted, abandon the name of Cummins for some professional pseudonym, complete my self-effacement, and—a thing of tricks and tatters, of posing and pretence—go upon the stage. It seems my only resort—"to hold the mirror up to Nature." For in the ordinary life, I will confess, no one now seems to regard me as both sane and sober. Only upon the stage, I feel convinced, will people take me seriously. That will be the end of it. I *know* that will be the end of it. And yet—I will frankly confess—all that marks off your actor from your common man—I *detest.* I am still largely of my Aunt Charlotte's opinion, that play-acting is unworthy of a pure-minded man's attention, much more participation. Even now I would resign my dramatic criticism and try a rest. Only I can't get hold of Barnaby. Letters of resignation he never notices. He says it is against the etiquette of journalism to write to your Editor. And when I go to see him, he gives me another big cigar and some strong whiskey and soda, and then something always turns up to prevent my explanation.

The Jilting of Jane

AS I SIT writing in my study, I can hear our Jane bumping her way downstairs with a brush and dustpan. She used in the old days to sing hymn tunes, or the British national song for the time being, to these instruments; but latterly she has been silent and even careful over her work. Time was when I prayed with fervour for such silence, and my wife with sighs for such care, but now they have come we are not so glad as we might have anticipated we should be. Indeed, I would rejoice secretly, though it may be unmanly weakness to admit it, even to hear Jane sing "Daisy," or by the fracture of any plate but one of Euphemia's best green ones, to learn that the period of brooding has come to an end.

Yet how we longed to hear the last of Jane's young man before we heard the last of him! Jane was always very free with her conversation to my wife, and discoursed admirably in the kitchen on a variety of topics—so well, indeed, that I sometimes left my study-door open—our house is a small one—to partake of it. But after William came, it was always William, nothing but William; William this and William that; and when we thought William was worked out and exhausted altogether, then William all over again. The engagement lasted altogether three years; yet how she got introduced to William, and so became thus saturated with him, was always a secret. For my part, I believe it was at the street corner where the Rev. Barnabas Baux used to hold an open-air service after evensong on Sundays. Young Cupids were wont to flit like moths round the paraffin flare of that centre of High Church hymn-singing. I fancy she stood singing hymns there, out of memory and her imagination, instead of coming home to get supper, and William came up beside her and said, "Hello!" "Hello yourself!" she said; and, etiquette being satisfied, they proceeded to talk together.

As Euphemia has a reprehensible way of letting her servants talk to her, she soon heard of him. "He is *such* a respectable young man, ma'am," said Jane, "you don't know." Ignoring the slur cast on her acquaintance, my wife inquired further about this William.

"He is second porter at Maynard's, the draper's," said Jane, "and gets eighteen shillings—nearly a pound—a week, m'm; and when the head porter leaves he will be head porter. His relatives are quite superior people, m'm. Not labouring people at all. His father was a green-grosher, m'm, and had a chumor, and he was bankrup' twice. And one of his sisters is in a Home for the Dying. It will be a very good match for me, m'm," said Jane, "me being all orphan girl."

"Then you are engaged to him?" asked my wife.

"Not engaged, ma'am; but he is saving money to buy a ring—hammyfist."

"Well, Jane, when you are properly engaged to him you may ask him round here on Sunday afternoons, and have tea with him in the kitchen." For my Euphemia has a motherly conception of her duty towards her maid-servants. And presently the amethystine ring was being worn about the house, even with ostentation, and Jane developed a new way of bringing in the joint, so that this gage was evident. The elder Miss Maitland was aggrieved by it, and told my wife that servants ought not to wear rings. But my wife looked it up in "Enquire Within" and "Mrs. Motherly's Book of Household Management," and found no prohibition. So Jane remained with this happiness added to her love.

The treasure of Jane's heart appeared to me to be what respectable people call a very deserving young man "William, ma'am," said Jane, one day suddenly, with ill-concealed complacency, as she counted out the beer bottles, "William, ma'am, is a teetotaller. Yes, m'm; and he don't smoke. Smoking, ma'am," said Jane, as one who reads the heart, "*do* make such a dust about. Beside the waste of money. *And* the smell. However, I suppose it's necessary to some."

Possibly it dawned on Jane that she was reflecting a little severely upon Euphemia's comparative ill-fortune; and she added kindly, "I'm sure the master is a hangel when his pipe's alight. Compared to other times."

William was at first a rather shabby young man of the ready-made black-coat school of costume. He had watery grey eyes, and a complexion appropriate to the brother of one in a Home for the Dying. Euphemia did not fancy him very much, even at the beginning. His eminent respectability was vouched for by an alpaca umbrella, from which he never allowed himself to be parted.

"He goes to chapel," said Jane. "His papa, ma'am—"

"His *what*, Jane?"

"His papa, ma'am, was Church; but Mr. Maynard is a Plymouth Brother, and William thinks it Policy, ma'am, to go there too. Mr. Maynard comes and talks to him quite friendly, when they ain't busy, about using up all the ends of string, and about his soul. He takes a lot of notice, do Mr. Maynard, of William, and the way he saves string and his soul, ma'am."

Presently we heard that the head porter at Maynard's had left, and that William was head porter at twenty-three shillings a week. "He is really kind of over the man who drives the van," said Jane, "and him married with three children." And she promised in the pride of her heart to make interest for us with William to favour us so that we might get our parcels of drapery from Maynard's with exceptional promptitude.

After this promotion a rapidly increasing prosperity came upon Jane's young man. One day, we learned that Mr. Maynard had given William a book. "Smiles' 'Elp Yourself, it's called," said Jane; "but it ain't comic. It tells you how to get on in the world, and some what William read to me was *lovely*, ma'am."

Euphemia told me of this laughing, and then she became suddenly grave. "Do you know, dear," she said, "Jane said one thing I did not like. She had been quiet for a minute, and then she suddenly remarked, 'William is a lot above me, ma'am, ain't he?"

"I don't see anything in that," I said, though later my eyes were to be opened.

One Sunday afternoon about that time I was sitting at my writing-desk—possibly I was reading a good book—when a something went by the window. I heard a startled exclamation behind me, and saw Euphemia with her hands clasped together and her eyes dilated. "George," she said in an awestricken whisper, "did you see?"

Then we both spoke to one another at the same moment, slowly and solemnly: *"A silk hat! Yellow gloves! A new umbrella!"*

"It may be my fancy, dear," said Euphemia; "but his tie was very like yours. I believe Jane keeps him in ties. She told me a little while ago, in a way that implied volumes about the rest of your costume, 'The master *do* wear pretty ties, ma'am.' And he echoes all your novelties."

The young couple passed our window again on their way to their customary walk. They were arm in arm. Jane looked exquisitely proud, happy, and uncomfortable, with new white cotton gloves, and William, in the silk hat, singularly genteel!

That was the culmination of Jane's happiness. When she returned, "Mr. Maynard has been talking to William, ma'am," she said, "and he is to serve customers, just like the young shop gentlemen, during the next sale. And if he gets on, he is to be made an assistant, ma'am, at the first opportunity. He has got to be as gentlemanly as he can, ma'am; and if he ain't, ma'am, he says it won't be for want of trying. Mr. Maynard has took a great fancy to him."

"He *is* getting on, Jane," said my wife.

"Yes, ma'am," said Jane, thoughtfully, "he *is* getting on."

And she sighed.

That next Sunday, as I drank my tea, I interrogated my wife. "How is this Sunday different from all other Sundays, little woman? What has happened? Have you altered the curtains, or rearranged the furniture, or where is the indefinable difference of it? Are you wearing your hair in a new way without warning me? I clearly perceive a change in my environment, and I cannot for the life of me say what it is."

Then my wife answered in her most tragic voice: "George," she said, "that—that William has not come near the place to-day! And Jane is crying her heart out upstairs."

There followed a period of silence. Jane, as I have said, stopped singing about the house, and began to care for our brittle possessions, which struck my wife as being a very sad sign indeed. The next Sunday, and the next, Jane asked to go out, "to walk with William;" and my wife, who never attempts to extort confidences, gave her permission, and asked no questions. On each occasion Jane came back looking flushed and very determined. At last one day she became communicative.

"William is being led away," she remarked abruptly, with a catching of the breath, apropos of table-cloths. "Yes, m'm. She is a milliner, and she can play on the piano."

"I thought," said my wife, "that you went out with him on Sunday."

"Not out with him, m'm—after him. I walked along by the side of them, and told her he was engaged to me."

"Dear me, Jane, did you? What did they do?"

"Took no more notice of me than if I was dirt. So I told her she should suffer for it."

"It could not have been a very agreeable walk, Jane."

"Not for no parties, ma'am.

"I wish," said Jane, "I could play the piano, ma'am. But anyhow, I don't mean to let *her* get him away from me. She's older than him, and her hair ain't gold to the roots, ma'am."

It was on the August Bank Holiday that the crisis came. We do not clearly know the details of the fray, but only such fragments as poor Jane let fall. She came home dusty, excited, and with her heart hot within her.

The milliner's mother, the milliner, and William had made a party to the Art Museum at South Kensington, I think. Anyhow, Jane had calmly but firmly accosted them somewhere in the streets, and asserted her right to what, in spite of the consensus of literature, she held to be her inalienable property. She did, I think, go so far as to lay hands on him. They dealt with her in a crushingly superior way. They "called a cab." There was a "scene," William being pulled away into the four-wheeler by his future wife and mother-in-law from the reluctant hands of our discarded Jane. There were threats of giving her "in charge."

"My poor Jane!" said my wife, mincing veal as though she was mincing William. "It's a shame of them. I would think no more of him. He is not worthy of you."

"No, m'm," said Jane. "He *is* weak.

"But it's that woman has done it," said Jane. She was never known to bring herself to pronounce "that woman's" name or to admit her girlishness. "I can't think what minds some women must have—to try and get a girl's young man away from her. But there, it only hurts to talk about it," said Jane.

Thereafter our house rested from William. But there was something in the manner of Jane's scrubbing the front doorstep or sweeping out the rooms, a certain viciousness, that persuaded me that the story had not yet ended.

"Please, m'm, may I go and see a wedding to-morrow?" said Jane, one day.

My wife knew by instinct whose wedding. "Do you think it is wise, Jane?" she said.

"I would like to see the last of him," said Jane.

"My dear," said my wife, fluttering into my room about twenty minutes after Jane had started, "Jane has been to the boot-hole and taken all the left-off boots and shoes, and gone off to the wedding with them in a bag. Surely she cannot mean—"

"Jane," I said, "is developing character. Let us hope for the best."

Jane came back with a pale, hard face. All the boots seemed to be still in her bag, at which my wife heaved a premature sigh of relief. We heard her go upstairs and replace the boots with considerable emphasis.

"Quite a crowd at the wedding, ma'am," she said presently, in a purely conversational style, sitting in our little kitchen, and scrubbing the potatoes; "and such a lovely day for them." She proceeded to numerous other details, clearly avoiding some cardinal incident.

"It was all extremely respectable and nice, ma'am; but *her* father didn't wear a black coat, and looked quite out of place, ma'am. Mr. Piddingquirk—"

"Who?"

"Mr. Piddingquirk—William that *was,* ma'am—had white gloves, and a coat like a clergyman, and a lovely chrysanthemum. He looked so nice, ma'am. And there was red carpet down, just like for gentlefolks. And they say he gave the clerk four shillings, ma'am. It was a real kerridge they had—not a fly. When they came out of church, there was rice-throwing, and her two little sisters dropping dead flowers. And some one threw a slipper, and then I threw a boot—"

"Threw a *boot,* Jane!"

"Yes, ma'am. Aimed at *her*. But it hit *him*. Yes, ma'am, hard. Gev him a black eye, I should think. I only threw that one. I hadn't the heart to try again. All the little boys cheered when it hit him."

After an interval—"I am sorry the boot hit *him*."

Another pause. The potatoes were being scrubbed violently. "He always *was* a bit above me, you know, ma'am. And he was led away."

The potatoes were more than finished. Jane rose sharply, with a sigh, and rapped the basin down on the table.

"I don't care," she said. "I don't care a rap. He will find out his mistake yet. It serves me right. I was stuck up about him. I ought not to have looked so high. And I am glad things are as things are."

My wife was in the kitchen, seeing to the higher cookery. After the confession of the boot-throwing, she must have watched poor Jane fuming with a certain dismay in those brown eyes of hers. But I imagine they softened again very quickly, and then Jane's must have met them.

"Oh, ma'am," said Jane, with an astonishing change of note, "think of all that *might* have been! Oh, ma'am, I *could* have been so happy! I ought to have known, but I didn't know—You're very kind to let me talk to you, ma'am—for it's hard on me, ma'am—it's har-r-r-r-d—"

And I gather that Euphemia so far forgot herself as to let Jane sob out some of the fulness of her heart on a sympathetic shoulder. My Euphemia, thank Heaven, has never properly grasped the importance of "keeping up her position." And since that fit of weeping, much of the accent of bitterness has gone out of Jane's scrubbing and brush-work.

Indeed, something passed the other day with the butcher-boy—but that scarcely belongs to this story. However, Jane is young still, and time and change are at work with her. We all have our sorrows, but I do not believe very much in the existence of sorrows that never heal.

The Lost Inheritance

"MY UNCLE," SAID the man with the glass eye, "was what you might call a hemi-semi-demi millionaire. He was worth about a hundred and twenty thousand. Quite. And he left me all his money."

I glanced at the shiny sleeve of his coat, and my eye travelled up to the frayed collar.

"Every penny," said the man with the glass eye, and I caught the active pupil looking at me with a touch of offence.

"I've never had any windfalls like that," I said, trying to speak enviously and propitiate him.

"Even a legacy isn't always a blessing," he remarked with a sigh, and with an air of philosophical resignation he put the red nose and the wiry moustache into his tankard for a space.

"Perhaps not," I said.

"He was an author, you see, and he wrote a lot of books."

"Indeed!"

"That was the trouble of it all." He stared at me with the available eye, to see if I grasped his statement, then averted his face a little and produced a toothpick.

"You see," he said, smacking his lips after a pause, "it was like this. He was my uncle—my maternal uncle. And he had—what shall I call it?—a weakness for writing edifying literature. Weakness is hardly the word—downright mania is nearer the mark. He'd been librarian in a Polytechnic, and as soon as the money came to him he began to indulge his ambition. It's a simply extraordinary and incomprehensible thing to me. Here was a man of thirty-seven suddenly dropped into a perfect pile of gold, and he didn't go—not a day's bust on it. One would think a chap would go and get himself dressed a bit decent—say a couple of dozen pairs of trousers at a West End tailor's; but he never did. You'd hardly believe it, but when he died he hadn't even a gold watch. It seems wrong for people like that to have money. All he did was just to take a house, and order in pretty nearly five tons of books and ink and paper, and set to writing edifying literature as hard as ever he could write. I *can't* understand it! But he did. The money came to him, curiously enough, through a maternal uncle of *his,* unexpected like, when he was seven-and-thirty. My mother, it happened, was his only relation in the wide, wide world, except some second cousins of his. And I was her only son. You follow all that? The second cousins had one only son, too; but they brought him to see the old man too soon. He was rather a spoilt youngster, was this son of theirs, and directly he set eyes on my uncle, he began bawling out as hard as he could. 'Take 'im away—er,' he says, 'take 'im away,' and so did for himself entirely. It was pretty straight sailing, you'd think, for me, eh? And my mother, being a sensible, careful woman, settled the business in her own mind long before he did.

"He was a curious little chap, was my uncle, as I remember him. I don't wonder at the kid being scared. Hair, just like these Japanese dolls they sell, black and straight and stiff all round the brim and none in the middle, and below, a whitish kind of face and rather large dark grey eyes moving about behind his spectacles. He used to attach a great deal of importance to dress, and always wore a flapping overcoat and a big-rimmed felt hat of a most extraordinary size. He looked a rummy little beggar, I can tell you. Indoors it was, as a rule, a dirty red flannel dressing-gown and a black skull-cap he had. That black skull-cap made him look like the portraits of all kinds of celebrated people. He was always moving about from house to house, was my uncle, with his chair which had belonged to Savage Landor, and his two writing-tables, one of Carlyle's and the other of Shelley's, so the dealer told him, and the completest portable reference library in England, he said he had,—and he lugged the whole caravan, now to a house at Down, near Darwin's old place, then to Reigate, near Meredith, then off to Haslemere, then back to Chelsea for a bit, and then up to Hampstead. He knew there was something wrong with his stuff, but he never knew there was anything wrong with his brains. It was always the air, or the water, or the altitude, or some tommy-rot like that. 'So much depends on environment,' he used to say, and stare at you hard, as if he half-suspected you were hiding a grin at him somewhere under your face. 'So much depends on environment to a sensitive mind like mine.'

"What was his name? You wouldn't know it if I told you. He wrote nothing that any one has ever read—nothing. No one *could* read it. He wanted to be a great teacher, he said, and he didn't know what he wanted to teach any more than a child. So he just blethered at large about Truth and Righteousness, and the Spirit of History, and all that. Book after book he wrote and published at his own expense. He wasn't quite right in his head, you know, really; and to hear him go on at the critics—not because they slated him, mind you—he liked that—but because they didn't take any notice of him at all. 'What do the nations want?' he would ask, holding out his brown old claw. 'Why, teaching—guidance! They are scattered upon the hills like sheep without a shepherd. There is War, and Rumours of War, the unlaid Spirit of Discord abroad in the land, Nihilism, Vivisection, Vaccination, Drunkenness, Penury, Want, Socialistic Error, Selfish Capital! Do you see the clouds, Ted?'—my name, you know—'Do you see the clouds lowering over the land? and behind it all—the Mongol waits!' He was always very great on Mongols, and the Spectre of Socialism, and such-like things.

"Then out would come his finger at me, and, with his eyes all afire and his skull-cap askew, he would whisper: 'And here am I. What do I want? Nations to teach. Nations! I say it with all modesty, Ted, I *could.* I would guide them; nay! but I *will* guide them to a safe haven, to the land of Righteousness, flowing with milk and honey.'

"That's how he used to go on. Ramble, rave about the nations, and righteousness, and that kind of thing. Kind of mincemeat of Bible and blethers. From fourteen up to three-and-twenty, when I might have been improving my mind, my mother used to wash me and brush my hair (at least in the earlier years of it), with a nice parting down the middle, and take me, once or twice a week, to hear this old lunatic jabber about things he had read of in the morning papers, trying to do it as much like Carlyle as he could; and I used to sit according to instructions, and look intelligent and nice, and pretend to be taking it all in. Afterwards, I used to go of my own free will, out of a regard for the legacy. I was the only person that used to go and see him. He wrote, I believe, to every man who made the slightest stir in the world, sending him a copy or so of his books, and inviting him to come and talk about the nations to him; but half of them didn't answer, and none ever came. And when the girl let you in—she was an artful bit of goods, that girl—there were heaps of letters on the hall-seat waiting to go off, addressed to Prince Bismark, the President of the United States, and such-like people. And one went up the staircase and along the cobwebby passage,—the housekeeper drank like fury, and his passages were always cobwebby,—and found him at last, with books turned down all over the room, and heaps of torn paper on the floor, and telegrams and newspapers littered about, and empty coffee-cups and half-eaten bits of toast on the desk and the mantel. You'd see his back humped up, and his hair would be sticking out quite straight between the collar of that dressing-gown thing and the edge of the skull-cap.

"'A moment!' he would say. 'A moment!' over his shoulder. 'The *mot juste,* you know, Ted, *le mot juste.* Righteous thought righteously expressed—Aah!—concatenation. And now, Ted,' he'd say, spinning round in his study chair, 'how's Young England?' That was his silly name for me.

"Well, that was my uncle, and that was how he talked—to me, at any rate. With others about he seemed a bit shy. And he not only talked to me, but he gave me his books, books of six hundred pages or so, with cock-eyed headings, 'The Shrieking Sisterhood,' 'The Behemoth of Bigotry,' 'Crucibles and Cullenders,' and so on. All very strong, and none of them original. The very last time but one that I saw him he gave me a book. He was feeling ill even then, and his hand shook and he was despondent. I noticed it because I was naturally on the look-out for those little symptoms. 'My last book, Ted,' he said. 'My last book, my boy; my last word to the deaf and hardened nations; ' and I'm hanged if a tear didn't go rolling down his yellow old cheek. He was regular crying because it was so nearly over, and he hadn't only written about fifty-three books of rubbish. 'I've sometimes thought, Ted—' he said, and stopped.

"'Perhaps I've been a bit hasty and angry with this stiff-necked generation. A little more sweetness, perhaps, and a little less blinding light. I've sometimes thought—I might have swayed them. But I've done my best, Ted.'

"And then, with a burst, for the first and last time in his life he owned himself a failure. It showed he was really ill. He seemed to think for a minute, and then he spoke quietly and low, as sane and sober as I am now. 'I've been a fool, Ted,' he said. 'I've been flapping nonsense all my life. Only He who readeth the heart knows whether this is anything more than vanity. Ted, I don't. But He knows, He knows, and if I have done foolishly and vainly, in my heart—in my heart—'

"Just like that he spoke, repeating himself, and he stopped quite short and handed the book to me, trembling. Then the old shine came back into his eye. I remember it all fairly well, because I repeated it and acted it to my old mother when I got home, to cheer her up a bit. 'Take this book and read it,' he said. 'It's my last word, my very last word. I've left all my property to you, Ted, and may you use it better than I have done.' And then he fell a-coughing.

"I remember that quite well even now, and how I went home cock-a-hoop, and how he was in bed the next time I called. The housekeeper was downstairs drunk, and I fooled about—as a young man will—with the girl in the passage before I went to him. He was sinking fast. But even then his vanity clung to him.

"'Have you read it? ' he whispered.

"'Sat up all night reading it,' I said in his ear to cheer him. 'It's the last,' said I, and then, with a memory of some poetry or other in my head, 'but it's the bravest and best.'

"He smiled a little and tried to squeeze my hand as a woman might do, and left off squeezing in the middle, and lay still. 'The bravest and the best,' said I again, seeing it pleased him. But he didn't answer. I heard the girl giggle outside the door, for occasionally we'd had just a bit of innocent laughter, you know, at his ways. I looked at his face, and his eyes were closed, and it was just as if somebody had punched in his nose on either side. But he was still smiling. It's queer to think of—he lay dead, lay dead there, an utter failure, with the smile of success on his face.

"That was the end of my uncle. You can imagine me and my mother saw that he had a decent funeral. Then, of course, came the hunt for the will. We began decent and respectful at first, and before the day was out we were ripping chairs, and smashing bureau panels, and sounding walls. Every hour we expected those others to come in. We asked the housekeeper, and found she'd actually witnessed a will—on an ordinary half-sheet of notepaper it was written, and very short, she said—not a month ago. The other witness was the gardener, and he bore her out word for word. But I'm hanged if there was that or any other will to be found. The way my mother talked must have made him turn in his grave. At last a lawyer at Reigate sprang one on us that had been made years ago during some temporary quarrel with my mother. I'm blest if that wasn't the only will to be discovered anywhere, and it left every penny he possessed to that 'Take 'im away' youngster of his second cousin's—a chap who'd never had to stand his talking not for one afternoon of his life."

The man with the glass eye stopped.

"I thought you said—" I began.

"Half a minute," said the man with the glass eye. "*I* had to wait for the end of the story till this very morning, and I was a blessed sight more interested than you are. You just wait a bit, too. They executed the will, and the other chap inherited, and directly he was one-and-twenty he began to blew it. How he did blew it, to be sure! He bet, he drank, he got in the papers for this and that. I tell you, it makes me wriggle to think of the times he had. He blewed every ha'penny of it before he was thirty, and the last I heard of him was—Holloway! Three years ago.

"Well, I naturally fell on hard times, because, as you see, the only trade I knew was legacy-cadging. All my plans were waiting over to begin, so to speak, when the old chap died. I've had my ups and downs since then. Just now it's a period of depression. I tell you frankly, I'm on the look-out for help. I was hunting round my room to find something to raise a bit on for immediate necessities, and the sight of all those presentation volumes—no one will buy them, not to wrap butter in, even—well, they annoyed me. I'd promised him not to part with them, and I never kept a promise easier. I let out at them with my boot, and sent them shooting across the room. One lifted at the kick, and spun through the air. And out of it flapped—You guess?

"It was the will. He'd given it me himself in that very last volume of all."

He folded his arms on the table, and looked sadly with the active eye at his empty tankard. He shook his head slowly, and said softly, "I'd never *opened* the book, much more cut a page!" Then he looked up, with a bitter laugh, for my sympathy. "Fancy hiding it there! Eigh? Of all places."

He began to fish absently for a dead fly with his finger. "It just shows you the vanity of authors," he said, looking up at me. "It wasn't no trick of his. He'd meant perfectly fair. He'd really thought I was really going home to read that blessed book of his through. But it shows you, don't it?"—his eye went down to the tankard again,—"it shows you, too, how we poor human beings fail to understand one another."

But there was no misunderstanding the eloquent thirst of his eye. He accepted with ill-feigned surprise. He said, in the usual subtle formula, that he didn't mind if he did.

Pollock and the Porroh Man

IT WAS IN a swampy village on the lagoon river behind the Turner Peninsula that Pollock's first encounter with the Porroh man occurred. The women of that country are famous for their good looks—they are Gallinas with a dash of European blood that dates from the days of Vasco da Gama and the English slave-traders, and the Porroh man, too, was possibly inspired by a faint Caucasian taint in his composition. (It's a curious thing to think that some of us may have distant cousins eating men on Sherboro Island or raiding with the Sofas.) At any rate, the Porroh man stabbed the woman to the heart as though he had been a mere low-class Italian, and very narrowly missed Pollock. But Pollock, using his revolver to parry the lightning stab which was aimed at his deltoid muscle, sent the iron dagger flying, and, firing, hit the man in the hand.

He fired again and missed, knocking a sudden window out of the wall of the hut. The Porroh man stooped in the doorway, glancing under his arm at Pollock. Pollock caught a glimpse of his inverted face in the sunlight, and then the

Englishman was alone, sick and trembling with the excitement of the affair, in the twilight of the place. It had all happened in less time than it takes to read about it.

The woman was quite dead, and having ascertained this, Pollock went to the entrance of the hut and looked out. Things outside were dazzling bright. Half a dozen of the porters of the expedition were standing up in a group near the green huts they occupied, and staring towards him, wondering what the shots might signify. Behind the little group of men was the broad stretch of black fetid mud by the river, a green carpet of rafts of papyrus and water-grass, and then the leaden water. The mangroves beyond the stream loomed indistinctly through the blue haze. There were no signs of excitement in the squat village, whose fence was just visible above the cane-grass.

Pollock came out of the hut cautiously and walked towards the river, looking over his shoulder at intervals. But the Porroh man had vanished. Pollock clutched his revolver nervously in his hand.

One of his men came to meet him, and as he came, pointed to the bushes behind the hut in which the Porroh man had disappeared. Pollock had an irritating persuasion of having made an absolute fool of himself; he felt bitter, savage, at the turn things had taken. At the same time, he would have to tell Waterhouse—the moral, exemplary, cautious Waterhouse—who would inevitably take the matter seriously. Pollock cursed bitterly at his luck, at Waterhouse, and especially at the West Coast of Africa. He felt consummately sick of the expedition. And in the back of his mind all the time was a speculative doubt where precisely within the visible horizon the Porroh man might be.

It is perhaps rather shocking, but he was not at all upset by the murder that had just happened. He had seen so much brutality during the last three months, so many dead women, burnt huts, drying skeletons, up the Kittam River in the wake of the Sofa cavalry, that his senses were blunted. What disturbed him was the persuasion that this business was only beginning.

He swore savagely at the black, who ventured to ask a question, and went on into the tent under the orange-trees where Waterhouse was lying, feeling exasperatingly like a boy going into the headmaster's study.

Waterhouse was still sleeping off the effects of his last dose of chlorodyne, and Pollock sat down on a packing-case beside him, and, lighting his pipe, waited for him to awake. About him were scattered the pots and weapons Waterhouse had collected from the Mendi people, and which he had been repacking for the canoe voyage to Sulyma.

Presently Waterhouse woke up, and after judicial stretching, decided he was all right again. Pollock got him some tea. Over the tea the incidents of the afternoon were described by Pollock, after some preliminary beating about the bush. Waterhouse took the matter even more seriously than Pollock had anticipated. He did not simply disapprove, he scolded, he insulted.

"You're one of those infernal fools who think a black man isn't a human being," he said. "I can't be ill a day without you must get into some dirty scrape or other. This is the third time in a month that you have come crossways-on with a native, and this time you're in for it with a vengeance. Porroh, too! They're down upon you enough as it is, about that idol you wrote your silly name on. And they're the most vindictive devils on earth! You make a man ashamed of civilisation. To think you come of a decent family! If ever I cumber myself up with a vicious, stupid young lout like you again—"

"Steady on, now," snarled Pollock, in the tone that always exasperated Waterhouse; "steady on."

At that Waterhouse became speechless. He jumped to his feet.

"Look here, Pollock," he said, after a struggle to control his breath. "You must go home. I won't have you any longer. I'm ill enough as it is through you—"

"Keep your hair on," said Pollock, staring in front of him. "I'm ready enough to go."

Waterhouse became calmer again. He sat down on the camp-stool. "Very well," he said. "I don't want a row, Pollock, you know; but it's confoundedly annoying to have one's plans put out by this kind of thing. I'll come to Sulyma with you, and see you safe aboard—"

"You needn't," said Pollock. "I can go alone. From here."

"Not far," said Waterhouse. "You don't understand this Porroh business."

"How should *I* know she belonged to a Porrohman?" said Pollock, bitterly.

"Well, she did," said Waterhouse; "and you can't undo the thing. Go alone, indeed! I wonder what they'd do to you. You don't seem to understand that this Porroh hokey-pokey rules this country, is its law, religion, constitution, medicine, magic— They appoint the chiefs. The Inquisition, at its best, couldn't hold a candle to these chaps. He will probably set Awajale, the chief here, on to us. It's lucky our porters are Mendis. We shall have to shift this little settlement of ours—Confound you, Pollock! And, of course, you must go and miss him."

He thought, and his thoughts seemed disagreeable. Presently he stood up and took his rifle. "I'd keep close for a bit, if I were you," he said, over his shoulder, as he went out. "I'm going out to see what I can find out about it."

Pollock remained sitting in the tent, meditating. "I was meant for a civilised life," he said to himself, regretfully, as he filled his pipe. "The sooner I get back to London or Paris the better for me."

His eye fell on the sealed case in which Waterhouse had put the featherless poisoned arrows they had bought in the Mendi country. "I wish I had hit the beggar somewhere vital," said Pollock, viciously.

Waterhouse came back after a long interval. He was not communicative, though Pollock asked him questions enough. The Porroh man, it seems, was a prominent member of that mystical society. The village was interested, but not threatening. No doubt the witch-doctor had gone into the bush. He was a great witch-doctor. "Of course, he's up to something," said Waterhouse, and became silent.

"But what can he do?" asked Pollock, unheeded.

"I must get you out of this. There's something brewing, or things would not be so quiet," said Waterhouse, after a gap of silence. Pollock wanted to know what the brew might be. "Dancing in a circle of skulls," said Waterhouse; "brewing a stink in a copper pot." Pollock wanted particulars. Waterhouse was vague, Pollock pressing. At last Waterhouse lost his temper. "How the devil should *I* know?" he said to Pollock's twentieth inquiry what the Porroh man would do. "He tried to kill you off-hand in the hut. *Now,* I fancy he will try something more elaborate. But you'll see fast enough. I don't want to help unnerve you. It's probably all nonsense."

That night, as they were sitting at their fire, Pollock again tried to draw Waterhouse out on the subject of Porroh methods. "Better get to sleep," said Waterhouse, when Pollock's bent became apparent; "we start early to-morrow. You may want all your nerve about you."

"But what line will he take?"

"Can't say. They're versatile people. They know a lot of rum dodges. You'd better get that copper-devil, Shakespear, to talk."

There was a flash and a heavy bang out of the darkness behind the huts, and a clay bullet came whistling close to

Pollock's head. This, at least, was crude enough. The blacks and half-breeds sitting and yarning round their own fire jumped up, and some one fired into the dark.

"Better go into one of the huts," said Waterhouse, quietly, still sitting unmoved.

Pollock stood up by the fire and drew his revolver. Fighting, at least, he was not afraid of. But a man in the dark is in the best of armour. Realising the wisdom of Waterhouse's advice, Pollock went into the tent and lay down there.

What little sleep he had was disturbed by dreams, variegated dreams, but chiefly of the Porroh man's face, upside down, as he went out of the hut, and looked up under his arm. It was odd that this transitory impression should have stuck so firmly in Pollock's memory. Moreover, he was troubled by queer pains in his limbs.

In the white haze of the early morning, as they were loading the canoes, a barbed arrow suddenly appeared quivering in the ground close to Pollock's foot. The boys made a perfunctory effort to clear out the thicket, but it led to no capture.

After these two occurrences, there was a disposition on the part of the expedition to leave Pollock to himself, and Pollock became, for the first time in his life, anxious to mingle with blacks. Waterhouse took one canoe, and Pollock, in spite of a friendly desire to chat with Waterhouse, had to take the other. He was left all alone in the front part of the canoe, and he had the greatest trouble to make the men—who did not love him—keep to the middle of the river, a clear hundred yards or more from either shore. However, he made Shakespear, the Freetown half-breed, come up to his own end of the canoe and tell him about Porroh, which Shakespear, failing in his attempts to leave Pollock alone, presently did with considerable freedom and gusto.

The day passed. The canoe glided swiftly along the ribbon of lagoon water, between the drift of water-figs, fallen trees, papyrus, and palm-wine palms, and with the dark mangrove swamp to the left, through which one could hear now and then the roar of the Atlantic surf. Shakespear told, in his soft blurred English, of how the Porroh could cast spells; how men withered up under their malice; how they could send dreams and devils; how they tormented and killed the sons of Ijibu; how they kidnapped a white trader from Sulyma who had maltreated one of the sect, and how his body looked when it was found. And Pollock after each narrative cursed under his breath at the want of missionary enterprise that allowed such things to be, and at the inert British Government that ruled over this dark heathendom of Sierra Leone. In the evening they came to the Kasi Lake, and sent a score of crocodiles lumbering off the island on which the expedition camped for the night.

The next day they reached Sulyma, and smelt the sea breeze; but Pollock had to put up there for five days before he could get on to Freetown. Waterhouse, considering him to be comparatively safe here, and within the pale of Freetown influence, left him and went back with the expedition to Gbemma, and Pollock became very friendly with Perera, the only resident white trader at Sulyma—so friendly, indeed, that he went about with him everywhere. Perera was a little Portuguese Jew, who had lived in England, and he appreciated the Englishman's friendliness as a great compliment.

For two days nothing happened out of the ordinary; for the most part Pollock and Perera played Nap—the only game they had in common—and Pollock got into debt. Then, on the second evening, Pollock had a disagreeable intimation of the arrival of the Porroh man in Sulyma by getting a flesh-wound in the shoulder from a lump of filed iron. It was a long shot, and the missile had nearly spent its force when it hit him. Still it conveyed its message plainly enough. Pollock sat up in his hammock, revolver in hand, all that night, and next morning confided, to some extent, in the Anglo-Portuguese.

Perera took the matter seriously. He knew the local customs pretty thoroughly. "It is a personal question, you must know. It is revenge. And of course he is hurried by your leaving de country. None of de natives or half-breeds will interfere wid him very much—unless you make it wort deir while. If you come upon him suddenly, you might shoot him. But den he might shoot you.

"Den dere's dis—infernal magic," said Perera. "Of course, I don't believe in it—superstition; but still it's not nice to tink dat wherever you are, dere is a black man, who spends a moonlight night now and den a-dancing about a fire to send you bad dreams—Had any bad dreams?"

"Rather," said Pollock. "I keep on seeing the beggar's head upside down grinning at me and showing all his teeth as he did in the hut, and coming close up to me, and then going ever so far off, and coming back. It's nothing to be afraid of, but somehow it simply paralyses me with terror in my sleep. Queer things—dreams. I know it's a dream all the time, and I can't wake up from it."

"It's probably only fancy," said Perera. "Den my niggers say Porroh men can send snakes. Seen any snakes lately?"

"Only one. I killed him this morning, on the floor near my hammock. Almost trod on him as I got up."

"*Ah!*" said Perera, and then, reassuringly, "Of course it is a—coincidence. Still I would keep my eyes open. Den dere's pains in de bones."

"I thought they were due to miasma," said Pollock.

"Probably dey are. When did dey begin?"

Then Pollock remembered that he first noticed them the night after the fight in the hut. "It's my opinion he don't want to kill you," said Perera—"at least not yet. I've heard deir idea is to scare and worry a man wid deir spells, and narrow misses, and rheumatic pains, and bad dreams, and all dat, until he's sick of life. Of course, it's all talk, you know. You mustn't worry about it—But I wonder what he'll be up to next."

"*I* shall have to be up to something first," said Pollock, staring gloomily at the greasy cards that Perera was putting on the table. "It don't suit my dignity to be followed about, and shot at, and blighted in this way. I wonder if Porroh hokey-pokey upsets your luck at cards."

He looked at Perera suspiciously.

"Very likely it does," said Perera, warmly, shuffling. "Dey are wonderful people."

That afternoon Pollock killed two snakes in his hammock, and there was also an extraordinary increase in the number of red ants that swarmed over the place; and these annoyances put him in a fit temper to talk over business with a certain Mendi rough he had interviewed before. The Mendi rough showed Pollock a little iron dagger, and demonstrated where one struck in the neck, in a way that made Pollock shiver; and in return for certain considerations Pollock promised him a double-barrelled gun with an ornamental lock.

In the evening, as Pollock and Perera were playing cards, the Mendi rough came in through the doorway, carrying something in a blood-soaked piece of native cloth.

"Not here!" said Pollock, very hurriedly. "Not here!"

But he was not quick enough to prevent the man, who was anxious to get to Pollock's side of the bargain, from opening the cloth and throwing the head of the Porroh man upon the table. It bounded from there on to the floor, leaving a red trail on the cards, and rolled into a corner, where it came to rest upside down, but glaring hard at Pollock.

Perera jumped up as the thing fell among the cards, and began in his excitement to gabble in Portuguese. The Mendi was bowing, with the red cloth in his hand. "De gun!" he said. Pollock stared back at the head in the corner. It bore exactly the expression it had in his dreams. Something seemed to snap in his own brain as he looked at it.

Then Perera found his English again.

"You got him killed?" he said. "You did not kill him yourself?"

"Why should I?" said Pollock.

"But he will not be able to take it off now!"

"Take *what* off?" said Pollock.

"And all dese cards are spoiled!"

"*What* do you mean by taking off?" said Pollock.

"You must send me a new pack from Freetown. You can buy dem dere."

"But—'take it off'?"

"It is only superstition. I forgot. De niggers say dat if de witches—he was a witch—But it is rubbish—You must make de Porroh man take it off, or kill him yourself—It is very silly."

Pollock swore under his breath, still staring hard at the head in the corner.

"I can't stand that glare," he said. Then suddenly he rushed at the thing and kicked it. It rolled some yards or so, and came to rest in the same position as before, upside down, and looking at him.

"He is ugly," said the Anglo-Portuguese. "Very ugly. Dey do it on deir faces with little knives."

Pollock would have kicked the head again, but the Mendi man touched him on the arm. "De gun?" he said, looking nervously at the head.

"Two—if you will take that beastly thing away," said Pollock.

The Mendi shook his head, and intimated that he only wanted one gun now due to him, and for which he would be obliged. Pollock found neither cajolery nor bullying any good with him. Perera had a gun to sell (at a profit of three hundred per cent.), and with that the man presently departed. Then Pollock's eyes, against his will, were recalled to the thing on the floor.

"It is funny dat his head keeps upside down," said Perera, with an uneasy laugh. "His brains must be heavy, like de weight in de little images one sees dat keep always upright wid lead in dem. You will take him wiv you when you go presently. You might take him now. De cards are all spoilt. Dere is a man sell dem in Freetown. De room is in a filty mess as it is. You should have killed him yourself."

Pollock pulled himself together, and went and picked up the head. He would hang it up by the lamp-hook in the middle of the ceiling of his room, and dig a grave for it at once. He was under the impression that he hung it up by the hair, but that must have been wrong, for when he returned for it, it was hanging by the neck upside down.

He buried it before sunset on the north side of the shed he occupied, so that he should not have to pass the grave after dark when he was returning from Perera's. He killed two snakes before he went to sleep. In the darkest part of the night he awoke with a start, and heard a pattering sound and something scraping on the floor. He sat up noiselessly, and felt under his pillow for his revolver. A mumbling growl followed, and Pollock fired at the sound. There was a yelp, and something dark passed for a moment across the hazy blue of the doorway. "A dog!" said Pollock, lying down again.

In the early dawn he awoke again with a peculiar sense of unrest. The vague pain in his bones had returned. For some time he lay watching the red ants that were swarming over the ceiling, and then, as the light grew brighter, he looked over the edge of his hammock and saw something dark on the floor. He gave such a violent start that the hammock overset and flung him out.

He found himself lying, perhaps, a yard away from the head of the Porroh man. It had been disinterred by the dog, and the nose was grievously battered. Ants and flies swarmed over it. By an odd coincidence, it was still upside down, and with the same diabolical expression in the inverted eyes.

Pollock sat paralysed, and stared at the horror for some time. Then he got up and walked round it,—giving it a wide berth—and out of the shed. The clear light of the sunrise, the living stir of vegetation before the breath of the dying land-breeze, and the empty grave with the marks of the dog's paws, lightened the weight upon his mind a little.

He told Perera of the business as though it was a jest,—a jest to be told with white lips. "You should not have frighten de dog," said Perera, with poorly simulated hilarity.

The next two days, until the steamer came, were spent by Pollock in making a more effectual disposition of his possession. Overcoming his aversion to handling the thing, he went down to the river mouth and threw it into the seawater, but by some miracle it escaped the crocodiles, and was cast up by the tide on the mud a little way up the river, to be found by an intelligent Arab half-breed, and offered for sale to Pollock and Perera as a curiosity, just on the edge of night. The native hung about in the brief twilight, making lower and lower offers, and at last, getting scared in some way by the evident dread these wise white men had for the thing, went off, and, passing Pollock's shed, threw his burden in there for Pollock to discover in the morning.

At this Pollock got into a kind of frenzy. He would burn

the thing. He went out straightway into the dawn, and had constructed a big pyre of brushwood before the heat of the day. He was interrupted by the hooter of the little paddle steamer from Monrovia to Bathurst, which was coming through the gap in the bar. "Thank Heaven!" said Pollock, with infinite piety, when the meaning of the sound dawned upon him. With trembling hands he lit his pile of wood hastily, threw the head upon it, and went away to pack his portmanteau and make his adieux to Perera.

That afternoon, with a sense of infinite relief, Pollock watched the flat swampy foreshore of Sulyma grow small in the distance. The gap in the long line of white surge became narrower and narrower. It seemed to be closing in and cutting him off from his trouble. The feeling of dread and worry began to slip from him bit by bit. At Sulyma belief in Porroh malignity and Porroh magic had been in the air, his sense of Porroh had been vast, pervading, threatening, dreadful. Now manifestly the domain of Porroh was only a little place, a little black band between the sea and the blue cloudy Mendi uplands.

"Good-bye, Porroh!" said Pollock. "Good-bye—certainly not *au revoir.*"

The captain of the steamer came and leant over the rail beside him, and wished him good evening, and spat at the froth of the wake in token of friendly ease.

"I picked up a rummy curio on the beach this go," said the captain. "It's a thing I never saw done this side of Indy before."

"What might that be?" said Pollock.

"Pickled 'ed," said the captain.

"What?" said Pollock.

"'Ed—smoked. 'Ed of one of these Porroh chaps, all ornamented with knife-cuts. Why! What's up? Nothing? I shouldn't have took you for a nervous chap. Green in the face. By gosh! you're a bad sailor. All right, eh? Lord, how funny you went! Well, this 'ed I was telling you of is a bit rum in a way. I've got it, along with some snakes, in a jar of spirit in my cabin what I keeps for such curios, and I'm hanged if it don't float upsy down. Hullo!"

Pollock had given an incoherent cry, and had his hands in his hair. He ran towards the paddle-boxes with a half-formed idea of jumping into the sea, and then he realised his position and turned back towards the captain.

"Here!" said the captain. "Jack Philips, just keep him off me! Stand off! No nearer, mister! What's the matter with you? Are you mad?"

Pollock put his hand to his head. It was no good explaining. "I believe I am pretty nearly mad at times," he said. "It's a pain I have here. Comes suddenly. You'll excuse me, I hope."

He was white and in a perspiration. He saw suddenly very clearly all the danger he ran of having his sanity doubted. He forced himself to restore the captain's confidence, by answering his sympathetic inquiries, noting his suggestions, even trying a spoonful of neat brandy in his cheek, and, that matter settled, asking a number of questions about the captain's private trade in curiosities. The captain described the head in detail. All the while Pollock was struggling to keep under a preposterous persuasion that the ship was as transparent as glass, and that he could distinctly see the inverted face looking at him from the cabin beneath his feet.

Pollock had a worse time almost on the steamer than he had at Sulyma. All day he had to control himself in spite of his intense perception of the imminent presence of that horrible head that was overshadowing his mind. At night his old nightmare returned, until, with a violent effort, he would force himself awake, rigid with the horror of it, and with the ghost of a hoarse scream in his throat.

He left the actual head behind at Bathurst, where he changed ship for Teneriffe, but not his dreams nor the dull ache in his bones. At Teneriffe Pollock transferred to a Cape liner, but the head followed him. He gambled, he tried chess, he even read books; but he knew the danger of drink. Yet whenever a round black shadow, a round black object came into his range, there he looked for the head, and—saw it. He knew clearly enough that his imagination was growing traitor to him, and yet at times it seemed the ship he sailed in, his fellow-passengers, the sailors, the wide sea, was all part of a filmy phantasmagoria that hung, scarcely veiling it, between him and a horrible real world. Then the Porroh man, thrusting his diabolical face through that curtain, was the one real and undeniable thing. At that he would get up and touch things, taste something, gnaw something, burn his hand with a match, or run a needle into himself.

So, struggling grimly and silently with his excited imagination, Pollock reached England. He landed at Southampton, and went on straight from Waterloo to his banker's in Cornhill in a cab. There he transacted some business with the manager in a private room; and all the while the head hung like an ornament under the black marble mantel and dripped upon the fender. He could hear the drops fall, and see the red on the fender.

"A pretty fern," said the manager, following his eyes. "But it makes the fender rusty."

"Very," said Pollock; "a *very* pretty fern. And that reminds me. Can you recommend me a physician for mind troubles? I've got a little—what is it?—hallucination."

The head laughed savagely, wildly. Pollock was surprised the manager did not notice it. But the manager only stared at his face.

With the address of a doctor, Pollock presently emerged in Cornhill. There was no cab in sight, and so he went on down to the western end of the street, and essayed the crossing opposite the Mansion House. The crossing is hardly easy even for the expert Londoner; cabs, vans, carriages, mail-carts, omnibuses go by in one incessant stream; to any one fresh from the malarious solitudes of Sierra Leone it is a boiling, maddening confusion. But when an inverted head suddenly comes bouncing, like an india-rubber ball, between your legs, leaving distinct smears of blood every time it touches the ground, you can scarcely hope to avoid an accident. Pollock lifted his feet convulsively to avoid it, and then kicked at the thing furiously. Then something hit him violently in the back, and a hot pain ran up his arm.

He had been hit by the pole of an omnibus, and three of the fingers of his left hand smashed by the hoof of one of the horses,—the very fingers, as it happened, that he shot from the Porroh man. They pulled him out from between the horses' legs, and found the address of the physician in his crushed hand.

For a couple of days Pollock's sensations were full of the sweet, pungent smell of chloroform, of painful operations that caused him no pain, of lying still and being given food and drink. Then he had a slight fever, and was very thirsty, and his old nightmare came back. It was only when it returned that he noticed it had left him for a day.

"If my skull had been smashed instead of my fingers, it might have gone altogether," said Pollock, staring thoughtfully at the dark cushion that had taken on for the time the shape of the head.

Pollock at the first opportunity told the physician of his mind trouble. He knew clearly that he must go mad unless something should intervene to save him. He explained that he had witnessed a decapitation in Dahomey, and was haunted by one of the heads. Naturally, he did not care to state the actual facts. The physician looked grave.

Presently he spoke hesitatingly. "As a child, did you get very much religious training?"

"Very little," said Pollock.

A shade passed over the physician's face. "I don't know if you have heard of the miraculous cures—it may be, of course, they are not miraculous—at Lourdes."

"Faith-healing will hardly suit me, I am afraid," said Pollock, with his eye on the dark cushion.

The head distorted its scarred features in an abominable grimace. The physician went upon a new track. "It's all imagination," he said, speaking with sudden briskness. "A fair case for faith-healing, anyhow. Your nervous system has run down, you're in that twilight state of health when the bogles come easiest. The strong impression was too much for you. I must make you up a little mixture that will strengthen your nervous system—especially your brain. And you must take exercise."

"I'm no good for faith-healing," said Pollock.

"And therefore we must restore tone. Go in search of stimulating air—Scotland, Norway, the Alps—"

"Jericho, if you like," said Pollock, "where Naaman went."

However, so soon as his fingers would let him, Pollock made a gallant attempt to follow out the doctor's suggestion. It was now November. He tried football; but to Pollock the game consisted in kicking a furious inverted head about a field. He was no good at the game. He kicked blindly, with a kind of horror, and when they put him back into goal, and the ball came swooping down upon him, he suddenly yelled and got out of its way. The discreditable stories that had driven him from England to wander in the tropics shut him off from any but men's society, and now his increasingly strange behaviour made even his man friends avoid him. The thing was no longer a thing of the eye merely; it gibbered at him, spoke to him. A horrible fear came upon him that presently, when he took hold of the apparition, it would no longer become some mere article of furniture, but would *feel* like a real dissevered head. Alone, he would curse at the thing, defy it, entreat it; once or twice, in spite of his grim self-control, he addressed it in the presence of others. He felt the growing suspicion in the eyes of the people that watched him,—his landlady, the servant, his man.

One day early in December his cousin Arnold—his next of kin—came to see him and draw him out, and watch his sunken, yellow face with narrow, eager eyes. And it seemed to Pollock that the hat his cousin carried in his hand was no hat at all, but a Gorgon head that glared at him upside down, and fought with its eyes against his reason. However, he was still resolute to see the matter out. He got a bicycle, and, riding over the frosty road from Wandsworth to Kingston, found the thing rolling along at his side, and leaving a dark trail behind it. He set his teeth and rode faster. Then suddenly, as he came down the hill towards Richmond Park, the apparition rolled in front of him and under his wheel, so quickly that he had no time for thought, and, turning quickly to avoid it, was flung violently against a heap of stones and broke his left wrist.

The end came on Christmas morning. All night he had been in a fever, the bandages encircling his wrist like a band of fire, his dreams more vivid and terrible than ever. In the cold, colourless, uncertain light that came before the sunrise, he sat up in his bed, and saw the head upon the bracket in the place of the bronze jar that had stood there overnight.

"I know that is a bronze jar," he said, with a chill doubt at his heart. Presently the doubt was irresistible. He got out of bed slowly, shivering, and advanced to the jar with his hand raised. Surely he would see now his imagination had deceived him, recognise the distinctive sheen of bronze. At last, after an age of hesitation, his fingers came down on the patterned cheek of the head. He withdrew them spasmodically. The last stage was reached. His sense of touch had betrayed him.

Trembling, stumbling against the bed, kicking against his shoes with his bare feet, a dark confusion eddying round him, he groped his way to the dressing-table, took his razor from the drawer, and sat down on the bed with this in his hand. In the looking-glass he saw his own face, colourless, haggard, full of the ultimate bitterness of despair.

He beheld in swift succession the incidents in the brief tale of his experience. His wretched home, his still more wretched schooldays, the years of vicious life he had led since then, one act of selfish dishonour leading to another; it was all clear and pitiless now, all its squalid folly, in the cold light of the dawn. He came to the hut, to the fight with the Porroh man, to the retreat down the river to Sulyma, to the Mendi assassin and his red parcel, to his frantic endeavours to destroy the head, to the growth of his hallucination. It was a hallucination! He *knew* it was. A hallucination merely. For a moment he snatched at hope. He looked away from the glass, and on the bracket, the inverted head grinned and grimaced at him—With the stiff fingers of his bandaged hand he felt at his neck for the throb of his arteries. The morning was very cold, the steel blade felt like ice.

The Sea Raiders

I

Until the extraordinary affair at Sidmouth, the peculiar species *Haploteuthis ferox* was known to science only generically, on the strength of a half-digested tentacle obtained near the Azores, and a decaying body pecked by birds and nibbled by fish, found early in 1896 by Mr. Jennings, near Land's End.

In no department of zoölogical science, indeed, are we quite so much in the dark as with regard to the deep-sea cephalopods. A mere accident, for instance, it was that led to the Prince of Monaco's discovery of nearly a dozen new forms in the summer of 1895, a discovery in which the before-mentioned tentacle was included. It chanced that a cachalot was killed off Terceira by some sperm-whalers, and in its last struggles charged almost to the Prince's yacht, missed it, rolled under, and died within twenty yards of his rudder. And in its agony it threw up a number of large objects, which the Prince, dimly perceiving they were strange and important, was, by a happy expedient, able to secure before they sank. He set his screws in motion, and kept them circling in the vortices thus created until a boat could be lowered. And these specimens were whole cephalopods and fragments of cephalopods, some of gigantic proportions, and almost all of them unknown to science!

It would seem, indeed, that these large and agile creatures, living in the middle depths of the sea, must, to a large extent, for ever remain unknown to us, since under water they are too nimble for nets, and it is only by such rare unlooked-for accidents that specimens can be obtained. In the case of *Haploteuthis ferox,* for instance, we are still altogether ignorant of its habitat, as ignorant as we are of the breeding-ground of the herring or the sea-ways of the salmon. And zoölogists are altogether at a loss to account for its sudden appearance on our coast. Possibly it was the stress of a hunger migration that drove it hither out of the deep. But it will be, perhaps, better to avoid necessarily inconclusive discussion, and to proceed at once with our narrative.

The first human being to set eyes upon a living *Haploteuthis*—the first human being to survive, that is, for there can be little doubt now that the wave of bathing fatalities and boating accidents that travelled along the coast of Cornwall and Devon in early May was due to this cause—was a retired tea-dealer of the name of Fison, who was stopping at a Sidmouth boarding-house. It was in the afternoon, and he was walking along the cliff path between Sidmouth and Ladram Bay. The cliffs in this direction are very high, but down the red face of them in one place a kind of ladder staircase has been made. He was near this when his attention was attracted by what at first he thought to be a cluster of birds struggling over a fragment of food that caught the sunlight, and glistened pinkish-white. The tide was right out, and this object was not only far below him, but remote across a broad waste of rock reefs covered with dark seaweed and interspersed with silvery, shining, tidal pools. And he was, moreover, dazzled by the brightness of the further water.

In a minute, regarding this again, he perceived that his judgment was in fault, for over this struggle circled a number of birds, jackdaws and gulls for the most part, the latter gleaming blindingly when the sunlight smote their wings, and they seemed minute in comparison with it. And his curiosity was, perhaps, aroused all the more strongly because of his first insufficient explanations.

As he had nothing better to do than amuse himself, he decided to make this object, whatever it was, the goal of his afternoon walk, instead of Ladram Bay, conceiving it might perhaps be a great fish of some sort, stranded by some chance, and flapping about in its distress. And so he hurried down the long steep ladder, stopping at intervals of thirty feet or so to take breath and scan the mysterious movement.

At the foot of the cliff he was, of course, nearer his object than he had been; but, on the other hand, it now came up against the incandescent sky, beneath the sun, so as to seem dark and indistinct. Whatever was pinkish of it was now hidden by a skerry of weedy boulders. But he perceived that it was made up of seven rounded bodies, distinct or connected, and that the birds kept up a constant croaking and screaming, but seemed afraid to approach it too closely.

Mr. Fison, torn by curiosity, began picking his way across the wave-worn rocks, and, finding the wet seaweed that covered them thickly rendered them extremely slippery, he stopped, removed his shoes and socks, and coiled his trousers above his knees. His object was, of course, merely to avoid stumbling into the rocky pools about him, and perhaps he was rather glad, as all men are, of an excuse to resume, even for a moment, the sensations of his boyhood. At any rate, it is to this, no doubt, that he owes his life.

He approached his mark with all the assurance which the absolute security of this country against all forms of animal life gives its inhabitants. The round bodies moved to and fro, but it was only when he surmounted the skerry of boulders I have mentioned that he realised the horrible nature of the discovery. It came upon him with some suddenness.

The rounded bodies fell apart as he came into sight over the ridge, and displayed the pinkish object to be the partially devoured body of a human being, but whether of a man or woman he was unable to say. And the rounded bodies were new and ghastly-looking creatures, in shape somewhat resembling an octopus, and with huge and very long and flexible tentacles, coiled copiously on the ground. The skin had a glistening texture, unpleasant to see, like shiny leather. The downward bend of the tentacle-surrounded mouth, the curious excrescence at the bend, the tentacles, and the large, intelligent eyes, gave the creatures a grotesque suggestion of a face. They were the size of a fair-sized swine about the body, and the tentacles seemed to him to be many feet in length. There were, he thinks, seven or eight at least of the creatures. Twenty yards beyond them, amid the surf of the now returning tide, two others were emerging from the sea.

Their bodies lay flatly on the rocks, and their eyes regarded him with evil interest; but it does not appear that Mr. Fison was afraid, or that he realised that he was in any danger. Possibly his confidence is to be ascribed to the limpness of their attitudes. But he was horrified, of course, and intensely excited and indignant at such revolting creatures preying upon human flesh. He thought they had chanced upon a drowned body. He shouted to them, with the idea of driving them off, and, finding they did not budge, cast about him, picked up a big rounded lump of rock, and flung it at one.

And then, slowly uncoiling their tentacles, they all began moving towards him—creeping at first deliberately, and making a soft, purring sound to each other.

In a moment Mr. Fison realised that he was in danger. He shouted again, threw both his boots, and started off, with a leap, forthwith. Twenty yards off he stopped and faced about, judging them slow, and, behold! the tentacles of their leader were already pouring over the rocky ridge on which he had just been standing!

At that he shouted again, but this time not threatening, but a cry of dismay, and began jumping, striding, slipping, wading across the uneven expanse between him and the beach. The tall red cliffs seemed suddenly at a vast distance, and he saw, as though they were creatures in another world, two minute workmen engaged in the repair of the ladder-way, and little suspecting the race for life that was beginning below them. At one time he could hear the creatures splashing in the pools not a dozen feet behind him, and once he slipped and almost fell.

They chased him to the very foot of the cliffs, and desisted only when he had been joined by the workmen at the foot of the ladder-way up the cliff. All three of the men pelted them with stones for a time, and then hurried to the cliff top and along the path towards Sidmouth, to secure assistance and a boat, and to rescue the desecrated body from the clutches of these abominable creatures.

II

And, as if he had not already been in sufficient peril that day, Mr. Fison went with the boat to point out the exact spot of his adventure.

As the tide was down, it required a considerable detour

to reach the spot, and when at last they came off the ladder-way, the mangled body had disappeared. The water was now running in, submerging first one slab of slimy rock and then another, and the four men in the boat—the workmen, that is, the boatman, and Mr. Fison—now turned their attention from the bearings off shore to the water beneath the keel.

At first they could see little below them, save a dark jungle of laminaria, with an occasional darting fish. Their minds were set on adventure, and they expressed their disappointment freely. But presently they saw one of the monsters swimming through the water seaward, with a curious rolling motion that suggested to Mr. Fison the spinning roll of a captive balloon. Almost immediately after, the waving streamers of laminaria were extraordinarily perturbed, parted for a moment, and three of these beasts became darkly visible, struggling for what was probably some fragment of the drowned man. In a moment the copious olive-green ribbons had poured again over this writhing group.

At that all four men, greatly excited, began beating the water with oars and shouting, and immediately they saw a tumultuous movement among the weeds. They desisted, to see more clearly, and as soon as the water was smooth, they saw, as it seemed to them, the whole sea bottom among the weeds set with eyes.

"Ugly swine!" cried one of the men. "Why, there's dozens!"

And forthwith the things began to rise through the water about them. Mr. Fison has since described to the writer this startling eruption out of the waving laminaria meadows. To him it seemed to occupy a considerable time, but it is probable that really it was an affair of a few seconds only. For a time nothing but eyes, and then he speaks of tentacles streaming out and parting the weed fronds this way and that. Then these things, growing larger, until at last the bottom was hidden by their intercoiling forms, and the tips of tentacles rose darkly here and there into the air above the swell of the waters.

One came up boldly to the side of the boat, and, clinging to this with three of its sucker-set tentacles, threw four others over the gunwale, as if with an intention either of oversetting the boat or of clambering into it. Mr. Fison at once caught up the boathook, and, jabbing furiously at the soft tentacles, forced it to desist. He was struck in the back and almost pitched overboard by the boatman, who was using his oar to resist a similar attack on the other side of the boat. But the tentacles on either side at once relaxed their hold at this, slid out of sight, and splashed into the water.

"We'd better get out of this" said Mr. Fison, who was trembling violently. He went to the tiller, while the boatman and one of the workmen seated themselves and began rowing. The other workman stood up in the fore part of the boat, with the boathook, ready to strike any more tentacles that might appear. Nothing else seems to have been said. Mr. Fison had expressed the common feeling beyond amendment. In a hushed, scared mood, with faces white and drawn, they set about escaping from the position into which they had so recklessly blundered.

But the oars had scarcely dropped into the water before dark, tapering, serpentine ropes had bound them, and were about the rudder; and creeping up the sides of the boat with a looping motion came the suckers again. The men gripped their oars and pulled, but it was like trying to move a boat in a floating raft of weeds. "Help here!" cried the boatman, and Mr. Fison and the second workman rushed to help lug at the oar.

Then the man with the boathook—his name was Ewan, or Ewen—sprang up with a curse, and began striking downward over the side, as far as he could reach, at the bank of tentacles that now clustered along the boat's bottom. And, at the same time, the two rowers stood up to get a better purchase for the recovery of their oars. The boatman handed his to Mr. Fison, who lugged desperately, and, meanwhile, the boatman opened a big clasp-knife, and, leaning over the side of the boat, began hacking at the spiring arms upon the oar shaft.

Mr. Fison, staggering with the quivering rocking of the boat, his teeth set, his breath coming short, and the veins starting on his hands as he pulled at his oar, suddenly cast his eyes seaward. And there, not fifty yards off, across the long rollers of the incoming tide, was a large boat standing in towards them, with three women and a little child in it. A boatman was rowing, and a little man in a pink-ribboned straw hat and whites stood in the stern, hailing them. For a moment, of course, Mr. Fison thought of help, and then he thought of the child. He abandoned his oar forthwith, threw up his arms in a frantic gesture, and screamed to the party in the boat to keep away "for God's sake!" It says much for the modesty and courage of Mr. Fison that he does not seem to be aware that there was any quality of heroism in his action at this juncture. The oar he had abandoned was at once drawn under, and presently reappeared floating about twenty yards away.

At the same moment Mr. Fison felt the boat under him lurch violently, and a hoarse scream, a prolonged cry of terror from Hill, the boatman, caused him to forget the party of excursionists altogether. He turned, and saw Hill crouching by the forward rowlock, his face convulsed with terror, and his right arm over the side and drawn tightly down. He gave now a succession of short, sharp cries, "Oh! oh! oh!—oh!" Mr. Fison believes that he must have been hacking at the tentacles below the water-line, and have been grasped by them, but, of course, it is quite impossible to say now certainly what had happened. The boat was heeling over, so that the gunwale was within ten inches of the water, and both Ewan and the other labourer were striking down into the water, with oar and boathook, on either side of Hill's arm. Mr. Fison instinctively placed himself to counterpoise them.

Then Hill, who was a burly, powerful man, made a strenuous effort, and rose almost to a standing position. He lifted his arm, indeed, clean out of the water. Hanging to it was a complicated tangle of brown ropes; and the eyes of one of the brutes that had hold of him, glaring straight and resolute, showed momentarily above the surface. The boat heeled more and more, and the green-brown water came pouring in a cascade over the side. Then Hill slipped and fell with his ribs across the side, and his arm and the mass of tentacles about it splashed back into the water. He rolled over; his boot kicked Mr. Fison's knee as that gentleman rushed forward to seize him, and in another moment fresh tentacles had whipped about his waist and neck, and after a brief, convulsive struggle, in which the boat was nearly capsized, Hill was lugged overboard. The boat righted with a violent jerk that all but sent Mr. Fison over the other side, and hid the struggle in the water from his eyes.

He stood staggering to recover his balance for a moment, and as he did so, he became aware that the struggle and the inflowing tide had carried them close upon the weedy rocks again. Not four yards off a table of rock still rose in rhythmic movements above the in-wash of the tide. In a moment Mr. Fison seized the oar from Ewan, gave one vigorous stroke, then, dropping it, ran to the bows and leapt. He felt his feet slide over the rock, and, by a frantic effort, leapt again towards a further mass. He stumbled over this, came to his knees, and rose again.

" Look out!" cried some one, and a large drab body struck him. He was knocked flat into a tidal pool by one of the workmen, and as he went down he heard smothered, choking cries, that he believed at the time came from Hill. Then he found himself marvelling at the shrillness and variety of Hill's voice. Some one jumped over him, and a curving rush of foamy water poured over him, and passed. He scrambled to his feet, dripping, and, without looking seaward, ran as fast as his terror would let him shoreward. Before him, over the flat space of scattered rocks, stumbled the two workmen—one a dozen yards in front of the other.

He looked over his shoulder at last, and, seeing that he was not pursued, faced about. He was astonished. From the moment of the rising of the cephalopods out of the water, he had been acting too swiftly to fully comprehend his actions. Now it seemed to him as if he had suddenly jumped out of an evil dream.

For there were the sky, cloudless and blazing with the afternoon sun, the sea, weltering under its pitiless brightness, the soft creamy foam of the breaking water, and the low, long, dark ridges of rock. The righted boat floated, rising and falling gently on the swell about a dozen yards from shore. Hill and the monsters, all the stress and tumult of that fierce fight for life, had vanished as though they had never been.

Mr. Fison's heart was beating violently; he was throbbing to the finger-tips, and his breath came deep.

There was something missing. For some seconds he could not think clearly enough what this might be. Sun, sky, sea, rocks—what was it? Then he remembered the boatload of excursionists. It had vanished. He wondered whether he had imagined it. He turned, and saw the two workmen standing side by side under the projecting masses of the tall pink cliffs. He hesitated whether he should make one last attempt to save the man Hill. His physical excitement seemed to desert him suddenly, and leave him aimless and helpless. He turned shoreward, stumbling and wading towards his two companions.

He looked back again, and there were now two boats floating, and the one farthest out at sea pitched clumsily, bottom upward.

III

So it was *Haploteuthis ferox* made its appearance upon the Devonshire coast. So far, this has been its most serious aggression. Mr. Fison's account, taken together with the wave of boating and bathing casualties to which I have already alluded, and the absence of fish from the Cornish coasts that year, points clearly to a shoal of these voracious deep-sea monsters prowling slowly along the sub-tidal coast-line. Hunger migration has, I know, been suggested as the force that drove them hither; but, for my own part, I prefer to believe the alternative theory of Hemsley. Hemsley holds that a pack or shoal of these creatures may have become enamoured of human flesh by the accident of a foundered ship sinking among them, and have wandered in search of it out of their accustomed zone; first waylaying and following ships, and so coming to our shores in the wake of the Atlantic traffic. But to discuss Hemsley's cogent and admirably-stated arguments would be out of place here.

It would seem that the appetites of the shoal were satisfied by the catch of eleven people—for so far as can be ascertained, there were ten people in the second boat, and certainly these creatures gave no further signs of their presence off Sidmouth that day. The coast between Seaton and Budleigh Salterton was patrolled all that evening and night by four Preventive Service boats, the men in which were armed with harpoons and cutlasses, and as the evening advanced, a number of more or less similarly equipped expeditions, organised by private individuals, joined them. Mr. Fison took no part in any of these expeditions.

About midnight excited hails were heard from a boat about a couple of miles out at sea to the south-east of Sidmouth, and a lantern was seen waving in a strange manner to and fro and up and down. The nearer boats at once hurried towards the alarm. The venturesome occupants of the boat, a seaman, a curate, and two schoolboys, had actually seen the monsters passing under their boat. The creatures, it seems, like most deep-sea organisms, were phosphorescent, and they had been floating, five fathoms deep or so, like creatures of moonshine through the blackness of the water, their tentacles retracted and as if asleep, rolling over and over, and moving slowly in a wedge-like formation towards the south-east.

These people told their story in gesticulated fragments, as first one boat drew alongside and then another. At last there was a little fleet of eight or nine boats collected together, and from them a tumult, like the chatter of a marketplace, rose into the stillness of the night. There was little or no disposition to pursue the shoal, the people had neither weapons nor experience for such a dubious chase, and presently—even with a certain relief, it may be—the boats turned shoreward.

And now to tell what is perhaps the most astonishing fact in this whole astonishing raid. We have not the slightest knowledge of the subsequent movements of the shoal, although the whole southwest coast was now alert for it. But it may, perhaps, be significant that a cachalot was stranded off Sark on June 3. Two weeks and three days after this Sidmouth affair, a living *Haploteuthis* came ashore on Calais sands. It was alive, because several witnesses saw its tentacles moving in a convulsive way. But it is probable that it was dying. A gentleman named Pouchet obtained a rifle and shot it.

That was the last appearance of a living *Haploteuthis*. No others were seen on the French coast. On the 15th of June a dead body, almost complete, was washed ashore near Torquay, and a few days later a boat from the Marine Biological station, engaged in dredging off Plymouth, picked up a rotting specimen, slashed deeply with a cutlass wound. How the former specimen had come by its death it is impossible to say. And on the last day of June, Mr. Egbert Caine, an artist, bathing near Newlyn, threw up his arms, shrieked, and was drawn under. A friend bathing with him made no attempt to save him, but swam at once for the shore. This is the last fact to tell of this extraordinary raid from the deeper sea. Whether it is really the last of these horrible creatures it is, as yet, premature to say. But it is believed, and certainly it is to be hoped, that they have returned now, and returned for good, to the sunless depths of the middle seas, out of which they have so strangely and so mysteriously arisen.

In the Modern Vein

An Unsympathetic Love Story

Of course the cultivated reader has heard of Aubrey Vair. He has published on three several occasions volumes of delicate verses,—some, indeed, border on indelicacy,—and his column "Of Things Literary" in the "Climax" is well known. His Byronic visage and an interview have appeared in the "Perfect Lady." It was Aubrey Vair, I believe, who demonstrated that the humour of Dickens was worse than his sentiment, and who detected "a subtle bourgeois flavour" in Shakespeare. However, it is not generally known that Aubrey Vair has had erotic experiences as well as erotic inspirations. He adopted Goethe some little time since as his literary prototype, and that may have had something to do with his temporary lapse from sexual integrity.

For it is one of the commonest things that undermine literary men, giving us landslips and picturesque effects along the otherwise even cliff of their respectable life, ranking next to avarice, and certainly above drink, this instability called genius, or, more fully, the consciousness of genius, such as Aubrey Vair possessed. Since Shelley set the fashion, your man of gifts has been assured that his duty to himself and his duty to his wife are incompatible, and his renunciation of the Philistine has been marked by such infidelity as his means and courage warranted. Most virtue is lack of imagination. At any rate, a minor genius without his affections twisted into an inextricable muddle, and who did not occasionally shed sonnets over his troubles, I have never met.

Even Aubrey Vair did this, weeping the sonnets overnight into his blotting-book, and pretending to write literary *causerie* when his wife came down in her bath slippers to see what kept him up. She did not understand him, of course. He did this even before the other woman appeared, so ingrained is conjugal treachery in the talented mind. Indeed, he wrote more sonnets before the other woman came than after that event, because thereafter he spent much of his leisure in cutting down the old productions, retrimming them, and generally altering this ready-made clothing of his passion to suit her particular height and complexion.

Aubrey Vair lived in a little red villa with a lawn at the back and a view of the Downs behind Reigate. He lived upon discreet investment eked out by literary work. His wife was handsome, sweet, and gentle, and—such is the tender humility of good married women—she found her life's happiness in seeing that little Aubrey Vair had well-cooked variety for dinner, and that their house was the neatest and brightest of all the houses they entered. Aubrey Vair enjoyed the dinners, and was proud of the house, yet nevertheless he mourned because his genius dwindled. Moreover, he grew plump, and corpulence threatened him.

We learn in suffering what we teach in song, and Aubrey Vair knew certainly that his soul could give no creditable crops unless his affections were harrowed. And how to harrow them was the trouble, for Reigate is a moral neighbourhood.

So Aubrey Vair's romantic longings blew loose for a time, much as a seedling creeper might, planted in the midst of a flower-bed. But at last, in the fulness of time, the other woman came to the embrace of Aubrey Vair's yearning heart-tendrils, and his romantic episode proceeded as is here faithfully written down.

The other woman was really a girl, and Aubrey Vair met her first at a tennis party at Redhill. Aubrey Vair did not play tennis after the accident to Miss Morton's eye, and because latterly it made him pant and get warmer and moister than even a poet should be; and this young lady had only recently arrived in England, and could not play. So they gravitated into the two vacant basket chairs beside Mrs. Bayne's deaf aunt, in front of the hollyhocks, and were presently talking at their ease together.

The other woman's name was unpropitious,—Miss Smith,—but you would never have suspected it from her face and costume. Her parentage was promising, she was an orphan, her mother was a Hindoo, and her father an Indian civil servant; and Aubrey Vair—himself a happy mixture of Kelt and Teuton, as, indeed, all literary men have to be nowadays—naturally believed in the literary consequences of a mixture of races. She was dressed in white. She had finely moulded, pale features, great depth of expression, and a cloud of delicately *frisé* black hair over her dark eyes, and she looked at Aubrey Vair with a look half curious and half shy, that contrasted admirably with the stereotyped frankness of your common Reigate girl.

"This is a splendid lawn—the best in Redhill," said Aubrey Vair, in the course of the conversation; "and I like it all the better because the daisies are spared." He indicated the daisies with a graceful sweep of his rather elegant hand.

"They are sweet little flowers," said the lady in white, "and I have always associated them with England, chiefly, perhaps, through a picture I saw 'over there' when I was very little, of children making daisy chains. I promised myself that pleasure when I came home. But, alas! I feel now rather too large for such delights."

"I do not see why we should not be able to enjoy these simple pleasures as we grow older—why our growth should have in it so much forgetting. For my own part—"

"Has your wife got Jane's recipe for stuffing trout?" asked Mrs. Bayne's deaf aunt, abruptly.

"I really don't know," said Aubrey Vair

"That's all right," said Mrs. Bayne's deaf aunt. "It ought to please even you."

"Anything will please me," said Aubrey Vair; "I care very little—"

"Oh, it's a lovely dish," said Mrs. Bayne's deaf aunt, and relapsed into contemplation.

"I was saying," said Aubrey Vair, "that I think I still find my keenest pleasures in childish pastimes. I have a little nephew that I see a great deal of, and when we fly kites together, I am sure it would be hard to tell which of us is the happier. By-the-by, you should get at your daisy chains in that way. Beguile some little girl."

"But I did. I took that Morton mite for a walk in the meadows, and timidly broached the subject. And she reproached me for suggesting 'frivolous pursuits.' It was a horrible disappointment."

"The governess here," said Aubrey Vair, "is robbing that child of its youth in a terrible way. What will a life be that has no childhood at the beginning?

"Some human beings are never young," he continued, "and they never grow up. They lead absolutely colourless lives. They are—they are etiolated. They never love, and never feel the loss of it. They are—for the moment I can think of no better image—they are human flowerpots, in which no soul has been planted. But a human soul properly growing must begin in a fresh childishness."

"Yes," said the dark lady, thoughtfully, "a careless childhood, running wild almost. That should be the beginning."

"Then we pass through the wonder and diffidence of youth."

"To strength and action," said the dark lady. Her dreamy eyes were fixed on the Downs, and her fingers tightened on her knees as she spoke. "Ah, it is a grand thing to live—as a man does—self-reliant and free."

"And so at last," said Aubrey Vair, "come to the culmination and crown of life." He paused and glanced hastily at her. Then he dropped his voice almost to a whisper—"And the culmination of life is love."

Their eyes met for a moment, but she looked away at once. Aubrey Vair felt a peculiar thrill and a catching in his breath, but his emotions were too complex for analysis. He had a certain sense of surprise, also, at the way his conversation had developed.

Mrs. Bayne's deaf aunt suddenly dug him in the chest with her ear-trumpet, and some one at tennis bawled, "Love all!"

"Did I tell you Jane's girls have had scarlet fever?" asked Mrs. Bayne's deaf aunt.

"No," said Aubrey Vair.

"Yes; and they are peeling now," said Mrs. Bayne's deaf aunt, shutting her lips tightly, and nodding in a slow, significant manner at both of them.

There was a pause. All three seemed lost in thought, too deep for words.

"Love," began Aubrey Vair, presently, in a severely philosophical tone, leaning back in his chair, holding his hands like a praying saint's in front of him, and staring at the toe of his shoe,—"love is, I believe, the one true and real thing in life. It rises above reason, interest, or explanation. Yet I never read of an age when it was so much forgotten as it is now. Never was love expected to run so much in appointed channels, never was it so despised, checked, ordered, and obstructed. Policemen say, 'This way, Eros!' As a result, we relieve our emotional possibilities in the hunt for gold and notoriety. And after all, with the best fortune in these, we only hold up the gilded images of our success, and are weary slaves, with unsatisfied hearts, in the pageant of life."

Aubrey Vair sighed, and there was a pause. The girl looked at him out of the mysterious darkness of her eyes. She had read many books, but Aubrey Vair was her first literary man, and she took this kind of thing for genius—as girls have done before.

"We are," continued Aubrey Vair, conscious of a favourable impression,—"we are like fireworks, mere dead, inert things until the appointed spark comes; and then—if it is not damp—the dormant soul blazes forth in all its warmth and beauty. That is living. I sometimes think, do you know, that we should be happier if we could die soon after that golden time, like the Ephemerides. There is a decay sets in."

"Eigh?" said Mrs. Bayne's deaf aunt, startlingly. "I didn't hear you."

"I was on the point of remarking," shouted Aubrey Vair, wheeling the array of his thoughts,—"I was on the point of remarking that few people in Redhill could match Mrs. Morton's fine broad green."

"Others have noticed it," Mrs. Bayne's deaf aunt shouted back. "It is since she has had in her new false teeth."

This interruption dislocated the conversation a little. However—

"I must thank you, Mr. Vair," said the dark girl, when they parted that afternoon, "for having given me very much to think about."

And from her manner, Aubrey Vair perceived clearly he had not wasted his time.

It would require a subtler pen than mine to tell how from that day a passion for Miss Smith grew like Jonah's gourd in the heart of Aubrey Vair. He became pensive, and in the prolonged absence of Miss Smith, irritable. Mrs. Aubrey Vair felt the change in him, and put it down to a vitriolic Saturday Reviewer. Indisputably the "Saturday" does at times go a little far. He re-read "Elective Affinities," and lent it to Miss Smith. Incredible as it may appear to members of the Areopagus Club, where we know Aubrey Vair, he did also beyond all question inspire a sort of passion in that sombre-eyed, rather clever, and really very beautiful girl.

He talked to her a lot about love and destiny, and all that bric-à-brac of the minor poet. And they talked together about his genius. He elaborately, though discreetly, sought her society, and presented and read to her the milder of his unpublished sonnets. We consider his Byronic features pasty, but the feminine mind has its own laws. I suppose, also, where a girl is not a fool, a literary man has an enormous advantage over any one but a preacher, in the show he can make of his heart's wares.

At last a day in that summer came when he met her alone, possibly by chance, in a quiet lane towards Horley. There were ample hedges on either side, rich with honeysuckle, vetch, and mullein.

They conversed intimately of his poetic ambitions, and then he read her those verses of his subsequently published in "Hobson's Magazine:" "Tenderly ever, since I have met thee." He had written these the day before; and though I think the sentiment is uncommonly trite, there is a redeeming note of sincerity about the lines not conspicuous in all Aubrey Vair's poetry.

He read rather well, and a swell of genuine emotion crept into his voice as he read, with one white hand thrown out to point the rhythm of the lines. "Ever, my sweet, for thee," he concluded, looking up into her face.

Before he looked up, he had been thinking chiefly of his poem and its effect. Straightway he forgot it. Her arms hung limply before her, and her hands were clasped together. Her eyes were very tender.

"Your verses go to the heart," she said softly.

Her mobile features were capable of wonderful shades of expression. He suddenly forgot his wife and his position as a minor poet as he looked at her. It is possible that his classical features may themselves have undergone a certain transfiguration. For one brief moment—and it was always to linger in his memory—destiny lifted him out of his vain little self to a nobler level of simplicity. The copy of "Tenderly ever" fluttered from his hand. Considerations vanished. Only one thing seemed of importance.

"I love you," he said abruptly.

An expression of fear came into her eyes. The grip of her hands upon one another tightened convulsively. She became very pale.

Then she moved her lips as if to speak, bringing her face slightly nearer to his. There was nothing in the world at that moment for either of them but one another. They were both trembling exceedingly. In a whisper she said, "You love me?"

Aubrey Vair stood quivering and speechless, looking into her eyes. He had never seen such a light as he saw there before. He was in a wild tumult of emotion. He was dreadfully scared at what he had done. He could not say another word. He nodded.

"And this has come to me?" she said presently, in the same awe-stricken whisper, and then, "Oh, my love, my love!"

And thereupon Aubrey Vair had her clasped to himself, her cheek upon his shoulder and his lips to hers.

Thus it was that Aubrey Vair came by the cardinal memory of his life. To this day it recurs in his works.

A little boy clambering in the hedge some way down the lane saw this group with surprise, and then with scorn and contempt. Recking nothing of his destiny, he turned away, feeling that he at least could never come to the unspeakable unmanliness of hugging girls. Unhappily for Reigate scandal, his shame for his sex was altogether too deep for words.

An hour after, Aubrey Vair returned home in a hushed mood. There were muffins after his own heart for his tea—Mrs. Aubrey Vair had had hers. And there were chrysanthemums, chiefly white ones,—flowers he loved,—set out in the china bowl he was wont to praise. And his wife came behind him to kiss him as he sat eating.

"De lill Jummuns," she remarked, kissing him under the ear.

Then it came into the mind of Aubrey Vair with startling clearness, while his ear was being kissed, and with his mouth full of muffin, that life is a singularly complex thing.

The summer passed at last into the harvest-time, and the leaves began falling. It was evening, the warm sunset light still touched the Downs, but up the valley a blue haze was creeping. One or two lamps in Reigate were already alight.

About half-way up the slanting road that scales the Downs, there is a wooden seat where one may obtain a fine view of the red villas scattered below, and of the succession of blue hills beyond. Here the girl with the shadowy face was sitting.

She had a book on her knees, but it lay neglected. She was leaning forward, her chin resting upon her hand. She was looking across the valley into the darkening sky, with troubled eyes.

Aubrey Vair appeared through the hazel-bushes, and sat down beside her. He held half a dozen dead leaves in his hand.

She did not alter her attitude. "Well?" she said.

"Is it to be flight?" he asked.

Aubrey Vair was rather pale. He had been having bad nights latterly, with dreams of the Continental Express Mrs. Aubrey Vair possibly even in pursuit,—he always fancied her making the tragedy ridiculous by tearfully bringing additional pairs of socks, and any such trifles he had forgotten, with her,—all Reigate and Redhill in commotion. He had never eloped before, and he had visions of difficulties with hotel proprietors. Mrs. Aubrey Vair might telegraph ahead. Even he had had a prophetic vision of a headline in a halfpenny evening newspaper: "Young Lady abducts a Minor Poet." So there was a quaver in his voice as he asked, "Is it to be flight?"

"As you will," she answered, still not looking at him.

"I want you to consider particularly how this will affect you. A man," said Aubrey Vair, slowly, and staring hard at the leaves in his hand, "even gains a certain éclat in these affairs. But to a woman it is ruin—social, moral."

"This is not love," said the girl in white.

"Ah, my dearest! Think of yourself."

"Stupid!" she said, under her breath.

"You spoke?"

"Nothing."

"But cannot we go on, meeting one another, loving one another, without any great scandal or misery? Could we not—"

"That," interrupted Miss Smith, "would be unspeakably horrible."

"This is a dreadful conversation to me. Life is so intricate, such a web of subtle strands binds us this way and that. I cannot tell what is right. You must consider—"

"A man would break such strands."

"There is no manliness," said Aubrey Vair, with a sudden glow of moral exaltation, "in doing wrong. My love—"

"We could at least die together, dearest," she said discontentedly.

"Good Lord!" said Aubrey Vair. "I mean—consider my wife."

"You have not considered her hitherto."

"There is a flavour—of cowardice, of desertion, about suicide," said Aubrey Vair. "Frankly, I have the English prejudice, and do not like any kind of running away."

Miss Smith smiled very faintly. "I see clearly now what I did not see. My love and yours are very different things."

"Possibly it is a sexual difference," said Aubrey Vair; and then, feeling the remark inadequate, he relapsed into silence.

They sat for some time without a word. The two lights in Reigate below multiplied to a score of bright points, and, above, one star had become visible. She began laughing, an almost noiseless, hysterical laugh that jarred unaccountably upon Aubrey Vair.

Presently she stood up. "They will wonder where I am," she said. "I think I must be going."

He followed her to the road. "Then this is the end?" he said, with a curious mixture of relief and poignant regret.

"Yes, this is the end," she answered, and turned away.

There straightway dropped into the soul of Aubrey Vair a sense of infinite loss. It was an altogether new sensation. She was perhaps twenty yards away, when he groaned aloud with the weight of it, and suddenly began running after her with his arms extended.

"Annie," he cried,—"Annie! I have been talking *rot*. Annie, now I know I love you! I cannot spare you. This must not be. I did not understand."

The weight was horrible.

"Oh, stop, Annie!" he cried, with a breaking voice, and there were tears on his face.

She turned upon him suddenly, with a look of annoyance, and his arms fell by his side. His expression changed at the sight of her pale face.

"You do not understand," she said. "I have said good-bye."

She looked at him; he was evidently greatly distressed, a little out of breath, and he had just stopped blubbering. His contemptible quality reached the pathetic. She came up close to him, and, taking his damp Byronic visage between her hands, she kissed him again and again. "Good-bye, little man that I loved," she said; "and good-bye to this folly of love."

Then, with something that may have been a laugh or a sob,—she herself, when she came to write it all in her novel, did not know which,—she turned and hurried away again, and went out of the path that Aubrey Vair must pursue, at the cross-roads.

Aubrey Vair stood, where she had kissed him, with a mind as inactive as his body, until her white dress had disappeared. Then he gave an involuntary sigh, a large, exhaustive expiration, and so awoke himself, and began walking, pensively dragging his feet through the dead leaves, home. Emotions are terrible things.

"Do you like the potatoes, dear?" asked Mrs. Aubrey Vair at dinner. "I cooked them myself."

Aubrey Vair descended slowly from cloudy, impalpable meditations to the level of fried potatoes. "These potatoes—" he remarked, after a pause during which he was struggling with recollection. "Yes. These potatoes have exactly the tints of the dead leaves of the hazel."

"What a fanciful poet it is!" said Mrs. Aubrey Vair. "Taste them. They are very nice potatoes indeed."

The Lord of the Dynamos

THE CHIEF ATTENDANT of the three dynamos that buzzed and rattled at Camberwell, and kept the electric railway going, came out of Yorkshire, and his name was James Holroyd. He was a practical electrician, but fond of whiskey, a heavy red-haired brute with irregular teeth. He doubted the existence of the deity, but accepted Carnot's cycle, and he had read Shakespeare and found him weak in chemistry. His helper came out of the mysterious East, and his name was Azuma-zi. But Holroyd called him Pooh-bah. Holroyd liked a nigger help because he would stand kicking—a habit with Holroyd—and did not pry into the machinery and try to learn the ways of it. Certain odd possibilities of the negro mind brought into abrupt contact with the crown of our civilisation Holroyd never fully realised, though just at the end he got some inkling of them.

To define Azuma-zi was beyond ethnology. He was, perhaps, more negroid than anything else, though his hair was curly rather than frizzy, and his nose had a bridge. Moreover, his skin was brown rather than black, and the whites of his eyes were yellow. His broad cheek-bones and narrow chin gave his face something of the viperine V. His head, too, was broad behind, and low and narrow at the forehead, as if his brain had been twisted round in the reverse way to a European's. He was short of stature and still shorter of English. In conversation he made numerous odd noises of no known marketable value, and his infrequent words were carved and wrought into heraldic grotesqueness. Holroyd tried to elucidate his religious beliefs, and—especially after whiskey—lectured to him against superstition and missionaries. Azuma-zi, however, shirked the discussion of his gods, even though he was kicked for it.

Azuma-zi had come, clad in white but insufficient raiment, out of the stoke-hole of the *Lord Clive*, from the Straits Settlements, and beyond, into London. He had heard even in his youth of the greatness and riches of London, where all the women are white and fair, and even the beggars in the streets are white; and he had arrived, with newly earned gold coins in his pocket, to worship at the shrine of civilisation. The day of his landing was a dismal one; the sky was dun, and a wind-worried drizzle filtered down to the greasy streets, but he plunged boldly into the delights of Shadwell, and was presently cast up, shattered in health, civilised in costume, penniless, and, except in matters of the direst necessity, practically a dumb animal, to toil for James Holroyd and to be bullied by him in the dynamo shed at Camberwell. And to James Holroyd bullying was a labour of love.

There were three dynamos with their engines at Camberwell. The two that have been there since the beginning are small machines; the larger one was new. The smaller machines made a reasonable noise; their straps hummed over the drums, every now and then the brushes buzzed and fizzled, and the air churned steadily, whoo! whoo! whoo!

between their poles. One was loose in its foundations and kept the shed vibrating. But the big dynamo drowned these little noises altogether with the sustained drone of its iron core, which somehow set part of the ironwork humming. The place made the visitor's head reel with the throb, throb, throb of the engines, the rotation of the big wheels, the spinning ball-valves, the occasional spittings of the steam, and over all the deep, unceasing, surging note of the big dynamo. This last noise was from an engineering point of view a defect; but Azuma-zi accounted it unto the monster for mightiness and pride.

If it were possible we would have the noises of that shed always about the reader as he reads, we would tell all our story to such an accompaniment. It was a steady stream of din, from which the ear picked out first one thread and then another; there was the intermittent snorting, panting, and seething of the steam-engines, the suck and thud of their pistons, the dull beat on the air as the spokes of the great driving-wheels came round, a note the leather straps made as they ran tighter and looser, and a fretful tumult from the dynamos; and, over all, sometimes inaudible, as the ear tired of it, and then creeping back upon the senses again, was this trombone note of the big machine. The floor never felt steady and quiet beneath one's feet, but quivered and jarred. It was a confusing, unsteady place, and enough to send any one's thoughts jerking into odd zigzags. And for three months, while the big strike of the engineers was in progress, Holroyd, who was a blackleg, and Azuma-zi, who was a mere black, were never out of the stir and eddy of it, but slept and fed in the little wooden shanty between the shed and the gates.

Holroyd delivered a theological lecture on the text of his big machine soon after Azuma-zi came. He had to shout to be heard in the din. "Look at that," said Holroyd; "where's your 'eathen idol to match 'im?" And Azuma-zi looked. For a moment Holroyd was inaudible, and then Azuma-zi heard: "Kill a hundred men. Twelve per cent. on the ordinary shares," said Holroyd, "and that's something like a Gord!"

Holroyd was proud of his big dynamo, and expatiated upon its size and power to Azuma-zi until heaven knows what odd currents of thought that, and the incessant whirling and shindy, set up within the curly, black cranium. He would explain in the most graphic manner the dozen or so ways in which a man might be killed by it, and once he gave Azuma-zi a shock as a sample of its quality. After that, in the breathing-times of his labour—it was heavy labour, being not only his own but most of Holroyd's—Azuma-zi would sit and watch the big machine. Now and then the brushes would sparkle and spit blue flashes, at which Holroyd would swear, but all the rest was as smooth and rhythmic as breathing. The band ran shouting over the shaft, and ever behind one as one watched was the complacent thud of the piston. So it lived all day in this big airy shed, with him and Holroyd to wait upon it; not prisoned up and slaving to drive a ship as the other engines he knew—mere captive devils of the British Solomon—had been, but a machine enthroned. Those two smaller dynamos, Azuma-zi by force of contrast despised; the large one he privately christened the Lord of the Dynamos. They were fretful and irregular, but the big dynamo was steady. How great it was! How serene and easy in its working! Greater and calmer even than the Buddahs he had seen at Rangoon, and yet not motionless, but living! The great black coils spun, spun, spun, the rings ran round under the brushes, and the deep note of its coil steadied the whole. It affected Azuma-zi queerly.

Azuma-zi was not fond of labour. He would sit about and watch the Lord of the Dynamos while Holroyd went away to persuade the yard porter to get whiskey, although his proper place was not in the dynamo shed but behind the engines, and, moreover, if Holroyd caught him skulking he got hit for it with a rod of stout copper wire. He would go and stand close to the colossus and look up at the great leather band running overhead. There was a black patch on the band that came round, and it pleased him somehow among all the clatter to watch this return again and again. Odd thoughts spun with the whirl of it. Scientific people tell us that savages give souls to rocks and trees—and a machine is a thousand times more alive than a rock or a tree. And Azuma-zi was practically a savage still; the veneer of civilisation lay no deeper than his slop suit, his bruises and the coal grime on his face and hands. His father before him had worshipped a meteoric stone, kindred blood, it may be, had splashed the broad wheels of Juggernaut.

He took every opportunity Holroyd gave him of touching and handling the great dynamo that was fascinating him. He polished and cleaned it until the metal parts were blinding in the sun. He felt a mysterious sense of service in doing this. He would go up to it and touch its spinning coils gently. The gods he had worshipped were all far away. The people in London hid their gods.

At last his dim feelings grew more distinct, and took shape in thoughts and acts. When he came into the roaring shed one morning he salaamed to the Lord of the Dynamos; and then, when Holroyd was away, he went and whispered to the thundering machine that he was its servant, and prayed it to have pity on him and save him from Holroyd. As he did so a rare gleam of light came in through the open archway of the throbbing machine-shed, and the Lord of the

Dynamos, as he whirled and roared, was radiant with pale gold. Then Azuma-zi knew that his service was acceptable to his Lord. After that he did not feel so lonely as he had done, and he had indeed been very much alone in London. And even when his work time was over, which was rare, he loitered about the shed.

Then, the next time Holroyd maltreated him, Azuma-zi went presently to the Lord of the Dynamos and whispered, "Thou seest, O my Lord!" and the angry whirr of the machinery seemed to answer him. Thereafter it appeared to him that whenever Holroyd came into the shed a different note came into the sounds of the great dynamo. "My Lord bides his time," said Azuma-zi to himself. "The iniquity of the fool is not yet ripe." And he waited and watched for the day of reckoning. One day there was evidence of short circuiting, and Holroyd, making an unwary examination—it was in the afternoon—got a rather severe shock. Azuma-zi from behind the engine saw him jump off and curse at the peccant coil.

"He is warned," said Azuma-zi to himself. "Surely my Lord is very patient."

Holroyd had at first initiated his "nigger" into such elementary conceptions of the dynamo's working as would enable him to take temporary charge of the shed in his absence. But when he noticed the manner in which Azuma-zi hung about the monster, he became suspicious. He dimly perceived his assistant was "up to something," and connecting him with the anointing of the coils with oil that had rotted the varnish in one place, he issued an edict, shouted above the confusion of the machinery, "Don't 'ee go nigh that big dynamo any more, Pooh-bah, or a 'll take thy skin off!" Besides, if it pleased Azuma-zi to be near the big machine, it was plain sense and decency to keep him away from it.

Azuma-zi obeyed at the time, but later he was caught bowing before the Lord of the Dynamos. At which Holroyd twisted his arm and kicked him as he turned to go away. As Azuma-zi presently stood behind the engine and glared at the back of the hated Holroyd, the noises of the machinery took a new rhythm, and sounded like four words in his native tongue.

It is hard to say exactly what madness is. I fancy Azuma-zi was mad. The incessant din and whirl of the dynamo shed may have churned up his little store of knowledge and big store of superstitious fancy, at last, into something akin to frenzy. At any rate, when the idea of making Holroyd a sacrifice to the Dynamo Fetich was thus suggested to him, it filled him with a strange tumult of exultant emotion.

That night the two men and their black shadows were alone in the shed together. The shed was lit with one big arc light that winked and flickered purple. The shadows lay black behind the dynamos, the ball governors of the engines whirled from light to darkness, and their pistons beat loud and steady. The world outside seen through the open end of the shed seemed incredibly dim and remote. It seemed absolutely silent, too, since the riot of the machinery drowned every external sound. Far away was the black fence of the yard with grey, shadowy houses behind, and above was the deep blue sky and the pale little stars. Azuma-zi suddenly walked across the centre of the shed above which the leather bands were running, and went into the shadow by the big dynamo. Holroyd heard a click, and the spin of the armature changed.

"What are you dewin' with that switch?"he bawled in surprise. "Ha'n't I told you—"

Then he saw the set expression of Azuma-zi's eyes as the Asiatic came out of the shadow towards him.

In another moment the two men were grappling fiercely in front of the great dynamo.

"You coffee-headed fool!" gasped Holroyd, with a brown

hand at his throat. "Keep off those contact rings." In another moment he was tripped and reeling back upon the Lord of the Dynamos. He instinctively loosened his grip upon his antagonist to save himself from the machine.

The messenger, sent in furious haste from the station to find out what had happened in the dynamo shed, met Azuma-zi at the porter's lodge by the gate. Azuma-zi tried to explain something, but the messenger could make nothing of the black's incoherent English, and hurried on to the shed. The machines were all noisily at work, and nothing seemed to be disarranged. There was, however, a queer smell of singed hair. Then he saw an odd-looking, crumpled mass clinging to the front of the big dynamo, and, approaching, recognised the distorted remains of Holroyd.

The man stared and hesitated a moment. Then he saw the face and shut his eyes convulsively. He turned on his heel before he opened them, so that he should not see Holroyd again, and went out of the shed to get advice and help.

When Azuma-zi saw Holroyd die in the grip of the Great Dynamo he had been a little scared about the consequences of his act. Yet he felt strangely elated, and knew that the favour of the Lord Dynamo was upon him. His plan was already settled when he met the man coming from the station, and the scientific manager who speedily arrived on the scene jumped at the obvious conclusion of suicide. This expert scarcely noticed Azuma-zi except to ask a few questions. Did he see Holroyd kill himself? Azuma-zi explained he had been out of sight at the engine furnace until he heard a difference in the noise from the dynamo. It was not a difficult examination, being untinctured by suspicion.

The distorted remains of Holroyd, which the electrician removed from the machine, were hastily covered by the porter with a coffee-stained tablecloth. Somebody, by a happy inspiration, fetched a medical man. The expert was chiefly anxious to get the machine at work again, for seven or eight trains had stopped midway in the stuffy tunnels of the electric railway. Azuma-zi, answering or misunderstanding the questions of the people who had by authority or impudence come into the shed, was presently sent back to the stoke-hole by the scientific manager. Of course a crowd collected outside the gates of the yard,—a crowd, for no known reason, always hovers for a day or two near the scene of a sudden death in London; two or three reporters percolated somehow into the engine-shed, and one even got to Azuma-zi; but the scientific expert cleared them out again, being himself an amateur journalist.

Presently the body was carried away, and public interest departed with it. Azuma-zi remained very quietly at his furnace, seeing over and over again in the coals a figure that wriggled violently and became still. An hour after the murder, to any one coming into the shed it would have looked exactly as if nothing remarkable had ever happened there. Peeping presently from his engine-room the black saw the Lord Dynamo spin and whirl beside his little brothers, the driving wheels were beating round, and the steam in the pistons went thud, thud, exactly as it had been earlier in the evening. After all, from the mechanical point of view, it had been a most insignificant incident—the mere temporary deflection of a current. But now the slender form and slender shadow of the scientific manager replaced the sturdy outline of Holroyd travelling up and down the lane of light upon the vibrating floor under the straps between the engines and the dynamos.

"Have I not served my Lord?" said Azuma-zi, inaudibly, from his shadow, and the note of the great dynamo rang out full and clear. As he looked at the big, whirling mechanism the strange fascination of it that had been a little in abeyance since Holroyd's death resumed its sway.

Never had Azuma-zi seen a man killed so swiftly and pitilessly. The big, humming machine had slain its victim without wavering for a second from its steady beating. It was indeed a mighty god.

The unconscious scientific manager stood with his back to him, scribbling on a piece of paper. His shadow lay at the foot of the monster.

"Was the Lord Dynamo still hungry? His servant was ready."

Azuma-zi made a stealthy step forward, then stopped. The scientific manager suddenly stopped writing, and walked down the shed to the endmost of the dynamos, and began to examine the brushes.

Azuma-zi hesitated, and then slipped across noiselessly into the shadow by the switch. There he waited. Presently the manager's footsteps could be heard returning. He stopped in his old position, unconscious of the stoker crouching ten feet away from him. Then the big dynamo suddenly fizzled, and in another moment Azuma-zi had sprung out of the darkness upon him.

First, the scientific manager was gripped round the body and swung towards the big dynamo, then, kicking with his knee and forcing his antagonist's head down with his hands, he loosened the grip on his waist and swung round away from the machine. Then the black grasped him again, putting a curly head against his chest, and they swayed and panted as it seemed for an age or so. Then the scientific manager was impelled to catch a black ear in his teeth and bite furiously. The black yelled hideously.

They rolled over on the floor, and the black, who had apparently slipped from the vice of the teeth or parted with some ear—the scientific manager wondered which at the time—tried to throttle him. The scientific manager was making some ineffectual efforts to claw something with his hands and to kick, when the welcome sound of quick footsteps sounded on the floor. The next moment Azuma-zi had left him and darted towards the big dynamo. There was a splutter amid the roar.

The officer of the company, who had entered, stood staring as Azuma-zi caught the naked terminals in his hands, gave one horrible convulsion, and then hung motionless from the machine, his face violently distorted.

"I'm jolly glad you came in when you did," said the scientific manager, still sitting on the floor.

He looked at the still quivering figure. "It is not a nice death to die, apparently—but it is quick."

The official was still staring at the body. He was a man of slow apprehension.

There was a pause.

The scientific manager got up on his feet rather awkwardly. He ran his fingers along his collar thoughtfully, and moved his head to and fro several times.

"Poor Holroyd! I see now." Then almost mechanically he went towards the switch in the shadow and turned the current into the railway circuit again. As he did so the singed body loosened its grip upon the machine and fell forward on its face. The cone of the dynamo roared out loud and clear, and the armature beat the air.

So ended prematurely the Worship of the Dynamo Deity, perhaps the most short-lived of all religions. Yet withal it could boast a Martyrdom and a Human Sacrifice.

The Treasure in the Forest

THE CANOE WAS now approaching the land. The bay opened out, and a gap in the white surf of the reef marked where the little river ran out to the sea; the thicker and deeper green of the virgin forest showed its course down the distant hill-slope. The forest here came close to the beach. Far beyond, dim and almost cloudlike in texture, rose the mountains, like suddenly frozen waves. The sea was still save for an almost imperceptible swell. The sky blazed.

The man with the carved paddle stopped. "It should be somewhere here," he said. He shipped the paddle and held his arms out straight before him.

The other man had been in the fore part of the canoe, closely scrutinising the land. He had a sheet of yellow paper on his knee.

"Come and look at this, Evans," he said.

Both men spoke in low tones, and their lips were hard and dry.

The man called Evans came swaying along the canoe until he could look over his companion's shoulder.

The paper had the appearance of a rough map. By much folding it was creased and worn to the pitch of separation, and the second man held the discoloured fragments together where they had parted. On it one could dimly make out, in almost obliterated pencil, the outline of the bay.

"Here," said Evans, "is the reef and here is the gap." He ran his thumb-nail over the chart.

"This curved and twisting line is the river—I could do with a drink now!—and this star is the place."

"You see this dotted line," said the man with the map; "it is a straight line, and runs from the opening of the reef to a clump of palm-trees. The star comes just where it cuts the river. We must mark the place as we go into the lagoon."

"It's queer," said Evans, after a pause, "what these little marks down here are for. It looks like the plan of a house or something; but what all these little dashes, pointing this way and that, may mean I can't get a notion. And what's the writing?"

"Chinese," said the man with the map.

"Of course! *He* was a Chinee," said Evans.

"They all were," said the man with the map.

They both sat for some minutes staring at the land, while the canoe drifted slowly. Then Evans looked towards the paddle.

"Your turn with the paddle now, Hooker," said he.

And his companion quietly folded up his map, put it in his pocket, passed Evans carefully, and began to paddle. His movements were languid, like those of a man whose strength was nearly exhausted.

Evans sat with his eyes half closed, watching the frothy breakwater of the coral creep nearer and nearer. The sky was like a furnace now, for the sun was near the zenith. Though they were so near the Treasure he did not feel the exaltation he had anticipated. The intense excitement of the struggle for the plan, and the long night voyage from the mainland in the unprovisioned canoe had, to use his own expression, "taken it out of him." He tried to arouse himself by directing his mind to the ingots the Chinamen had spoken of, but it would not rest there; it came back headlong to the thought of sweet water rippling in the river, and to the almost unendurable dryness of his lips and throat. The rhythmic wash of the sea upon the reef was becoming audible now, and it had a pleasant sound in his ears; the water washed along the side of the canoe, and the paddle dripped between each stroke. Presently he began to doze.

He was still dimly conscious of the island, but a queer dream texture interwove with his sensations. Once again it was the night when he and Hooker had hit upon the Chinamen's secret; he saw the moonlit trees, the little fire burning, and the black figures of the three Chinamen—silvered on one side by moonlight, and on the other glowing from the firelight—and heard them talking together in pigeon-English—for they came from different provinces. Hooker had caught the drift of their talk first, and had motioned to him to listen. Fragments of the conversation were inaudible and fragments incomprehensible. A Spanish galleon from the Philippines hopelessly aground, and its treasure buried against the day of return, lay in the background of the story; a shipwrecked crew thinned by disease, a quarrel or so, and the needs of discipline, and at last taking to their boats never to be heard of again. Then Chang-hi, only a year since, wandering ashore, had happened upon the ingots hidden for two hundred years, had deserted his junk, and reburied them with infinite toil, single-handed but very safe. He laid great stress on the safety—it was a secret of his. Now he wanted help to return and exhume them. Presently the little map fluttered and the voices sank. A fine story for two stranded British wastrels to hear! Evans' dream shifted to the moment when he had Chang-hi's pigtail in his hand. The life of a Chinaman is scarcely sacred like a European's. The cunning little face of Chang-hi, first keen and furious like a startled snake, and then fearful, treacherous, and pitiful, became overwhelmingly prominent in the dream. At the end Chang-hi had grinned, a most incomprehensible and startling grin. Abruptly things became very unpleasant, as they will do at times in dreams. Chang-hi gibbered and threatened him. He saw in his dream heaps and heaps of gold, and Chang-hi intervening and struggling to hold him back from it. He took Chang-hi by the pigtail—how big the yellow brute was, and how he struggled and grinned! He kept growing bigger, too. Then the bright heaps of gold turned to a roaring furnace, and a vast devil, surprisingly like Chang-hi, but with a huge black tail, began to feed him with coals. They burnt his mouth horribly. Another devil was shouting his name: "Evans, Evans, you sleepy fool!"—or was it Hooker?

He woke up. They were in the mouth of the lagoon.

"There are the three palm-trees. It must be in a line with that clump of bushes," said his companion. "Mark that. If we go to those bushes and then strike into the bush in a straight line from here, we shall come to it when we come to the stream."

They could see now where the mouth of the stream opened out. At the sight of it Evans revived. "Hurry up, man," he said, "or, by heaven, I shall have to drink sea-water!" He gnawed his hand and stared at the gleam of silver among the rocks and green tangle.

Presently he turned almost fiercely upon Hooker. "Give *me* the paddle," he said.

So they reached the river mouth. A little way up Hooker took some water in the hollow of his hand, tasted it, and spat it out. A little further he tried again. "This will do," he said, and they began drinking eagerly.

"Curse this!" said Evans, suddenly. "It's too slow." And, leaning dangerously over the fore part of the canoe, he began to suck up the water with his lips.

Presently they made an end of drinking, and, running the canoe into a little creek, were about to land among the thick growth that overhung the water.

"We shall have to scramble through this to the beach to find our bushes and get the line to the place," said Evans.

"We had better paddle round," said Hooker.

So they pushed out again into the river and paddled back down it to the sea, and along the shore to the place where the clump of bushes grew. Here they landed, pulled the light canoe far up the beach, and then went up towards the edge of the jungle until they could see the opening of the reef and the bushes in a straight line. Evans had taken a native implement out of the canoe. It was L-shaped, and the transverse piece was armed with polished stone. Hooker carried the paddle. "It is straight now in this direction," said he; "we must push through this till we strike the stream. Then we must prospect."

They pushed through a close tangle of reeds, broad fronds, and young trees, and at first it was toilsome going; but very speedily the trees became larger and the ground beneath them opened out. The blaze of the sunlight was replaced by insensible degrees by cool shadow. The trees became at last vast pillars that rose up to a canopy of greenery far overhead. Dim white flowers hung from their stems, and ropy creepers swung from tree to tree. The shadow deepened. On the ground, blotched fungi and a red-brown incrustation became frequent.

Evans shivered. "It seems almost cold here after the blaze outside."

"I hope we are keeping to the straight," said Hooker.

Presently they saw, far ahead, a gap in the sombre darkness where white shafts of hot sunlight smote into the forest. There also was brilliant green undergrowth, and coloured flowers. Then they heard the rush of water.

"Here is the river. We should be close to it now," said Hooker.

The vegetation was thick by the river bank. Great plants, as yet unnamed, grew among the roots of the big trees, and spread rosettes of huge green fans towards the strip of sky. Many flowers and a creeper with shiny foliage clung to the exposed stems. On the water of the broad, quiet pool which the treasure-seekers now overlooked there floated big, oval leaves and a waxen, pinkish-white flower not unlike a water-lily. Further, as the river bent away from them, the water suddenly frothed and became noisy in a rapid.

"Well?" said Evans.

"We have swerved a little from the straight," said Hooker. "That was to be expected."

He turned and looked into the dim, cool shadows of the silent forest behind them. "If we beat a little way up and down the stream we should come to something."

"You said—" began Evans.

"*He* said there was a heap of stones," said Hooker.

The two men looked at each other for a moment.

"Let us try a little down-stream first," said Evans.

They advanced slowly, looking curiously about them. Suddenly Evans stopped. "What the devil's that?" he said.

Hooker followed his finger. "Something blue," he said. It had come into view as they topped a gentle swell of the ground. Then he began to distinguish what it was.

He advanced suddenly with hasty steps, until the body that belonged to the limp hand and arm had become visible. His grip tightened on the implement he carried. The thing was the figure of a Chinaman lying on his face. The *abandon* of the pose was unmistakable.

The two men drew closer together, and stood staring silently at this ominous dead body. It lay in a clear space among the trees. Near by was a spade after the Chinese pattern, and further off lay a scattered heap of stones, close to a freshly dug hole.

"Somebody has been here before," said Hooker, clearing his throat.

Then suddenly Evans began to swear and rave, and stamp upon the ground.

Hooker turned white but said nothing. He advanced towards the prostrate body. He saw the neck was puffed and purple, and the hands and ankles swollen. "Pah!" he said, and suddenly turned away and went towards the excavation. He gave a cry of surprise. He shouted to Evans, who was following him slowly.

"You fool! It's all right. It's here still." Then he turned again and looked at the dead Chinaman, and then again at the hole.

Evans hurried to the hole. Already half exposed by the ill-fated wretch beside them lay a number of dull yellow bars. He bent down in the hole, and, clearing off the soil with his bare hands, hastily pulled one of the heavy masses out. As he did so a little thorn pricked his hand. He pulled the delicate spike out with his fingers and lifted the ingot.

"Only gold or lead could weigh like this," he said exultantly.

Hooker was still looking at the dead Chinaman. He was puzzled.

"He stole a march on his friends," he said at last. "He came here alone, and some poisonous snake has killed him—I wonder how he found the place."

Evans stood with the ingot in his hands. What did a dead

Chinaman signify? "We shall have to take this stuff to the mainland piecemeal, and bury it there for a while. How shall we get it to the canoe?"

He took his jacket off and spread it on the ground, and flung two or three ingots into it. Presently he found that another little thorn had punctured his skin.

"This is as much as we can carry," said he. Then suddenly, with a queer rush of irritation, "What are you staring at?"

Hooker turned to him. "I can't stand—him." He nodded towards the corpse. "It's so like—"

"Rubbish!" said Evans. "All Chinamen are alike."

Hooker looked into his face. "I'm going to bury *that*, anyhow, before I lend a hand with this stuff."

"Don't be a fool, Hooker," said Evans. "Let that mass of corruption bide."

Hooker hesitated, and then his eye went carefully over the brown soil about them. "It scares me somehow," he said.

"The thing is," said Evans, "what to do with these ingots. Shall we re-bury them over here, or take them across the strait in the canoe?"

Hooker thought. His puzzled gaze wandered among the tall tree-trunks, and up into the remote sunlit greenery overhead. He shivered again as his eye rested upon the blue figure of the Chinaman. He stared searchingly among the grey depths between the trees.

"What's come to you, Hooker?" said Evans. "Have you lost your wits?"

"Let's get the gold out of this place, anyhow," said Hooker.

He took the ends of the collar of the coat in his hands, and Evans took the opposite corners, and they lifted the mass. "Which way?" said Evans. "To the canoe?

"It's queer," said Evans, when they had advanced only a few steps, "but my arms ache still with that paddling.

"Curse it!" he said. "But they ache! I must rest."

They let the coat down. Evans' face was white, and little drops of sweat stood out upon his forehead. "It's stuffy, somehow, in this forest."

Then with an abrupt transition to unreasonable anger: "What is the good of waiting here all the day? Lend a hand, I say! You have done nothing but moon since we saw the dead Chinaman."

Hooker was looking steadfastly at his companion's face. He helped raise the coat bearing the ingots, and they went forward perhaps a hundred yards in silence. Evans began to breathe heavily. "Can't you speak?" he said.

"What's the matter with you?" said Hooker.

Evans stumbled, and then with a sudden curse flung the coat from him. He stood for a moment staring at Hooker, and then with a groan clutched at his own throat.

"Don't come near me," he said, and went and leant against a tree. Then in a steadier voice, "I'll be better in a minute."

Presently his grip upon the trunk loosened, and he slipped slowly down the stem of the tree until he was a crumpled heap at its foot. His hands were clenched convulsively. His face became distorted with pain. Hooker approached him.

"Don't touch me! Don't touch me!" said Evans, in a stifled voice. "Put the gold back on the coat."

"Can't I do anything for you?" said Hooker.

"Put the gold back on the coat."

As Hooker handled the ingots he felt a little prick on the ball of his thumb. He looked at his hand and saw a slender thorn, perhaps two inches in length.

Evans gave an inarticulate cry and rolled over.

Hooker's jaw dropped. He stared at the thorn for a moment with dilated eyes. Then he looked at Evans, who was now crumpled together on the ground, his back bending and straitening-spasmodically. Then he looked through the pillars of the trees and net-work of creeper stems, to where in the dim grey shadow the blue-clad body of the Chinaman was still indistinctly visible. He thought of the little dashes in the corner of the plan, and in a moment he understood.

"God help me!" he said. For the thorns were similar to those the Dyaks poison and use in their blowing-tubes. He understood now what Chang-hi's assurance of the safety of his treasure meant. He understood that grin now.

"Evans!" he cried.

But Evans was silent and motionless now, save for a horrible spasmodic twitching of his limbs. A profound silence brooded over the forest.

Then Hooker began to suck furiously at the little pink spot on the ball of his thumb—sucking for dear life. Presently he felt a strange aching pain in his arms and shoulders, and his fingers seemed difficult to bend. Then he knew that sucking was no good.

Abruptly he stopped, and sitting down by the pile of ingots, and resting his chin upon his hands and his elbows upon his knees, stared at the distorted but still stirring body of his companion. Chang-hi's grin came in his mind again. The dull pain spread towards his throat and grew slowly in intensity. Far above him a faint breeze stirred the greenery, and the white petals of some unknown flower came floating down through the gloom.